225

James Tennant

FRE3DOMPRESS
INTERNATIONAL

Freedom Press International Inc.
12-111 Fourth Ave., Suite 185
St. Catharines, ON L2S 3P5

Printed in the United States of America

Cover Design: David Strutt

Book Design: David Bolton

ISBN: 978-1-927684-11-5

James Tennant

*T*his is late, I know. I finally completed it.

    I'm not sure really, why I labored over it so. I guess I just needed to explain why I made the decision I did… to somebody. That seemed over-ridingly important somehow.

So this is my story. I've rendered it from the outside looking in, like a novel. It seemed the best way to relate the account truthfully and dispassionately. I'm sure the Committee would have appreciated the creative touch. It was something I was striving to do—to gain their notice and enhance my prospects. Who would have anticipated it would have ended this way though?

Obviously, there are many details I dare not recount and names I cannot disclose here. Also, there are many things that were only revealed, or became apparent, to me afterwards. Some of the events I relate here must be of the conjectural sort.

It has been a turbulent three years since I made the decision that has so altered the course of my life. It hasn't been a steady ascent from certitude to ironclad certitude; still less a soaring to sublime heights. The reversals and regressions have been incessant; the questions and doubts: was my reasoning sound or did I just respond emotionally, with the rash conviction of youth, to unsettling circumstances? Did events even occur as I remembered them? Was the path I took worth it in the end?

But through each tormented restless night, each bout of regret for lost af-fection and prospect, the loneliness of the outcast, through all the desper-ate questionings—day by day—I've become more and more sure of that for which I hope. I know, as well as one can be able. I know I would never choose again otherwise than what I did choose then.

I have found peace.

In those rare periods of calmness I think about how it was before. We all thought we were building a shining future; a great new age. I was so ideal-istic, arrogant and sure—typical scion of these times of ours.

But I was changed. This is the story of why I changed.

I'm writing this to those who possess an, as yet un-extinguished spark of humanity—those who can still listen to the voice and hear its message. There are others who will never listen, or listening, can never hear. I do not write for them. They will cling to the darkness and, in the end, become the darkness.

Anyway, I have to go now; I know they are coming.

I'm leaving this. I hope you will read it and it will somehow make sense to you.

One last thing:

'Everyone must choose.' That's what they told me.

Choose carefully.

—Obadiah

Prologue

World Era 230.
Five years after Ascension…

Shards of glass ricocheted menacingly off the sidewalk sending pedestrians cowering into doorways or scurrying onto Richmond Street, sparsely trafficked at that early hour. The clamor emanating from the smashed fifth floor window attested to a frantic and violent struggle between an indeterminate number of persons. Witnesses on the sidewalk opposite strained their necks to catch a glimpse of a flailing arm and flash of jet black hair. A screaming head appeared pressed painfully against the window frame above the precipice; its cry echoed and re-echoed in the enclosed space formed by the surrounding high-rises. It wrenched free and the scene proceeded into another flurry of arms and fists. More voices cried out, there was a loud crash and then silence.

Seconds later the fire escape door burst open and two grappling men, one a blue-shirted policeman, tumbled unto the metal landing. Their struggle sent them on a perilous slide down to the next landing. Two other cops appeared in the doorway a flight up and started to clang down the stairs to their comrade's aid, but the fugitive had wrenched free and was hurling down the stairs a flight at a time. Upon reaching the bottom he darted a glance back to his pursuers, then sprang over the rail lithely and dropped the dozen or so feet to the dank alleyway only to be tackled immediately by another two blues who had moved in to cut off his escape. The three slammed to the greasy concrete in a jumble of grasping, tearing fingers, flashing fists and pirouetting eco-containers.

The fugitive possessed a desperate and uncommon strength. He struggled to his feet and, despite one officer's restraining grip, shot an elbow to his startled comrade's midsection, crumpling him to his knees rasping hoarsely. He appeared poised to shake off his remaining assailant when the three policemen on the fire escape fell upon him, the weight of their bodies slamming everyone to the concrete again. Two more cops approached, truncheons at the ready. There would be no escape.

Still, the runner raged like a tempest trying to blow free. His fist cracked on the jaw of one cop, sending him reeling backwards, and his nails raked the eyes of another and tore at his ear. The officers rejoined with equal fervor; clutching and scrapping, trying to corral the berserker. A nightstick impacted his forearm with a dull thud, deadening the nerves. Finally, one cop managed a head lock and the others were able to evade his telescoping legs and pin his wildly bucking body. One enraged cop with a bloody face aimed a jackbooted foot cruelly at his defenseless ribcage. Blows from the nightsticks buffeted his limbs and body but still he fought on with a rabid ferocity that exasperated his subduers. A crunching boot to his temple ended the combat. The young body went limp and quiet.

"Damn crazy bastard—" Bloody Face gave the body another resounding kick.

"Stop! He's out already," another groaned, massaging a painful jaw.

The blues disentangled from the pile and lay on the pavement, feeling for loosened teeth, attending to abrasions, sucking in the sour humid air. With the scrum's dispersal, the bruised broken body of the fugitive was revealed, tossed puppet-like on the ground. It was suddenly animated by a spring of warm scarlet gurgling up from its ear canal, spilling over, tracing the contour of its cheek and dribbling onto the steaming concrete.

In the sudden silence the word "devo" could be discerned in the whispering voices of the gathered spectators.

"Cordon!" a burly sergeant bellowed as he hustled up with reinforcements. Officers moved to seal the crowd off from the alley with a portable steel barricade.

Sergeant O'Connor closed on the nearest cop who struggled hastily to his feet. "Officer Bolton, what the hell went down here?!"

"We tried to apprehend this runner. Fought like a pit bull," Bolton barked back to the stout figure confronting him. "I think maybe he's dead," he added in a subdued voice.

"Crap!" The sergeant wheeled around to take in the scene. "You know the protocol," he scowled, turning back to Bolton. "This is supposed to be a quiet pickup and you go off, what, making a grand spectacle..." He glanced nervously at the crowd. "Where's the wagon?"

"It's coming up Sarg; ETA thirty seconds," a cop with a headset responded. "Sarg, squad blue has got the other runner cornered in a building out back." O'Connor re-activated his own headset.

"Figured this one would be bound for KIDS anyway," Bolton mumbled.

The sergeant snarled an undecipherable riposte and fixed Bolton with a censorious glare.

Soon a navy blue van was passing through the police cordon. The sergeant flagged it down. "Okay, get this off the street," he said pointing out the broken body. He turned to Bolton and ordered him curtly to "Clear the area."

The van pulled up alongside the body, shielding it from the gawking spectators, and three white clad attendants leaped out and began to seal it away in a black nylon bag.

Sergeant O'Connor let out a tired sigh and mopped his damp forehead with the back of his hand. "Damn, I wish MoT would handle these things," he muttered.

"What's that Sergeant?"

The sergeant swung around. "Who-the-f... oh, Facilitator Lanton, didn't see you there sir," he fumbled, adjusting his forage cap and drawing himself up smartly.

The apparition before him was hatless, in a gray uniform and black tie. A copper-colored command badge with the One World logo—a circle with '225' emblazoned—was pinned to the lapel. The body filling the uniform was physically unremarkable: under 1.8 meters in stature and of modest musculature. The head above the stiff wide collar belonged to a middle-aged man, square with full lips and white hair, eyebrows and moustache. The face was distinguished by brilliant blue eyes which seemed to be endeavoring always to corner one's own gaze, seeking there the signs of a shared sensibility. Facilitator Lanton was flanked by two herculean escorts in blue uniforms of a lighter shade than the cops' and with multicolored armbands—the familiar livery of the Ministry of Tolerance.

Probably a grade school teacher before the Ascension, O'Connor sneered silently, noting the gray uniform lacked the spic-and-span of a career officer's. The Facilitator looked more like a rumpled political commissar from another era than a soldier. Outwardly O'Connor maintained a posture of strict deference, however. He knew better than to betray even a hint of his disinclinations to MoT. O'Connor would have guffawed at an accusation of his being 'political,' but he knew how to play the game.

The blue eyes peered into O'Connor's and the brow above them furrowed as if puzzling out a riddle of momentous depth and importation. "What has happened here?" He mouthed his words mechanically, conscious to maintain an officious tone.

O'Connor was reminded of a yapping mutt. *Little snot,* he thought. *Civilian playing soldier.*

"We cornered some devos up there sir," he reported. "We figured they were operating in the area but weren't able to nail any until this morning's tip. Word is they have a nest in the neighborhood. Unfortunately, we weren't able to apprehend this one but we've got another contained in the next building."

Lanton's face remained serious and his eyes dropped for an instant, then his expression softened and the blue eyes rose to recapture O'Connor's. He smiled awkwardly. "Yes, yes, good, good. It's a difficult job I know, but we all understand the necessity of freeing Metro from those who would, ummm, well, enemies of progress." He flushed slightly, like an actor conscious of a mediocre script. "We all need to pull in the same direction these days, eh sergeant?" Those big azure eyes searched O'Connor's face for affirmation.

O'Conner obliged him. "Yes Facilitator Lanton, we're steadily clearing things, block by block." He let out a long sigh. "They know the city as well as we do, so it…"

Lanton was nodding quickly. "That's what is important—steady progress; that's what they are expecting downtown." He peered directly into the sergeant's face and added in a sanctifying tone, "The dedication to this mission displayed by you and your men has been noted."

"Thank you, Facilitator Lanton, that means a lot—"

"May I have a look at this one?"

"Oh? Oh yeah, yes sir." He turned and called to the white uniforms who were about to deposit the body bag into the back of the wagon. "Hold that for a moment! The Facilitator wants to take a look at him."

With a stone-faced sentry on either flank, Lanton approached the idling van. One of the attendants drew the zipper down, exposing the young man's head and upper torso. Lanton studied the face. Once again his eyes grew steely and his brow hardened. He hadn't seen this one before. *Humph, he is not so old. Just a kid during the Ascension*, he thought. *I wonder why they behave so. Madness.*

Lanton had served the people of the city—his city—all his life. He was committed to their welfare and determined to ensure that government provided for their needs. At one time, immediately after the ascension of One World to national governance, he had had a real sympathy for those who resisted being integrated into the planetary society that was being forged. He understood their insecurities, their feelings of being torn away from their old traditions and societal trappings, the apparent loss of control of their own affairs with the abolition of their national democracies. He could understand how threatening the new reality of global governance would seem to the less-enlightened. Personally, he still held out hope for them—that proper re-education would bring them around. Left to his own, he would have let things go on the way they had been. The devos would, in time, dwindle away anyway, the young replacing the old. Although his magnanimity had been attenuated by the years of dealing with these people—it was their dogged irrationalism that was causing all their problems after all—he still regretted it had all come to this. In any case, global directive GG001-0Y125-56130 had come down, so there was nothing left to do—the Integrated World had to be purged of subversive elements.

He had issued the necessary orders to bring Metro into compliance, requisitioning the manpower of the Metro police force to bolster MoT field strength.

While he occasionally doubted the soundness of some of its decisions, Lanton had confidence in the One World Government generally. He knew it employed the best and brightest, the most enlightened. It was the world's best chance—the government he had hoped and fought for all his life.

But as he peered into the youthful visage emerging from the bag he felt uneasy. From time to time certain occurrences prompted these feelings of disquietude. He prided himself on his ability to read the human animal, to ascertain its fears and discern its underlying motives—of course, it was vital to the competent performance of his job that he be able to do so—but, sometimes, he couldn't reduce a behavior to a rationalization. Some people baffled Lanton.

Today the thing that disturbed him was the apparent age of the

devo—barely beyond adolescence. He was young enough to have bene-
fitted from the One World Curriculum, yet had rebelled against the new
order which promised a suitable place for everyone; universal inclusion.
What made a person behave so? What pernicious impulse?

Suddenly the sun peeped into the alley and fell across the body. A
tiny flash of reflected light alerted Lanton's eye to the link of silver peeping out from the young man's collar; there was a chain around his neck.
Lanton reached down and pulled it out. When he saw the silver pendant
dangling from the end he quickly released it as if stung by a viper.

O'Connor watched him straighten up and stand there a moment
pondering, a hard frown on his face. As he began to walk away the sergeant heard him mumble one word: "*Madness.*"

This incident was not reported in the media, local or global. The
glass fragments littering Richmond Street and the sticky garnet puddle
in the alley remained the sole evidences of what had transpired there
that morning. Soon the rain would sweep these away and nothing would
mark the young man's passing.

But this was a common and necessary occurrence, even at that time.

Twelve years later...

1

THE BEGINNING

M r. Lichter rose to speak just as the bell sounded. Thirty chairs were pushed back, and thirty bodies clambered to their feet. Thirty pairs of arms moved to pack up their things.

"Hold on everyone!" he called out, his body unconsciously edging a step toward the classroom door to discourage the threatened exodus. The students paused where they were and looked askance at him. He flashed an apologetic smile. "I know you are all anxious to get out of here, but there's one more thing. Please take your seats for a moment," he said, motioning them down. Thirty bodies reseated themselves in unison.

Sidney Lichter was a product of the One World revolution in education, and now, as an educator himself, one of its facilitators. He was conscious of the commission he shared with other educators and cognizant of the unique opportunity present at this point in human history to instill a global consciousness and universal values structure in the young.

Yes, education was the instrument to build the great new society beginning with its individual atom—the child. Education: in the past it had *served* the public but now it would *fashion* it.

Lichter was nine years old when the One World Curriculum was instated, so he hadn't been a product of the Life Center Early Training. In fact, it wasn't until he was ten that he was selected for a teaching role, but he had taken to the profession like a fish to water. It was exhilarating to be at the center of the new planetary culture rapidly encompassing the world and to be responsible for shaping the next generation during this historical transition.

He was now twenty-five and it was his fourth year teaching; he was just hitting his stride.

This morning Lichter was a bit nervous. He didn't care to make speeches, but today the matter was close to his heart—*Really, it is the point of the whole academic undertaking,* he thought.

He scanned the faces peering back at him quizzically. He had grown to know them well these last four years and, although he knew they belonged to One World, they were his kids in a sense; his creation; his contribution to the cause; a source of personal pride.

He cleared his throat and began. "Okay. Firstly, I just wanted to say how great it's been working with you all. I hope you feel you have grown from the experience, as I have. We've been a great team. I know that sounds corny, but I really mean it. I feel we—you and me—have all striven to rise to our potentials and we've all been true to the vision with which we've been entrusted." He broke into a broad smile. "We can all be proud." He paused and surveyed his mute audience with their chins resting on hands or sitting straight with arms crossed or hands cupped on the desk before them; all watching intently; all wonderfully compliant.

He continued. "Well, as you well know, this upcoming semester is your last here, then you'll be heading off to university." His clear lecturer's voice became more serious. "It's an important time for each of you," he said scanning the room to make eye contact with as many as he could. "Yes, it's an exciting time. I know. You, no doubt, see your future lives becoming clearer. I remember how that was." He flashed a quick smile then his voice grew more earnest and compelling. "It's an exciting time to be young, to be here... in this country... now. You live in an historic period. You will, each of you, look back one day, when you are old—" His mouth drooped and a sour mock-serious expression materialized on his face momentarily before he produced a grin returned by many of the students. "—when you are older you will look back and realize this."

His tone grew earnest again and his hands joined the appeal. "Each of you will be integrating into our society, taking your place and becoming part of its future—shaping its future—especially you: the politicals, our future leaders." He looked at them pointedly. "I imagine you all think about that a lot." A few nods, a few compressed lips. "Near the end of next semester, at your Induction, you'll make an explicit commitment to this society and this society will commit to you."

"We'll get chipped!" one brave student spoke out, a sentiment endorsed by a communal "Yay!" Quiet laughter filled the room.

Lichter smiled an acknowledgment in the general direction of the comment. "Yes, *yay*. Well, we've talked about that already. I hope you've all thought about it—what it means to be taking your place in One World." He paused and scanned the room, attempting to capture their eyes again, willing an aura of introspection. "You will be participants in the realization of the greatest achievement in human history; the first global civilization," he said with arms outstretched and eyes wide. "Think about it." The room was silent and still for a long moment.

Lichter interrupted the reverie. "Okay everyone; keep all this in mind when you are considering your final paper. We talked about this before: each of you must submit a ten thousand word essay pertaining to the general topic *the evolution of civilization* next semester. You can write about future trends in science or a particular scientific discipline, for instance. Or you can write on cultural trends, or political organization, art or sport—whatever you like. We want you to show us your vision of where our culture is going, or should be going." He paused and surveyed the room for questions. There were none. "Remember to have your outline submitted for review before August eighth. You can post them to the oopolitics channel."

He paused and stood with hands clasped tightly in front. Then he smiled, thrust his arms wide and whooped, "Vacation time!" The class erupted in a clatter of chairs and animated discussion.

Lichter stood at the door remarking to some smilingly and nodding to others as they poured out of the room. He was still standing there grinning after the last student had departed.

It was at times like this he wished he could have known his own progeny.

* * *

Paul wandered along, gym bag in hand. He loved this time of year, with the warmer weather coming on. The sunshine and spring air lifted his spirits after the long gray winter that seemed to stretch October to April.

He meandered along in a semi-delirious mood smiling and casting a glance at each pretty girl, all with the giddy assurance of being master of one's destiny that adheres to the young.

A couple of cops passed on the opposite sidewalk but didn't scan him, thankfully.

When he rounded the corner at Davisville an older women caught his eye. She was wearing tight slacks and a low cut spaghetti strap top that displayed her mature curves invitingly.

Many younger men preferred older woman—there was less of a chance of an incompliant entanglement with them and they were usually sterile as a result of FreeDom use too. Most seemed pretty thankful for the attention given the competition from younger women and HotTube.

She smiled behind her dark sunglasses as they drew near. Paul returned a grin and glanced back over his shoulder boldly as they passed to survey her body from another angle. For a second he considered dogging her, but he was determined not to miss a workout and had already committed to meeting some friends downtown afterward.

He arrived at Davisville Gym, found a locker and changed without breaking the spell. Minutes later he was mounting one of the familiar crosstrainer machines.

He had been awarded a club membership there in his junior year. It had a lot more equipment than the school gym and there was a much more interesting crowd. The presence of the body builders provided the hardcore attitude—it was a *real* gym. He liked that authenticity. And there were lots of girls too.

It was early afternoon but the crowd was surprisingly light. *Probably all taking advantage of the weather*, he thought, looping his towel around the neck of the machine and punching up the hill program—twenty minutes. The machine's pedals started to grind and its arms to alternate back and forth. He intended to do a warm up, then a little stretching before hitting the weights. It was important to warm the body up before stretching in order to prevent injuries; he didn't want to pop a hamstring just before vacation.

Throughout his high school years he had made it a practice to work out regularly. Originally, his intention was to add muscle to his spare frame to attract girls, but he had soon discovered that the sweat and blood rush also served to clear his mind and dissipate the stress of the day. He did his best thinking on the crosstrainer.

He was restless today, though, with the summer approaching and the anticipation of how his life would be changing with graduation and university away from Aquarius City.

The monitor on the wall opposite was replaying the zone leader's speech from Tuesday previous. Paul flipped to the SpaceFleet news on the smaller screen in front of him but soon found studying the other patrons more engaging. It was a great place to people-watch and the human species had always fascinated Paul—a propitious trait for someone in the political career stream.

Here humanity paraded itself in all its shapes and sizes and myriad of mannerisms. There were the heavily-muscled body builder types flexing their chests and biceps in front of the mirrors between sets, or swaggering off, traps spread bat-like, to get a drink at the fountain. In contrast to this display was that of the gaunt runners grouping up to hit the streets. A gaggle of pony-tailed girls, animated, chatty, and oblivious—likely Betas—would bounce by heading for the fountain whenever an aerobics class let out. He took stock of their tights and shorts, their pink headbands and other girlish paraphernalia. There was an obvious attention to appearance, whereas the body builders tended to wear nondescript gray sweatpants and tee or muscle shirts, sometimes threadbare and often in dire need of laundering; their vanity invested in their bodies solely.

In any case, it was a way for both species to achieve their weekly activity quota.

An attractive sandy-haired pony-tailed girl over at the ballet barre caught Paul's attention. He could see her reflected in the mirror to his right, but it took him a moment's orientation to realize she was in the stretching area behind and off his right shoulder. She was wearing a lime green body suit with a thong style bottom and sneakers. The shimmering spandex fit like a second skin revealing a firm curvy body, obviously not a stranger to the weight room but not at all like the blocky masculine physique of the hardcore musclehead; she was juicy.

Paul entertained himself watching her stretch routine. He had to smirk noticing that she would often shift her eyes and sneak a peek at her own image in the mirror self-consciously. This was something he noticed often, the insecurity of the opposite sex concerning their bodies. It amazed him at times. *I wonder if she thinks her bum is too big,* he mused.

The crosstrainer program expired and he noted his calories burned, kilometers covered and other stats on the monitor, then swabbed his forehead and shoulders, took a drink at the fountain, and wandered casually over to the stretching area.

The girl in the sexy green thong was doing some cat stretches. She was probably around his age, but he couldn't recall seeing her before; she didn't go to Eastview. As she lunged forward a gold chain around her neck shifted and a cross slipped out from between her breasts and dangled free. As she regained her feet her hand stuffed it back into her top nimbly.

Paul was bemused by the amulet. He had seen a few other girls wearing them around and thought it strange they choose to wear the symbol of an archaic religion. While not listed as incompliant officially, such displays had the spirit of rebellion about them, like daring to exhibit a swastika. *Rather immature. Likely one of those pretentious spiritual types.*

Of course, it was a bit hypocritical denouncing the girl over an illicit religious talisman considering the trinkets he had squirreled away in the box—his 'treasure box'—under his dresser at home: the Bible; the old American dollar bill; the newspaper clipping of the World Trade Center incident…

The girl had finished her stretch and Paul watched her sashay off to another room so the mystery of the ornament was not pursued.

He moved over to the pulley row machine and adjusted the pin on the weight stack. Sitting on the padded chair with legs slightly bent he took hold of the handle, inhaled, then exhaled as he drew it to his stomach. "One," his mind registered. He inhaled again and let the machine pull his arms straight in a controlled descent. At the bottom his torso leaned forward slightly as the machine stretched his latissimus muscles taunt. He exhaled again and drew the handle to his stomach once more, returning his torso to an upright position. "Two."

After ten reps he stood up and shrugged a few times to relax his lats then reached across his body and grasped one of the struts of the row machine and leaned back on his heels allowing his body weight to stretch his back. It felt good to feel his pumped-up muscles unfold. His back felt huge. He stretched the other side then sat down on the chair again and repeated this sequence three more times, increasing the weight for the next two sets, dropping it back a bit for the fourth. Then he moved over to the pull down machine. He was really getting into a zone now.

He glanced around to check out the other action. Two humungous builders were doing bench presses on one of the Olympic benches. They had three of the big black plates and one dime on either side of the bar— 190 kilos; impressive. One was pumping the bar up and down piston-like while the other hung over him mouthing encouragement. They might have been Kappas, but he knew Kappas were not issued memberships there. A more modest physique sat on a flat bench resting between sets and watching the reflection of the two giants going at it in the mirror. Another was humping out reps with an easy-curl bar.

He turned back to the pull down machine. The scene from his final class today, the speech by Mr. Lichter, leapt to mind. *Ah, I have to come up with a topic for my final paper… something original, relevant… something to really impress the placement office.* He sat with a faraway look on his face for a minute, then blinked. *I'll ask Bev and Roland what they are going to do.*

He glanced at the clock. *Wow, three twenty-five! I'd better get a move on if I'm going to meet up with Mo and Cal.* He grasped the cambered bar firmly and began his first set.

2

VOCATIONS

Calvin Wong looked around at the four white walls, yawned, and wandered over to the window. From his third floor perch he could look down on Darwin Street and the mid-afternoon traffic, the cars mostly dark blue governmental issue, and the bicycles. The weather was fine, the temperature climbing into the low twenties; summer was coming on. He hoped to get some time off to think about things and get away from the music for a while; maybe do some painting. Another troop of soldiers marched past heading eastward toward the Portlands base— strong impressive physical specimens—Kappas. They had been streaming past all day such that it seemed the sprawling army base north of the Junction must be left vacant. It was like a World Day parade.

He wondered if the soldiers ever resented their occupational assignment.

There were rumors of former Betas being re-evaluated to the ranks. He studied their faces. A few of them seemed to project a superior intelligence.

The muted intonations of an aspiring soprano filtered through the door intruding into his musings and drawing his mind back to the present. The recital was in four days; he could relax after that. Today and tomorrow would be used to polish everything up and there would be a light practice and time to sleep on Saturday.

Just another hour practice then he'd meet some friends for dinner.

He stretched his fingers and shrugged to release the tension in his shoulders, then turned away from the window, crossed the creaky hardwood floor and settled behind the worn Steinway. A score for Rachmaninoff's Prelude in G minor was on the rack before him—his assignment for Sunday's recital—a sure crowd pleaser.

He was lucky to have the use of the practice room away from the watchful eye of Petya. It came courtesy of a friend who knew a teacher at the World Conservatory of Music who was down with the flu.

He paused a moment, perched on the front half of the bench with the balls of his feet on the pedals. A mischievous grin appeared on his face and his fingers began to run through the G minor scale. He was remembering what a teacher had told him when he was a child those many years ago: *Always practice the scale of the key of the piece you are currently studying.* Back then it had lessened the drudgery of learning the scales and provided an additional memory aid.

He had been having thoughts about the past a lot lately—many of them incompliant.

A sigh escaped his lips. He looked at the score one more time—at the frayed edges of the paper marked up with his old fingering notes. Once again his mind wandered back to the beginning of the musical odyssey that had brought him to this present venue and moment.

He had commenced studying piano when he was three years old—an early age by convention but, of course, he was not an ordinary student. He was bred to play the piano—an early product of the One World Eugenics Institute. Once, success had depended upon talent and hard discipline; now it required genetic selection and manipulation also.

Although not officially sanctioned before the Ascension—indeed, often proscribed then, at least publicly—eugenics programs had been around for many years supported by certain well-to-do progressive circles operating quietly in the background. In fact, since the nineteenth century and the rise of the modern understanding of man's place in the animal kingdom, rooted in evolutionary theory, eugenics had been a persistent preoccupation of Progressive thinkers: If we employed scientific methods to improve our animal stock, to make them stronger and less vulnerable to disease, why not employ the same methods to improve the human species?

This and other initiatives to liberate scientific exploration in general from irrational influences accelerated as the proto-One World era proceeded. With the Ascension of One World an unfettered science could now realize its promise of defeating humankind's ailments—disease, pollution, food shortage and, ultimately, its own mortality.

Such was the promise of the science of eugenics: In the great global culture there would be smarter engineers, faster, more agile athletes, and yes, exceedingly refined pianists. The potential of the species would be realized; humanity would seize responsibility for its own evolution from Nature.

He had learnt all this in school.

Although Calvin had been bred to play, he still had to work hard to realize his man-given potential. For this he was well tempered—he labored harder than anyone and his musical progression was rapid.

He remembered it all: his early years counting the rhythm with the click, click, click of the metronome; learning the scales and arpeggios; developing the proper hand techniques—*Find the natural position*—and training each digit—*No lazy fingers*; coordinating the left with the right; learning to unlearn mistakes. There were the long hours sight reading, memorizing, studying the styles of the composers and the history of music. He experienced the joyfulness of Mozart, the masculine intensity of Beethoven, the humor of Prokofiev, and always there was Bach to meld the mind and hands. He was always taking up new pieces to build repertoire, with Petya there to coax him off any comfortable plateau. As he matured he acquired the artistry necessary to stamp his own personality on the pieces without transgressing the composer's intentions.

He remembered his first venture into public performance at the old hall in the west end—now in the restricted zone if it indeed still stood. It was the beginning of the long process honing his performance muscles that saw him evolve from the scared jittery boy to the masterful performer: *If you are convinced, everyone else will be.*

By age eight he had conquered the grade ten repertoire—Special Program—with distinguished honors. At twelve he was an acclaimed prodigy, already making the concert rounds and building a name. He was awarded the One World Artist designation at fourteen, one of the youngest ever. Now, thirteen years from the beginning, he had emerged a seasoned musician.

As he played his eyes would wander over to the Kandinsky print mounted on the wall opposite. He had never been partial to Kandinsky—he thrilled to the colors but the composition baffled him. He preferred other artists, feeling a special affinity to the mystical ambience of the dark Rothkos. Like many pianists, he often had a painting within his field of vision, usually right in front of him, through his long hours of practice. It provided a venue in which to refocus the weary mind, like the clearing of one's palette at a wine tasting. He had gradually acquiesced to the companionship of the Kandinsky this afternoon.

It was something he appreciated about painting—you could sit and ponder a work. Another day, or even after many years, you could return to a canvas with a different perspective and experience it anew. He liked the permanence of painting. It was so different from the immediacy of the musician's art where one's struggle is to animate a bulky block of wood and steel, and bring the long dead composer back to life—for an instant. Then it was over. The musician was always making and remaking, never completing. He could never hang his creation on the wall and savor it.

Calvin wanted to hang his own Kandinskys or, perhaps more to the point, he wanted to find his own way and make his own choices. He longed for freedom.

These thoughts were incompliant of course, but he had ceased to care.

A fleeting memory caused him to smile. At one time, when he was very young, he had thought Petya his mother—an absurdity given his prototypical mongoloid features: yellow skin, black narrow eyes, shiny black hair.

This life he led: somewhere he had forgotten what it was all for. What *was* it all for? The glory of the revolution? That was an abstraction too amorphous to command his allegiance. The sheer pleasure of music? Maybe; at one time. But at this point he felt he needed a break. He was tired and oppressed; a Shostakovich with a boot on his chest. He had to get away from music, regenerate and refresh his mind. He had never had time to pursue other interests, the piano consumed his life: *The more you play, the more musical you become.*

He knew that less than a kilometer to the south, in the huge birthing complex—*Mother* everyone called it—technicians were crafting the next generation of musicians. They would be improved models no doubt—

a further milestone in human progress. He would need to work even harder to stay ahead of them.

He tried to raise his concentration to performance level—he needed to be *two hundred percent ready* as Petya would say—but his efforts were unavailing. In a few minutes he was once again sitting idly staring at the water pipe running across the ceiling before refocusing back on the Kandinsky.

He wished that, in time, he might hope to move on to another vocation.

But he knew that time would never come. He was designed to be a piano player; there could never be anything else for him.

* * *

Morris Keller sat immobile, hunched over the chessboard, alone in the small lecture room in Hart House at the University of Aquarius.

His mind selected a list of candidate moves and then proceeded in its highly disciplined way to march through the variations and sub-variations.

Computers can examine millions of moves a second, nominating candidates, generating responses, applying complex formulae to evaluate the resultant positions, pruning out the weak positions to give more time to pursue the better ones in the next ply. It was a brute force approach.

In contrast, the human mind, that mysterious 1.4 kilogram slab of protoplasm, can examine perhaps two positions per second, so it is obliged to approach the problem from a different perspective. Unlike the computer, it learns over time which characteristics of a position—a *weak* pawn structure or square, a *dominant* knight, a *promising* initiative— make it a *good* or *bad* one. It knows, seemingly intuitively, which candidate moves are promising without calculating further move sequences because it can draw on its experience and the ability to apply rules of thumb, or break with these rules. It can recognize patterns—positions that are similar to other, known, positions; signposts of promising positions.

Morris was seeking such a signpost, a familiar position or one that could be directed to transpose into one, or one from which he could force disadvantage upon his opponent directly. His mind considered a promising move, followed the procession of responses and counter-responses until it could sense it was diverging from a favorable path; then discarded it and proceeded to the next variation, never going back to reconsider those already examined. He was sharpening his endgame play; conditioning his brain.

It was almost time to break and kick the ball around the field behind University College for a while. About five o'clock he was to meet Paul and maybe Calvin up on Darwin. After that he would spend some time with the computer affirming his opening preparation: English with white; Indian complex—Nimzo or Queen's—against the queen pawn with black, and French against the king pawn. He admired attacking players such as Alekhine, Kasparov and Ming, but he knew his talents lay more in a solid positional style of play along the lines of a Karpov or Petrosian. His was a striving to be the immovable object rather than the irresistible force. It meant he would never be the kind of swashbuckling player the public delighted in, but he did not mind this; he just wanted to win.

After opening analysis he would finally head home in the darkness. Such had been his routine for the last two months. He would be glad when the Zonal was over and he could relax for a few weeks; maybe go down to College Park and play some blitz games. His trainer would berate him for that he knew—*Speed chess blunts your mental discipline*—but it was his preferred way to unwind. It had to be better than junking out on SpaceFleet or HotTube anyway.

OWG had recognized chess as a catalyst in developing critical thinking skills, and so included it in its One World Curriculum. It established zonal chess leagues to provide viable employment, and the world tournaments which led to the summit: the One World Chess Championship. One World's Eugenics Institute, at Mother, had achieved some success in developing players, and Keller himself was a product of that. In many ways, the chess player was a benchmark subject for the Institute.

The OW Zone Fifty-Three Closed tournament would start tomorrow. The winner would represent zone fifty-three in the OW Domain Five Championship to be held in September in New Frankfurt, a very desirable venue for an up-and-coming player like Keller—a planetary stage.

Keller knew exactly where he was going. He could see the progression of his life before him. Being a professional chess player was hard work and the pressure of obtaining results was immense, but he thrived on these. The twentieth century artist and obsessive chess player Marcel Duchamp had once remarked that chess players were "completely cloudy, completely blind, wearing blinkers. Madmen of a certain quality, the way the artist is supposed to be, and isn't in general." Keller was cast from this mold.

So now, just a few hours more…

* * *

Calvin and Paul were already seated on the patio under the canopy when Morris arrived.

Paul looked up and grinned wryly, "Learn any new moves today, Mo?"

Morris plopped down on the remaining chair. "All the moves have already been discovered, as you well know friend. It is my fate—all our fates—to repeat the moves of those who have come before." He added the aside, "Hopefully in a more effective order," nodded solemnly and picked up a menu. "Truly, there is nothing new under the sun."

"Hmmm, yes. And while we struggle to appreciate the hidden depths of the profound utterances just, um, uttered, let's check out the burgers," Paul said spritely.

"I think the skins look good from here," Morris ventured. "What's up, Cal?"

Calvin responded morosely, "Oh, y'know, same old crap."

"He's playing at the Conservatory on Sunday—part of the run-up to the Leader's celebration. Always a little edgy before a show I think," Paul offered from behind a menu. "How're you doing?"

"I'm feeling pretty good about my preparation… gonna kick butt," Morris trumpeted.

"Way to go. Hey, look me up when you are famous," Paul bantered.

"Fame isn't all it's cracked out to be," Calvin mumbled.

"Yeah, but fame or no fame, I'm gonna kick butt!"

"Hey fame's okay," Paul interjected. "Chicks dig fame. Right, Cal?"

Calvin smiled helplessly. Everyone laughed.

"What would you guys like?" A pretty Beta girl in jeans and tee shirt with wavy black hair cropped at her jaw line had appeared.

"Oh, hi there," Paul perked up, "I'm for the Belfast Burger with a Coke—cheese and onions on top." The cheese had been a spur of the moment addition; he and Morris liked to flaunt their fat quota to each other. He pressed his palm to the register so the girl could confirm he was within dietary restrictions.

Morris cast a knowing glance at him. "I'll do the loaded skins—lots of sour cream," he winked at Paul. "You have Sprite?"

"Seven-Up," said the girl tilting her head and offering a crooked smile.

"Awk! Okay, make it a Coke too."

She giggled and confirmed his order. "And for you?" She looked at Calvin.

Calvin was peering into the menu with screwed up eyes. Finally he waved his arm in a "don't care" attitude and said, "Just the chicken salad please. I'm not too hungry. Oh, and some iced tea."

"Sure." She tripped off with their order.

Paul watched her walk away. "Cutey."

"Yes, very," Morris affirmed, "probably a low grade Beta though."

"Augh! You're such a racial snob," Paul laughed.

"Whatever," Morris said dismissively. He took a deep breath. "I can tell you I'll be happy when the tourney is over. I'm going stir crazy locked up in Hart House all day. I guess it must be like that for you too, eh Cal?"

Calvin was slow to respond. "I don't know. Yeah, I'm tired of the practicing." He went silent for a moment. "I'm just tired."

"You sound like you need a change of scenery," Paul said. Calvin hadn't been close to rising to the modest heights of even his usual melancholic state lately. He always seemed lost in thought; a million kilometers away. "There's a party at Julius' on Sunday; it's in Roncesvalles. They say you can see the West Wall from their second floor. You could drop in after your concert."

Calvin sighed and shrugged his shoulders resignedly, "Yeah. I suppose. We'll see."

"I hear they got a diet waiver too; you can eat whatever you want."

"Yeah, go figure. How did they manage that?" Morris cut in.

"Paige's enabler; he's MoC."

"Oh yeah. Right. Oh, I hear Suzanne and her sidekicks are going," Morris offered significantly.

"Ha, yeah. Of course they would show up; anywhere there's a party," Paul replied drily. His eyes scanned the street as he talked. The venue was close to the university, so there were a lot of young women out and about. A tall black girl with wide hips, heavy breasts and an impossibly slim waist drew Paul's attention. *Wow. I'd like to see that on the beach,* he thought.

"You gonna be around tomorrow afternoon?" Morris asked. "We could kick the ball around, maybe get a scrimmage going."

Paul responded without interrupting his surveillance, "Well. Ah, no. I have the Mother tour tomorrow."

"Oh, you're going to see where babies come from. Swell," Morris drawled. He glanced over his shoulder and spotted the black girl. "Yikes! Wonder how she manages to restrain those puppies!"

Calvin turned to see what had caused the outburst. The corner of his mouth drew down and he turned back, apparently unimpressed.

"Whew!" Morris whistled softly. "Don'tcha just love summer."

The girl passed out of view and the waitress re-appeared and dropped off their drinks. "Back in a minute with your food," she said, hurrying off again.

Paul took a sip of Coke. The mention of Mother had caused his stomach to lurch. He hated that feeling. He longed to be free from irrational psychological baggage—to *be clear* as his Spirituality professor would say.

The girl brought their food and Paul and Morris wolfed it down, pausing at intervals to chat about the Jays, SpaceFleet, or to remark on an interesting pedestrian. Calvin picked at his salad and said little.

Paul's wandering eyes spotted the black sedan with tinted windows drifting past. He shivered and his expression became grave.

"What's up?" Morris turned to see what Paul was looking at. "Oh," he said quietly.

Cal turned too.

Everyone referred to them as *black marias.* They were used by the Ministry of Equality. It was common wisdom that if you went into one you would never be seen again.

The three watched until it slipped out of view, then returned to their meal, subdued.

When they were finished Paul motioned to the waitress who brought the scanner over. Morris pressed his palm to the reader and it whirled for a few seconds then beeped.

"Um, could you help me out, Paul?" Calvin said timidly. "I don't have any credits. Petya wouldn't give clearance."

Paul's eyebrows shot up. "Oh, no problem buddy. What's wrong with her anyway?" he scowled. Calvin shrugged sheepishly. Paul placed his palm on the reader. "I'll get both," he said, indicating his and Calvin's plates. The girl nodded hesitantly, not wishing to be drawn into an incompliancy, but the food had been eaten already. After her reader whirled and beeped its assent she had Cal press his palm to register his meal statistics too, though. "Thank you," she chimed and hustled off to another table. Paul grinned after her.

Morris rose and drew his jacket from the back of his chair. "See you guys later; I gotta get back to work—big day tomorrow."

"Yeah, see ya. I should be heading out too. You going my way, Cal?"

"Back to the subway? Yeah."

They decided to walk back to Morgentaler where Paul could catch the northbound and Cal would head east.

The traffic at that hour consisted of a steady flow of bikes and minicars mostly, with the usual smattering of government vehicles and police cruisers. A marching column of khaki-clad soldiers overtook them after a few blocks.

"They've been marching along Darwin all day," Calvin observed.

"Probably something to do with the Galton expedition?"

"No, I don't think that's on," Paul replied. "I'd guess Africa."

The buildings grew taller as they continued and they soon found themselves hiking through a shadowy urban canyon. They walked on in silence for a block, then Paul said, "How are you making out with the Rach?"

"Oh, no problem; it's ready to go. I'm just putting in time really."

"I can't believe Petya is being so tight with the money," Paul continued. "You really should have your authorization already, like Mo. I mean, you are out there making your living." Paul smiled at an attractive Alpha girl passing in the other direction.

"Yeah, I know. When I'm eighteen, they say. I don't mind really." Calvin's voice trailed off as he looked away.

Paul spotted the two policemen scanning pedestrians before he saw the handcuffed offenders, a young man and a teenager, being led away by some other cops. By their manner Paul guessed they must be high Betas at least—quite respectable. He wondered what they had done.

He lowered his shoulders intending to pass through but one of the cops stepped into his path. "Comply!" he demanded, thrusting a tablet into his face. Paul glared at his own reflection in the dark visor and pressed his palm to the register. It beeped and the officer said, "Okay, now you" to Calvin who pressed his palm absent-mindedly to achieve the affirming beep. The officer brushed past like a hound on a scent allowing the two friends to move on.

"I hate having those guys in my face," Paul griped. Calvin wasn't paying attention.

They arrived at Morgentaler and descended to the subway. "How are things looking for you?" Paul ventured in a concerned tone of voice. "I mean, y'know, how's life?"

"Well, to tell you the truth, I don't know anymore," Calvin sighed. "I need to take a break. I'd really like to try something else." He paused then added awkwardly, "I've been painting, you know? When Petya lets me…"

"Oh?" Paul startled.

Cal brightened up. "Yeah, I've been doing it in my spare time for about five years now. I think I could contribute in that field."

Paul was confused. "What do you mean?"

Cal slunk back into a somber state. Paul was alarmed at his friend's emotional changeability. He sounded dangerously incompliant.

Cal sighed again and shrugged his skinny shoulders and looked straight at Paul. "I don't want to do it anymore—to be a musician, I mean," he confessed. Paul could see it was a weight off his shoulders to have finally said it out loud. Cal lifted a hand and dropped it helplessly. "I wish I could be a painter."

Paul was nonplussed. It was crazy talk; could he be serious? He glanced around to make sure no one was listening.

"I know it's incompliant," Cal continued as if eavesdropping on his thoughts, "I know there is no way. I'm a piano player. That's what I was made for—what my life has been geared towards." His voice wavered and Paul could see his eyes misting over. "There are others who have been raised to be painters. I can't take their place." He was silent for a moment. "But I never had a chance… we never have a chance to choose…" He turned away from Paul. His shoulders lurched and Paul could tell he was crying. He put his hand on his shoulder.

"C'mon, Cal…" Although he felt sorry for his friend he was embarrassed for him also. Despite his musical maturity, Cal was still just a mixed up sixteen year old who still had a lot of growing up to do, he knew. In a few years he would be beyond the 'feeling sorry for oneself' stage.

By the time the two arrived on the lower level Cal had grown calmer and his voice had resumed that familiar tone again—of helpless resigna-

27

tion. "No, it's just the way it is." He glanced towards the escalator to the Darwin line. "I'd better get going."

"Try to make it to the party Sunday, eh?" Paul called after him hopefully.

"Yeah maybe," Calvin answered as he stole away.

Paul watched his head bobbing in a sea of other heads until he was lost in the jam.

He knew Calvin wouldn't be going to the party.

3

DAY 145

ASCENSION

Lanton marched briskly along Kinsey Street. He seldom rode the
streetcar anyway—service was generally unreliable—but today he
felt a particular desire to walk. The exercise would do him good and
there would be ample opportunity to mull things over.

It was bit cooler this Thursday morning—a blip in the warming
trend—and the gray skies portended rain so he had donned a gray trench
coat over his black uniform. At Marcuse he turned north.

The air was more tranquil here and he noticed the chirping of the
birds above. Spring.

As he crossed Emerald and turned westward the cool breeze blew up
again, stirring his senses and threatening to dislodge his cap. It tossed
the long flaps of his coat as he strode along; it was like flying. The streets
were un-crowded and few troubled to cast a second glance at the passing
Ministry Of Equality officer.

He remembered a time when you would, more likely than not, be ac-
costed by panhandlers as you walked this stretch, but he never saw street
people anymore. Of course, panhandling had been rendered pointless
by the abolition of currency but, still, he wondered what had happened
to them all.

The traffic light was red at Community Street, so he was left there
looking up at the towering steeple of the old cathedral occupying the
block opposite. *Such a beautiful building*, he thought, tracing up the

soaring neo-Gothic lines, inadvertently comparing it to modern efforts. It was used as an art gallery now, he knew. It had opened under the auspices of the Ministry of Truth about five years previous. It was so confusing, MoT being the Ministry of Truth. He still remembered his old Ministry of Tolerance. *Recycled acronyms.*... Some LifeFormers were shepherding a class of fourth or fifth-graders into line in front of the entrance where there was a large sign announcing the featured attraction: a modern Earth art exhibit entitled *Mother Gaia*. The children were probably Betas; low to mid-grade he guessed.

He knew that the great windows, now plain, had once been spectacular stained glass. They had all been smashed one night, the interior vandalized and the great organ pounded to splinters despite the rainbow banner hanging above the entrance.

Once, Community Street had been called Church Street, he knew; no doubt because of all the great cathedrals along its lower stretch. He didn't often recall the old street names; it was incompliant to do so. Reluctantly, his eyes peered up the road toward Shuter where one of the grandest cathedrals had stood. What memories he had of that night so long ago, just before the Ascension.

He had been thirty-five then; working at City Hall. Recent years had been difficult, but events reached a critical point that year.

The harvest had been poor everywhere, causing shortages of basic foodstuffs—a shock to a largely urban citizenry isolated from the land and accustomed to plenty. No one starved, but rationing had to be introduced. This had followed five years of radical weather which was widely believed to be caused by global cooling. He remembered all the celebrities and academics in the media denouncing the government for its inadequate response to the repeated warnings from scientists, and calling for the suspension of parliament and empowerment of a United Nations panel of experts to manage the crisis. They laid the blame for the planet's blight on resisters of global regulation—social conservatives and certain religious groups, mostly. Progressive politicians urged massive demonstrations in support of a unified global response.

Then the X15 virus had struck consigning one in four to their beds. The hospitals were overwhelmed and, in the end, thousands had perished in the city. This stoked the flames of discontent still higher, and the voices demanding the total suspension of any regulations restricting medical research and experimentation joined the rising chorus of dissension.

As the bonds of civil society began to unravel there was increased violence and general lawlessness in the streets coupled with widespread vandalism against government, corporate and religious property, all exacerbated by police indifference and a politicized judiciary.

The outcry reached a crescendo when the stock market crashed, the result of continual deficit budgeting and the hollowing out of industrial and intellectual bases that had been proceeding for decades along with the natural depopulation and market shrinkage. The government manipulated the available levers of finance and pumped more capital into failing institutions until it could do no more, then the banks folded and the whole system of Western financing came tumbling down. Savings were rendered worthless overnight; the bank card scanners went dead.

In all major population centers the people, driven by fear, took to the streets in huge numbers and the government, no longer confident of its capacity or mandate to rule, sat paralyzed.

Finally, everything exploded in a great conflagration that night seventeen years ago, a release of long pent up rage and frustration.

Lanton remembered looking out his third floor window and seeing smoke rising into the twilit sky to the west. After dark he could see throngs of people heading downtown—a city on the move. He left the house and wandered along Kinsey Street following the others. The night was aglow with the makeshift torches carried by many, often by those wearing the multi-colored armband of the Equality movement.

Lanton remembered his disgust at the destruction he saw perpetrated by those taking advantage of the situation to indulge their baser impulses.

Just down the road from his house there was a beautiful little church built in the Gothic style by the people of that industrial district in the 1840s, which made it Aquarius' oldest. He had fond memories of that building with its arched windows and doors and its tall square bell tower with octagonal buttresses at the corners extending above the parapet into the sky. He could still recall the charm of its bells on Sunday morning while he walked the dog; it was still common for people to have dogs then. He didn't care for the particular brand of religion practiced there—they were of the devo sort: biblical literalists—but he welcomed the elegance the building lent to the area which was otherwise dominated by claptrap cottages, dusty tumbledown factories and the newer boxy high-rises to the south.

That night he saw the glow of the church as soon as he stepped outside. When he came to the corner its smoldering ruin filled his field of vision. The tower still stood, alight by an almost-full moon, but the roof had fallen and the walls were a jagged shambles. Flames licked the debris and white smoke poured from everywhere.

Some stood silent vigil over the dying structure and Lanton lingered with this group at first, with a genuine empathy. Despite his goodwill, he felt out of place within this final melancholic vespers and so allowed himself to be pulled along by the passing crowd, ending up on Shuter Street in front of the Roman Catholic cathedral.

Everyone stood delirious as the apocalyptic vision of the flames consuming the great behemoth flickered on their glazed retinas. The wild eruptions of the incendiaries thrilled the beholders. Lanton saw the fire department units standing by or positioning to protect adjacent properties but doing nothing to intervene in the church's destruction. It hadn't been clear to Lanton whether they were in collusion with the mob or just afraid of intervening. He didn't really think about it at the time—the Catholics were pretty much hated by everybody.

There was a muffled explosion and the crowd let out a tremendous cheer when a tower staggered then thundered to the ground in a great cloud of dust and sparks. They were all singing rapturously, howling like wolves, crying "Freedom!" to the conflagration in drunken exuberance. To his dismay and astonishment Lanton realized he was wailing too.

Four tumultuous weeks later, the elected government went the way of all the others throughout the western world and One World ascended to power. The bells that used to ornament the neighborhood were silenced forever.

Lanton had never walked Shuter again.

The light turned green and he roused himself and crossed. At Morgentaler he was delayed by another light. *At least they are all working today.* A glance at his watch told him there was still plenty of time. The Emerald streetcar pulled up and let its passengers off, mostly shoppers headed for the Layton Center. Then the light changed and he continued on his way.

He thought about his mission this morning. A devo of some importance—a pastor—had been caught down by the ravine so, as senior investigator, he had assumed the interrogation.

He was passing old City Hall now—another architectural piece d'art in the Romanesque Revival style, Aquarius' third city hall built in the late nineteenth century—but the ornate arches, gray and brown stonework, gargoyles and towers failed to capture his interest now. As he approached his destination his pace quickened.

Now he entered the square. Aquarius' fourth city hall used to stand here, but now the monolithic Strong Building, headquarters of One World Zone Fifty-Three, towered fifty-five floors above the street, its stainless steel and reflective glass bulk protected by a ring of reinforced concrete stanchions occupying the whole city block north to Ecology.

The sun peeked through the clouds causing the giant One World logo above the blockhouse entrance to radiate brightly, momentarily blinding Lanton. Two mammoth guards, resplendent in black uniforms and bearing machineguns, nodded to him as he approached, their scanners having confirmed his identity. He acknowledged them by touching his hand to his cap as he entered the revolving door. The tired-looking guard at the desk inside glanced up for a moment as the wraith-like figure flew out of the turnstile. Lanton hastened past him and the first bank of elevators, crossed a court decorated in marble and garnished in brilliant gilding to a second bank and pressed his right palm to the sensor. The silver doors hissed open and he shot up to the heights of 53 HQ West.

Exiting, he traveled down the lavishly carpeted hallway, around a corner and down another hallway to office 38-302. The brass plaque on the door read 'Chief Inspector Lanton, Zone 53 Section D, Ministry of Equality.' He pressed his palm to the sensor and the lock clicked.

The room was small and sparsely furnished with a desk to the left, a few tall bookcases on the far wall, two leather chairs in the corner facing the desk and a drab green carpet—all the necessities of the work habitat with nothing extraneous. He lodged his coat and hat and went over to the window which offered a commanding view of the courthouses along University Avenue. To the south the definitive landmark of Aquarius, the Lawrence Tower, rose five hundred fifty-three meters into the dappled sky. Its navigation lights blinked red and white in the overcast but gradually brightening sky. The tower had been a tourist attraction before the sequestering directives; now only government bigwigs and others with elevation clearance could ride up to the observation deck.

The wild weather suited his mood, and he would have liked to have gone for a stroll down by the waterfront and perhaps take the ferry across to Ward's Island. He enjoyed being there, standing by the northern shore looking back at the city or strolling across to the boardwalk to lean on the sea wall with the exhilarating sea breeze in his face and the panorama of Lake Obama and the lighthouse across the channel on the Leslie Street Spit before him. He could imagine the cacophony of the sea gulls and the dart and play of the sailboats being buffeted along by the whitecaps. He was gladdened that these entertainments—the ferry, the Island—had been retained.

But he had more pressing matters this morning. The black leather chair creaked familiarly as it took his weight and he adjusted the monitor and pressed his palm to the sensor on the side of his desk. In a few seconds the One World logo appeared.

He withdrew the black folder he had left in his drawer the previous night and reviewed the pages inside. Satisfied, he placed them back in the folder and deposited it into the regulation black leather satchel slung from his shoulder.

"Dial sub nine," he pronounced. The logo disappeared and a dingbat icon appeared briefly. Then there was a beep, and the head of a square jawed, gray-eyed man appeared on the screen. "Block nine. Morning sir."

"I'm coming down in few minutes to question P838506," Lanton said.

"Yes sir. He is being moved to room three now."

"Excellent. Com off." The screen made a doodle-ee-do then went black again. Lanton swept it aside and retrieved his hat from the rack. The lock clicked behind him when he left.

His black-uniformed image confronted him in the reflective doors as he waited for the elevator. He always felt self-conscious when he wore the uniform—the 'gestapo suit' he called it. Fortunately he was only required to wear it to formal events and at headquarters; at other times he wore the all-gray field uniform of the MoE.

He rode the elevator back down to the ground floor and strode along the brightly lit hallway, his boots clicking on the marble floor as he marched along, eyes forward. He turned left, then immediately right and came to another door that clicked and opened when he placed his palm on the sensor. Now he was proceeding down the long narrow hall-way which, he knew, very few individuals ever travelled. He could see the heavy steel door flanked by two guards holding automatic weapons about thirty meters ahead.

They stepped aside and hovered as he placed his palm on the sen-sor there. A few tense seconds later the clack of a withdrawing bolt was heard and the door began to swing open ponderously. Lanton proceeded inside and the door clanged shut and re-bolted behind him like a vault.

He was in a small dazzlingly lit room containing just a monitor and a steel door. "Identify," the head on the screen said.

"Chief Inspector Lanton. Interrogation room three. Subject P838506."

The eyes on the screen shifted to the side for a moment then snapped back. "Cleared." The heavy metal door hummed open and Lanton stepped into the elevator. His stomach lurched as the elevator plunged far beneath the streets.

There was a camera in the corner above him; his mind wandered to imagining who was watching from the other side. The cameras were ev-erywhere. The younger generations probably didn't even notice them but he remained uncomfortable beneath their unblinking scrutiny. He felt the vibration of the floor and, for a hair-raising second, in his mind's eye he saw an image of the black, fathomless shaft beneath his feet. In a mo-ment the vision receded. He had never been comfortable in elevators—a residual from a childhood incident. His body quaked and his groin stiff-ened enabling rubbery legs to grip the floor more securely.

Finally, the elevator decelerated and the door slid open. He was in another small brightly-lit room facing another steel door. It raised im-mediately and Lanton found himself walking along another corridor, deeper and deeper into the sepulchral bunker, his boots clicking on the concrete floor, the sound echoing in the dead air as he proceeded. In this labyrinthine environment it was impossible to calculate one's position relative to the streets above. Another steel door raised as he approached and he couldn't help smiling faintly, recalling a similar scene in the intro of a farcical secret agent TV serial re-run he had watched when he was a boy.

The door clanged shut behind him and the guard behind the bullet-proof glass eyed Lanton briefly before the heavy steel door to the left of his station clanked and swung open. A short man in a blue uniform was standing there behind a chain-link fence. "Chief Inspector, Sergeant Baader sir, I will take you to your meeting," he announced smartly.

The barricade slid back, pocket style, and Lanton followed him inside.

Caged recessed lights in the wall provided intense illumination for the round white-washed concrete vault of a hallway the two travelled. The place always reminded Lanton of photos he had seen of the Maginot Line. Marching down its corridors was like walking into a steel trap. They passed through numerous metal doors promptly unlocked and rebolted by the attending guards until they stopped in front of a gray steel door with a plaque: *Interrogation Room 3*. Below the plaque, at eye level, there was a small square window and a box containing a tablet situated below it. "Sir," the escort said. He removed the tablet, and Lanton pressed his palm to it and replaced it, then the escort opened the door and Lanton brushed by him into the room.

Interrogation Room Three had a claustrophobic feel due more to its rigid dimensions than its size. It was a perfect square with a low ceiling that seemed to press down on its occupants and the gray walls and chalky recycled air added to this impression. Lanton sensed an irony in the subdued lighting—as if intended to soften the overall effect, like a silk glove covering a mailed fist.

The furnishings consisted of a heavy steel military-looking table and two chairs—a padded leather one on Lanton's side and another, the apparent mate of the ponderous table, opposite. A guard stood at a second, windowless door beyond the table.

Lanton withdrew the folder from his satchel and sat down on the leather chair. He whisked through the papers again, then placed the folder on the table and nodded to the guard. The guard pivoted and rapped on the door, which immediately opened, and two other guards entered with a prisoner shackled and fettered between them.

With practiced dexterity, they secured the prisoner to the metal chair with nylon straps, then left through the rear door smartly. Lanton nodded to the remaining guard who immediately turned and exited by the same door which, clanging shut behind him, returned the room to silence.

The prisoner did not raise his head. Lanton looked him over. He was an older man—fifty-eight according to his file. His head had been shaved and he was wearing the gray and black striped togs of the institution's inmates. Lanton knew from the photos of his arrest that he had had long, unkempt hair and a thick beard and mustache—a kind of Rasputin-like physiognomy.

Lanton clicked his tongue for effect, then opened the folder and perused the leaves inside. He paused for a moment, looked up to survey the inmate once again, then started in a knowing voice: "Nathan Eaton. Age fifty-eight. Born 184 w.e. in Harlow, Essex England. Father civil engineer; mother dental hygienist. Two older brothers James and Caldwell; one sister Fern, younger. The family came over when you were age ten. Settled in Waterloo. Attended Eastwood Collegiate Institute… graduated honors 202. Six years at McMaster University…awarded Masters of Science, Biology, 208. Proceeded to wed one Mary Adler, artist. Taught biology various schools 210 to 219… almost ten years." Lanton paused and glanced at the inmate who remained motionless with head bowed.

"Now it gets interesting. Quit teaching job and enrolled in Wycliffe College here in Aquarius… a strange career move… awarded Master of Divinity 222. Ordained 222… priest from 222 to 225 at Westminster Station, a particularly rigid fundamentalist congregation." Lanton had raised his eyes and uttered the last accusingly before returning to his brief. "Denomination ruled seditious—hum, 'non-adhering to equality directives and obstructing societal reform'—banned 225, assets redeployed to the Inclusion Church."

Lanton paused and shot another glance at the prisoner who remained still. He continued. "After that, you disappear for a few years. We next hear from you in 228 when you are implicated in a plot to seize Media One on Kinsey. Efforts to apprehend fail. In 229 a tract *Not My Mother* advocating the destruction of the Life Center in Aquarius appears, believed authored by you. Once again, dragnet launched but no arrest. The next year another pamphlet, *KIDS Sick*, a long rant against the supposed evils of euthanasia and abortion appears, signed by one *N. Eaton*." Lanton raised his eyes to address the prisoner again. "You were a bit cocky there." Eaton made no indication he had heard, so Lanton continued. "Efforts to track down the author again fail. Subversive activity on the west side increases—street surveillance camera destruction, anti-societal graffiti, defacement of government postings—the usual stuff—and more 'revolutionary' tracts. Rumors of devo cell believed led by *Reverend Nathan*. Picked up on a counter-insurgency sweep a week ago." Lanton closed the folder and slapped it down on the table. "And here we are."

There was no response from the prisoner. Lanton sighed audibly.

He reached into his bag and tossed a black leather-clad book and a small stack of pamphlets on to the table. "You had these with you when you were captured."

The prisoner maintained his inanimate posture.

Lanton read the titles of the pamphlets. "*Evilution. Love Not Death.*" He held a gray pamphlet up to Nathan. "What exactly is 'The Culture of Death'?" The prisoner did not stir. Lanton rummaged through a few more. "Hrumph! Then there is this one: *ProgreSS.*" He slapped the offending document on to the table roughly. "Pretty crude—the Nazi runes." Lanton's voice rang with disgust and he had risen from his chair. "Do you seriously think that One World is comparable to Hitler's regime? Do you?" he spat at his sphinx-like captive. Lanton sat down and glared at him, his fingers drumming on the table testily.

Suddenly, Lanton's body gave a jolt as he recalled an item of importance. "And then," he said brightly, retrieving a small navy blue book from his bag, "there's this little item: *Holy Bible, NRSV.* I haven't seen one of these in years." He smiled triumphantly at the prisoner. "I thought they had all been disposed of long ago." He leafed through the pages jauntily emitting a 'tsk' or disapproving 'hmmm' at intervals. Then he snapped it shut and deposited it on to the table between them.

The prisoner's eyebrow twitched ever so slightly. Lanton smiled. "Well *Pastor Nathan* do you deny your involvement in activity against the state?"

The prisoner's head rocked slightly to the side as if trying to find an angle from which to digest the question satisfactorily. The voice was a deep clear baritone when it answered. "No, there is nothing I care to deny."

So, he would talk… good, Lanton thought. He leaned forward and asked sternly, "So you admit to waging a campaign to undermine governmental authority?"

The prisoner shrugged. "Yes, of course. It has been my work to attempt to wake people up to the evil that is One World," he answered matter-of-factly with a proper British accent.

Lanton was speechless for a moment and his complexion reddened. "I see, I see… you're one of those self-righteous Bible thumpers come to show us all the error of our ways," he enunciated imperiously. "That's what you mean, eh?" His voice rose. "I know you… I know your type," he accused, nodding his head sharply. "You hold humanity back with your anti-reasoning, anti-science, anti-progress ideology. You divide men into tribes and set them at each other's throats. You sabotage any efforts at brotherhood, at unity," he scowled. He shook his finger and hissed, "You teach them to feel guilty about their natural drives and to wallow in morbid self-hatred." Lanton's eyes glared blackly at the prisoner. "You claim to be for 'love' but you are *really* driven by hatred towards your fellow man." He tapped his forefinger on the surface of the table sternly. "What needless suffering your type has inflicted on humanity throughout the ages."

"Ah, so you've perused all my work," Eaton replied dryly without raising his head.

Lanton leaned back in his chair and crossed his arms. His heart was racing, so he paused to let it settle. These kinds of people had always gotten his dander up—self-righteous *religious* people—fundamentalists. He had fought them all his life. When he continued it was in a calmer voice, though. "What is it that you want? What do you hope to accomplish by stirring up dissension?"

The prisoner responded haltingly. "I want us to turn… to go back to chastity… to marriage, to families… human dignity… sanctity of life… to virtue…"

Lanton cut in. "What you are describing are the moribund platitudes of your moribund religion. Why should we want to go back to that? Haven't we seen the results of that way of thinking? All through history…"

"What about *your* history?" Eaton responded quietly. He raised his head and Lanton found himself peering into two large sad gray eyes resembling a bloodhound's.

The look disarmed Lanton momentarily and he mouthed automatically, "My history?"

Eaton leaned towards him. "Yes, you know, your life's work: the concerned defender of the destitute and the helpless; the voice of the downtrodden; the champion of so many worthy causes." He uttered this in a tone of apparent sincerity.

A shaken Lanton sat with lips pressed tightly shut, leaving the field to the prisoner.

"Remember the hospice up on Huntley Street? You set that up in, what, 210, 215? How are they doing? Have you been over there lately?"

Lanton knew that the center no longer existed as such; the house was used as a neighborhood surveillance center by the MoE. AIDS cases were covered by the Health and Compassion directives now so there was no longer any need for extended care facilities.

Eaton shrugged. "How about the men's hostel on Seaton? How's it going?"

Lanton recalled the drop-in for street people he had been instrumental in establishing in the decade before the Ascension. But now the government ensured everyone was deployed and appropriately nourished so there was no longer a need for them.

"I guess you've not kept touch," Eaton concluded. "How about the taxi service for the disabled or the home for those with MS and MD…"

"All this is public knowledge… my record is there for anyone who cares to know," Lanton replied dismissively. This wasn't true of course, but it was the official line. He was uneasy at the prisoner's familiarity with his particulars—the other side had dossiers too, apparently.

Eaton was undeterred. "Have you been to see your clients down on Sherbourne; you know, just north of Emerald there? Or down on River—your old stomping grounds? You know, the street people."

Lanton hadn't been there in decades; there hadn't been time. It would be incompliant anyway—to fraternize with un-integrates.

Eaton smiled kindly. "Oh, your people are still there, hiding in the shadows. You can find them if you want to, you know. Just settle in to one of the side streets there after two in the morning and you'll see, well, a remnant." He nodded adding, "Don't wear your uniform."

Lanton didn't see the point of the conversation and was getting increasingly agitated.

"Of course, aid for Africa is pretty much out of the question now…" He looked at Lanton. "Tell me, how are your parents? How are Victor and Jillian? See them much?" he asked, leveling those great doleful gray disks at him. "How do you think they would feel about your career choices thus far?"

This was too much. Lanton was embarrassed at having known his parents. He had been born long before the Ascension, of course, and long before global directive GG001-1B895-20813 made parenting illegal, so it wasn't his fault, but he still felt a tinge of guilt.

The interrogation had taken an unexpected path, but Lanton wasn't particularly alarmed; there would be time to get it back on track—as much time as he wanted. "I don't know why you've taken such an interest in my personal history," he said, clearing his throat. Eaton was some years older than he, but to Lanton, he seemed younger, more robust and resplendent with life despite his melancholic demeanor. He had a certain presence and power. "Why have you?"

Eaton's gaze was penetrating. "You are an interesting person… an interesting person, Mr. Lanton. As one who has chosen a different path entirely, I find myself wondering what your thoughts are after all these years pursuing this mission of yours—this quest for the perfect human society, I mean. That's what you've expended your life on, yes?" Lanton sat immobile. Eaton continued, "So I wanted to ask you about those things you have sacrificed to achieve it." He paused for a moment. "What are your feelings now that you've destroyed your family; yours and everyone else's?" This was rendered not as an approach but as a statement of fact. "And the people you sacrificed your life to help, well, they've all been swept away by your revolution—made obsolete and, shall we say, 'put down.' How do you feel about that?" Nathan asked mildly, without malice.

Lanton rolled his eyes and the tips of his lips curled upward, slightly effecting the look of an adept encountering an unsophisticate. It was a forced gesture, more of a defensive tactic than aggressive maneuver. He clicked his tongue. "Aw yes, the same old arguments: breakup of the 'traditional' family portending the demise of liberty—no more mommy and daddy, so the evil state steps in. What else? Oh yes, abortion, leading to euthanasia, leading to state-sanctioned murder. That's it, eh?" he fired behind a patronizing smile.

Eaton stared unwaveringly into Lanton's face. His eyebrows furrowed in empathetic duress as his huge eyes scrutinized Lanton in penetrating detail to arrive, in time, at a studied conclusion: "What darkness," he said, sadly, lowering his eyes again.

Lanton crossed his arms and hardened his stare. He sighed impatiently. "You cling to old ways as your world fades away," he explained as to a tiresome child. "Everything changes, progresses, civilization evolves…"

"*Evolve, evolve*, ah yes, the 'E' word," Eaton interjected, "the new teleology: the cosmos has no meaning, no destination, but we are rushing to get there." He dismissed Lanton's comments with a sweep his head. His intense stare returned to Lanton. "Your baby mills turn out more material submissive to your ruling cabal's whims—mere drones—while you exterminate the old and infirm and other *inefficiencies*," he pronounced grimly, "and you call this *progress.*"

Lanton remained impenetrable with arms crossed at his chest. "You don't understand. They're not *inefficient*; they're unhappy. We've eliminated all the suffering. One World has been the best thing for everyone. Our scientists are—"

Eaton interrupted Lanton's apologetic with an emphatic shake of his head. "*You*," he moaned. "Look at what it has done to *you* Mr. Lanton. Can't you see?" He stared beseechingly at his interrogator.

Lanton winced and warded off the stare with a shake of his head. However he tried to pass off the prisoner's insinuation lightly, the stirrings in the pit of his stomach continued to unsettle him.

Eaton sensed Lanton was at the point of terminating the interview. "One question, if you will, Chief Inspector Lanton." Lanton looked into those huge sorrowful eyes. "Is this what you intended? Did it all turn out the way you wanted?"

Lanton challenged his gaze for a long moment, but finally looked away and tapped the button on the edge of the table. The door behind the prisoner opened immediately and the three guards re-appeared. Eaton relaxed his gaze to look longingly at the blue book on the table, then raised his eyes once more to Lanton. "Can I please have that back?" Lanton remained mute.

The prisoner's hands were cuffed, and Lanton heard his ankle chains clink as he was led away. The door clanked shut behind them and the room was quiet again.

Lanton sat for a while staring distantly at the gray door. He was perturbed but determined not to allow his feelings to dictate his action. He knew what Eaton was. His kind didn't encourage armed insurrection but they were far more dangerous than those who did. They worked by sowing doubt and undermining confidence, eating away at the very foundations of society like a cancer. Left unattended, the poison would metastasize into a general dissent impossible to eradicate and terminal in its consequence. Eaton was more dangerous than a loaded pistol.

He picked up the blue book, opened it and, his mind still far away, let the pages rifle through his fingers autonomously. When Lanton finally glanced down it had fallen open about three-quarters through. He focused his eyes on the text: *And because of the increase of lawlessness, the love of many will grow cold.*

He shivered as if the 'cold' had escaped the pages. "A strange book," he muttered. He stood up and returned the pamphlets and other papers to his satchel along with the Bible. Perhaps he would study it one day if he ever had the time. Taking up his cap he turned to leave.

Outside Lanton took the tablet from the box on the door and paused for a moment wrestling with his options. Finally he tapped in some instructions and handed the tablet to the escort.

The escort's mouth registered a twitch of surprise as he scanned the order. "We will return him to the holding area then, sir."

Lanton nodded curtly and allowed himself to be guided back to the exit. It would be awkward to justify his decision if challenged, he knew—standard procedure dictated that the prisoner be terminated—but he felt that perhaps there was something to be learned about the insurgents' mindset from this man.

He was certainly an engaging character, this *priest*. It was understandable how some would be taken by him.

As he marched back through the underground passages towards the black shaft he reviewed his thoughts. It was all nonsense of course, the bits about state murder and societal regression. One World had given everyone freedom to live without want, without suffering. It represented the apex of human society.

But, however he tried to discourage the feeling, part of him still longed for the old days campaigning for the poor and disenfranchised.

4

MOTHER

Paul emerged from the underground at Emerald station. It would have been faster to go around the loop and get off at Life or to have simply walked over from College, but he enjoyed strolling through the downtown core.

He passed Old City Hall and turned up Cosmos. As he strode along his eyes were fixed on the awesome Strong Building to his left, radiant in the morning sun, its countless windows glittering like the facets of a giant diamond. All those people there, behind those windows, all allied in the Great Mission. Two dark blue sedans emerged from the back and raced up Cosmos. His eyes widened to take it all in.

The Strong Building was where the real power lay, he knew. One day, if he followed the course, he would have a place there. It was the goal of every aspiring politico, to secure a station at the local zone HQ. From there you might rise to Domain in New Frankfurt or even Capricorn Central.

He winked at the black-uniformed sentinels standing rigidly at the east gate. "See you guys later."

The morning was warming so he doffed his jacket over his shoulder. There was little breeze and the air was dry and carried an odor of dust and ozone. He skirted a Kappa work party repairing a fissure in the sidewalk.

It was mandated that each candidate of the Alpha or upper Beta level tour the Life Center in their graduating year. A cross-section of students from many disciplines—political science, biology, media, psychology, historical interpretation, etc.—were brought together to gain a personal experience of the convergence of knowledge. This morning it was his group's turn to 'do the tour'.

Paul proceeded with an exaggerated élan and firmness of step to disguise a rising disquietude. He was seldom nervous at gatherings like this, being never more in his element than when plunging into a party of unfamiliar personalities, but on this occasion a feeling of unease clung to him like a wet tissue. It wasn't the other students that disturbed him, it was the Life Center itself. The Life Building, *Mother*, that great white children's-building-block-of-a-structure in Life Square, tended to provoke a response quite opposite to that of the Strong Building—he was repulsed by it.

It was a troubling reaction because the Life Center, more than any other institution, captured the essence of One World. It embodied the rational scientific, holistic, and spiritually integrated approach to life in the unfolding new age. It was iconic.

Mother was an apt moniker because everyone, except those originating in the un-integrated areas, passed into this life through a Life Center. You were nursed by its humming surrogate mothers and your rudimentary instruction was administered by its Early Lifeformer technicians in the confines of its nurseries and classrooms.

Paul knew the Life Center model constituted a more scientific child-rearing regime than had been possible before the Ascension; each child received the training tailored to its unique genetic disposition and was directed into the vocation most harmonious with its evolutionary traits and to societal needs. Each child had its place in the community. What could be wrong with that?

When they were five, children were assigned an appropriate family collective for the next stage of their development. This reduced the chance of incompatibility between child and parent on an evolutionary/spiritual developmental plane, endemic in earlier cultures; surely a good thing. The adult enablers in the collective were vetted and trained in right-thinking and child-forming, and all this was directed from Mother. Mother's technicians monitored each child's progress, so while one might change enablers during one's developmental phases—indeed it was inevitable since adult couples were licensed for five years unless there existed extenuating circumstances—Mother was always there: overseeing your unfolding, encouraging positive growth and attitudes and correcting undesirable ones. It was the constant in one's upbringing—one's true parent, in fact.

This scientific management of child development had other ramifications beyond the provisioning of the basic building blocks of society; it set the tone for everything.

For instance, it was understood that the key to having a harmonious culture was to ensure that the various public goods—education, parenthood, employment, health, entertainment, even self-esteem—were created and made available to each citizen on a fair and equitable basis. This is what promoting equality meant: determining people's valid desires and aspirations and providing them. Equality would eliminate the injustices that led to the jealousies, antipathies and violence of unmanaged cultures. It would calm the restless energy of the population and direct it along productive channels.

It made everything fair.

In the Life Center model those who were biologically incapable of conceiving children were not disadvantaged because all children born at Mother entered the adoption pool from which anyone could draw, providing they acquired the requisite parental training credentials. In this way, parenthood was awarded on the basis of personal desire and competency, not on an uncontrollable factor like fecundability.

Where once biological parents had had a controlling influence in the determination of their children's worldview—often instilling them with unenlightened attitudes detrimental to the civilization—the Life Center model of expertly managed child forming ensured shared values and the resultant societal harmony.

Paul had absorbed all this in his studies at Eastview, and before that in grade school, and he acknowledged the correctitude of the system and the benefits it accrued to society. It was all very logical after all, but it still felt like—how could he describe it?—*like my environment fits like a strait-jacket.*

He had arrived at Ecology Street without being cognizant of the route taken. Traffic was light, but he waited for the light anyway; he had been trained to be compliant in minor matters as this led to compliancy in greater ones. A warm breeze whiffed by and he could smell the distinctive odors of Chinatown a few blocks over. It had been reconstituted with humans from Agincourt a few years back.

He continued in a reflective mood. Having this societal-shaping instrument under governmental control gave society the agility to respond to unfolding conditions. New experiments in social engineering could be devised and tested rather than leaving the evolution of society to happenstance.

When the light turned green he zigzagged up some side streets and emerged on University Avenue. The great glowing white block that was Mother loomed in the distance. His anxiety increased, so he tried to concentrate on his breathing, taking deep draughts. At College the light was red again forcing him to stand there, uncomfortably surveying the building whose round portal windows strung around its blank walls challenged his gaze.

The light changed and he proceeded across the footbridge over University into Life Square. As he advanced along the wide sidewalk leading to the north entrance of the complex, he remained sensitive to the oppressive presence on his left. Armed guards flanked the huge revolving door which collected people from the park and dispensed others from the interior. They scanned everyone who approached. He took a final deep breath and slotted himself into its mechanical maw.

The temperature rose ten degrees as he passed the threshold; it was like walking into a large incubator. The vast sanctuary of pale marble was all spic and span. *Perhaps that's why this place gives me the creeps*, he thought to himself. *It's like a hospital.* The slight scent of chloroform, real or imagined, that hung in the air reinforced this hypothesis.

"Comply," an efficient worker instructed as he approached the reception desk. He pressed his hand to the tablet and she nodded and gave directions to the students' tour, pointing out the correct elevator bank. He waited there with six others, one of whom drew much attention because he was blind. Severe dis-function was seldom permitted so Paul guessed he must be an exceptionally high Alpha.

The elevator disgorged four or five people allowing he and the others to push on. He managed to snake his arm between the bodies of a nervous-looking, bespectacled man and a bored white-uniformed intern to hit the button for the third floor. It looked like he would be the first one off. The elevator lurched and glided up two floors and the door opened with a ping. Paul jostled off and the door swooshed shut marooning him in the middle of another spotless corridor, blindingly white but for the giant poster mounted on the wall opposite. It declared 'EVERY GENERATION: BETTER' in triumphant 60cm black letters on ivory ground.

Below that, in an identical pitch, the sponsors were announced in blood red: *The Life Center.* The poster's message barely registered on his mind, so ubiquitous were the declarations of One World from early childhood on that one grew saturated and insensitive to their prodding.

He turned left, as instructed, and traveled along a pristine hallway with rows of identical white doors all with small rectangular black plaques beside them on the wall, like a mausoleum, until he came to *Reception Room 12.* He paused for a brief instance and looked around quickly before chancing a turn of the burnished knob.

The quiet was broken by a chorus of animated youthful voices; most of the others had arrived before him. There were to be ten students altogether Paul knew: a politico like himself, two biologists, one chemist, two engineers, a social engineer, and two others in the medical profession. He guessed the Chinese girl lounging on a chair with her attention absorbed in a journal to be one of the med-eds; and the slight anxious-looking black-haired girl standing on the periphery of the group with her folder held to her chest, rocking back and forth on the balls of her feet, to be the soc-eng. He was quite sure the tall brown-haired male standing, legs planted broadly and grinning from ear to ear, was the politico. He tried to make the acquaintance of all the other politicos he could at these gatherings but didn't recall seeing this one before. That wasn't particularly surprising though, it was a big city. The other four huddled with the politico looked like science types, so that left one med and one engineer unaccounted.

Paul implanted himself opposite the other politico who was bantering about the upcoming SpaceFleet campaign. One of the science students was holding forth fervidly for the Metaloids while the other two backed the Argonites. Although he didn't follow the show very closely, Paul joined to level out the sides and in the course of the conversation discovered the other politico's name to be Cranston.

Meanwhile the other med-ed, another Chinese girl, had arrived. She glanced around quickly at the company and appeared relieved upon discovering her fellow sitting by herself and went to join her. Her colleague didn't acknowledge the newcomer's presence so she took out her own book and ruffled through it restlessly, stealing glances at the others periodically. Paul caught her eye once and grinned and she smiled back hesitantly before turning back to her book. She was cute.

Suddenly a middle-aged man with salt-and-pepper hair and goatee, black-rimmed glasses poorly mated to his facial structure and wearing a lab coat—looking very much the harried scientist—barged through the door and strutted towards the group gesturing wildly with his arms. "Students! I'm Doctor Bright. I'll be conducting your tour this morning," he announced. "Ah, everyone is here already. Oh! There's one missing."

"He's sick," one of the science types said.

"Oh okay. We're all here then. Good! Follow me then," he said spinning around and tossing the door open again. "Oh, just leave your coats here; it's okay."

The students stumbled down the corridor after him. An elevator whizzed them up two floors and deposited them into another long white hallway. Paul wondered that the inmates didn't get snow blindness travelling these corridors every day.

"Come along everyone," Bright urged as he motored along, "we'll start at the selection chambers." They turned into a large atrium that had a glass wall on one side and stared goggle-eyed into the huge brilliantly-lit cavern beyond. It was astounding. There was row upon row of white incubators, each containing a tiny body—there must have been a thousand at least. Legions of attendants in white coats and masks were methodically traversing the aisles servicing each cell, adjusting a knob there, checking a reading there, updating a chart, communicating quietly into their microphones—a hive of activity. One couldn't help being amazed at what humanity could achieve.

"This is Newborn Room One," Bright announced proudly. "There are more rooms like this on the other floors. The newborns are cared for here for the first ten days," he explained. "During this time they are inspected for physical deformities, organ dis-function, disease, etcetera—not all of these are detected pre-birth of course." As if on cue, one of the white attendants lifted a tiny body out of its bed and deposited it in the passing trolley wheeled by another attendant in a salmon colored uniform before moving on to the next subject. "If the evaluation determines they are likely to be incapable of living a normal happy life, they are discontinued so as to spare them the anguish of a degraded existence," he said without embellishment. Paul now noticed quite a number of unoccupied cribs sprinkled throughout the room.

"Of course, not all the newborns you see here are part of the population program, as important as that is; many are earmarked for therapeutic uses—to produce replacement body parts for patients for instance. We've been quite successful in this area," he noted to his attentive audience.

The young biologist raised his hand and the doctor nodded to him.

"How does it work?" he asked nervously. "I mean, how do you get organs that will be accepted by the patient's body?"

Bright smiled knowingly. "As I believe you've been taught"—he winked at the student—"whenever possible, we fabricate new tissue by growing a genetically-matched body from the DNA of the patient." He turned to the others. "You see, we take an egg from a female, remove the nucleus—that's the part where the DNA resides—and replace it with the nucleus of a cell from the patient. The egg is then implanted within a host uterus and grows into a fetus having the same genetic makeup as the patient. This procedure is called *cloning*—you've likely heard of it," he smiled to them. "Since the harvested tissue is genetically identical to the patient's there is virtually no chance of rejection."

The budding biologist put up his hand again. "Didn't we try to use embryonic stem cells to regenerate organs?"

"Ha, yes," Bright chuckled turning to the others, "*embryonic stem cells*—cells from a human organism in its earliest stages of development—were thought to be the counteractant to degenerative disease because of their pluripotency, that is, their ability to grow into any type of cell. We thought with these we would be able to regenerate any organ." He scanned their faces to affirm their comprehension. "But"—he held up his finger—"the problem with embryonic stem cells—'as *you* well know" to the biologist—is that they are unstable. Although they can be stimulated to grow into the desired cells there is an unacceptably high rate of other malignant growth: cancer," he explained. "So we simply allow the embryo to mature to the fetus stage instead, by which time the cells have stabilized, then harvest the tissue. In any case, it just makes more sense; I mean, why inject the stem cells into the patient and wait for him to grow the necessary tissue when the fetus can grow it without risk to the patient?" he nodded pointedly. "This procedure has led to the much greater capacity to treat degenerative diseases over the past decade." He raised his fist in a triumphant salute. "In time we will be able to offer them to the general public."

One of the med-eds spoke up. "Alzheimer's and cancer, how are these investigations coming?"

Bright responded, "Alzheimer's hasn't been a focus as it is restricted to the aged, but cancer"—his face became more serious—"well, we are making progress on that front—slow progress yes, but progress. We are quite optimistic about the future of successful therapeutic courses for many difficult conditions—lung and pancreas included." He nodded to the group. "That's how it goes in this field—step by step progress. I think people will consider the advances in disease control and regeneration that will be achieved in this upcoming decade to be, well, quite miraculous." His eyes peered off onto space as if seeking the precise coordinates of that future Eden.

Returning to the present he continued, "In any case, we can eliminate many deceases at selection time—we've been very successful there." He nodded to the group again. "We detect the genetic predisposition for disease in the newborn and remove the host immediately. Yes, well, let's move on."

As they walked he returned to the discussion concerning the processing of the newborn. "The healthy ones go on to stage two where they are tested to confirm their evolutionary progression, classified accordingly and tagged." The students understood 'tagging' to mean the implantation of the collective microchip in their right palms. "A training regime tailored to their classification is created for each one." He smiled at the assemblage. "Everyone is set on the best path right from the get-go."

"How many units are we producing?" Cranston queried. The soc-eng nodded eagerly.

Bright clapped his hands with enthusiasm. "We are producing ten thousand citizens a month currently. We will ramp this up to twelve thousand five hundred by year's end. But the really exciting thing happens next year when the first Genesis block comes online—that will double our capacity. The following year, when the second block is activated, we will double again." Bright was aglow. "By then Zone Fifty-Five will be one of the largest producers of human organisms in the world and we will be able to deploy them to Europe and elsewhere—wherever re-population is required."

Then he nodded gravely. "Of course this is contingent on the availability of birthing hosts. We use Kappas for the most part, as their physical robustness lends itself most appropriately to the role." He glanced around at their young inquisitive faces. "After birth there's a six month recuperation period before the next implantation." He clasped his hands. "We've greatly improved the safety of this procedure for the host units and are working on an artificial host, but that's a way off yet.

"Currently seventy percent of our production is Kappa."

"Why so high?" one of the scientists blurted out.

Bright smiled ruefully. "Yes, of course we'd love to turn our full capacity to producing higher forms," he acknowledged, "but society requires all types to meet its different vocations. I mean"—he smiled to them—"things wouldn't function too efficiently if we were all Alphas would they?" Everyone laughed. "The Kappa type is still in high demand for menial tasks and of course there is a continuing necessity for military units." He tsk-tsked. "In these times of human shortage we even have to pass mild to moderately defective Kappas into the workforce," he admitted. "Yes, it's not perfect, but we are improving things step by step. We will succeed," he concluded confidently with a broad smile. "Are there any more questions?"

The dark curly-haired girl with a white face and colorless lips—the social engineer—flashed her hand and Bright nodded to her. "What about the tagging? I heard that the new *White Night* low emission chips were imminent."

"Ah," the doctor nodded fervently, delighted to elaborate on details concerning his discipline. "Yes, there's been a big push to get those deployed." He turned to the others. "The White Night chips will replace the current One World collective chips. They will have an extremely low radiation emission and so eliminate the stochastic effects consistent with long and early exposure," he explained. "So, instead of waiting until the subject reaches the age of seventeen, we will be able to activate the transponder very early, well before they leave Mother for citizen mentoring. This will enable us to locate anyone, anywhere." He rubbed has hands together savoring the eventuality. "It will be impossible for anyone to get lost, and it will reduce the possibility of foul play."

"It will make it harder for devo runners to go undetected," the social engineer offered.

"Yes, that too," Bright confirmed spryly. "Anyway, they will be out before year's end I'm told. But we are getting ahead of ourselves…" He turned quickly and headed down the pristine hallway waving his arm in a 'Come follow me' motion. "This way please."

His exposition continued as they proceeded down the hallway. "At five they are released to the adoption pool where qualified enablers are assigned. Oh here we are." He drew up to another window and the students lined up along it peering into a cavernous chamber, awesome in its dimensions—it was about the size of six football fields.

Bright's hand swept over the panorama. "This is one of our play rooms. The children spend most of their time here, or in the classroom or dorm." He turned to the students. "We need absolute control of the first five years, that most vital period of mental formation. We do everything in-house so there are no distractions." He turned back to the glass. "Over there the Alphas and Betas are in their exercise period," he said, pointing out the soccer fields in the distance where a hundred or so children were playing under the supervision of the Play Technicians. "We instill a physical training regime so they will maintain their bodies and also to encourage group cooperation," he explained. "These become life habits."

He pointed to a park-like area containing trees and bushes and paths and several ponds where young children, little girls in tiny bikinis and little boys in briefs, were playing in the sand, splashing in the water, or wandering off into the garden all under the un-intrusive watch of the LifeFormer monitors. "That's a group of Alphas and Betas in play period. They're encouraged to explore nature and their own bodies, and each other. We want to break down any impediments to healthy sexuality." He stroked his goatee as he watched a little blond girl heading towards some bushes with a hesitant little boy in hand.

"What are they doing over there?" Cranston asked, pointing out a group of older children in khaki green, each with a wooden rifle on their shoulder, drawn up in four columns on a concrete square.

"Oh, the Kappas are parading," Bright chuckled. "Basic military training."

Just then an officer, who was barely older than the others, barked an order and all the other visitors turned to watch the unit advance smartly. They could hear the officer's commands clearly however muted by the glass. "Left wheel!" The column turned and proceeded along the right edge of the square, each arm rising and falling with the one behind, each leg in perfect cadence. "Left… turn!" the command sounded and the marchers all turned and advanced in four perfect ranks down the center of the square. "About… turn!" the officer bellowed and they reversed their direction as one. It was all quite impressive. Paul remembered the marching soldiers on Darwin Street.

"They drill until they can do it in their sleep," Bright beamed. "It's no wonder the devos are no match for them."

He turned to his charges. "We regulate the quantity of physical interaction between the evolutionary classes. The Betas are given more time with the Alphas; the Kappas less with either. It's a carefully-monitored variable—too little interaction and society fragments; too much familiarity and the chain of authority breaks down." The class looked thoughtful. He roused them with a "Let's go see some classrooms" and started back towards the corridor.

The hallway branched into several corridors each servicing a multitude of classrooms.

"Oh, this one is good," Bright said in a hushed voice. "Quiet now." He opened the door gingerly and they filed into the back of the room and sat in the row of seats raised and segregated from the students' area by a low wall. From there they had a good vantage point from which to audit the proceedings.

There were about two hundred children in the class all wearing the navy-blue uniforms and red armbands of the Beta cadre. They were older than Paul had expected; likely grade three or four. A lean androgynous woman in a gray uniform was presiding over the class which was on 'worldview and values'. There were three large monitors behind her displaying the identical message: *Who is my friend?*

"Students," she announced when they entered, "Doctor Bright from the human engineering department is present in the classroom." She emphasized the 'doctor'. All eyes turned reverently to Bright and he graciously nodded an acknowledgment.

The lesson continued. "So, we know that we should always love our fellow citizen," she said in summary, "but should we love everyone, then?"

A murmured 'no' swept across around the room.

"No," echoed the teacher, "no, that wouldn't make sense would it? Why should we help those who are bad?" The students nodded. "But how do we know who is bad and who is good? How do we know who we should love?" She waited a moment for the class to think about the question then continued, "here's how." The message on the monitors changed to 'Love those who love. Hate those who hate.' The members of Paul's group glanced at each other and nodded, recognizing one of the basic propositions of One World.

"Now, who do we mean by *those who love*?" she asked the students. A number of hands were raised.

"Yes, citizen 536?" she said pointing to a dark haired girl in the second row.

"We mean those who like tolerance and in-clu-si-vi-ty."

"Yes," the teacher affirmed. "And who are these people?" More hands were raised. "Yes, citizen 238?"

The sandy-haired boy in the fourth row replied, "I think it's people who love One World. They want everyone to be able to live in One World."

"Yes, certainly," the teacher affirmed. "Yes, citizen 105?"

A serious-looking girl close to the boy said, "It's people who follow the laws of One World."

The teacher clapped. "Yes, exactly, it's people who follow the laws of our society—people who are compliant. Why is that so important—to be compliant? Citizen 412?"

"Because the leaders are good and they know what is best for everyone," a black boy answered. "They are smart, so we should do what they say."

The teacher smiled. "Yes, citizen 412, the leaders are the smartest people—they're scientists—and they have calculated what the best thing is for everyone so everyone can be happy. So if we love people, we follow the laws of the leaders, which are made by scientists, so everyone can be happy." She raised an ominous finger. "So, who are the ones who don't love people? Citizen 629?"

"They're all the haters," a small Indian boy answered.

The teacher nodded. "And who are these haters? What else do we call them? Citizen 323?"

"Traditionalists," a red-haired boy answered.

"Very good," the teacher smiled. "Yes, people who are against science and progress. And you, citizen 202?"

"Familialist," the bright freckle-faced girl offered boldly.

"Yes!" she laughed encouragingly, "people who only love some but not all. They often try to parent and pass their fixations on to their children. Very good citizen 202. And you, citizen 212?"

The girl blushed and said, "mono-sexist." Another girl cast a glance at Doctor Bright but turned away shyly when he returned her gaze.

The teacher nodded encouragingly. "Of course; people who have sex with only one person. They are often familialists and even religious." The students snickered derisively.

A small boy raised his hand shyly and the teacher nodded to him, "Yes citizen 739?"

"Un-ti-grates," he said unsurely.

"Yes, citizen 317," the teacher acknowledged, "but is there one thing we can call all of them?"

The students looked quickly at each other, then responded as one:

"DEVOS!" The big screens changed to display 'DEVOS' in flashing red letters.

"Yes!" the teacher clapped, flashing a triumphant glance at Doctor Bright. "The word 'devo' encompasses all these people. They seek to destroy science and freedom and everything that binds us; everything that is good, peaceful, happy," she assured them. She swept the room with a finger inclusively. "We are for the evolution of humanity..." She pointed at the monitor. "...they are for devolution."

She stood there pointing accusingly at the flashing 'DEVO.' "They are incompliant." She turned and addressed her charges earnestly. "Remember students, it is important to love and support One World, but it is equally important to hate those who would hurt people and try to destroy One World. So we say, 'It is important to love correctly; it is important to hate correctly.'" The slogan *Love correctly. Hate correctly* appeared on the screens and the students dutifully repeated it. "We can all strive to be better at this," the teacher counseled them solemnly. Each of the student's faces manifested an appropriate display of repentance.

Bright winked at his group and they slipped out the side door.

"That was one of the review classes," he explained. "We have older kids back periodically to make sure everyone is progressing as they should when they are away from the Center."

He led them up another floor where they viewed a dormitory containing row upon row of beds each with a sleeping little body and micro-speaker to etch the tenets of One World upon the mind of its unconscious occupant.

"So that is a typical day for our children," Bright told them as they led them back towards the elevators. "They are taught the basic social skills—working with others, establishing the correct attitude concerning authoritative figures and the correct outlook on moral issues and, of course, to recite the One World Invocation—basic compliancy training. By the time they leave here they will be ready to assume their positions as budding new citizens of One World." Bright's hands were clasped in from of him like a curator presenting a cherished and masterful canvas. Then he set off abruptly. "Come this way please."

"What's down there?" a sci-ed asked, pointing to another hallway leading to a double door.

"Oh, that's the cross-breeding unit. We're not visiting that today," Bright smiled quickly and shepherded them along.

As he waited impatiently at the elevators he continued in a lowered voice as if speaking confidentially. "So, so far you've seen human generation from cradle to schooler." They drew closer to hear him. Suddenly he exploded with: "But that is nothing compared with what we are achieving in cybergenics!" startling the students standing nearest. "Come come; follow me." He was a whirlwind of flailing arms rushing off to the stairwell, his white coat twisting in wild disarray. The med-eds looked at each other and giggled.

Two floors up he held the door allowing them to pile into the corridor. "This is my favorite initiative," he gushed. "You see, although we are improving the human stock, we are still limited by the frailty of our bodies. Our species is still bound by limited physical capabilities, but"— he held up a finger triumphantly—this state of affairs is being rectified."

They hurried down another long hallway that had few doors on either side. He approached one and scanned in. "This is where we employ our brightest technicians," Bright whispered. Another man in a white lab coat passed them going the other way. "Doctor Gruter," Bright nodded reverently and the other returned the acknowledgement like two monks passing along a cloistered walk.

They came to a small white room. "Here we are. Squeeze in everyone."

They were bundled together peering through a portal into a giant lab, or rather, a honeycomb of labs on many levels divided by glass partitions. Paul could see a group of technicians in, what looked like, space suits working silently and diligently at their benches.

I'm afraid we can't go in—cleanroom restrictions," Bright explained. "See the technician there?" He pointed to one close by. "He's testing a synthetic heart." The students could barely make out the sleek oval specimen. "It's made of a special alloy that will never wear out... well, in all practicality. Behind him they are working with synaptic interface components," he whispered. "Over there they are fabricating optical components—replacement eyes," he whispered with excitement rising in his voice. "They'll allow much greater range than natural eyes and are sensitive to a wide range of light spectra." He looked to his charges, "You'll be able to see in the dark." The students craned their necks to catch a glimpse of the ocular miracle. "Hmmm. It's hard to see," Bright said disappointedly. "Well, let's go next door and see the movie, it will give you a greater appreciation of the work that is being accomplished here."

The students paraded into the adjacent screening room, the lights were dimmed and a promotional documentary on the science and technology of cybergenics was shown. The movie offered a futuristic vision of a world without suffering or death or physical limitation. Beginning with the replacement of limbs and proceeding, as the technology advanced, through the internal organs until finally the mind itself would be loaded into a super-dense memory core—the finite human clothed in an imperishable body of alloy and silicone.

Bright appeared at the front of the studio as the lights came on. "You see students, we are not just improving the species, we will be creating an immortal life form; a *new* species!" He beamed so intensely Paul thought he might go supernova.

"Like God," the young biologist said.

Bright laughed at the analogy offered. "Yes, like God. That's the power of our techno-centric society: we can control our own destiny. We can dictate the path our evolution will travel."

Paul wasn't sure he shared Bright's enthusiasm for the vision presented. He raised his hand. "Doctor Bright, sir?"

"Yes?"

"But won't it mean, in all practicality, the extinction of the human race? What you are describing, doesn't it mean this robot race displacing humanity?" Several of the others looked curiously at Paul.

Bright smiled condescendingly. "Yes, of course. But why should you regret that?" He addressed all the students. "Such is the fate of all species—the inferior gives way to the superior. In our case, we will actually be the enabling agent in the emergence of our successor species. The human species will become extinct, as all have before it," he conceded, "but we will be the first species to have realized our place in the grand evolutionary mission and to have actively assisted the cause of evolutionary progress." He beamed at Paul. "What prouder legacy could a species have?"

Paul didn't trust himself to respond. Bright's thinking was undoubtedly rational, but something inside him balked at the idea of pursuing the means to one's demise. There was something pathological, or perhaps religious, in the idea. He tried to make contact with some of the others but they averted their eyes, unwilling or unable to question the goodness of Progress.

The tour continued for another hour with visits to the adoption center and the enabler school. Afterwards, when they had returned to the reception room to retrieve their coats and baggage, Paul found himself lingering with several of the science students. The other politico, Cranston, had left quickly so he hadn't a chance to speak with him. He wandered over to where the med-eds were sitting and caught the word "preg-ref" in their whispered conversation, but they went quiet when he sat down. It was strange, in retrospect, that Bright had not taken them though the pregnancy relief facilities. He chatted with the med-eds for a while and managed to extract the handle of the cute one before setting off for home.

When he passed through the ponderous revolving door out into the park he experienced a great barometric release, and his spirits rose with every additional meter of separation from Mother.

When he got to Cosmos he paused at the lights and looked back at the great flawless leviathan in the distance staring unblinkingly back at him through the trees. "Busy with the next cohort," he muttered.

The light changed and he hastened on his way.

The morning had done nothing to dispel his uneasiness concerning Mother.

5

Party

Paul was in the kitchen with a few others, one of whom was a very attractive black-haired olive-skinned girl whose genes surely originated in the subcontinent. He was captivated by her pitch black eyes whenever they turned his way. It would still be a while before the pizzas would be ready and it didn't look like he would get a chance to talk to the girl alone so he went out to the living room and drifted in the crowd.

Morris was sitting on a sofa chair in the corner with his head lying on the back, closed eyes aimed at the ceiling, headphones blaring and a beer on the table beside him. *Typical Mo*, Paul smiled to himself, *on a different planet altogether.* Calvin hadn't shown, as anticipated. *Maybe he couldn't get away from Petya*, he thought, but he knew these parties weren't his thing anyway—Cal was becoming more and more a recluse.

The living room was crowded, so he wandered down the dimly lit hallway where he had seen some others go. The doors to the rooms on one side of the hallway were shut and he could hear moaning coming from one of them; he'd found the kennels. He peeped into the only open door and saw some guys gathered around a monitor and stopped to listen in. It was a newscast. The screen showed soldiers shooting at some unseen enemy and some burning buildings. The narrator was talking about another push in Guangxi province which was holding out against One World forces.

Then it switched to another scene, in Africa where a long raggedy line of prisoners was being marched off by One World troops. They were part of a devo force that had been beaten in east Africa. An army officer was optimistic that the rebels would be crushed by fall. A third story announced the re-establishment of another World Zone in central Africa—Zone 394. It had been seized by insurgent forces three years earlier following the mass rioting that swept the continent in the wake of order GX819-4V52-09297, the so-called 'culling' directive. The small local One World forces had been overwhelmed by the mob and some devo warlords had taken control. The One World military response was ruthless and decisive, however. The major towns were quickly recovered and governance reestablished. The insurgent forces had fought a fierce guerrilla campaign in the countryside ever since, but now the last of their leaders had been executed and his remaining forces isolated. The newscast showed the celebration at One World Plaza in New Frankfurt. The unvarying theme of the newscast was of One World advancing triumphantly and bringing the un-integrated areas under control.

Paul examined the faces and physiques of the young men who were all absorbed in the newscast. *They are all Kappas*, he thought. *Their kind will be doing most of the fighting so it's no wonder they are so interested.* He remembered the khaki-clad marching children at Mother.

The newscast was a minimum Beta level that was obviously not compliant for Kappas, but Paul didn't feel any motivation to challenge them. While he was curious to know their opinion about the military situation, he had always been reserved around the lower grades and doubtful as to the possibility of really connecting with them. They might even think he was talking down to them if he tried.

A low rumble of voices could be heard whenever someone opened the side door, so he headed outside to take a look.

It was dark and confining at the side of the house, but he could hear voices, lots of them, and see light coming from the back yard as he picked his way along the stone walk. The yard was aglow in shimmering moonlight, but the crowd there was so tightly packed he had to push through to see what was happening.

In the center there was a white circle drawn on the grass—it looked like chalk or maybe salt, he couldn't tell exactly. Four large candles, each on a platter mounted on a pole, were on opposite sides of the circle—at twelve, three, six and nine o'clock. About forty people were sitting inside the circle and a hooded figure in a long black skirt and lacey bodice was moving clockwise around its circumference tracing it out with her staff. She paused at each candle and drew a pentagram in the air with her long finger and rhymed out an incantation while the seated participants followed her progress. The candlelight illuminated her face as she came around, and he recognized Cassandra, a Spirituality student at Eastview. Her bell-like voice carried clearly in the sultry air. "Guardians of the West, of Water and Love, the torrential rain and the morning dew, life and regeneration, I call upon your presence at this place, your protection, Love and Light for this circle." Then in a firm voice: "So mote it be."

The celebrants affirmed: "So mote it be," in unison.

She traced along the circle to the last candle and invoked the protection of the 'Guardians of the North, of Earth and Stability….' The electricity in the air was heightened with each chorus of 'So mote it be.'

She arrived back at three o'clock, raised her arms and called out into the night sky, "Oh Mighty Ones, Lord of the East, Lord of the North, Lord of the West, Lord of the South, I summon thee to protect this rite! I bid thee hail and welcome!" She lowered her arms and announced, "The circle is closed."

On cue those inside the ring rose to their feet, joined hands and began to move in a great serpentine swirl around its circumference and through its middle, the leader finally clasping the hand of the trailer. Around and around they danced, a drum beat setting the rhythm, while Cassandra lit the candles in their midst.

Paul was agitated, as he often was at spiritual events. He knew One World sanctioned compliant religious expression—whether Hinduism, Buddhism, Shamanism, Paganism or other earth religion—whatever facilitated the perception of oneness and banished individuality, but he had always thought worship irrelevant to Alphas; it was something for the less-evolved.

Meanwhile the scene was becoming increasingly frantic. The bodies of the dancers collaborated in a primal synchronicity, chanting "The Goddess is in everything; everything is in the Goddess," faster and faster, heightening the energy with every lap. The kaleidoscope of bodies was mesmerizing and the beat set the spectators nodding and swaying but Paul resisted its pull.

All the dancers were female. He recognized one from Eastview: a cute grade eleven with long sandy-brown hair wearing a candy-stripe tee shirt. Her name was Melanie; Beverly knew her. Her eyes were ecstatic like the others' and her body stalked the primitive beat with the same animal abandon. Faster and faster, round and round, faster and faster.

Suddenly, Cassandra's voice broke through the bedlam like a thunderclap. "She descends! She descends! She descends!" The dancers stopped and thrust their linked hands into the sky and a chant like swift water dashing over boulders streamed from their lips. Cassandra threw back her hood and raised her arms to the full moon. "Goddess of the moon, Mother of all Creation, guide me in your Love," her ruby lips called above the storm. "Keeper of the ancient mysteries, Beautiful One, come down into me!" Her skin glowed white in the full moon's radiance and the smoky oval amulet swinging from a silver chain around her neck flickered scarlet in the shadow of her cloak. "Queen of Heaven, fill me with your presence…"

Paul felt the hair on the back of his neck rise; the tension was unbearable. The others standing with him were entranced, spellbound, so he edged back from the circle between their comatose bodies and managed to stumble back to the house in the darkness.

When he had gained the sanctuary of the hallway and closed the door behind him securely, relief rushed over him. He drifted down the dark hallway in a stupor, vaguely aware of two others peeking into the TV room bemusedly. One whispered the answer to a question that had crossed his mind earlier: "Paige invited them; she has a thing about the under-classes."

The bright light of the living room disoriented him further as he emerged from the dim hallway. It took a few moments to regain his equilibrium.

At first he saw some girls and guys huddled in the corner wiped out on SOMA but then spotted Morris and Roland talking to a petite artsy-looking girl wearing mod black glasses and a leopard print top. He went over to them.

"Hey, Paul, whazzup?" Morris greeted him and they grasped hands. "Hey, you look like you've seen a ghost."

"Hi, Paul," Roland said. "This is Cat. She's from Northview."

"She likes chess," Morris added.

Paul settled himself and extended a hand, "Meow." Cat snickered and shook it. "There's a few others from Northview here I think."

"I came with Cranston," the girl said. "He goes to Northview too.

"What's that?" a tap on her shoulder caused her to startle.

"Oh you! You scared me!" she said with a laugh. "We were just talking about the Life Center. Oh, this is…"

"It's Paul, we were at Mother on Friday," Cranston said extending a hand.

Paul shook the proffered hand. "Ha, small world. How'd you hear about this party?"

"Oh, Cat is buddies with Paige." he explained. "So Paul, what did you think of the Life Center?"

The question was unexpected and sent Paul's confused mind spinning. "Oh, well, it was interesting."

"Just 'interesting'? Einstein there thinks it's 'the crowning achievement of our enlightened society,'" Cranston said ironically.

"Ha, Bright," Paul laughed. "He's quite the character."

"I was pretty much blown away by the whole experience," Roland interjected earnestly. "I was there last month. I mean, what they can do with the cell, and the whole re-engineering of our species. In the next ten years, twenty tops, we'll be seeing stuff we can only dream of—artificial organs, greatly extended lives, maybe indefinitely." Roland's goggle-eyed gaze reminded Paul of Bright.

Cranston rolled his eyes. "You sound like Doctor Bright." Paul laughed at hearing his thoughts given voice. "He's the guy who did our tour."

"Yeah, so I gathered."

Cat had tucked herself under Cranston's arm and was rubbing against his body, like her namesake, as he talked. They were a cute but physically discordant couple Paul chuckled to himself—like a brown tie with a navy blazer—as he beheld the tall athletic square-jawed figure of Cranson encompassing her diminutive frame with her studious and slightly rodent-like visage peeping out. Her squirming finally caused him to pause and look down. "Hey what's up with you?" he laughed.

"I want to go for a walk," she purred, peering up at him.

Cranston winked at Paul, "Guess I'd better take the Cat for a walk. Nice meeting you."

"Yeah nice," Cat grinned, and they scooted off.

Paul wished he could have spoken with Cranston for a while because it seemed they would have a lot in common. He wished Beverly had come. Suddenly, he remembered his thesis assignment and turned to Roland. "I've been trying to think of a topic for my exit paper. Have you decided on anything?"

"I'm doing something on eugenics," Roland replied, "I think on the role of DNA manipulation in accelerating the evolutionary process."

"Sounds right up your alley," Paul said. "I'm still drawing a blank here."

"Why don't you write something on Mother? 'Why We Should All Raise Kids' or something," Morris deadpanned.

Paul grimaced. "Yeah, thanks for the tip friend."

"Anytime buddy," Morris sniffed and slipped his headphones back on.

Throughout the conversation Paul had kept an eye on the raven-haired girl he had seen earlier in the kitchen. She was standing near the window chatting with two guys and he managed to overhear her name 'Andrea'. She seemed a bit older than the others—the way she held herself and the confident way she conversed. She was a little more sophisticated. He liked that. All night he had been hoping to catch her alone, so when the two males moved off he crossed the floor.

"Hi, you are Andrea, right?" Paul grinned winningly as he drew close.

Her long, shiny black hair tossed as she turned her head towards him. "Oh hi. Yeah. Paul?" she said. Her white white teeth were brilliant against her dusky skin as she smiled pleasantly. Paul could see she had a single chocolate brown pin stripe highlight on the left side of her shiny pitch-black hair. He thought she was perhaps the most beautiful girl he had ever seen.

"You are good with names," Paul smiled charmingly.

"Oh, well, sometimes," she grinned. "Umm, it was interesting what you were talking about—about Mother I mean."

Paul's eyebrow arched. "Oh, really? You overheard that all the way over here? What's your interest in it?" Her eyes were so deep and black, mesmerizing—like falling into Walden Pond; twice.

She cast quickly to the right and left before returning her gaze to Paul. "Well, I'm just completing the Enabler training there. Next week I should be done."

"Oh really? That's great!" Paul said mustering more enthusiasm than he felt. "So you are planning to enable a child?"

"Well, for a few years anyway," she said reservedly.

"Wonderful!" Paul enthused. "What made you decide to? It's a big commitment."

"We felt it was the right thing to do. We have the time now. We both wanted to do our part for society." She smiled sheepishly. "Well, we need the points too…for the apartment you know?" She looked at him with raised brows, seeking affirmation.

"Oh. You mean you're short community merits?"

"Yeah," she said a bit flustered, as if she had committed an incompliancy, "we like where we are. You know how hard it is to get a nice place downtown. We have three years in our coupling," she added awkwardly. "Petre's an artist, Beta type y'know," she winked and rolled her eyes. "I think he will do okay. He's kind. Anyway we're happy to do our part for society. It will only be a few years," she consoled herself.

"Well, for sure there's nothing more important than guiding the next generation. Our society sure needs more people willing to shoulder that responsibility. I think it's really great what you're doing," Paul assured her. *She really is a pretty girl.*

"Yeah, yeah," she mused, "thanks." She gave a quick smile, "How about you? You ever thought about it?" She stared expectantly at him with those pit-bottomless eyes.

"Oh well, ah boy. No, ah, I haven't really got that far yet. I'm just graduating this year. Then it's, y'know, off to university," he fumbled.

"Oh," she laughed, "I thought you were older."

Paul laughed too. "Yes, people often think that. How old are you?" he asked cheekily, happy for a chance to change the subject.

She grinned back but said not a word. Her lips pressed together pensively. "Y'know, I just wish we could choose the child. I guess the technicians know best though."

"Yeah they're trained for that sort of thing." Paul answered, "It's all done very scientifically."

"Yeah," she said pensively. She grinned, "Chinese kids are so cute though."

"Hey, Andrea, pizza's done!" a voice bellowed from the kitchen.

Andrea rolled her eyes and smiled, "Petre's calling. Nice meeting you Paul," she said with a brilliant smile.

"Yeah, see ya." He watched her sashay across the room to vanish into the kitchen.

"Whew," he whistled and wandered off to check out the rest of the party.

A group had gone off to the TV room to watch SpaceFleet, thinning the crowd out a bit. He noticed Suzanne had arrived and was sitting on the couch sipping a drink with her friends Kim and Belinda. They looked as if they had come from another party. Predictably, Morris had settled into a chair opposite and was trying to chat her up while stealing glimpses at her cleavage. She was wearing a bronze-colored chemise over shiny white spandex pants with a snakeskin pattern woven in—a costume that invited such scrutiny.

Next to her, Kim, a beautiful Chinese girl, reclined back on the chair, her face flushed and her eyes closed. She had never held her liquor well. Beside her, Belinda, a busty full-figured black girl in cream halter and snug pink slacks was snickering as the white guy beside her patted her thigh and whispered in her ear.

"Soooo, Suzanne," Morris crooned, "what's in the glass?"

Suzanne swirled an ice cube around the perimeter of her glass with her finger. "Scotch," she said quietly without returning his gaze.

"Oh, that's my drink too." He looked down at his glass, "Well maybe after British brews. You into Islays? Lagavulin—puts hair on your tongue."

"Umm just Glenlivet," she stammered.

"Oh, good call. The eighteen year old is smooth like silver—real sophisticated one."

"You can get that?" Suzanne ventured skeptically.

Morris shrugged nonchalant. "Yeah sure. I know people…"

Suzanne looked doubtful.

"Hey, my gene strain is from Aberdeen. I used to play the Scotch Opening even."

"That's not a real chess game," Suzanne groaned.

"Sure it is. I'll show it to you later back at my place."

Suzanne fixed him with a hard stare. "There's not much chance of that, really."

"Okay. Not your thing? How about I show you my French Defense?" he said with a plausible Gaulish accent.

"You're always horsing around," she chuckled reluctantly.

"*Me* horsing around?" he said with mock sensitivity. "Well, actually I'm *monkeying* around—I only *horse* around on weekdays."

Suzanne suppressed a smirk. "God you're weird."

Morris was unfazed. "So you're finishing up at Eastview and moving on to U of A? Looking forward to starting out in the world of high business?"

"She wants to go into fashion," Kim piped in without stirring from her recumbent position.

"Kim!" Suzanne slapped her on the thigh.

"What about you? What do you want to be when you grow up? Oh hi, Paul," Suzanne smiled as he stepped up behind Morris' chair.

Paul nodded and saluted, "Hi."

Morris cocked his head up. "Hi. We're just talking about vocations."

"What about you, Mr. Politico, did you ever think you'd like to do something else?" Suzanne asked playfully.

"Oh, I guess I've thought about other careers at times," he responded gamely.

"Like what," Suzanne prodded. Just then Belinda giggled prompting Suzanne to grin ruefully and look skyward.

"Oh, maybe something in sports… a hockey coach."

"Whoa! That's some leap from politics!" Suzanne laughed.

"When I was young I wanted to be a Tyrannosaurus Rex," Morris confided, "I later realized the impracticality of it—what with the extinction of suitable prey and all."

Suzanne guffawed despite herself. "Is he always like this?" she asked Paul.

"Yeah, that's him… pretty much." He didn't want to intrude in on his friend's play, but Suzanne seemed bent on drawing him in. She was certainly attractive and available, but he just didn't feel any resonance with the person behind that striking figure. He was ashamed he had these feelings; like he suffered from sexual inhibition or something.

"You're EVIL!" Belinda blurted out in response to something her admirer had whispered in her ear, and burst into a riotous laughter which proved contagious. Even Kim sat up and giggled emphatically. Belinda's unself-conscious laughter sent convulsions through her body that threatened to dislodge her heaving breasts from her flimsy top.

"Belinda dear, you are causing a scene," Suzanne giggled.

Out of the corner of his eye Paul noticed a stream of people pouring in from the hallway. *The séance, or whatever it was, must have concluded*, he thought. When he saw Melanie emerge he took the opportunity to duck out.

Melanie was standing on the threshold waiting for her eyes to adjust to the lighting when Paul approached. "Hi there," he smiled warmly. "The night's conjuring has finished I guess."

Her cheeks dimpled up, "Yeah, we sent the spirits back to bed." She exalted, "Wow! Cass is so good at it!" Her sea blue eyes had accommodated to the brightness of the living room. "Hey, I know you from school, right?" she quizzed, raising her pencil line brows.

"Yes, I think so. You go to Eastview too."

"Ha, yeah! Well actually, there's probably quite a number from Eastview here." She bobbed her head, "I'm Melanie."

"Paul," he replied, bobbing back. "I'm a politico, senior."

"Wow! I'm doing Environmental Management; third year. So you'll be graduating in the winter?"

"Yeah, just one more semester."

"Where will you be going after?"

"I'm going to the University of Trudeau. Well, that's what I hope for anyway."

"Oh right!" She tapped herself on the forehead. "That would be the place to go, I mean, for politicos. It will be five years for you there then."

"Yeah, six with the probation."

"Boy, long time to be in school," she sighed. "I'm just as happy to have my four and be done."

"You don't like school?" Paul asked.

"Oh, well, no it's okay." She pinched her lips together dimpling her cheeks. "I just think I'll be ready to get out there in the real world, y'know? Do something to make a difference."

"Yeah, I can relate."

As their conversation progressed Paul was aware of how comfortable he felt with her and sensed the feeling was reciprocated. A synchronicity of expression and social cadence graced their intercourse. He was charmed by her dimpled smile and innocent looking pale blue eyes.

They chatted for the better part of an hour about music, books, travel, art, even flowers. Often she would touch his arm while relating a story or explaining something and stare fixedly into his eyes when he was talking. They shared a lot of laughter.

He was disappointed when Cassandra appeared at her side.

"Oh hi, Cass, you ready to go?"

Cassandra eyed Paul from head to toe with a darting flash of her large onyx eyes. "Yeah, I've got to be back by eleven-thirty at least, you know." She tossed a black lace throw across her shoulders. Her eyes were ebony like Andrea's, but wild, almost fierce, like an animal's, and without warmth. Andrea's pulled you in; Cassandra's cut like a knife.

"Yeah right, I'm ready," Melanie replied. This is Paul by the way. He goes to Eastview too."

"Yeah, I've seen you around," Cassandra acknowledged him.

Paul found Cassandra's presence unsettling for some reason. There was something creepy about her, like a clock running backward. Melanie didn't seem to sense it though. Perhaps it has something to do with the scent she threw off: a strange herbaceous fragrance he could not identify. "Yes, me too," he said awkwardly. He thought maybe it was just her reputation as a mystic slash spiritualist that caused him to imagine the weird aura she seemed to project. Perhaps if he knew Cass better, as Mel did apparently, he wouldn't feel so odd.

"It was great talking to you, Paul." Melanie said, smiling shyly. "Maybe I'll see you at school."

"Oh. Yeah. I'll look for you," he smiled back, not at all shyly.

She grinned, "You do that."

Paul's eyes followed her as she zigzagged through the crowd, skittering behind her formidable friend. *Yes. I surely will*, he thought.

* * *

As he left the train to switch to the northbound line Paul caught a glimpse of a lone figure sitting on a bench with head lowered. An inertia borne of weariness carried him a few more paces before he stopped and looked back. "That looks like…it's Calvin," he muttered. He reversed course and approached the forlorn figure.

"Hey Cal, what's up? Missed you at the party," he said in an upbeat manner. Calvin didn't stir. Paul sobered and sat down beside his friend.

He waited a few moments. At the other end of the platform two men were leaning against the tiled wall, necking.

"Things not going so good I guess?" he finally said.

Calvin emitted an undecipherable grunt.

Paul waited for a continuation in vain. Three others approached from the other direction; the woman's heels tap-tapped on the polished floor.

"How did the concert go?" he said finally.

Calvin was silent. He shrugged but still said nothing.

A girl and two guys walked by holding hands. They must be a coupling, Paul thought. He watched them pass. He could see others gathering on the westbound platform.

"It didn't," Calvin's voice pronounced quietly.

Paul turned to his friend. "What's that?"

"The concert; I didn't play. I couldn't," Calvin said in a hollow voice.

"What happened?" Paul said, befuddled.

Calvin sighed wearily. "I just couldn't," he repeated.

"What do you mean?"

Calvin's voice was barely auditable. "I mean I just couldn't. I can't anymore."

Paul sat staring at the stone floor as he tried to fathom the enigma beside him. The approaching westbound train screeched in the distance. "You mean something happened at the concert, so you couldn't play?" he ventured.

"No. Nothing happened. It's me. I can't play," Calvin anguished.

An artificial wind blew down the tunnel as the train thundered into the station crashing into their conversation. It unloaded and loaded its passengers and Paul watched the windows speed by like a string of pearls as it clambered off again. He was left staring at the advert panel hung between the tracks opposite. It was an enabling poster from the Life Center showing two smiling women and a man with two children. "TAKE TIME FOR THE FUTURE" the caption below read.

Paul resumed, "Calvin, what's wrong? What happened?"

"I tried to play, but I couldn't." His voice faltered. "I just sat there in front of them all."

"Oh." Paul's consternation was unalleviated, and he didn't know how to proceed. Calvin was talking at least, so he thought he should try to keep the conversation going and everything would work itself out. "Has anything like this happened before?"

Calvin sighed again. "It's not just 'something that happened.' It's not like a case of stage fright," he said, a note of exasperation in his voice. He paused, seeking words. "I can't live like this anymore."

A woman in a business suit standing nearby must have caught part of the conversation because she looked around curiously. For a second Paul was alarmed she might denounce them to the operators—everyone was subject to official reprimand and even possible genetic reevaluation if implicated in socially delinquent thinking. They both fell silent.

The eastbound train approached pushing a cool column of air. In a few moments it rumbled into the station and screeched to a halt. The doors swooshed open, bodies staggered out and others began to board.

Calvin rose suddenly. "I have to go," he muttered and rushed for the closing doors, just in time.

Paul's final vision was of his friend hunched over in his seat as the train started out. Soon its rumble faded out in the distance leaving Paul in the surreal silence of the empty platform.

He sat on the bench staring down the long black tunnel.

6

DAY 130

HARMONY

Paul hadn't talked to Calvin for almost two weeks although he thought he had spotted him on a passing subway train once. Someone said he was undergoing psychiatric treatment. He didn't respond to Paul's messages and was never online.

Morris had re-located to New Frankfurt. He had won the zonal tournament and plunged immediately into training for the Domain Five Championship, studying ten hours a day. Paul wondered how he managed to keep up the pace.

He had made contact with Melanie and they had gone out twice. She invited him to go to the Lammas celebration in August. It was some kind of Sun festival—probably something witchy. He hadn't committed to it yet, though.

Their meetings had affirmed his feelings of complementariness. He was looking forward to meeting up with her this afternoon.

He knew he should go out with other girls, so they couldn't be accused of having an exclusive relationship—an incompliancy—but he hadn't the interest.

But for the mandatory four-day stint with the World Pioneers, the rest of his time was spent relaxing and recharging for next semester. He worked out regularly, intending to add a few more pounds to his chest and arms and thicken up his legs for the beach season.

One night he went out with a few of the guys for a beer and Beverly had shown up. He always enjoyed it when she came along; her presence took the edge off the conversation and it was cool that she liked to guzzle beer too. Zone Fifty-Three was a major beer exporter so it was one commodity in plentiful supply.

Bev talked about getting up to the summer Jazz Festival in Foucault, and that Roland and she planned to go canoeing for a week in Algonquin Park late July, before the black fly season and after the mosquitoes. Paul had gone camping with them twice before and had a great time—it was nice to just hang out and party and not be required to attend the endless doctrinal sessions you got at the Pioneer camps. He was pretty sure of getting a travel permit but didn't know whether he would be up for it this summer; there was a lot to think about.

The business concerning his final essay was weighing on his mind. A topic had to be submitted by August eighth, so there was still plenty of time, but he was ambitious to get a head start on it and write something that would really impress the Committee. Such were his thoughts this Friday morning as he proceeded along Davisville Avenue en-route to the gym.

At times he felt his mind was on the verge of a suitable topic, but he could never quite coax it up into the light of day. He started into his warm up still preoccupied. An aerobics class let out and the girls skipped by on their way to the fountain, but he was too distracted to take notice.

What would really stand out? he wondered. *What makes our culture different from all the others? I mean, what REALLY captures the essence of One World?*

A hot pink leotard flashed by catching his eye. The girl had a body, that was for sure—lots of curves and bounce. He realized it was the girl in the green leotard he had seen before—the one with the amulet. He hadn't seen her since.

I could just write about political trends—maybe the emerging synergies at the zonal level. That would be okay—he grimaced—*I guess.* It was a meager prospect. *Man! There's got to be something better....*

The pink leotard came back heading the other way, towards the weight room. She looked at him, compressed her lips in a simulated smile and quickly passed on.

"Nice," he mumbled as he watched her sashay away. *Too bad about the devo pendant though.* No sooner had that thought subsided then another pushed itself forward. *The devos: what about* their *culture?* His mind stirred. *They came before One World. Really, the devo culture dominated the West until the beginning of the World Era.* His thoughts began to race. *So,*—he stopped pedaling—*so, the philosophy that underpinned it must have had some good points.* It was strange how little he knew about it. In school there had been a brief synopsis of devo beliefs—mostly ridicule of its prudish sexual ethic and superstitions—but not much else. *The question then is: What were the flaws in that worldview that led to its demise? How did One World displace it? THAT would be an interesting study,* he thought. *How would I present this?* His face lit up. *Yes! Of course! It's so obvious! I just have to make a study of the devo worldview, distill it down into its essentials, its axioms—that's where its flaws will be exposed—and compare them with their One World counterparts! Wouldn't that illustrate cultural evolution brilliantly!* He started to pump the pedals again. *I should check out WorldLib to see what material is available before I submit my topic though—do a bit of preliminary research.* He remembered the Bible stashed way in his treasure box. *That might come in handy too although I'll have to be careful not to reveal I have it.*

After the couple weeks off he was warming up to getting back to the books; he didn't like to be idle. This topic could be very interesting. In any case it would, for sure, make him more appreciative of the One World civilization after examining it in the light of a less evolved one.

The crosstrainer timer ran out. Initially, he thought to go for another ten minutes since he had not been pedaling the whole time, but then he remembered the girl in the pink leotard. *Hmmm... I wonder if it would be worthwhile to talk to her; she might have some insights into devo religion.* He recalled a news item a while back about some official from the 'Inclusion Church,' or some such organization, assuring everyone that Jesus, an important devo figure, would have blessed the unburdening of un-integrated vagrants, so he knew there were still people taking about it. He smiled to himself knowing that her appearance didn't lessen his motivation for approaching her—she was a looker—before hopping off the crosstrainer, making a quick stop at the fountain and sauntering off towards the weight room in search of her.

The sounds of training filled the room: the controlled breathing, clatter of barbell returning to cradle and thud of dumbbells hitting the rubber floor while the zip of pulleys and clack of their weights against their stacks kept time. A reviving breeze wafted down the aisles driven by the overhead fans. It was quite busy.

She wasn't occupying any of the machines in the back training area, so he peered around the lat machine into the free weight zone. She wasn't there either. He thought perhaps she had retired to the showers but then caught a flash of pink in a mirror. There she was, in the squatting area behind the chest machines, working with a Smith Machine. Paul looped around the other side of the long row of IronGym equipment, approached from the other direction and settled into the chest press close by.

The bar resting across her shoulders had a twenty kilo plate on either side. She descended in a uniform motion all the way down until her butt almost touched her heels. *She sure is flexible*, Paul noted. He watched her buttocks clench in their semi-opaque tights as she began the ascent back to a standing position. She continued with controlled precision for fifteen reps. He pressed out twelve reps with a light weight in order to avoid looking too conspicuous. There were others waiting for machines, and he didn't want to lose his seat. In between sets she stood and eyed her image in the mirror, seemingly unconscious of the frenetic activity all around her.

She had earphones on. *I wonder what she is listening to.* They made it more difficult to approach her. *How to get her attention?*

She finished another set, patted her forehead and shoulders down with her towel, and moved down a few places to a standing leg curl machine. Paul did another set with a heavier weight and kept tabs on her out of the corner of his eye. When the incline press machine opposite her came free he changed stations.

She finished one leg and switched to pump out fifteen reps on the other. Paul pressed out ten reps on the incline in the meantime. In between sets she did a few toe touches. As she was positioning herself on the machine again she glanced in the mirror and caught him looking. Her eyes met his for a moment but her face remained expressionless as if there were an opaque barrier between them. She quickly looked away and went on to another set. Paul was a bit discouraged but added more weight to the stack and pressed out eight reps.

When she finished her set she did a few lunges to stretch out her hamstrings before taking her position at the leg curl machine again. Again she glanced in the mirror and again her eyes found his. Paul thought he detected a slight amused buckling of her lips before she looked away and launched into her next set.

Paul did another and was finished well before she completed her second leg. She dried herself off with her towel and turned to study her profile in the mirror. To Paul's surprise she cast a sideways glance at him and smirked as she moved off. *Wow. Things are looking up*, he thought. He coolly did another set, toweled down then set off in her direction.

He located her in the corner struggling on the shoulder press machine. *Now or never.* When she had finished her set he stepped up. "Mind if I work in?"

She raised then furrowed her eyebrows before lowering her headphones. "Yes?"

"I was wondering if I could work in with you," Paul repeated.

"Oh. Yeah. Sure." She grinned. "Sorry, I didn't hear you." She got up and stood beside the machine allowing him to sit. The seat was warm. He resisted the masculine urge to really load up the weight, instead deciding to start moderately light. As he went through his reps he could see her in the mirror rotating her arms like a windmill.

After he had finished he moved the weight setting back up to where she had left it and stepped aside so she could do another set. She hadn't replaced her headphones, so he surmised she wouldn't mind talking.

"I haven't seen you around."

"No, I usually work out at school. I come here on the weekend," she said, then added, "Of course in the summer time I'm mostly here." She fidgeted with her hair and tossed a long blond tress over her shoulder. "I think I've seen you here before."

"Well, I usually come here weeknights. Sometimes during the weekend but I'm usually too busy then." He extended his hand. "I'm Paul by the way."

"Harmony," she answered. She had a firm handshake for a girl.

"How long have you been coming here?" he asked.

"Oh, a couple of years… since grade nine. One of my, uh, boyfriends worked out here and he got me in." She sat down and moved the pin down one plate. "One moment," she said, took a breath and began to press the weight overhead. They stopped talking while she executed her twelve repetitions. Paul stepped in to aid with the last two as her deltoids fatigued.

"Whew! Tough one!" she said breathlessly.

"Good set," Paul said. "You didn't wear your bandana today. Aren't you afraid your hair will get caught?"

"Oh, so you have seen me before," she said grinning mischievously.

"Yeah," he chuckled, "I guess you found me out."

She smiled. "You don't go to Northview do you?"

"No, Eastview. Politics," he answered.

"Eww, a politico! You must be smart," she laughed.

"Ha, yeah I guess. Where do you go?"

"Parkside. I'm a business student," she answered.

"Graduating soon?" he asked.

"I have one more year. I can't wait. You?"

"I'm going into my last semester."

"Must be nice," she said longingly. "Out on your own, free from your enablers." She mouthed the last word with a sarcastic intonation.

He changed the topic. "Do you meet at lot of people at the gym?"

"Oh. Ha, ha. Yeah, a fair number I guess."

"I find it hard meeting people. Everyone has earphones on so it is hard to talk," Paul said.

"By 'everyone' you mean the girls," she grinned. "Yeah, I know what you mean. I wear them so that I'm not distracted when I'm working out—you know: all the noise and the god-awful music on the speakers." She snickered and nodded her head, "Yeah, and it keeps the guys at bay too."

"Thar ya go," Paul laughed, "I suspected there was something of that afoot."

"Well, you didn't seem to have too much trouble getting my attention anyway," she laughed.

"Yes well, when I set my mind to things…"

"I'm sure," she grinned. "Your set by the way."

Paul grinned back, sat down and loaded up the stack. He pumped out seven reps then struggled for an eighth. Harmony looked on intensely.

"It's not fair," she said as he rose from the seat.

"What's that?"

"Guys can lift so much. It doesn't matter how hard I train, I'll never be able to do that."

"Well, vive la difference," Paul beamed. "We have to have some redeeming qualities to make up for our other shortcomings, don't you think?"

"We-ell, since you put it that way…" She grinned and added coyly, "Not that I've noticed any obvious shortcomings."

Paul flashed a winning smile. "What are your training goals anyway? Why do you work out?"

"Oh, I'm on the gymnastics team at school for one. Strength and flexibility training is mandatory there."

"And for two?"

She grinned evilly. "I like how it makes my body look." She arched her back and struck a centerfold pose in the mirror.

"Yup. I, uh, see what you mean," Paul stammered. Harmony laughed, pleased.

"What else do you like to do," he asked.

She smiled and twirled one of her long locks around her finger. "Well, let's see. Besides working out, I like to listen to music, I like to dance and hang out on Emerald West. Oh! I saw Captain Ewing—from SpaceFleet, you know?—one night," she gushed wide-eyed. "Anyway, my friends and I like to go to the beach. We go to concerts at Suzuki Place and the Unity Dome downtown, and check out the clubs around town." She paused and added with a smirk, "Oh, and I like to shop."

"That goes without saying," Paul interjected.

Harmony grinned. "I'm sure I don't know what you mean."

Paul chuckled then cut to the chase. "Do you have any spiritual interests?"

Harmony looked surprised. "Oh, wow... change of topic," she laughed. "Yeah, well, several of my friends are into meditation, so I go to some of their classes and enviro events," she said. "I do yoga, and I also attend an Inclusion church on Sundays..."

"Oh, that's interesting," Paul said seizing the opening, "I don't think I know any other Inclusionists. How did you come to take that up?"

"Ha! You probably think I'm a little weird!" Harmony laughed knowingly. "It just happened by accident for me, really. I just wandered in one day." She checked herself. "Oh! Actually, I heard about this really cool pastor, Gretchen Teasdale, who was presiding at a church downtown—they had a poster in the cafeteria at school. I went to check it out and, well, I'm still going there after three years."

"Whereabouts is it?"

"It's called the Church of the Affirming Spirit, just behind the Layton Center. Did you know there's about fifty-thousand Inclusionists in zone fifty-three?"

"Wow. Why is it so popular?"

Harmony furrowed her brow a moment. "Well, I think it's mostly because the IC has kept up with cultural trends, you know—stayed relevant. We're always changing to satisfy society's evolving spiritual needs and we're always looking to incorporate other spiritualities and traditions into our worship, to expand our horizons and keep everyone's interest up," she nodded. "And then there's Gretchen—she's so good at making people feel great about just who they are, you know? She's so affirming! You should meet her."

Paul leaped at the opportunity. "Well, could I come along to one of your meetings? Maybe this Sunday?"

"Oh! That would be great!" Harmony bounced excitedly. "Gretchen is always telling us to bring others along." She stopped short and put a finger to her lips, "Oh! But I can't go this week. How about next Sunday? It's at ten a.m."

"Sure, sounds good," he answered. He had planned to go to the ball game that afternoon but didn't want to miss a chance to get a leg up on his essay. "Let's exchange contacts after. We can talk during the week and figure out how to coordinate things."

Harmony gave him an arch look. "Aaaaah. So you'll be getting my handle then? Pretty smooth," she laughed.

Paul grinned. "I'm like an open book, I see."

"Hmmm. I think it's my set," she said.

They finished off the military press, then did four sets of flys and called it a day. Paul waited for her in the lounge afterwards with his eye on his watch. After a twenty-five minute wait she appeared in pink sweatpants and jacket with a black gym bag in hand. They exchanged com numbers and walked to the door.

When they got outside Harmony said, "there's a juice bar around the corner, wanna get some?"

Paul was anxious to be off but answered, "Uh, okay, I know the place you mean. I could use a protein shake." He should still be able to get downtown in time to meet Melanie.

Their conversation was limited to reflections on music and nutrition. She didn't offer anything more about her religion, but Paul didn't press since he figured he had done well enough to secure the invitation to worship the following Sunday.

Frankly, he judged Harmony to be less evolved than himself—she was religious after all—perhaps a low Alpha or maybe even Beta. Of course, her evolutionary deficit wasn't really a big deal—she was charming and sexy and definitely screwable—but he was anxious to get downtown.

When she asked him if he wouldn't like to see her place he paused for a moment, tempted, but said he really couldn't as he had a friend waiting for him downtown. "How about next week sometime?" he offered.

Harmony tilted her head then finally grinned, "Yeah, maybe."

He rushed off to keep his rendezvous with Mel.

7

LANTON

L anton sat at his desk on the 38th floor of the Strong Building, eyes glued to his monitor. He had scanned over the daily reports from Europe and Africa, and the news was not good in his estimation. Despite official communiques detailing an improving security situation, Europe was still worryingly restless with more insurgencies breaking out in the inhabited zones east of the Rhine and below the Pyrenees. Plans to re-enter South Galton were on hold as One World lacked sufficient forces to maintain security, even with the buffer provided by the nuclear zone to the north. It was depressing: everywhere the desire for peace and progress smothered by the inexorable pull of war.

He pushed his chair back and reclined with his hands behind his head. He had been thinking about things at lot lately—about the politics at headquarters, the wars, about the direction the world was going in general. About the devos.

He got up and shuffled over to the window. His head ached, probably due to the changing weather. Outside, the sun was dropping lower in the sky igniting the windows of the buildings opposite in a golden glare. Down below the Kappas were busy sinking the stanchions for a second barricade. He frowned. The government was to be safely walled in and secure from the citizenry it 'served.'

The people and traffic hurried along Emerald Street—another work week over. His thoughts turned to retirement—what he would do then.

Early in his career he had imagined devoting himself to a charitable organization when his working life was through—something with street people probably. But there were no clients anymore.

Then he wondered if perhaps he might get clearance to write a book. Surely his experiences working for the Justice and Equality organizations in the early years, the Rainbow Coalition later on, and finally One World security forces, would be riveting reading for some and informative historical study for others. After all, he had been active in the transformation of society from the beginning all the way through to Ascension and beyond.

But now the work of the early years was judged to be largely misguided, naïve and inefficient—unscientific in its execution. It had been full of incompliancies; everyone saw that now.

Neither was the Coalition's legacy esteemed as it had been during the opening years of One World. In fact, it was a bit of a joke now—few would advertise their prior complicity. He clicked his tongue. History had sunk into irrelevancy: its verities went in and out of fashion like women's clothing.

His Ministry work could not be discussed candidly in the present environment either.

It seemed that any book he could write would be ruled incompliant and never published anyway.

He had to smile, remembering the time before Ascension when the Internet still existed, and one could self-publish. Anyone could. *How the world had changed.*

His mind turned to friends of those times, so long ago seemingly. Many of them had served alongside in the old Ministry of Tolerance and later some had also been conscripted into the MoE. But as the years went by their ranks had thinned. Where had they all gone? He had lost touch.

Now the senior positions were filled with younger people—the progeny of Mother. The world had changed. He imagined all generations had this feeling as they neared the end of their working lives—the feeling that the world they had known existed no longer. It was difficult to retain the sense that one really had a stake in it anymore.

But he wasn't ready to drift off yet. There were too many things happening—things he had worked a lifetime to bring to fruition and wanted to see through. He wanted to see the planetary culture consolidated—the end of the wars; the end of the struggle; the beginning of the new era of unity and progress.

His mind shifted to a more pressing matter: what to do about Eaton.

He had been interviewing the priest for about two weeks now and it had not gone the way he had anticipated. He had allowed Eaton a broad swath hoping to draw him out and, remarkably, their meetings were proving interesting—alarmingly interesting; beyond their professional relevance perhaps. His initial curiosity had grown to an overriding desire to understand the man, even on a personal level. Why that was so, he didn't know. Perhaps it was his stage in life. In any case he found himself actually anticipating their talks with some keenness.

It was surprising that, as one became familiar with Eaton's thought processes, one could begin to comprehend his creed. He actually made sense if you would but suspend your rational faculties to assume the existence of God for a time. At least his beliefs were coherent.

Despite all this he knew the interrogation should have wrapped up days ago. It would be awkward if he were audited.

He glanced at his watch: 18:20. They would be moving Eaton to the interrogation area now.

"But why not work within the system?" Lanton pressed.

Eaton licked dry lips and shot a look of exasperation at his interrogator. "How, exactly? What could you do? What challenge to its dogma would One World tolerate? When the only permitted criticism of its policy is to decry that it isn't stringent enough; that its control will be left not so absolute but that some facet of life could escape its oversight—that some doctrinal aberration could still exist, even hypothetically—when critical examination, no matter how benevolent, is heinous heresy, then what could you possibly say?"

Lanton shook his head, "It's not like that. We're not a government of closed minds. What about the Inclusivity Church…?"

Eaton appeared shocked for an instant before responding in a completely unexpected way: he burst out laughing. "Poeticized One-World-ism! I've known many of them—the Inclusionists. Their sole occupation is the subjugation of their thinking to the dictums of One World: 'If the world hates you, conform to the world, so that it will love you as its own' kind of thing."

"At least they are trying to be a constructive voice," Lanton protested, "not like…"

"*A constructive voice?*" Eaton echoed incredulously. "You mean 'submissive lackey' or 'sycophant.' 'Mouthpiece,' 'appendage' perhaps but hardly a constructive voice. They don't even have to trouble to prostitute their religion to One World; One World *is* their religion." Eaton expanded on the point: "You believe our origins are in the primordial soup—so do they. You believe in an unrelenting progress towards a better world—salvation through science and human intelligence; they also. You might even believe that religion is useful in some situations—to tranquilize your fear of death for instance—that's about as far as they get too." He shook his head. "They do not, cannot, offer counsel to this society because their worldview is identical to, to…"—he glanced quickly to the ceiling—"the devoted apparatchiks in the building above us."

When his eyes returned to Lanton they beamed wide and his voice climbed to a feminine parody: "Jesus wants me to fornicate! Jesus wants me to kill my baby!" he wailed falsetto. "Jesus wants me to be happy! Oh Jesus, Lord Jesus, the one who takes away the world's obligation to adhere to the precepts of God! Blessed be Lord Jesus!" He answered in a tone of mock authority: "You have heard that it was said, 'Do not commit adultery,' but I tell you that anyone who looks at another lustfully has a healthy sex drive. Whoever has my commands and obeys them is being too legalistic, so ignore the plank in your brother's eye and he will ignore yours—and we'll all get along just fine, for this is true religion: to keep oneself from being polluted by the Word." His eyes rolled heavenward. "…and lead us not into contrition, but deliver us from repentance. For thine is the inclusiveness, the tolerance, and the affirmation…"—his eyes fell in reverent salutation—"My will be done. Amen."

Lanton couldn't quite suppress a smile. Eaton's reaction, visceral as it was, had astonished him because he had maintained an emotionally restrained posture all along. The Inclusionists touched a tender spot apparently.

Eaton continued: "Of course, this shouldn't astonish us—that the Inclusionist is in lock step with One World moralisms—they get their ethic from the same place everyone else does after all—Network One, World-Pedia, the nurturing embrace of Mother—not from Christ. They're as zealous for One World as you are, they just employ Christian nomenclature to proclaim that *Kingdom*. They hate Jesus just as much as you do."

"I don't *hate* anyone," Lanton responded wearily. "I just want the world to be a better place for everyone"—he nodded to Eaton—"devos included."

"Yes I'm sure the Inclusionists do too. Everyone does. Me also. I don't doubt your or their motivations."

Eaton fell silent for a moment, thinking. His raised his eyes to Lanton again. "You think that by correct human management, providing the right environment, you can overcome man's limitations—his self-interestedness, greed, callousness…?"

"Yes, in time, with the right education…"

"Education?" Eaton rolled his eyes. "Listen. You've dwelt at some length on how 'devos' allegedly supported Hitler, but there was one group that positively *embraced* his regime and all the racist pseudo-science and murder that went with it: the German scientists. No, it was hardly uncommon in the 1930s CE to see a German anthropologist running around with calipers measuring the skulls of 'inferior' humans. How wholeheartedly they took to the myth of the Aryan man! And how about his fellow world molder, Stalin? He murdered tens of millions of people while the 'progressive' western intelligentsia applauded from their exalted posts at the institutes of higher learning, lauding the achievements of the 'worker's paradise' and pooh-poohing any attempt to expose its excesses." He warmed to the subject. "Then there's the rule of Science and Reason at the end of the eighteenth century in France—tens of thousands sent to their grizzly deaths in less than a year—more than those killed in all the centuries of the Inquisition." He rolled his eyes skyward. "Ah, but the twentieth century… so much murder and bloodletting in that time…"—he looked at Lanton—"the century of rationalism and atheism." He looked away again. "All through history it has been the educated, clever people who have laid the foundations for mass murder, all in the pursuit of their 'enlightened' goals. They would not let humanity stand in the way of their plans for humanity's betterment; they would not be restrained by *mere* morality." Eaton shook his head vehemently. "No, God save us from the sophisticated educated class!"

He leveled his heavy gaze on Lanton once more. "No, you are wrong there. Man doesn't suddenly become virtuous through education. Education, like science, is merely a tool to be wielded for purposes good or evil, depending on the character of the one wielding it. There are millions of educated criminals and murderers. The problem is not ignorance; the problem is human nature. You believe humanity is basically good; that with the correct handling you can dispel its dark side. But humans are not *good*. You—all of us—can verify this by looking into ourselves… honestly look inside yourself. You can verify it—"

"We are making progress: genetic screening, Early Childhood Training, Mother…"

Eaton's face took on a resigned look. "*We are making progress.* Are we? We were just remonstrating about the evils of Hitler's regime, but how many in One World would even acknowledge the validity of this critique? How many would discern the criminal nature of the Nazi state's actions?" he asked. "You grew up in a Christian culture, however faded and masked; the new generation hasn't. How many of them would balk at the extermination of the weak? How many would suffer the presence of inferior humans after the numbing decades of abortion and euthanasia, and other state-sanctioned murder?" He looked challengingly at Lanton. "Indeed, what coherent argument could One World make for preserving the lives of the *unwanted*? Can you offer one?" Lanton remained grim-faced with arms crossed at his chest. Eaton grimaced. "The Peace Center, the Re-Education camps, Mother... what direction do you think your society is heading? Are we heading for a 'kinder gentler society'? Is One World on the road to heaven... or to hell?"

He looked to Lanton for a response, but Lanton remained motionless and mute.

"You see, Mr. Lanton," he continued again, "the repression and murder you see—you have to see—One World perpetrating is not incidental to its foundational humanist rationalist philosophy—your creed," he nodded sternly. "It is indispensable to it. It all makes sense to it. Historically, all regimes of that genre—I mean Utopias—must engage in just the same kind of savagery to enforce conformity. Anyone can consult the history books to confirm this. Oh, yes," he added, "that's right; they cannot consult the history books; *ist verboten*—another characteristic of said regimes."

Lanton's only response was to frown slightly.

Eaton's voice took on a more conciliatory tone. "This is the great insight that Christians have—what you lack Mr. Lanton—the one thing One World needs to have any chance of success: knowledge of the true nature of man. We really do need a redeemer. But it's so easy to obtain— this knowledge. You can verify it by looking inside yourself," he urged again.

Lanton shook his head. "No. No, I don't buy into your guilt trip; all your talk about everyone 'being a sinner.'"

"So you don't acknowledge your own brokenness, and the world's, and your own complicity in it all?"

"Look," Lanton replied with a rising impatience, "all I see is people trying to do their best. We're not perfect, but we are hardly the brutes you make us out to be."

"No…not 'brutes' to be sure…" Eaton's eyes lowered and he pondered for a moment. Then his deep voice said quietly, "You were at St Mike's that night. I saw you."

Lanton stared at him. He knew the night Eaton was referring to—the night they burned the cathedral down. Eaton's eyes gleamed as they caught the concession in Lanton's. "I saw what was really inside that night," he said softly. "I'd venture you saw it too."

Lanton felt the weight of those eyes upon him. "I did not approve…" he muttered weakly.

"You didn't *approve*?" Eaton's gaze remained steady.

Lanton didn't know what he thought about that night anymore; the person he was then had been obliterated by a lifetime.

"I opposed all of that—the burning and looting, the violence," Lanton said, "the… the purging."

"Oh?" Eaton replied mildly, his large gray eyes cutting into Lanton's "We both know that, in the end, when our talking time is through, you will kill me Mr. Lanton. I'm merely a cancer to your society after all." Lanton opened his mouth, but no words of protestation would form.

"Yes, I suppose you find that duty distasteful," Nathan continued. "But you are colored by the environment you were raised in; an environment still tainted by Christian ethics. You still think it's 'wrong,' but you cannot give a coherent justification for thinking so. It's just your 'feelings'. You can still feel that way, but each generation of One World feels this less and less. Even you are ashamed of having such feelings—yes?—that you lack the ruthlessness to excise the cancer with an untroubled conscious? You lack the commitment. The *faith*." Lanton stared hard at him. "You are no longer one of them—what they have become. You are tainted now; defective." Both men were staring firmly at the other. "It's a world gone insane, Mr. Lanton—the inevitable consequence of its rejection of the Ground of Truth and so of morality."

"We can have morality," Lanton protested weakly.

"Oh, of sorts," Eaton acknowledged. "Rule by the stronger, that's all—'might makes right.' Right now you have the might; therefore, you can murder me without moral offence."

"So we should adopt *your* morality," Lanton spat back.

"No," Nathan corrected him, "not *my* morality; I'm a sinner as much as you. The difference between us is I acknowledge the fact. It's what keeps me from joining your 'heaven-on-Earth' mission—putting my trust in the perspicacity and benevolence of your leaders. It allows me to recognize your worldview for what it is: a culture of darkness and death."

Lanton glared angrily. "Why do you call it that?"

Eaton raised its eyebrows. "Abortion over life, euthanasia over caring, temporal Man over immortal God—it's not hard to figure out, really. As with anything, you can know it by the fruit of its endeavors." He paused for a moment. "It always chooses death over life."

That utterance hung in the air for a long time.

Finally Lanton broke the silence, attempting to nudge the interrogation back to a standard form. "Why did you leave your teaching position and enter the church?"

"Oh. I switched from biology because I realized it wasn't important. It wasn't real." He added in explanation, "By my time science, biology in particular, was just a contrivance for disseminating One World creed. Real science had long since deserted the classroom and laboratory. I wanted to find something real in the midst of the ignorance and falsity I knew permeated my world." He paused for a moment. "Jesus was a lone figure against the appalling darkness."

They lapsed into silent reverie again. Lanton tried to make sense of Eaton's ramblings. Finally he sighed. "So what's the answer? What should we do? How should we proceed?"

Eaton answered immediately, as if responding to a catechism. "Believe in the One who made you fearfully well. Follow His ways. Do not steal. Do not kill…"

Lanton crinkled his face. "I can't believe in him. How can I believe in him? I *don't* believe in him. I don't see how you, a man of science, can believe in him."

Eaton pressed back in his chair as if he had known all along they would arrive at this point eventually. "Perhaps you can't…not by yourself," he said quietly. "But there's one thing you can do."

"What's that?" Lanton asked hopelessly.

"Pray."

The word caused Lanton's body to shiver involuntarily. He sighed, "I can't do that." He massaged his temples; his eyes ached. "I just want … peace."

The two were quiet for a moment then Nathan spoke. "This peace you have chosen to pursue—One World's peace—it's not the peace of heaven; it's the peace of the graveyard—for you and all its adherents."

Lanton didn't respond. He tapped the button and the guards entered through the steel door behind Eaton. They disengaged the prisoner from the chair and cuffed him.

Lanton looked up just as they as they began to lead Eaton off and caught him looking down at him. His big eyes shone sorrowfully. "You cannot expiate your sins through your utopian project. You must see that." The guards moved him out.

8

Day 128

Thesis

Paul rolled out of bed early and went to sit on the porch to eat his cereal. He enjoyed the calmness of a summer Sunday morning before the cooling mist lifted and the city shook itself awake. It was the quietest day of the week.

He finished his breakfast and reclined in his chair. His muscles were sore as a result of the workout the day before but it was a satisfying soreness, signifying progress.

It had been a good week all around. Things were going great with Melanie and a weight had been lifted from his shoulders with the settlement of the essay topic question. He had tried to contact Harmony a few times unsuccessfully but was still confident she would make their church date the following Sunday. It could just be another glitch in the Net for all he knew.

Today he planned to search World Library and determine the direction his research should take—maybe come up with an initial outline for his paper.

After a few hours scanning Worldpedia he had a good overview of his proposed topic.

He found that devo religion had been instrumental in initiating most of the wars throughout history. Noteworthy were the Crusades, launched at the end of the eleventh century CE which disrupted a peaceful and more advanced society and bred so much strife in subsequent centuries. In fact, the trauma inflicted on the Muslim civilization was a major contributor to the animus of Muslims towards the West until the twenty-first century when One World asserted itself. Apparently, Muslims equated 'The West' with Christendom that had launched the crusades, so it was understandable that they fiercely resisted Western encroachments down through the centuries.

There was also a clear record of devo intolerance of other religions. It ruthlessly crushed alternative belief systems and lifestyles whenever it had the power to do so. He was surprised to discover that there had been many other varieties of Christianity in the first and second centuries CE which disagreed with the views of the Bible authors—whether Jesus was God; the subservience of women; the puritan morality, etcetera. Of course, these rival viewpoints had been stamped out by the so-called 'orthodox' Christians, their adherents massacred, their books burned.

In 391 CE the devos even burned the great library at Alexandria, and many priceless works of antiquity were lost forever.

Then there was the Inquisition and witch burnings where millions lost their lives.

Throughout the centuries, devo dogma that some people would go to heaven and others to hell promoted an exclusory, tribalistic worldview and led to societal strife. Paul wondered how many people must have suffered psychologically under this cruel doctrine. How many children were left damaged, trembling in fear of hell in those superstitious times?

Worst of all, it had been anti-science, teaching its adherents to rely on blind faith and reject reason and empirical evidence. They even denied the existence of Darwin's Subatomic Teleological Force. People were forced to believe in many absurdities because 'the Bible said so.'

In the twentieth century devos sought to deprive woman of reproductive equality—denying them access to preg-refs—and still endeavored to force them into families to be ruled over by husbands. It imposed a 'one man one woman' pair bonding to the exclusion of other, more natural, ones. It fact, it was pretty hung up about sex, insisting the people limit their sexual partners to just one person for one's whole lifetime! It was no wonder they sounded so grumpy all the time.

They also tried to prohibit life relief—even voluntary life-ref—saying that even useless old or disabled people's lives were 'sacred.' They didn't even want to relieve mentally dysfunctional children!

Paul was amazed that people of a mere hundred years ago had actu-

ally taken a three thousand-year old book of dubious authorship so seriously. He flipped through the thin leafs of his Bible. He had bartered an
old Batman comic for it from Alan Kuipers when he was in grade nine.
He never asked Al where he got it; it was better not to know.

It was one of his proudest possessions, but he had never felt the urge
to read it. It was just exciting having something so incompliant in his
possession.

With this book the devos had held mankind in thrall for two mil-
lennia. It was only in the eighteenth century, with the triumph of rationalism and critical thinking, that primitive superstition could finally be
expelled and the way paved for the explosion of knowledge and progress
that ultimately brought humanity to One World.

So far, all his reading had confirmed his understanding of events.

It would be easy to contrast the devo worldview with the more enlightened One World one. He could just pick a few case studies to illustrate his points. For instance, he could show instances where the tribalism of the devos led to civil and international strife and compare it
with the inclusive planetary perspective of the One World worldview
which obsoleted nationalistic competition and affirmed all beliefs, treat-
ing them as equally valid.

In the realm of human interaction he could show how the devo
worldview, with its narrow insistence on traditional 'one man one woman' permanent relationships was prejudicial towards those of different
sexual orientations—non-monogamous, homosexual, polysexual, intergenerational—and imposed a stunting, guilt-ridden restraint on man's
natural drives.

In science, he could use the Galileo case to demonstrate devo opposition to rational thought versus the One World worldview which es-
chewed blind faith and celebrated science, and so had achieved so much
to elevate man's living standards.

Yes, it would be easy to demonstrate the superiority of the One World
worldview versus devo culture; perhaps too easy.

In fact, it was disappointing that they couldn't provide a more worthy foil; it was like pummeling a dwarf. Although such a paper would
probably satisfy the selection committee it wouldn't make scintillating
reading, certainly.

He considered changing his topic, but he had had such hopes for this
one it was hard to cast it aside. The thought of starting over was a daunting one. *What to do?*

There were some things that bothered him about his research thus far. He knew, despite the contrary concordance of the One World library, that many of the pioneers in the scientific revolution were Christians, or at least had professed being such. He knew this from his own reading and certain utterances he had snared in passing within the One World Curriculum that rendered the point implicitly. Reading between the lines, he would often pick up on items like that although they appeared to go unnoticed by his peers. *So why*, he asked himself, *did these people, who must have been so clever, adhere to such a dumb religion?* Another thing: he couldn't understand how the Enlightenment, with its commitment to reason and experiment, had suddenly sprung out of the arid soil of the devo West. *Why not out of the seemingly more hospitable atheist soil of China for instance?*

Overall, he was nettled by the suspicion that he could not really present the devo viewpoint accurately because he had not really grasped the devo mind. However he tried it continued to elude him.

He pushed himself to read on, but as he read more and more of the history of the devos and explanation of devo thought from One World sources, he yearned more and more to read some books written by devos themselves—to have them explain their beliefs in their own words. How would a devo justify his religion's rejection of science and rational thought or its persecution of other religions or marginalization of women and non-monogamous people? That's what Paul really wanted to know. Unfortunately devo books written before Ascension were not accessible with his security clearance.

So how could he get a partisan devo viewpoint? He hoped Harmony could help him out or at least point him in the direction of someone who could—perhaps this Gretchen person she was so enthralled with.

* * *

The long day spent in front of his monitor had wearied his mind and eyes. Fortunately, Melanie's link was open when he called that afternoon and she would be able to meet him downtown after helping her enablers with some chores.

He was sitting under the awning at a cafe on Kinsey mulling over the day's readings when he spotted her standing on the other side of the street a block away waiting for the light to change. He could always distinguish her person long before she drew near: her restless body motions and the way she lifted her head and thrust her chin out slightly while surveying her surroundings. He smiled to himself as she skipped off the curb and sashayed across the road.

His smile broadened as she approached.

"What's so funny, you?" she laughed as she drew up to his table.

He laughed back. "Oh I don't know. You're kinda cute."

Her cheeks dimpled as she laughed again.

"C'mon, sit down," Paul said rising. She looped around the fence and they kissed before sitting down opposite each other. Paul pushed the menu aside so they could clasp hands across the table.

"Were you able to get away without any fuss?" he asked.

She rolled her eyes. "Well, Doris wanted me to stay and help her weed the garden, but I sulked and carried on until she let me go," she laughed.

"You have her wrapped around your little finger I reckon."

"Oh, I wish," Melanie snickered. "She can sure put her foot down when she wants. How's your day been? What have you been up to?"

Paul grimaced. "Trying to get some work done on my exit paper."

"Oh, your final paper. You were doing it on devo culture."

"Yeah, well, I'm trying to anyway. I'm not sure there's enough to go on. Say, you wouldn't know anyone who knows about Christianity would you?"

Melanie's eyes widened incredulously. "Christianity? Are you crazy?" She blushed prettily. "Why would I be into anything like that?"

"Yeah, there's this Inclusion Church still—they are Christianist. I was just wondering if you knew anyone. Maybe Cass knows someone?"

Melanie's eyebrows shot up. "Ha! No, I don't think so. She wouldn't be seen dead with someone like that!"

"Right. Just asking."

"Oh, that reminds me: we are on for Tuesday, right? Remember, the summer solstice..?"

"Oh yeah. With Cass. Sure, right." He was distracted by a female figure striding in their direction. She looked familiar but Paul could not place her right away. She was middle-aged with a bolt-straight patrician carriage. He could discern eastern European features as she drew near: thick dark eye brows, brown hair, cream skin. She wore a stylish, crisply-tailored, mid-length, black skirt with green-gray blouse, and her expression evidenced intelligence. It was, almost certainly, an Alpha face—a masterful image. Then he had it: it was Petya, Cal's piano mentor. Petya's searching eyes saw him just then and passed on briefly before snapping back in recognition. She altered course to bring herself to the fence in front of him.

"You are Paul, yes? Calvin's friend?" she asked rhetorically.

Paul stuttered, "Uh yeah. You're Petya. We met at David—"

"Yes, I remember," she interrupted. She darted a side glance at Melanie then continued, "Have you seen him?"

"Who? Oh, you mean Cal?" Paul flustered. "No. Well, not since June. Is anything wrong?"

The opalescent eyes fixed him for a long moment. "No. Excuse me," she said and turned and marched away.

Paul watched her recess down the street.

"Who was that?" Melanie ventured.

She disappeared from Paul's view and he slowly turned back to Melanie. "Her name is Petya. She is Calvin Wong's piano teacher."

"Oh, yeah, I remember now. So that's Petya. She's looks pretty tough."

"Yeah, from what I understand," Paul muttered absently. "I wonder what's up."

9

DAY 121

WORSHIP

The subway train thundered into the station and Paul ascended to Ecology Square. It was just after nine-thirty, but the heat was radiating off the asphalt already; it was going to be another sizzling day.

Aquarius' answer to New Frankfurt's Times Square, Ecology Square presented an urbanscape awash in lights and signage. It was quiet now, but he knew it would be rocking with street performers, vendors and their clients later. He loved the energy of the place.

He spotted Harmony and another girl on the opposite side of the street waving and hustled to join them.

"Hey, Paul," she laughed and they hugged. "This is Anne."

Anne was a bit shorter and of much slighter build than Harmony. She wore a very short claret tartan skirt with a white blouse, white socks and red sneakers—the retro schoolgirl attire that was popular in some cohorts. Straight reddish-brown hair emerged from beneath her green beret and fell past her shoulders. Her ears protruded from it giving her an elfin look which her green eyes and freckled nose did nothing to dispel. "Hi, Paul," she said shyly, grinning a crooked girlish grin which caused him to think of Cat.

"Hi Anne," he nodded and shook her hand, trying not to stare back at the jade eyes surveying him steadily.

"You've got great timing," Harmony said "We just got here too." She was wearing a white, wide-brimmed sun hat, silver camisole and a pair of white spandex jeans that sheathed her luscious thighs like a coat of paint. "We can go this way." They headed west along Ecology Street, Paul flanked by the two.

"Do you come here every Sunday?" Paul asked as they walked.

"Mostly," Harmony answered. "Well, not so much in the summer. We like to go to the beach or go blading, or just hang out, y'know?" She looked up at him. "Have you ever bladed on the Island?"

"No, I never have," Paul confessed.

"It's great! We skated from Hanlon's Point right to the Eastern Channel last year. Remember Anne?" The other girl nodded and continued to smile. She hadn't stopped grinning since they had met; *miles of smiles,* he thought.

"We like to blade beside the boardwalk in the eastern beaches and watch the volleyball players too," Harmony said, smirking at Anne who grinned back significantly.

"Do you both go to Parkside?" Paul asked.

"Yeah. Anne's a year behind me. We met last year at a Green Godiva concert."

So Anne must be sixteen anyway. He had been wondering..

"This way," Harmony said, and they turned down an alleyway between two skyscrapers. It was shady and cooler there.

"How long have you been coming here?" Paul asked.

"I think I mentioned that to you before," Harmony laughed. "I think it's been about three years for me; Anne for just this past year."

Anne nodded affirmatively. "We like the pastor."

"Yeah," Harmony agreed, "I really became interested when Gretchen took over. She's so spiritual! Wait till you meet her!" she gushed. "Here we are."

They had emerged from the alleyway into a compact square where a pretty gray stone church stood among the lofty office towers. Paul realized he had passed by many times without noticing the structure, dominated as it was by its surrounding office buildings. He mused on the extent to which the height and grandeur of an edifice indicated its perceived importance.

The square provided a tranquil space ideal for quiet reading, and there were two elderly men perusing newspapers on one of the benches scattered around the small enclosure.

The muffled undulations of otherworldly music stirred the atmosphere close to the church and poured out when Harmony nudged the door ajar.

It was cool, moist and dim inside; like a crypt. Beams of colored light, mostly green, streaming from the stained glass windows bisected the shadows of the chamber. He shivered and his nostrils twitched at the pungent aroma permeating the air. The music had a pulsing psychedelic rhythm and, with the incense and lighting, induced a slight disorientation. A multitude of voices bubbled in the dark sanctuary. He recalled the uneasiness he had experienced at the ritual at Julius' place—the one Cass had officiated. It was all very *spiritual* and unsettling.

The elderly woman just inside the door greeted the arrivals and provided them programs. "Hello Vera. Glad you could make it… Mr. Demeter, nice to see you," she said as she passed each a lavender slip. To his relief, Paul noticed there were quite a few young people filing in.

"Hi Holly," Harmony said spritely as she took the program from the woman's hand.

"Oh hi, Harmony," the other answered with a wide smile, "and Anne, I see."

"We brought a friend, Paul, too," Harmony announced proudly.

"Oh wonderful! Welcome Paul," she beamed, offering him a program. "I hope you enjoy our service."

The thin carpet underfoot muffled their footfalls as they proceeded up the aisle with the others. The light from the windows tinted the air an astral mauve or green which baffled one's senses—it was difficult to determine where one object ended and other began. Paul stepped carefully, leery of stumbling in the magenta twilight.

It was only when he was ensconced in his seat about mid-way back that he finally had an opportunity to survey his surroundings in detail.

The side walls were richly paneled and had, what looked like, marble plaques on them. He couldn't read their inscriptions. The walls were broken by several arched doors likely leading to side chapels. The church was larger than expected.

The high ceiling was concealed in shadow, but here and there mobiles hung down like stars in the heavens.

At the front there was a raised semi-circular floor with an elevated pulpit to the left. A small altar table stood in the center of the dais, washed green by the light from the windows. There was a large globe mounted on a brass stand on one side of it—Paul could make out the continents etched on its surface—and another smaller silver item that looked like an inverted teacup beside it: a bell. Next to these were four large silver chalices covered with white napkins. "Oh, it's Community" he heard Harmony murmur. There were also several covered baskets. A white candle burned on either side of them.

Two stands, each supporting a vase of red roses, stood in front and to the side of the altar and there was a small podium between them. To the right were various musical instruments—a drum set, guitar and bass. A forlorn piano stood off to the left, at the foot of the stage.

The dais was flanked by several more rows of pews. It looked like the designer's intention had been to place the raised stage in the middle with the seating encircling but the restricted dimensions of the building had denied that configuration. Paul could see some musicians convoking off to the right of the stage.

There was a screen on the wall behind the altar displaying an idyllic image of a mountain and lake. It remained for about twenty seconds then changed to a picture of the Earth from deep space, then a black and white picture of, what was probably, Tibet, with a line of monks streaming towards a Buddhist temple. The music, whose source Paul could not determine—it saturated the air—complemented each scene.

He strained his eyes to make out the images of trees and plants and various animals in the colored glass of the windows. Strangely, he didn't see any cross symbols anywhere. The large space on the wall behind the stage was occupied by a giant One World logo.

As his eyes grew accustomed to the darkness he could make out, perhaps, one hundred fifty in the pews. Most were chatting to their neighbors above the hum of the music, but others sat quietly here and there. One woman, illuminated by a green beam, moved her lips in silent prayer as she sat with closed eyes, hands arrayed mudra-style.

He examined the books on the shelf on the back of the seat in front of him. There was a blue one with 'The Inclusion Bible' inscribed in silver block letters on its cover. Another contained excerpts from the Hindu scriptures and there was a red hymn book *Songs of Love and Unity*.

Two girls moved into the pew beside him. The nearest glanced at Paul, smirked, then looked away quickly.

The music suddenly changed from aqueous fluidity to a more deliberate march, and Paul looked to the stage to see a figure in a silver-white flowing robe floating in from the choir. The voices hushed, and the music abruptly ceased as the congregation rose from their seats as one. The silver figure was bathed in green from the large rosette window opposite her position before the altar. Her attentive flock waited expectantly in the darkness for guidance. She raised her arms and a clear beacon emitted from her mouth, "May the light from the mind of god stream down and enlighten our minds!"

"May we gain god's knowledge," they responded. Paul tried to read the program in the dim light before Harmony nudged him and he realized the liturgy was being projected onto the screen.

"May the love of god stream down and saturate our hearts!" the silver voice sang out.

"May we exude god's love!" came the response.

"May the will of god be done on earth as in the realms beyond!" the leader's voice crescendoed.

"May god's will be done!" was the reply.

"Amen," the oracle sealed their pronouncement. "We are the people of the light, trusted by the powers to carry their message. May we be the instruments to further their plans on Earth!"

Everyone resumed their seats in unison.

When they were all seated the priestess bid welcome to visitors. Paul squirmed in his seat as a few eyes turned his way. She then pressed on to point out the highlights in the Activities section of the bulletin: an upcoming workshop on meditation techniques; Bible studies; an art class for 'tapping into the power of the Ground of Creativity.' A church dignitary of some renown—a *star*—would be delivering a lecture entitled *The Evolution of Human Spirituality: The Next Stage* in a few weeks' time and the congregants were entreated to take advantage of the opportunity to hear him and to bring another *seeker* if possible. The items were summarized on the screen as she elaborated on each.

The announcements concluded, she raised her arms and the music beckoned the assembly to worship (the musicians had taken the stage unobtrusively). "And now rise to sing to the Oneness that makes us whole," she exhorted, "*The Spirit of Unity*."

They rose to their feet and their voices erupted:

> *In the morning,*
> *In the evening,*
> *The winding pathway,*
> *All the day.*
> *We remember,*
> *We surrender,*
> *Service render,*
> *to the Way.*

The music had an infectious beat. Paul glanced over and saw that Harmony was bobbing and shaking her hips as she sang. She had a pretty voice too. Anne was on Harmony's other side out of earshot. Some of the older people looked bemused at the exuberance of the younger set's celebration but soldiered on gamely.

The driving tempo propelled them into the intro:

> *In the misty dawn*
> *of the forest of Eden*
> *To the victory won,*
> *by the Rising Ones.*

…and broke like a wave on the rocks for the chorus:

> *We are the minds.*
> *We are the voices,*
> *speaking the Word.*
> *We are the light,*
> *We are the plan.*
> *One community,*
> *in the Spirit of Unity.*

They sang four more songs after that, each launching immediately after the previous. The dancing imagery on the big screen provided accompaniment. The second hymn was *Praise Everyone* with the chorus alternating between accenting the *praise* and the *everyone* leaving the object of its worship unresolved. The third was a soulful—Paul thought sentimental—tribute to the Earth: *Mother of Us All*. The fourth was a rollicking anthem, similar to *Spirit of Unity*, that left his ears ringing—*We Are One*, which drifted into the final offering, a soulful ballad entitled *Freedom From Want*. The band faded until only a lone flautist remained to play counterpoint to the singers. Many in the congregation were holding hands and swaying in unison.

The final strains of the flute died out leaving them in a state of emotional ecstasy. Some of them were crying. The rush the others were experiencing eluded Paul, excluding him from the fellowship.

The priestess had returned to her place of prominence and consoled them all. "In the great realm we'll all be One."

"We are the image of the enlightened masters," came the communal reply. They reseated themselves. The priestess moved to the rear of the stage and sat on one of the throne-like chairs there while an elderly woman mounted the steps and proceeded to the lectern. "The first reading today is from Matthew 5, chapter 5, verses 14 to 16." The girl to Paul's right picked up the blue book and flipped quickly to the designated verse. She darted a side glance as if to confirm he had witnessed her proficiency in locating it.

The reader cleared her voice. "You are the light of the Earth. A city on a hill cannot be hidden. Neither do people light a lamp and put it under a bowl. Instead they put it on its stand, and it gives light to everyone in the house. In the same way, let your light shine before everyone, that they may see your good deeds and praise the god within us."

She left the stage and a young man, about Paul's age, replaced her at the podium. "Our second reading for today is from Sigmund Freud's *The Future of an Illusion*," he announced. He paused a moment, cleared his throat and read, "When the growing individual finds that he is destined to remain a child forever, that he can never do without protection against strange superior powers, he lends those powers the features belonging to the figure of his father; he creates for himself the gods whom he dreads, whom he seeks to propitiate, and whom he nevertheless entrusts with his own protection."

A minute of silence followed the reading. Paul looked around at the heads all bowed in contemplation. Harmony's eyelids were pressed tightly shut to repulse worldly intrusion. Paul fidgeted in his seat. *How hard it is to sit silently*, he noted.

The priestess was mounting the steps to the high pulpit. Paul was delighted to see that the sermon was entitled *The Evolution of Christianity* which promised to be eminently relevant to his investigation. He wondered momentarily if Harmony had forewarned the priestess about his attendance.

Reaching the summit now, the priestess stood there a moment solemnly surveying them all. "People of the light. Welcome to this assembly of the people seeking a better way—the way of unity. For this is why we gather here: to strengthen the bonds of community; to draw strength from the whole for the journey we are taking—all of us." She spread her hands over her flock. "It's an arduous journey, fraught with misdirection, which calls for patience and endurance." Her manner lightened. "We might remember the times we have failed in this our duty (she smiled at them all encouragingly), but we know we are forgiven our failings." Paul observed many shaking their heads affirmatively. "We come here to re-focus our spirits on our mission. May my words encourage and aid each one on that sacred journey. Amen."

"Amen," they echoed earnestly.

Her voice shifted into a prayerful tone and the congregation bowed their heads once more.

As we come before the life force
may we hear its voice
and discern its intentions.
May our pulses be quickened
that we may be moved by its Truth.
May our mortal souls awaken to the presence
of the power that guides our steps.
On the morrow
let the spirit of god lead us to the other place,
of unity, love and peace.

"Amen."

Once more the congregation sealed the *amen.*

The priestess paused for a moment, smiled mischievously and began. "In the pre-Ascension Bible"—she raised a black book—"Paul says 'But Christ has indeed been raised from the dead,'"—she acknowledged the smattering of laughter—"'the first fruits of those who have fallen asleep. For since death came through a man, the resurrection of the dead comes also through a man. For as in Adam all die, so in Christ all will be made alive.'" The couple in front of Paul exchanged a grin and wink.

"Don't blame Paul," the priestess counseled them. "He lived in a primitive age: before astronomy, psychology, critical history, anthropology, biology, archaeology—when ignorance and credulity ruled. It was a world that believed in demons and monsters, miracles and magic—in dead bodies getting up and continuing on their way." More laughter. She leaned closer to her audience and took them into her confidence. "A fearful society desiring a powerful god to protect them from the unknown." Her face took on a pitying expression immediately reflected in the faces of the listeners.

"And what has been the fruit of that way of thinking? How did civilization get on under its sway?" she asked. "Progress held back for hundreds of years," she answered. "Blind obeisance in place of enlightened reasoning. From the earth-centric universe right down to the"—she rolled her eyes and waved her arms chaotically—"'random mutations and natural selection' superstition." The audience laughed. "What absurdities have these 'Christians' not foisted on the world?"

"So much for our scientific and cultural progress," she waved her hand. "But what of our spiritual progress? What mark has this Pauline attitude left on our spiritual psyche?" She stared askance at them. "He thought that God loved some more than others." She stared out to her audience her arms extended downward, palms open in supplication, a look of profound sadness arrayed on her face. They shook their heads dolefully.

"He believed that people would suffer in hell—forever—because of their 'sins'," she pronounced indignantly. Many shook their heads defiantly.

She drew herself up, crossed her arms at her chest and declared proudly, "We are not evil. We are divine."

"Yes!" voices in the audience whispered. There was a smattering of applause.

"This vengeful God of his—who demands unthinking obedience; who punishes people for following mere natural human instinct; who demands blood to sate its appetite for vengeance—is this our god?" In the audience heads shook back and forth vehemently. "The murder of the innocents, animal holocaust, tribalism, chastity, genocide. The flood. How is such a god worth worshipping?" She held a challenging gaze to them. "No," she said firmly, "Paul didn't see clearly. He knew 'only in part.' For how can a loving god be so cruel? How can an authoritarian god be loving?" she asked rhetorically. In the audience heads were shaking back and forth.

She smiled and reached out to them. "You see, Paul was not special. He was a person just like you and me. We are all god," she pronounced decisively. "But we know more than Paul. We need no supernatural authority to tell us what is right." she declared. "Science and reasoning— science, the fount of all knowledge—has propelled us to heights Paul couldn't have imagined."

She smiled assuredly. "We know from Freud that traditional religion evolved out of man's feeling of helplessness in the face of an inhospitable world. God was the childish projection of his need for a dependable, strong, sheltering parent presence. That's where Paul's thinking originates—in the longings of a child." Harmony stole a side glance at Paul and grinned. "But"—she tap-tapped the pulpit sternly with her index finger—"we know it is time to put away childish things."

The audience was nodding fervently.

"To put away the things that divide us."

Her long white fingers gripped the front edge of the pulpit. "Christianity, like all human creations, is forever changing, evolving. We use our creative power to create the future." She pointed off into the horizon with one hand. "We, all of us, created Christianity, evolved it, and continue to do so." She paused to allow this thought to sink in.

"We do this by learning and by acting. By fostering relationships, shaping values that are solidly rooted in our best selves. Social justice. By supporting One World initiatives for greater unity. Humanitarian values."

"Yes!" the voices in the audience affirmed.

"We discard everything that suppresses the human spirit—the patriarchal, the familial, the nationalist, the gender chauvinistic—and keep whatever is life-enhancing."

"Yes!" the voices rose.

"We believe in forgiveness, not confession; compassion, not suffering; affirmation, not sin; goodness, not grace; ecology, not dominion; kindness not holiness; love, not rules."

"Yes! Yes!"

"So we focus on whatever is true, whatever is noble, whatever is right, whatever is pure, whatever is lovely, whatever is admirable. By this we elevate our spiritual consciousness and we draw together—we, who are in the vanguard of this new Enlightenment; we are open to everything. We watch diligently for ways to encourage the Good which is in us to grow. We don't look to heaven, for how can anyone who believes in heaven care about the Earth? No, we work in the world, to bring about a better world. We take up our own tools: the breastplate of goodwill; the helmet of intelligence; the sword of Science; and above these, the Spirit of Unity. With these we create our own heaven."

"Yes!"

"Love, compassion, affirmation, forgiveness, tolerance, goodwill, equality"—she tapped out the virtues on her palm. "These are what make life worthwhile." She pumped her arm in the air. "No everlasting punishment! We want a heaven that everyone can get to. This is the true

Gospel!"

"Yes!" The crowd broke out in general applause and cheering.

"We know god, not in the dead word"—she held up the Bible—"but in the heart"—pounding her chest—"and in our minds." She tossed the book aside.

At this point many rose to their feet spontaneously, applauding and drawing others to do the same. Paul finally had to stand too.

The priestess motioned them to be reseated and her voice returned to a calmer tone. "That's our religion: an ecologically sound religion for all creation's creatures, for all life is holy; inclusive of all; relevant to people's lives; effective in the world. Isn't that the purpose of true religion: to address the world's needs? To help people find meaning? To provide spiritual fulfillment?"

Everyone nodded. *Yes.*

"We can take our lead from other great saints—people who did what they had to do, what was asked of them—and in so doing changed the world; elevated our existence."

She went on to sketch the lives of others who had facilitated the world's spiritual unfolding: Doctor Henry Morgentaler, an early pioneer in the struggle to release women from the scourge of motherhood;

MP Mary Wiltshire who, more than any other in the pre-Ascension Northern states, advanced the Future Family campaign leading to the final abolition of marriage and the traditional family hegemony, and the implementation of inclusive coupling and scientific child breeding—the Life Center model;

Justice Howard Stennle and Justice Marilyn Wavel, who persevered, often against fanatical religious resistance, in writing many of the progressive policies into law—the Coexistence laws mandating inclusive social interaction; the Progress Laws protecting science from litigious interference; the Compassion Laws governing end of life and quality of life issues; the Great Ape Laws establishing rights for other species—the list went on and on;

And finally: Michael Warlinger, the great social justice reformer, founder of the Equality movement and so, enabler of all that proceeded from that: the abolition of currency and private property; the instatement of gender and racial quotas; judicial affirmative action.

The listeners sat still, focused on her words, inspired by the precedence set by these titans of Progressive forbearance.

"So shine your light that the world might see," she challenged them. "Who knows what you may accomplish!"

The crowd sat pensive, heads resting on folded hands.

"Friends"—she held her arms towards them—"since we have a great cloud of witnesses bearing testimony to the work of the Spirit, let's not slacken our efforts; let's not grow weary of the task. Let's not be found idle, without accomplishment, on that day when the christ returns to Earth." She stood rigid, her gaze roaming steadily, challengingly, over the mute assembly.

She assumed a more relaxed posture and concluded in a business-like tone: "And so we keep proclaiming and pursuing the way of unity and love." She raised her arms. "And this is why we always say 'May the will of god be known. May we further its plan of salvation.' Amen."

The congregation echoed the *amen.*

The priestess descended from the pulpit like a prophet returning from the mountain, and settled into the chair again. The congregation sat still, absorbed, pensive.

The screen changed to a picture of a ring of people, laughing singing, hands joined in a scene reminiscent of a Matisse. The words 'The Order of Community' materialized in the center of their circle.

The priestess took up station behind the altar. "People of the dawning light, draw round." She picked up the silver bell and rang it three times.

"Jesus called his followers to inclusivity—to a celebration of diversity. To a oneness based on their oneness in the Spirit of Unity." She held her hands in front of her with her forefingers and thumbs touching, forming a circle. "And so we draw this ring to symbolize our oneness in the Spirit of Unity."

"Everyone who is in sympathy with this vision has a place at our table." She called them with outstretched arms, "Come to the Community!" She rang the bell twice more.

The members rose row by row and filed towards the stage. Harmony grinned and cocked her head and motioned Paul to follow her and Ann but he demurred. They laughed and joined the column of people streaming to the stage. The other girls stole quick curious glances at him as they squeezed by.

He looked around and was reassured seeing a few others lingering in the pews.

When they had taken their places around the altar the lighting there allowed Paul to see them more clearly and he noticed how few men there were—perhaps one in five. Age wise, they seemed to be either in the very old or in the teenager category with few between. It was probably because of the great decline in religious observance before Ascension he reasoned. Of course children wouldn't be allowed in a service such as this.

The priestess' voice echoed supernaturally in the chamber. "We are gathered around this table, over a meal, as people have done from time immemorial, in recognition of the work of the human spirit. Face to face, looking into each other's eyes, we give and receive nourishment for the journey. Bread and wine to symbolize life and sharing." She removed the napkins from the chalices and baskets and passed them to others.

Each ate of the bread and drank the wine then offered the plate and cup to the one adjacent. "May the peace of Unity rest upon you," they would say. "And also with you," was the response.

When the final person had eaten, all joined hands. The actuation of the imagery that had suggested Matisse to Paul's mind produced instead a remembrance of Cass' ritual and the serpentine ring there.

The priestess concluded the rite. "We celebrate this gift of fellowship, this company of believers. We offer ourselves, our bodies and talents to the Holy Mission. And we look for future progress and the life to come when we will all be in perfect oneness; the everlasting kingdom: One World."

"One World," the celebrants responded as one. They hugged their neighbors, then began to file back to their seats. Harmony smirked at Paul as she and Anne squeezed by to regain their places.

"Our closing hymn is, oh, one of my favorites, *The Church's One Foundation*," the priestess announced when they had all settled. The band struck up and a hundred voices joined in:

The Church's one foundation
is unity, divine.
It is the true creation
of true love, yours and mine...

All sang the achingly soulful tune earnestly, absorbed in its drama and pathos—a suitable paean to the icons of progress. Many threw up their arms to reach out rapturously to the ascended paragons of unity. They wailed, they laughed, they cried, as the emotional pitch climbed verse upon heartrending verse, and ended triumphantly on a note of great hope and longing:

> O happy ones so admired!
> Oh, give us grace that we
> like them, the heav'nly inspired,
> in life may further peace.

As the final strains faded out, the priestess appeared at the podium. "Yes, like them, may we all further peace on Earth." She made to press on then recalled, "Oh, remember to mark your calendars for the *Evolution of Human Spirituality* presentation everyone." She waggled her finger at them with an admonishing smile.

She composed herself once again. "We close with a familiar poem by Annie Besant."

They all chanted the, what seemed to be, familiar words:

> O Hidden Life, vibrant in every atom;
> O Hidden Light, shining in every creature;
> O Hidden Love, embracing all in Oneness;
> May all who feel themselves at one with Thee,
> Know they are therefore one with each other.

She raised her arms in final benediction. "Go forth and shine your light!"

"So mote it be," the girls next to Paul responded.

The priestess floated off the stage and disappeared into the choir and the slideshow resumed on the screen. A moment later the rumble of many voices released from sober confinement filled the chamber.

"Hey, there's Emily!" Harmony shouted to Anne. They jumped up and pushed through the crowd dragging Paul along.

Emily was a long held acquaintance of Harmony's, but Paul quickly lost the flow of the conversation in the plethora of names, places and events.

He noticed a kindly-looking old women standing nearby glancing around happily at no one in particular. "It's a bit of a madhouse in here," he ventured.

"Oh. Hello," she laughed inclining towards him. "Yes, they do carry on after the service," she said gaily. She looked at him carefully. "You are new here I think." She extended a hand. "I'm Violet."

"Paul. Yes, well, two friends brought me along. Have you been coming here long?"

"Oh goodness, I've been here since, I think, well, before the Ascension. It's so hard to keep track of time," she smiled apologetically. "Life is a blur. There's coffee downstairs by the way."

Paul returned the smile. "Yeah, I was wondering what it was like back then, before the Ascension I mean. Has the worship changed much?"

"Oh," Violet startled. She massaged her chin and furrowed her brow to think. "Well. I don't know…"

Harmony nudged him and he saw the priestess moving towards them, like an angel on a float.

Her iridescent eyes fell on Harmony and her mouth gleamed wider. "Harmony dear!" a silvery voice exclaimed. "And Anne!" She hugged each girl in turn.

Her arrival had caused Paul to forget about Violet as he endeavored to master the cipher before him. Her age was difficult to determine—she could be anywhere from thirty to sixty. Her hair was silver and fell in a long sweep just short of her shoulders. Her eyes were a serene pale gray, barely colored at all. Her face bore the features of an older lady—smile lines around the eyes, creases between the eye brows, a softer jaw line— if one looked closely, but it was milky white and unblemished, like a bar of soap. Her nose was small and delicately formed, and her bow-shaped lips, curled up at the end in a perpetual smile, were parted to display a double row of ivory teeth adequate for a more predatory species.

"Yes, this is Paul; he's a politico student at Eastview," he heard Harmony announce proudly.

Those entrancing eyes fell upon him. "Delighted to meet you, Paul." Paul was momentarily suspended staring at her pristine mouth, the porcelain teeth and active lips. He had a fleeting longing to kiss it.

"He is writing a paper on Christianity and wanted to meet you," Harmony said.

"Oh, really?" that gleaming mouth pronounced. The face remained placid, a slight widening of the eyes the only sign of surprise.

"Yes, I wonder if I could ask you a few questions about it," Paul managed to sputter. "You know, basic doctrine, theodicy, morality." He grimaced slightly upon realizing he had used the word *theodicy*.

"Of course," Gretchen nodded, "but today is not a good day unfortunately. The best thing is to contact the office—there's a number in your bulletin; they can set up an appointment." Gretchen looked squarely into Paul's face and smiled pleasantly. "It's so nice that young people are taking an interest in spiritual matters," she said, regarding him with those titanium eyes.

Paul ruffled his bulletin. "Oh yes, I'll do that then. Thanks," he fumbled.

Gretchen smiled serenely and floated off to converse with a group of young people talking animatedly in the back. Paul watched her go.

"Come on," Harmony said tugging at his arm. She dragged him towards the door.

It was about 11:15 when they emerged into the bright sunshine. Harmony lowered her sunglasses and put her hat on and they began to retrace that morning's steps.

"Man! I always feel so upbeat after church. I feel I can take on the world. Isn't she great!"

Paul was lost in thought and Harmony's comment didn't fully register in his mind. "You mean Gretchen?"

Harmony threw her head back in exasperation. "Of course, silly!"

Paul shrugged. "Yeah, she's pretty unique... for sure," he said impassively.

Harmony cast him a hard look. "Well, at least now you can make an appointment and get all your questions answered."

"Yeah. I'll do that," Paul replied non-committal.

They started up the alleyway in silence, their cadence kept by the sound of Harmony's thighs rubbing together in her tight jeans.

Finally, Paul said, "I was surprised at the tone of the service. I thought there would be more moralizing and exhortations to 'be a good person' and dogmatic stuff, you know; 'Jesus is my saviour' and 'repent or perish' or regaling us about our 'sins'."

Harmony giggled and Anne grinned back. "It's not like that at all," she laughed. "No one talks like that anymore."

"Isn't Jesus supposed to be, y'know, our savior?" Paul asked. "Isn't he supposed to 'save us from our sins'?"

Harmony looked skyward. "Oh brother. Listen: Jesus had some good ideas, like loving people and stuff like that, but he wasn't the be-all-and-end-all. There's been lots of other good people. Like the Dalai Lama, and Jung, and Buddha, and Sanger." She pronounced the last with particular reverence.

"Or Gandhi," Anne chipped in.

Harmony pointed an acknowledging finger at her friend, "Right. And of course Darwin. Gretchen has told us about lots of famous people," she assured him. "We learn. We listen to them all while seeking our own truths. We're not dogmatic about anything. You understand?"

No, Paul didn't really understand. It wasn't that he disagreed with Harmony's philosophy, but that he thought Christians, if their religion resembled what he had encountered in the Bible, should—they were moral absolutists. He ventured a more direct line: "But, in the Bible he says he is the only way to life—I heard that in my Cultural Evolution class. Jesus said if you don't believe he's God you will die." The girls stared blankly at him; mystified. He turned to a topic closer to home: "He said you should only have sex with, well, with only one person."

"Hahaha!" Harmony burst out and Anne giggled. "It depends on how you interpret it," Harmony explained.

"We don't take it literally," Anne contributed.

"They didn't know any better back then; they didn't have science and all that," Harmony explained. "Anyway, Jesus wanted people to 'live their life to the full' so he wouldn't have been against having a fun sex life," Harmony assured him. "You should read the Inclusion Bible; it's the most up to date on Christian beliefs. We're more enlightened now."

"We're more evolved," Anne added, staring into his eyes with a sweet smile.

"But this Bible, isn't it the only record we have of what Jesus taught?" Paul persisted.

Harmony shook her head. "Well, lots of the stuff in the Bible is totally against what we believe now. Besides, the writings we have are just the ones that the people who came to be called *orthodox* favored. There were lots of other writings about the christ that were suppressed by them because they only wanted their own version to be accepted. They just made up a bunch of stuff and said Jesus said it." She nodded sternly to him, "You need to hear more of Gretchen's sermons, then you'll understand."

"But why would they want to push a religion they knew to be false?" Paul asked, bewildered. "After all, they were there when Jesus was supposed to have resurrected."

"Oh, they just wanted to control everyone" Harmony sneered. "What better way than to control their sex lives?"

Paul thought it was strange that they would endeavor to lord it over people by promoting a religion that restricted their sexual liberty. It seemed to him one would be more successful pushing a religion that endorsed sexual license.

Once more they emerged into the sunlight at Ecology.

Paul's investigation hadn't gone the way he had anticipated. He had imagined confronting a host of irrational Christian platitudes, but he was having difficulty seeing where these Christians' beliefs bore any resemblance to the documented ones. He was beginning to have doubts about the usefulness of meeting with Gretchen and aggrieved that his proposed thesis appeared to be in a shambles for want of substance.

Perplexed, he tried one more time. "I'm not sure why you would call yourself *Christian* if you really don't believe most of the things Christ apparently said. If you think the writers of the Bible got it all wrong, why call yourselves 'followers of Christ'? I mean, how do you know what he taught at all?"

Harmony fidgeted with the brim of her hat. "Oh, why do we have to talk about this now?" she pouted. "Why don't you ask Gretchen all this when you see her? She can explain about how we know."

It was obvious Harmony wasn't in a mood to continue the conversation so Paul let it go.

Meanwhile, they had arrived back at Ecology and Morgentaler, busy with weekend shoppers now. Paul had planned to part with them there and take the subway back to Davisville but Harmony said, "We can just walk up to Anne's; she lives above a store on Morgentaler." Anne, hands clasped in front of her, looked at Paul measuredly. Her girlishly innocent mannerisms, studied or otherwise Paul was unsure, exuded a 'come thither' magnetism. "Bruce and Jermaine are away, right?" Harmony asked her friend.

Anne grinned, "Yeah. They won't be back until tomorrow night." She fidgeted with her hair and stared at Paul shyly still smiling all the while. He wondered if she smiled when she was sleeping.

"They're Anne's enablers," Harmony explained. "You should see their place!" She nodded at Anne. "And they're well stocked with everything. We can hang out on the roof!"

"Well, I don't know," Paul said hesitantly. "I had a few chores I wanted to get done this afternoon." He noticed some cops scanning pedestrians on the other side of the street.

Harmony pouted, "Oh come on." She lowered her glasses and smiled mischievously, "It will be fun." The preceding conversation had been erased from her mind apparently.

Paul hesitated a moment. "Well, okay, I guess I can do it later," he stammered with a grin.

"Alright!" Harmony whooped while Anne bounced up and down gleefully. "Hey, the light's changing, let's go!" Each looped an arm around Paul's and they started uptown against the throng. Paul looked over his shoulder to where the cops had taken up their station and frowned.

The girls walked and chattered, always with one eye on the window displays seemingly. They stopped whenever something caught their interest, which was frequently. It took twenty minutes just to walk to College.

"Born to shop!" Harmony exclaimed. Anne laughed. Paul smiled.

"Oh wow, look at those!" Harmony squealed pointing at some pink high-heeled shoes that had caught her eye.

"Oh so cute!" Anne gushed. "They'd go with your pink tube!"

"Pink tube?" Paul quizzed.

"A dress, silly," Harmony grinned. "Maybe I'll show it to you sometime… if you're a good boy," she smirked.

Paul raised his eyebrows. "Woof!" The girls giggled.

Just as Harmony turned to walk on, her hip struck the hand of an elderly woman who was passing by in the opposite direction, knocking a cane from her grasp. Harmony exploded, "Ow! Why don't you watch where you're going, stupid old bitch!" The frail lady cowered in the path of the enraged and formidable younger woman.

"She didn't mean anything," Paul started. "She didn't expect you to turn so quickly."

"Oh f---," Harmony exclaimed. "What's she doing hobbling around taking up the sidewalk when other people are trying to walk." She gave the fallen cane a boot sending it clattering on to the busy street and marched on with Anne.

Paul looked back at the old lady standing on the edge of the sidewalk sobbing helplessly as traffic passed over her walking stick. Others jostled past without stopping. Finally she sat on the sidewalk crying piteously. Paul had an urge to go back and rescue her but continued on after the girls instead.

They were silent for a while then Harmony said, "Sorry, I get peeved when I run into people like that."

"People like what?" Paul asked.

"Y'know, old people. Hangers-on."

Paul didn't reply.

"It's just, I mean, they've had their time. Why do they hang on when they can't do anything but suffer? What good is their life anyway? I'd never let myself get to be like that."

"They use up resources and don't contribute anything to society," Anne added. "Hey, here's the shop I told you about!"

Harmony brightened up immediately and skipped over to join her friend before the storefront. It featured lingerie, swimwear and skanky dresses—the kind worn to the mingle clubs downtown. "Let's go inside and try on some things," she giggled to Anne with a surreptitious glance back at Paul. Anne giggled back and they charged through the door with a wide-eyed Paul following.

For the next hour or so Paul was treated to a lascivious pageant of miniskirts, bikinis, gym togs and improbable accessories. In the end Harmony's blue dress was too dark, and she couldn't really afford the red sequined one, so she bought a bright white microknit bodysuit with a lace up front instead. It was sure to be a hit at the gym, Paul thought. Anne bought some cream-colored fishnet stockings, black garter belt, and a red choker.

They emerged from the store in high spirits with their little shopping bags in hand. The conversation was animated, and Paul was enjoying walking and bantering with them. It was hot, they were wearied from the walk, and were all getting quite silly.

A little north of Gandhi Anne stopped at a door, rummaged in her bag and retrieved a single brass key. "This darn thing is always tricky," she said in a fluttery voice as she fumbled with the lock. "Oh, here we go." Paul reached over her and held the door so she could withdraw the key. A breath of her candy sweet perfume tickled his nostrils as she slipped under his arm and stepped inside. He followed after and Harmony closed the door behind them.

There was a long narrow uncarpeted staircase just inside leading up to the third floor apartment. They started up in silence, their gay mood having sobered suddenly.

Anne's little skirt floated in the draft as they climbed revealing her skinny white legs all the way to her upper thigh to Paul below. Half-way up the flight Anne suddenly bolted ahead of them. "The key is under the mat, if you can believe it!" she tittered breathlessly. She stopped on the top stair and immediately bent over to retrieve the key from beneath the rubber doormat so that her skirt hiked up offering Paul a glimpse of tight white panties riding up a plump girlish bottom.

"Got it," she said huskily. She straightened up and rattled the key

120

into the lock then shot a quick glance back at him, smirked and ducked inside. Paul noticed the tips of her ears had turned a rose color. He and Harmony followed inside and the door locked with a click.

He didn't return home until the next morning.

10

CENSOR

"**W**ell, there are a lot of other worthwhile subjects."

"But I've already begun my research; I'm finding it pretty interesting," Paul protested. Mr. Lichter was getting increasingly agitated as they talked.

"Haven't you heard enough about that worldview in class already? Won't you just be going over old ground—regurgitating old news?"

"Well, that's one thing that surprised me. When I think about it, I haven't really learnt much about it; at least, I haven't heard much that makes sense," Paul began. "I've read a lot about the devos, but I can't really understand how their culture could have preceded the great scientific revolution which ushered in the modern era, given their irrational outlook." He tried to sound as consolatory as possible: "Could it be that we have not presented their worldview accurately?"

Lichter's eyes flamed up. "You think the OWC panels would not have investigated this area thoroughly; worse, that they would misrepresent facts!"

Paul braced himself. "No, not deliberately, but—"

The self-mastery that had restrained Lichter's passions broke like a breached dam. "This is preposterous!" he roared. "How could you think such a thing? We check and re-check all publications. Everything is vetted by the Ministry of Truth."

"—but everyone is influenced by the culture they live in—that's what you said—why would our writers be any different?" Paul contended. He didn't know why he suddenly felt so strongly about pursuing the paper given the difficulty he was having finding reliable sources; it made sense just to drop it. Maybe he just didn't like being forbidden to explore something.

Lichter clenched his fist. "But our society is not like any that has come before; ours is rooted in rational thought, impartiality—science." He thumped his fist on the desk emphatically.

"But the devos were people, like you and me. Whatever their shortcomings, they must have had a reason for believing the things they did and I can't fathom it based on what I've read."

Lichter sighed and cupped his fingers and looked hard at Paul. He sighed again. "Okay, what do you want to do?"

"I'd like to read what they thought, in their own words."

Lichter eyes blinked several times rapidly.

Paul continued, "After all, you taught us that societies always find their beginnings in those that came before. There must be something about the devo culture that could evolve into One World."

"Well, I meant our society came after but… well, it didn't necessarily owe anything to theirs," Lichter sputtered. "The transformation was more of a revolution than an evolution."

"Well, okay. In my paper I intended to contrast their worldview with ours—to reveal the failings of Christianity in the light of One World achievements. I could point out these revolutionary events that ushered in One World."

"Christianity?"

"Yeah. I mean, like devo philosophy."

Lichter drummed his fingers on the desk and his eyes roamed around the room.

Paul buried his hands in his pockets. "I've scanned the library, but I don't see any original Christian material. Why do we restrict access to their writings?" The words had barely left his mouth when he regretted not phrasing them differently.

Lichter's face flushed. "Restrict access? *Restrict access!* You make it sound like we have something to hide; that we're afraid of devo ideas or something!" His eyes had taken on a wild look again. It was a strange sight, to see the normally unflappable Lichter ruffled.

"Why are you so angry?" Paul asked.

Lichter's body was rail straight and he had dug his fingers into the desk involuntarily. He exerted himself to relax and then sat silently staring at his desk, his arms folded across his chest. *How did this bright young man—my student—get these ideas?* he thought. He felt… incompetent.

Long seconds ticked off the clock on the wall as they both sat mute.

"Okay," Lichter finally said in a quiet voice, "let's make a deal."

Paul stared at his teacher who now raised his eyes to him.

"You need higher access to World Library to continue your assignment. Without this you have no means of producing a credible paper because you believe the material available to you, at your present access level, is *tainted* with bias…"

"I didn't…"

Lichter put up a restraining hand. "You say you need to read the, um, *Christians* themselves, yes?"

"Yes, I need access," Paul conceded.

"Well then," Lichter said, unfolding his arms, "it's simple. I will request the access for you from One World Library. If you get it, you can continue with your paper. If not, you must pick another topic. Doesn't that sound reasonable? I mean, as you yourself said, without access you cannot continue anyway."

Paul balked. It was unlikely that a high school student would be granted higher security clearance. He was being asked to abandon a matter he had taken a personal interest in. Neither was he completely trusting of Lichter to submit the access request in good faith. He had never thought to question Lichter's integrity before, but now, having seen the fiery passion this topic aroused in him, he had lost some of that confidence.

"But I've already put in a lot of time on this. I don't know if I could begin again and still complete the essay before graduation."

Lichter waved his objection away. "Oh, don't worry about that. I know you've been working hard on this—it's very commendable—but I can give you an extension given the circumstances. You can complete it later," he assured him. "Just submit a progress report."

Paul's resources were exhausted, he knew; he didn't really have a choice.

"Deal?" Lichter pressed.

Paul hesitated. "Yes," he muttered finally.

Lichter's face brightened. "Okay, good. I'll submit your request this afternoon and we should know by Wednesday," he said extending his hand.

Paul grasped his hand and Lichter shook firmly. "You can continue for now with your paper, but you should think about another topic just in case clearance is not given."

"Yes. Okay," Paul replied weakly.

He left the classroom dejected. His paper had effectively been cancelled.

11

SUMMONS

Lanton sat in his office on the thirty-eighth floor of the Strong Build-ing staring at the ceiling. It was a slow Tuesday afternoon in July.

He roused himself and focused on the monitor in front of him. "Dial sub nine," he ordered. The spinning One World logo replaced the ding-bat momentarily, then the head of a guard appeared. "Block nine, sir."

"Prep P838506," Lanton said, "I'll be there at"—he looked at his watch—"fourteen hundred."

"Yes sir," the head answered and lowered its gaze to register the ap-pointment.

"Com break," Lanton pronounced and the logo re-established itself. Almost immediately the monitor made three rapid beeps indicating an incoming call. Lanton could see it was from the containment area. "Com pickup," he said impatiently. The head reappeared.

"Sir. There's a problem with your request."

"What is it?" Lanton said with a sigh.

"The prisoner, P838506, was transferred out this morning, sir."

Lanton's body stiffened. "Transferred? Where?"

"Yellow-two-two," the head replied significantly.

It was the code for KIDS. Lanton's mouth hung wide open in shock. A rage seized him. "By whose order!"

The guard hastened to locate the answer. "It was Superintendent Banderjee, sir."

Lanton slunk back into his chair as if impacted by a steel girder. He had known all along his handling of Eaton would lead to this day. All the while he had set that certainty aside hoping that the moment would pass if he banished it from his thoughts.

"Sir?"

"Com break," Lanton ordered, restoring the One World logo.

He reclined heavily, his body pinned to the chair, his hands grasping the arms, thoughts paralyzed. The aching between his eyes grew more pronounced.

His body lurched when the triple beep sounded again. The call was from a command office. His body remained rigid for a moment as if to avoid detection. "Com pickup," he pronounced in a shaky voice. A young man appeared on the screen—Banderjee's secretary.

"Inspector Lanton," Lanton said hoarsely.

"Chief Inspector Lanton," the authoritative voice corralled him, "you are to report to Superintendent Banderjee's office at fourteen hundred."

Lanton's stunned mind took a moment to digest the message. "Yes sir," he willed his voice to say calmly. "Is there a, um, agenda for this meeting? Some preparation required?"

The gray eyes on the screen riveted on Lanton's. "Fourteen hundred hours," he repeated. The screen beeped and returned to the One World logo.

Lanton sat stark still for a long while as if a flinch would send the ceiling crashing down. The clock on his screen advanced, second by second, towards two o'clock. Second by second…

Unable to sit there passively any longer he pulled himself up to the screen and glanced through his in box and selected an item. It was a request from a high school teacher for L7 World Library clearance for a bright politico student who was doing a paper on, of all things, Christianity. The corners of Lanton's lips curled up at the irony.

The room seemed so confining. He wandered over to the window to survey the city below. Should he run away? But where was there to flee? He could just go to the boardwalk and wait for them to find him there; the cool wind on his face would feel good.

At least he had been summoned; they hadn't sent the police. That was a good sign.

His mind sunk into reverie. Where was Alice at that moment? He had met her a few years after Julia left. They had gone out a few times; shared each other's world for a while. They had enjoyed each other's companionship and the talk, the common sensibility. He smiled faintly. It was a silly thought though—she wasn't anywhere. The reminiscing calmed him though.

He glanced at his watch. It was 13:45—time to go.

He put on his forage cap. "Com…" He stopped before completing the order and looked at the request displayed there on the screen. He rubbed his fingers nervously, his mind occupied. Then he shrugged and typed his response and closed the session. The door clicked behind him and the lights went off as usual as he left.

He exited the elevator on the fifty-third floor Northwest Wing and strode to the office at the end of the hall; number 53-040. An adjutant passed him going the other way without acknowledging his presence. Lanton settled into one of the chairs opposite and stared at the brass plaque on the door: *Superintendent Banderjee, Internal Bureau.*

Banderjee was one of the young ones he had been thinking about earlier that day. He had known her predecessor well—they had both been members of the downtown MoT civil security corps early on—but he had never met Superintendent Banderjee. She wasn't one to show up at the Lion after hours for a drink with the cadre; the younger ones—the ones from Mother—were never that way. He had only seen her on parade or presiding over council meetings.

He placed his cap on his lap.

There was something unsettling about his having to defer to someone so much younger and, he imagined, less refined—something indecent.

The door to 53-040 clicked and two stern-looking black-clad officers with holstered side arms emerged. Lanton's heart skipped when he saw them, but they hurried off without paying him any attention. *They must be on street duty.*

His anxiety refused to abate. It was two o'clock. He climbed to his feet, re-placed his cap and knocked firmly.

"Enter!" a youthful feminine voice commanded from within. Lanton turned the knob and went inside.

The door clicked shut behind him and he found himself standing in front of a huge black metal desk polished to a brilliant sheen. The occupant was marking up the document before her with a red pen.

"Chief Inspector Lanton," he announced crisply.

"Sit down, Officer Lanton," she replied without glancing up.

He removed his cap and settled into one of the dark green cushioned chairs and tried not to look at Banderjee who remained occupied. He used the time to wrestle his nerves down.

She raised her head to review the document, gave a nod and set it aside. Finally she looked up and her black eyes inspected her visitor rapidly and expertly.

"I don't believe we have met, Officer Lanton."

"No Superintendent Banderjee." He was thankful to be sitting some distance away from her desk—she perhaps wouldn't detect the odor of the sweat saturating his underarms and trousers.

"Hmmm." She picked up a dossier. "You have a good service record," she commented. "Quite good." She put it down on the desk and her hard black eyes latched onto him. "You've been active in the One World movement since its inception; a loyal soldier. We owe a lot to your efforts." It was clear to Lanton that the 'we' meant the post-Ascension generation—that people like Lanton, the trailblazers of the movement, were no longer in its vanguard. He was an outsider in this brave new world. It was the first time he had felt such a powerful awareness of this fact.

She continued. "Without the persistence of visionaries like you, well, who knows if Global Governance could have come about. We are indebted to you." It was said in an officious voice of a political superior. She shifted in her chair and reversed the crossing of her legs. "Despite your commendable service you haven't risen above the rank of Chief Inspector. Why do you think that is?" she asked pointedly, fixing him again with her laser-black eyes.

"I haven't thought about it. I've just been doing my job," he said plainly. Of course, he couldn't confide what he believed to be the actual cause—that he was perceived as doctrinally unreliable.

She stared hard at him. Lanton observed that she was quite attractive—almond skin, handsome face dominated by those jet black eyes, even teeth, full lips, shiny black hair, shapely feminine figure—but all this feminine allure seemed incidental to her person which was defined completely and solely by her station. She was a sexless machine in an enticing encasement, like a nine millimeter pistol—cool to the touch and lethal.

Banderjee uncrossed her legs and stood up. "Let's just cut to the chase," she said as she paced over to the window. She glanced down on the city briefly then turned to him. "We have determined to send you back to Counter-Subversion."

Lanton buried his astonishment beneath an impassive facade. It was one outcome he had not imagined—that the leadership would assign him back to the street. There must be something afoot.

Banderjee's alert eyes searched him for a reaction but discovered none.

"You'll take command of Blue section in the downtown core," she said authoritatively. "It's a sensitive zone—the west side—as you know." She glanced at Lanton then looked away again. "We need you to settle things down; to ferret out the troublemakers."

She stole a side glance at him and, still not drawing any revelations from his impassive figure, continued. "I know you might consider this a demotion—back to patrol—but we need experienced officers there."

Lanton was unfazed. "I've always been in the service of One World, in whatever capacity required," he answered factually.

Banderjee forced a smile. "Yes Citizen Lanton," she said without obvious irony. She moved back to her desk, reseated herself and activated her console.

"You'll receive orders on the channel by tomorrow morning. Dismissed." She returned to her work. Lanton rose, replaced his cap and exited the office smartly.

Immediately after his departure Superintendent Banderjee looked up from her work and frowned at the closed door. She had adamantly opposed the decision to move Lanton to Counter-Subversion—it came from higher up the chain of command. *Probably an old hand*, she mulled, *seeking to prove their old comrade's loyalty.* She despised the system that still allowed sentimentality to determine the placing of an operative of dubious loyalty in such a position. Lanton should be exposed for the pernicious agent he was. She would make a point to find out where the decision originated.

She had been sincere in her acknowledgment of Lanton's role in bringing One World to power—she respected his kind for that—but the old guard lacked the dedication of the younger generation raised in the culture of One World. Their stupid idealism left them prone to procrastination and wavering in their duty. They were soft, inefficient. One day his cadre would be purged completely...

In any case, she would make sure Lanton was closely monitored in his new posting. One misstep on his part and the case of Chief Inspector Lanton would be resolved to her satisfaction.

Lanton regained the sanctuary of his office and sat at his desk replaying the encounter with Banderjee in his mind while his unfocussed eyes stared blankly at the wall opposite.

Suddenly, his body convulsed, sweat oozed out of his pores and his limbs shook violently. He buried his face in his hands on the desktop and sobbed, the nervous energy draining out of him.

He didn't know why, exactly, he was crying. Perhaps in thankfulness for his narrow deliverance; perhaps for his uncertain future; perhaps, more, for the world he had lost—for Frank, his parents, Julia. Alice. Even Nathan Eaton.

He quieted and just sat with his head in his hands, reminiscing. He remembered old Julian Malanski and recalled the circumstances of their meeting. They were trying to get a homeless shelter running in the East side. Man! The hoops they had had the jump through, but in the end they succeeded. Those were the happiest times of his life—those days before the Ascension. You felt like it all mattered.

He hadn't had that feeling for a long time. The hospice wasn't there anymore, he knew. The need for palliative care had gone out the window when the Compassion Directives came out. So many things that he had fought so hard for just didn't matter anymore; they just didn't compute in the new world.

Then there was his high school teacher, Mr. Samba, his first mentor; Janet Thompson from the Corktown drop-in and the other social workers—all wonderful people. The others at City Hall. They were all gone now. Irrelevant.

Why was he having these thoughts so often lately—going over the same story in his mind, over and over?

Painfully, he remembered his son. Frank had been a journalist in the early years after the Ascension—a rising star, likely to have made senior official of some sort in the MoT by now. But his penchant for candor doomed that in the end. One day he just vanished. Julia urged him to inquire through official channels, but he had kept quiet through it all; compliant. Many of the old guard—he knew many of them personally— were disappearing at that time as the world government consolidated its power. Swept along with them were the intelligentsia, teachers, politicians, celebrities, religious figures—anyone considered unreliable—and to Lanton's anguish, one brash youth—his son. His wife Julia was gone before the year was out. She had blamed him.

He continued on—over the years—patiently doing his part. No longer in control; just following orders.

Is it what you wanted? That's what Eaton had asked. He didn't know anymore.

He wondered if the person whose name adorned the building he sat in would have 'wanted it this way.' If they were all culpable, Strong's guilt was certainly more excusable than his own—he couldn't have foreseen where it was all going. They had all been caught up in it.

In that moment he hated the devos for forcing him to become what he was; forcing him to do things; leaving him no choice.

It wouldn't do, to be having these thoughts, he knew—it was incompliant. It was stupid; they would be scrutinizing his every move now. He couldn't afford to have his mind jumbled with philosophical musings.

He didn't really reproach the hierarchy for sacking him—they had to keep security tight—but he couldn't fathom why he was being transferred back to Counter-Subversion. He judged it hadn't been Banderjee's decision; the jargon about 'needing experienced officers' was clearly a thin rationalization spoken through her teeth. He had recognized her type immediately—the new zealots. In his time he had been considered one of those, he knew, but this latest breed surpassed his generation in One World zeal as his had surpassed its predecessor.

So there must be someone else up the chain looking out for him. Who might that be? Who was there to watch over one such as he?

Suddenly, he remembered the young man who had applied for World Library access and was remorseful he had granted it so thoughtlessly; his carelessness could put him in danger. The authorization must be revoked immediately.

He hastily activated his com. The twirling One World logo appeared, but it was promptly overlaid by a flashing 'Access Denied' message.

He paused, dumbfounded, for a moment. Not bothering to attempt entry again, he pushed himself away from the desk and stared at the blinking signal and shrugged in resignation. "Well, we are efficient."

It was 15:44. There wasn't much he could do there anymore. He placed some papers in his satchel and donned his overcoat and cap. The door clicked and the lights went off as he left 38-302 for the last time.

12

DAY 118

GRETCHEN

Paul approached the Church of the Affirming Spirit re-tracing the route he had taken with Harmony and Anne the Sunday prior.

The feeling of apprehension remained with him as he searched out the side door. He gripped his M-Brain tightly; all the important points he wanted to cover were recorded there. He half-wished he could have brought Harmony along but knew she would just impede the discussion.

The ancient wooden door opened easily and he found himself standing in a small alcove peering into the main sanctuary which was dimly lit by sunlight filtering through colored glass. It was so deathly still he imagined hearing the falling dust particles impacting the sun beams.

When his eyes had adjusted to the lighting he was able to make out a lone figure sitting motionless with head bowed in a pew a few rows back. It was an old woman, not Gretchen. There didn't appear to be anyone else there.

Suddenly an amber glow appeared against the wall opposite. A chapel door had opened spilling a soft warm illumination into the sanctuary. A ghostly figure emerged from the light and floated silently along an aisle between two banks of pews in the direction of the praying woman. Paul knew it was Gretchen without seeing her face. She stopped, apparently detecting the other woman and stood there in the darkness surveying the room. Paul could just make out her white garment in the shadows.

Suddenly a feeling of vulnerability gripped him. She was looking at him in the darkness—he could sense those platinum eyes on him. The phantom moved back along the way it had come then advanced up the aisle towards him.

She emerged from the darkness like a schooner out of the mist. Her pallid hand extended to take his. Its gossamer touch felt neither warm nor chilled to Paul; it was like holding nothing at all. "Paul, you've come." An echo that seemed to originate inside his mind said, "You are punctual." She smiled serenely and turned to lead him back into the sanctum. "Come this way." The lustrous eyes left him and the vaporous fingers released his hand and he followed her into the darkness.

Gretchen led him back to the chapel. It was bathed in green light from the windows and a pungent incense permeated the air. There was, what Paul supposed to be, Eastern religious music wafting in faintly from somewhere. A simple bench about a foot high made of unpainted wood occupied the center of the cement floor. The seat was inclined slightly towards the back. Paul had seen some of the students at school using them when they meditated. Gretchen settled onto it with her legs bent under, like a Buddhist monk.

"I so enjoy coming here to meditate in the morning," she said, smiling perpetually. "It is so peaceful." You can sit there if you like." Paul sat cross-legged on a cushion before her. The lines of the labyrinthine pattern on the floor ran between them.

The chapel walls were constructed of wooden panels with intricate carved edges. There was an ornate lectern at the front with an ancient volume upon it. When his eyes returned to his host he found her staring fixedly at him. Her lips were perpetually curled up at the tips giving the impression of a suppressed smile.

"So, you met Harmony at school?"

Paul shook his head. "Oh. Oh no. We don't go to the same school. We're in different grades actually. I met her at the gym," he explained. He blushed slightly as if that admission had somehow compromised his standing.

Gretchen's lips curled up at the corners, "Oh, I see." Paul wondered uncomfortably what it was she had *seen*.

"Did she give you any insight into our religion? You are writing a graduation paper on the Christian worldview, I believe."

Paul cringed slightly. "Yeah, we discussed some things…"

"But you had other questions that Harmony couldn't answer to your satisfaction?" Gretchen concluded.

"Yes. She said I should ask you."

Gretchen flashed a smile and turned her head casting a side glance his way. "Would you like some green tea? I think it is ready."

Paul startled. "Oh. Okay. Yeah, sure."

Gretchen rose easily and drifted noiselessly behind him returning with a reed tray holding a small Japanese tea pot and two ceramic cups. She placed this on the floor and resumed her position. Paul thought she was going to pray when she brought her hands together before her, but instead she pressed her fingers together and made a quick bow with her head before taking up the tea pot and pouring the steaming amber liquid into each cup.

She closed her eyes and took a sip then turned her attention back to him. "So, what is it you would like to know?"

Paul raised his cup to his mouth trying to organize his thoughts. The tea burned his lips but he did his best to conceal the pain. Suddenly he remembered his notebook. He was conscious of those alabaster eyes on him as he tried to pull up his questions.

"Okay. I guess I'd like to clarify something," he fumbled and cleared his voice. "I wanted to clarify Christ's mission. The Bible says that humans are full of sin…"

"And so we are. We are all full of hate and selfishness," Gretchen concurred.

"…and that Jesus died for our sins in order to reconcile us with God."

"But what do you mean 'he died for our sins'?" Gretchen asked guardedly.

Paul thought for a moment. "Well, I mean, there was a price to pay for our sins so we don't have to go to hell. Christ offered to pay the penalty for us—to die in our stead—so that we might be reconciled…"

Gretchen's body tensed and her smile disappeared in a flash. "Jesus Christ did not die for my sins!" she pronounced sternly. It was the first time Paul had seen her placid façade falter. However, in a moment her body relaxed again and the smile re-appeared. "That's not what it means," she said waggling a finger at him. "Jesus came to bring a message of love and hope to humankind. His message wasn't welcomed by everyone—especially by the *orthodox* religious establishment—and so they had him silenced. So, in that sense he did die to bring us life—the message of love and tolerance and equality. That's what it means."

She paused and took a sip of her tea then set it down on the floor again. "Tell me, would you want an innocent man to die for something you had done?"

"Well no…"

"So why would you think that God, the Great Living Force, would demand such a thing?" Her eyes burned the question into his brain. "The idea of a god demanding that someone be killed so horribly to sate his wounded pride—his own son at that!" Her lips turned down sourly. "Who would think such a god worthy of worship?"

Paul was silent.

Gretchen gave out a *humph!* then lifted up her cup and took a sip.

Paul glanced quickly at his notes. "What about the resurrection?" he offered timidly.

"You are talking about Christ's arising from the grave; his body getting up and walking away?" Gretchen said amusedly.

Paul shrugged sheepishly. "John and the others said it—the apostles." He felt ridiculous.

"That's just silly; it's against everything we know." She put her cup down. "People back then might have thought that, before the advent of modern technology and learning made such beliefs impossible." She nodded quickly. "But we are evolving, and with our evolution has come greater faculty for higher understanding. Jesus showed us the way. He was the most evolved of all. But we can all be what Jesus was; we *will* all be like Jesus if we just keep learning, keep evolving." She smirked at Paul. "The apostles misunderstood this."

Paul looked mute at her.

Gretchen pressed her lips then smiled playfully as if addressing a naughty schoolboy. "And so, in that sense, we can all be 'resurrected'."

Paul was reluctant to let the idea go. "But why were his followers, people like Paul and Peter, willing to go to their deaths for that belief—I mean that Jesus rose bodily from the grave?" he asked. "Isn't it possible that they saw something that scared the…, well, showed them that Jesus was something supernatural?" He gulped as the crystal eyes probed. "I mean," he went on weakly, "why be so dogmatic about what was a practical joke?" Paul was repeating an argument he had read somewhere but couldn't remember the rebuttal.

Gretchen rolled her eyes skyward momentarily. "But, as you know, people have sacrificed themselves willingly for all kinds of beliefs. Consider those who famously dove the airplanes into the World Trade Center or the Eifel tower attack. Look at the devos today…" Her mouth soured. "People have always been willing to sacrifice themselves if the belief is strong enough. It doesn't mean it's true."

It was obvious she had been through this all before, many times. "Also, we do not know if anything happened the way the Bible says it did. There were many others back then with other opinions—we have their accounts too. In any case, human nature being what it is, people can talk themselves into believing anything.—like people walking on water or rising bodily from the dead," she laughed. "We don't even know if this John figure really lived."

"So you say the Bible is just a lot of made up stories? That none of it is true?"

"What do you mean by *true*?" she smiled condescendingly. "The events may not have happened in reality, but the scriptures often speak to deeper truth. They were not meant to be read literally."

Paul couldn't credit the point—didn't 'not meant to be read literally' simply mean 'not factual'?

Discarding his notes he asked, "What does the Bible mean by 'eternal life' then? It says that Jesus gave us eternal life."

Gretchen lips curled slightly and her eyes shimmered with amusement. "What do *you* think?"

Paul thought for a moment. "Well, if Jesus did not rise from the grave, I don't see how we would either. So I guess that's pretty much out."

Gretchen smiled kindly. "But we do have eternal life; all of us," she said archly.

Paul's brow furrowed questioningly.

"Don't you see?" Gretchen smiled. "Our genes have been alive for millions of years." She waved her hand expansively. "In that sense, each of us is immortal. We live on in the lives of our progeny. Isn't that a more wonderful vision than dead bodies emerging from the ground?"

Paul wasn't sure. In truth, it didn't seem as appealing—living through your offspring—than his original understanding of eternal life; it was easier to accept but not as satisfying. He wondered why the Christians made such a big deal about eternal life at all if that is all that was meant, that your progeny—whoever they might be—carried your genes onward in time. *How banal is that?*

Gretchen was still looking at him expectant of an answer. He referred quickly to his notes. "So what would Jesus want us to do with our lives?" he asked awkwardly.

Gretchen turned her head and cast a side glance at him. Her placid face turned back. "As I said, as humanity has evolved. So has its religions," she explained. "In our distant past we went around in animal skins killing others of different tribes. I mean, at one time Christianity supported slavery! But, as humanity progressed, gaining knowledge, we forged a higher morality of love and affirmation. And we grow higher still—day by day! Just think of what is coming to pass, in our own time" she said elatedly. "A planetary culture of inclusivity and equality." She raised her hands above her shoulders as if grasping for the stars. "It is the duty of all of us to further this evolution—to further this aspiration to oneness and love. This is our mission—Jesus' mission. In a way, God *is* evolution," she pronounced with finality.

Paul let his notebook rest on his knees having abandoned any hope of pursuing his intended line of inquiry. The questions he had prepared seemed irrelevant now. It was as if he had swotted up for a biology exam and found upon arriving at the examination venue that the test was on English literature. He went quiet.

"What about you?" Gretchen picked up the conversation. "Have you been developing your own spirituality?"

Paul blushed slightly, "Well…"

She smiled understandingly. "Do think about it. We have lots of interesting things going on. The scripture group is learning about the Upanishads—it's a twelve week introduction—every Wednesday at seven thirty. I'm leading the meditation class on Friday. Harmony and Anne have been coming," she smiled knowingly. "We've been contemplating starting a youth group."

"Um, well, I'm really busy right now, trying to get this paper moving along—it's my last semester at school you know…" He rose and stood over the Buddha-like figure. "Thank you for speaking with me."

Gretchen waved the imposition aside. "Whenever you'd like to talk, just phone the office," she smiled.

Paul glanced back as he let himself out of the chapel to see Gretchen reposed with eyes closed, that serene, assured smile still playing at the corner of her lips.

13

SAMUEL

The sun was dazzlingly bright when Paul emerged from the church. He tried to collect his thoughts and determine the significance of the meeting for his paper.

As long as he could remember—on TV, in books, at school—Christianity had always been described as the antithesis of One World. Devos were just people who had not evolved beyond the Judeo-Christian worldview. Left unchecked, they could drag everyone back into the pre-Ascension dark ages, before science and reason; all progress would be abrogated.

He had hoped to be able to detect traces of this subversive element in Gretchen's Christianity but, as far as he could determine, contemporary Christians—Harmony, Anne and Gretchen—believed what everyone else believed and their answers to the great existential questions would be identical to any One Worlder's: How did human life come about? *From a warm primordial pond,* he was sure they'd say. What is the purpose of human life? *They would answer, to promote unity and happiness.* How can we do that? *Answer: Goodwill and scientific progress.*

What happened to God creating man? What about revelation as a source of knowledge? What about pursuing 'holiness'? Where was all the supernatural stuff? On no significant point would they fail to achieve ready concurrence with any One World atheist. How, then, can I draw any contrast between the two worldviews?

He saw why this was so, this convergence of opinion between the Christian Inclusionists and One World: the Inclusionists might appeal to Biblical authority to invest their opinions with Godly authority when they coincided with scriptural teaching, but when the Bible's directives run counter to their own they didn't take its prescriptions 'literally'— that is, they ignored them. In the end they trusted in their own reasoning, just like non-Christians, so it wasn't surprising that they held the same views—they lived in the same environment after all, heard the same news, read the same books and watched the same TV shows.

He crossed the square and headed uptown on Cosmos without taking stock of his surroundings. When he came to Ecology he turned left instead of heading back to the subway because he still wanted time to think.

So how could he gain insight into the pre-Ascension period? The thought crossed his mind: *There were still devos around, in hiding.* Everybody knew that, although it wasn't talked about. Were they the key then—his conduit to pre-Ascension Christian thought?

If only I could make contact with one of them. Maybe I could get clearance to interview one in…well, wherever they are kept when captured. He was amazed he was even entertaining the idea; his body shivered at the thought of being in the same room with one. *At least, if I could get access to pre-Ascension writings.*

A rusty male voice in close proximity startled him. "Hmmm, yes, that would be the thing—get access to One World Library. But isn't that impossible? Well, unless you know somebody important."

Paul realized he had been thinking out loud. He glanced over his right shoulder to see who the owner of the voice was.

It was an elderly man, stout of figure but not exceeding average height. His hair and beard were long, white and tangled, like an unkempt Santa Claus. His slacks were baggy and gray. His worn lumberjack jacket, also gray, had a barely discernable plaid pattern. He wasn't looking at Paul but was intent on watching the traffic light. Paul shrugged and turned to wait for the light also. He hoped the stranger hadn't overheard too much of his monologue.

It was taking a long while for the light to turn and the silence was becoming awkward. Paul felt the presence of the old man beside him, although he wasn't making any sound, and had to suppress the urge to jaywalk since there was so little traffic. He didn't want to commit an incompliancy in front of a stranger, though.

The man's boldness was startling—to comment on such a topic to a stranger. Covertly Paul stole a glance to confirm he was still there. He was, rooted to the curbside looking at the red light. Paul quickly looked away again.

"I'm still here," he heard the ancient voice say.

Paul turned his way. "Pardon me?"

"I said, *I'm still here.*"

"Yes, so you are." Paul looked away again, impatient for the light to change. He was worried the stranger might be maneuvering him into buying a hit of SOMA or a bottle of wine. A yellow taxi slowed down and the driver looked Paul over.

"Hmmm. It's strange that pre-Ascension Christian writings are classified, don't you think?" the old man asked. Paul glanced over and caught his eye. "I mean, aren't we all about rationality and science—pursuing the facts, no matter where they lead, in the service of Truth?"

"Yeah, I guess," Paul said, looking away again. He discerned an element of sarcasm in the old man's speech although his voice didn't betray any.

"Yes, why the secrecy?" the old man mused. "Unfortunate." His demeanor insinuated that he knew something about the things Paul had been pondering.

Would the darn light never change? Inexplicably he found himself asking, "What do you know about pre-Ascension writings anyway?" Immediately the light turned green and he started off without waiting for a reply.

"Perhaps we could chat a while and you could determine that for yourself," the man continued behind him. Paul could tell by the strain in his voice that he was extending himself physically to keep up. "I have been a follower of The Way for many years... many years."

The Way caught Paul's ear. He knew that some of the earliest devos referred to their religion as The Way. *Did he really say he was a 'follower' of The Way not just someone who had studied it?* Paul slackened his pace a bit.

"I mean, if you are really curious about the matter—a *true* seeker, not just one of those... well, one of those who pan for idle amusement," the old man said breathlessly.

Paul wheeled around to face him. "If I was a 'true seeker' as you say, why should I want your opinion on the subject? What expertise do you have?"

"Oh! Well," the old man stammered and stroked his beard. "*Expertise.* Credentials. Yes, I suppose that's what's important now," he said absently. "An accreditation from the Ministry of Truth and you're certified to mentor the world."

Paul reviewed the figure before him and had to smile to himself. He was a kindly-looking specimen, a little Hobbit-like of physique, with his flat feet and bulbous nose—a bit comical. Something about his carriage and the diction he employed ruled out dismissing him as a crank out of hand though. Paul was wondering about this when the old man said, "Well that's it then," shrugged and started to move off.

Paul hadn't expected that reaction and stood dumbfounded as the old man stole away. His intuition alerted him that he was losing an opportunity to make contact with someone who might know something about pre-Ascension times—if not the old man himself, perhaps he knew someone who did. He looked street-wise—maybe he even knew some devos! Paul he roused himself and called after the retreating figure, "Who was Amos?"

The old man waved his arms without turning or slowing. "The Lord roars from Zion and thunders from Jerusalem," he bellowed, "but they won't listen! Who in this God-forsaken place will listen?"

The words rang familiar to Paul from his Bible perusing so he stepped after him quickly. "Okay, maybe we should talk. I see you know something about the devo scriptures. How did you come by your knowledge?" An unlikely thought entered his mind. "Were you a priest before Ascension?"

The old man halted as if shot and wheeled to face Paul. "How?"

"Yes, how did you come to study the Bible?"

The man tilted his head side to side. "I will tell you, if you like… sometime."

Paul waited for further elaboration but it was not forthcoming. He had heard that many renegade priests had gone underground after Ascension and it was rumored some were still around, on the margins of society. It could all be an urban myth of course and the old man cut an unlikely figure as a priest but, then again, what should one expect a rebel priest to look like? "Okay then, if you are willing, how about we just go over some of the tenants of pre-Ascension religion. There are a few things that confuse me."

"But we can't talk out here," the old man said, darting a nervous glance about. "I live just on the next block. Let's go there."

His corpulent body set off at a pace exceeding its apparent capability. Paul hustled after him wondering if he had been faking difficulty
in keeping up before.

In the middle of the next block he approached an unadorned wood-
en door, worn with peeling brown paint, nestled between a hardware
store and a flower shop. "Here we are," he said punching in the combination. The door opened with a squeak and he motioned to Paul, "Come
come. Just inside here we can talk." He passed beyond the threshold.

Paul hung back for a moment. The old man seemed kindly however
eccentric. It was unlikely he could harm Paul in any way. *In any case,
maybe the old guy does know something. He must have been around a
long time—since way before the Ascension for sure*, he thought. So he
cast a quick glance up the street and ducked inside.

It was pleasantly cool there. Paul found himself standing in a single
room, wider than it was deep; likely a tiny shop at one time. There was
a table with books and other paraphernalia strewn across it just ahead,
and a small seating area with a couch and two chairs, one wooden and
one in a faded green damask, to the right. The old man shuffled over
to the refrigerator to the left where the room was lit by a single light
bulb and drew out a pitcher of orange juice and took a glass from the
cupboard above the sink. "Want some?"

Paul was still standing just inside the door. "Uh, no. No thanks."

The other grunted then poured half a glass and put the pitcher back
in the fridge. Then he shuffled over to the couch and sat down at one
end of it with a weary sigh. "Have a seat," he said taking a sip.

Paul advanced hesitantly, his eyes panning the room. There were
papers and books stacked on every available horizontal surface in a
sort of ordered chaos and a musty odor of dust and old newspaper
drifted in the air. It was the habitat of someone devoted to matters of
the mind and little concerned with physical amenity. He was surprised
to see so many books in one place; books were tracked closely in One
World.

As he settled into the green chair opposite his host, Paul noted a
silver cross on the wall above a calendar that looked to have a print of
a Van Gogh painting.

The old man looked directly at him. "My name is Samuel."

"Paul."

"Hmmm…Paul," the other echoed. "A good Christian name." He
smiled showing small regular teeth.

Paul jostled uncomfortably. "Okay. What if I just ask you a few general questions about your beliefs, just to see if I understand them."

"Shoot," Samuel answered. He stooped to take another sip of his juice then set the glass on the table between them and offered his undivided attention.

Samuel had not objected when Paul had referred to Christian beliefs as *your* beliefs. *Could he really be a believer, not just someone who studied devo religion?* He thought for a moment then ventured, "Okay, so you believe that God created two people, a man and a woman, and they populated the whole earth?"

"Yes," Samuel answered smartly, "don't you? I mean, isn't that what your science tells you?"

Paul let the question pass. "You believe this guy Jesus rose from the dead?"

"I think the evidence points that way, yes," Samuel answered immediately. He looked hopefully at Paul. "Have you ever considered the evidence?"

Paul wasn't really interested in the old man's 'evidence.' He wanted to determine if Samuel really believed what the people in the Bible believed. So far, he seemed to be in sync with them as near as he could tell. *It was too good to be true—a Bible Christian!*

"You believe the Bible came from God."

Samuel flipped his gray eyebrows. "I believe it to be written by men guided by the Holy Spirit. So, I guess yes, it is from God."

"You believe that this Jesus will come back to Earth and judge everyone, the living and the dead. The good people will go to heaven, the bad to hell."

Samuel shook his head quickly. "No. There are no 'good' people. Those saved by the blood of Christ will enter heaven, not 'good' people." Samuel looked wide-eyed at him. "Does that offend you?"

Samuel's exposition of the heavenly requisites passed Paul by without impact, he was so stirred at having discovered someone who might actually believe all this stuff.

The question that had most troubled Paul about Christians bubbled up. "Tell me, why do you associate yourself with such a movement?"

Samuel's bushy wide eyebrows rose and a concerned expression descended over his face. "What do you mean *such a movement*?"

Paul felt his temples flush warm. "Let me be frank with you…"

"Yes please," Samuel nodded eagerly.

Paul plunged in. "Aren't you ashamed of identifying with a religion that has killed so many people? I mean, think of the Crusades and the Inquisition and witch burnings?" Immediately, he regretted wording the question so harshly. In a more consolatory tone he added, "I mean you seem like a nice fellow."

"Are *you* ashamed to associate yourself with a religion that kills so many every day?" Samuel replied.

"What do you mean?" Paul responded with surprise.

Samuel picked up his glass. "Oh, never mind".

He leaned back in his chair. "The Crusades and the Inquisition you say. Okay, let's talk about the Crusades. But first I would like to know, when you say *the Crusades,* do you mean the military campaigns of Christendom against the Islamic lands in the twelfth century, or do you mean the Christian invasion of the Muslim mid-eastern countries that ignited the religious wars between Muslim and Christian that ultimately led to the bloody and bitter reprisals of Islamic militants in the twenty-first century?"

Paul shrugged, "Both. Aren't they the same thing?"

"Not at all," Samuel replied. "One is a fact of history, the other a myth of modernity."

"What do you mean?" Paul said, bewildered.

"I mean, the first is historic record: the peoples of western Europe, after enduring four centuries of Islamic military conquest which swallowed up their lands in the middle east, Africa, Spain and even half of France, launched an ultimately unsuccessful campaign to re-conquer some of those lost lands, in particular their most hallowed place, Jerusalem."

Paul had always understood the Crusades to be a murderous campaign by Christian zealots against the peaceful, more sophisticated and scientifically advanced Muslim empire, not a response to an aggressive foreign power. Samuel's synopsis ran counter to everything he believed about that period; his revisionism breathtaking in its audacity.

"This, the historical Crusades, contrasts sharply with the modern Progressive myth which is: a mob of Christian religious fanatics launched a bloody assault on the peace-loving people of Jerusalem, slaughtering them in such numbers and with such savagery that it birthed a hatred and distrust of the Muslims towards the West which proved to be the cause of perpetual conflict down to the twenty-first century."

Paul flushed slightly, recognizing his own understanding of the events in Samuel's 'myth.'

Samuel continued before he could issue a challenge. "The first, historic, Crusades were a series of campaigns launched in response to a sustained assault by an implacable enemy bent on the conquest of the world for its god Allah. These Crusades were unsuccessful and forgotten for hundreds of years while militant Islam pressed on with its mission of world subjugation."

Samuel paused a moment to catch his breath then continued. "The second, mythic, Crusades were stories drummed up by anti-clerical Progressives in eighteenth and nineteenth century Europe to tarnish the image of their opponents, and later adopted by nationalist forces in Islamic countries to rouse their people against perceived ancient wrongs. 'Remember the Crusades' became a rallying cry for them."

Paul was flabbergasted. "Let me get this straight," he said with more agitation in his voice than he wished. "You are blaming the Crusades, the bloody wars of the Christians, on nineteenth century Progressives?"

"No, you have to listen to what I say," Samuel said gently. "I'm saying that the historical wars were fought to repulse a determined foe. They were not against a peaceful neighbor," he emphasized. "I am also stating that, the enmity between the West and Muslim countries in the twenty-first century, if it had anything to do with the Crusades, had little to do with the historic Crusades but more to do with the mythic Crusades created by so called 'enlightened' opponents of the Church in the nineteenth century and adopted by Muslim leaders as a rallying myth in the twentieth. The Muslims of that time—I mean just after the Crusader period—didn't really think much about them, and when they did it was in positive terms—they had won after all. Understand that I am not denying the bloodshed of the Crusades, except to say it was not a remarkable occurrence for that time and the situation was more nuanced than the modern myth would concede."

"So you think we've been duped into believing fairy tales?" Paul said in a defensive tone of voice.

"Not *fairy tales*, myths," Samuel repeated. "A narrative created by Progressives and Muslims to justify their antipathy towards Christianity."

Paul sat, arms folded across his chest, strangely affronted by it all.

"Why are you so opposed to that?" Samuel asked. "All cultures have their myths. Is Progressive culture immune to that charge?"

The remembrance of his own assertion of that very point—the universality of societal-supporting myth—with Mr. Lichter caused Paul to cringe. Even though he believed it as a general concept he couldn't really bring himself to permit another to apply it to his own worldview. He understood Samuel to be referring to One World culture when he said *Progressive*.

"I would have to think about that," he said haltingly. Then, more firmly, "I'd have to read up a bit on that history to check out these things you are saying. Maybe it's you that has been fooled."

Samuel flashed a quick grin. "Yes, yes, investigate everything."

Paul was surprised Samuel didn't take offence at his reluctance to believe his testimony. He expected a Bible Christian to be more fiery in the presence of dissention.

Meanwhile Samuel's face had returned to a neutral thoughtful expression and he pressed on without leaving Paul opportunity to reflect further. "Now let's talk about the Inquisition, and 'witch burnings' as you called it." He nodded to Paul. "How many witches do you think were burned during the four hundred-odd years the Inquisition existed?"

Paul shrugged impatiently. "I don't know for sure. I think millions—maybe twenty million."

Samuel tsk'd. "The actual figure of people executed for witchcraft, as far as we know from the historical record, is around fifty thousand—a bit more than one hundred people per year on average."

Paul shook his head, "That doesn't sound right."

"Well, of course we don't know for sure, but that's the estimation historians have arrived at by extrapolating from extant trial documentation," Samuel explained. "But most of these were not burnt by the Inquisition, less than two percent of them in fact."

"What do you mean? You said fifty thousand were killed by the Inquisition!" Paul protested.

"No, I said about fifty thousand were executed; less than one thousand of these were victims of the Inquisition; the overwhelming number were killed by secular authorities."

"But why would they do that?" Paul sputtered. "It was the Church that started the belief in witches. It promoted the witch hysteria."

Samuel shook his head. "No. No, that's simply not true. Belief in witches was present in societies throughout ancient times. The Romans and other pre-Christian societies—the German and Celtic for instance—had statutes concerning the prosecution of witchcraft. The

149

western Church arose in an environment where belief in the efficacy of witchcraft was already widespread."

Paul stared open-mouthed.

"Witchcraft prosecutions picked up during trying times—the Black Plague years of the fourteenth century being a notable one—when a superstitious people looked for answers to the dire afflictions that were assaulting them. They didn't have scientific explanations, you see? So, often it was the strange, the decrepit and the loner, living on the margins of society, who were accused of bringing these calamities upon their societies. Also, of course, there were many prosecutions driven by petty jealousies or ambition, often political, which used witchcraft as a pretense. What better way to crush one's rivals than to have them implicated in malignant activity?" he nodded to Paul. "The church was the first organization to view the existence of witchcraft skeptically."

Paul's head nodded slowly, unbelieving.

"Yes, it's true," Samuel asserted. "The Church consistently spoke against the prosecution of 'witches.' It believed that God had control of the universe and ordered its functioning and that humans were powerless to usurp this control. So it thought the power of witchcraft imaginary. Defendants who persisted in the belief that they wielded magical powers were routinely dismissed as delusional."

Paul looked doubtful.

Samuel was unperturbed. "What was the Inquisition like?" he continued. "Unlike secular courts, it demanded a fair trial with representation and due process. It dismissed charges if they were motivated by animosity. The defendant was required to list his enemies before his trial and their testimony was received with skepticism. Accordingly, the conviction rate in the Inquisition's courts was miniscule compared with the secular ones and generally led to penitential prescription—reciting the psalms, say, or for extreme cases, excommunication—rather than capital, or even corporal, punishment. Also, we should note, while the Inquisition used torture sparingly, it was commonly used in the secular courts and it was much harsher. This was only natural since the secular courts were concerned with protecting society from the offender exclusively—getting rid of the threat—whereas the Inquisition was more concerned with rehabilitating him and preserving his soul."

Paul crossed his arms at his chest again and looked hard at Samuel, who continued. "So, as far as 'promoting witch hysteria,' it was actually the Church that did the most to defuse it. The number of prosecutions were actually much less where the Church was strongest—in Italy and Spain for instance—than where it was weak; in Germany say, or Switzerland. And as the civic power of the Church faded throughout the fifteenth and sixteenth centuries and the Enlightenment forces began to stir, the number of witch burnings increased dramatically."

"That can't be true," Paul muttered plaintively.

Samuel sighed. "Just check the historical record." Twisting his lips wryly he added, "Well, if One World will permit you."

He continued. "Most of the burnings took place in the sixteenth century, when the Church's power had largely been superseded by that of the secular state.

"Did you know that there wasn't really an *Inquisition* as such?"

Paul sighed irritably. "You aren't going to tell me it never existed?" His head was reeling from all the alleged facts.

"No, the Church had many inquisitory courts—there was one in Rome, one in Portugal, one in Venice, etcetera. The bloodiest one was in Spain. It accounted for about 4500 executions—mostly heretics; very few witches—perhaps one hundred. An inquisitory court was one in which experts sat in judgment. It was a common arrangement in that day, as it is now. Your One World Tribunal is an inquisitory court—One World's Inquisition."

Paul grimaced. "So you are saying there wasn't an Inquisition—capital 'I'—but many inquisitory courts. That's quite interesting, but I don't see how it is relevant to the charge your Inquisition, or inquisitory courts—whatever you want to call it—murdered innocent people because of the Church's superstitious beliefs—beliefs recorded in your Bible by the way: 'Do not let a witch live.' And what about the others, the non-witches, killed? So I don't see how the Church can be excused even if what you say, that *only* a thousand witches—which I seriously doubt—were murdered, is true."

"Oh, so you have access to a Bible." Samuel winked.

Paul nodded 'yes' uncomfortably.

Samuel continued, "No, of course not. But your original point, if I understood it, was that Christians perpetrated these evil deeds in history—in the age of the Inquisition—so the position of the non-Christian is preferable. That is, the world would have been a better place had Christianity not existed and everyone had been irreligious. But, as you see, the non-Christian courts of the time murdered far more people than the Inquisition's and were much crueler in their interrogations than it was. So if you are contending that the non-Christian position is preferable to the Christian one based on the events of the Inquisition then you are saying that you prefer the situation where people are murdered in much greater numbers and tortured more severely to the one where few are murdered and torture is sparingly used and of less severity. You prefer a situation where people can be executed on the flimsiest of evidence—mere prejudice—to one where an accuser is tasked with proving his case in a court with due process and representation. You prefer a situation where—"

Paul raised a hand. "Enough! Like I said, I would have to check your facts. They don't square with what I understand about the period. How do you know all this anyway?"

Samuel smiled sagely, "Reading, study." He patted the stack of books on the table beside him. "The information is all available if you have the will to search it out."

Paul nodded, "We'll see." He added, in a conciliatory note, "At least we agree that the Church did a lot of evil things."

"Yes, for sure; it is composed of sinful people after all. The Church has apologized many times for the role its adherents have played in the dark periods of history, and rightly so. The irreligious have yet to do so, however."

Paul overlooked the jab. "Can we agree that the Church used its power to silence other points of view? The Inquisition was created to silence people who dissented from its narrow beliefs. If I, an atheist, had lived where the Inquisition was active I would have been burned for sure."

"No. No," Samuel replied, "the Inquisition was created to restrain Christians who professed beliefs which were not in accordance with what the Church believed to be the genuine teachings of Christ—Christian heretics in other words. This is why it executed so few witches—it was concerned about Christian doctrinal heterodoxy, not folk superstition. Its victims were overwhelmingly Christian. The Inquisition did not persecute atheists—it had no jurisdiction to do so because atheism is not a heresy. The Inquisition was not at all like Progressive tribunals which persecute the adherents of *other* religions."

An annoyed grimace flashed momentarily on Paul's face. "I'll never believe the Inquisition just attacked Christians."

Samuel extended his palms in a supplicatory gesture. "Please investigate it yourself."

"Okay, okay. I will research that and get back to you," Paul replied testily. "I have other questions anyway." He rubbed his hands together in anticipation. "What about the supernatural stuff—Jesus rising from the grave, for instance—how can you believe that?"

"Why is that so hard for you to believe?"

"Because such things don't happen. A dead person can't come alive again."

"But you are speaking from within your worldview. Certainly, if there is no God then a person can't rise from the dead. But if there is a God then why should it be surprising? If He could create life then surely He can return life to a body."

"But everyday experience tells us…"

"But we are not talking about *everyday* experience," Samuel countered "We're talking about something quite extraordinary."

Paul crossed his arms. "Okay, if there is a God, why doesn't he just reveal himself, then we could all believe in him?"

"Is that what you think God wants? Is that *all* he wants?" Samuel said, casting a probing gaze at him.

Paul warded it off with, "Well that's what your religion says: if people believe in Him they will go to heaven. If they don't they will be tormented in hell. So it must be pretty important to him that people believe."

"Yes important…" Samuel echoed vacantly. He clasped his hands in front of him. "But what if he wants more from us? What if he wants us not just to believe in him—even the demons do that—but he wants us to choose him?"

"What do you mean?" Paul asked.

"Maybe he wants us to follow him voluntarily—to accept him for what he is, not out of personal desire for gain or out of fear but because we find him just, noble, lovely and attractive in every way? That is, because we love him."

Paul was nonplussed.

"Well what would you do?" Samuel continued engagingly. "If you were God, and you wanted people to come to you of their own volition. What would you do?"

"Well, I'd certainly let them know in no uncertain terms that I existed!" Paul replied curtly.

"Would you? Do you think that would be best?" Samuel persisted.

Paul mustered a sarcastic "Umm, *yes!*"

Samuel thought for a moment. "Okay, let's look at it from a different perspective. Let's say you were a young prince, the ruler of a kingdom, and you had life and death authority over your vassals." He turned to

Paul. "You can imagine how frightened and deferent they would be to-wards you."

"Yeah, I suppose."

"Okay. Now say you were peering out of your castle one day and your eyes alighted on a girl—the most beautiful creature you had ever seen. You were smitten and fell helplessly in love. You wanted to have her for yourself."

"Ha ha, it sounds so antiquated: 'fall in love,' 'have her for yourself.' You really are a relic," Paul laughed.

"A *romantic* relic," Samuel corrected. "So how would you proceed to capture this rare prize of charm and beauty? You could just send your guards down to scoop her up and bring her to you and, well, so on. But being the noble fellow you were you didn't want to force the lady's hand. You didn't want to coerce her. You wanted her to fall in love with you, not because you were the prince, but because you were you. What course of action would you take?"

"I suppose I'd, um, *woo* her like anyone else."

"But remember, you are her all-powerful lord. Wouldn't she feel obliged to, hum, succumb to your advances? The poor thing would be so frightened of refusing you she would submit to anything, affirm all your virtues, even laugh at your weak jokes."

Paul smiled. "Yes, of course. So I wouldn't let her know who I was. I'd dress like a commoner to conceal my identity and try to win her heart with my charm and good looks." He smiled winningly.

"Yes, exactly," Samuel concurred. "Enough light to accept; enough darkness to reject." He sat back and happily sipped his juice.

Paul realized the point he was making. "So you are saying that God hides himself from us because he wants us to choose him freely; that, he does not reveal himself because, by doing so, he couldn't help but oblige us to accept him?"

Samuel nodded. "Something like that."

Paul shook his head. "But that's crazy. How can we choose him if he doesn't reveal himself to us?"

Samuel sat up spryly. "Has he not revealed himself?" He sprang to his feet and swept his arms across the room in a wide arc. "When you look into the night sky; when you ponder the intricate movements of the heavenly bodies, the laws that govern their movements, or the fine engineering of the microscopic world; if you look closely and don't deny the evidence, is it not plain, can you not discern His presence?" He stared at Paul with glowing eyes. "The resplendence of the flowers, the chorale of the birds, the artistry of the bees, the sublime dance of life. Life!—is it not clear?" he asked again and continued. "The orderly succession of the seasons. The vitality of the rain." He glanced briefly at Paul and proceeded to pace. "Consider the superfluous harmony and color, the exorbitant beauty of it all!" He was growing increasingly animated. "Music. Art. Yes, science." He extended his open hands to Paul. "How is it that our minds"—he tapped his temple—"pieces of flesh that they are, comprehend all this?" His voice reverberated with jubilance. "When you look at man—our minds, our emotions, our bodies—can you not see the mind that animates yours, the spirit that speaks to your inner being? Aren't His fingerprints all over our DNA?" he beseeched the younger man. Samuel stilled himself and held up a solitary finger. "But mostly, when you look at this man, Jesus, can't you recognize the author of all that you experience? Can't you sense with your inner light the light that illuminates your life? Doesn't your soul resonate with his? Can you not hear the Father who calls you to himself?" He looked hopefully at Paul.

"Oh brother," Paul groaned, "if that is the best you can do…"

Samuel's countenance fell and he stared sadly at his almost empty glass. "Are you sure you wouldn't like some?" he said raising it. "It's pretty hot out."

Paul sighed. "Um, sure. Thanks." Paul watched him shuffle over to the refrigerator. He took another glass down from the cupboard, filled it then topped up his own and returned to the sitting area.

When he had settled Paul asked, "What about the absolutist nature of Christianity? Doesn't that cause a lot of hatred and civil unrest? I mean, Christians think they have all the answers—Jesus is 'the only way' and all that—but other religions thought theirs was the *only* way too. What about them?"

"Yes. *What about them*?" Samuel replied. "How does their believing something else disprove the truth of Christianity? Surely one has to examine each and weight its merits? Your worldview is not automatically invalidated because Christians disagree with it; why should the Christian one be because you disagree with it? As for Christians 'thinking they have all the answers,' I think that is more true of other worldviews."

"That's ridiculous," Paul countered, "One World welcomes all perspectives, whereas Christianity represses any that don't go along with its narrow unreasoning ideology." He immediately felt uneasy about saying so.

"*All perspectives*?" Samuel echoed. "Which, besides its own, does One World 'welcome'? The Muslim? The Christian?"

"Both of those," Paul replied glibly.

Samuel grinned infuriatingly ironically at him for a moment then pressed on. "Christians acknowledge that they are finite creatures of limited understanding and intellect—here for a short time then gone; mere dust. It's because of this they acknowledge the fallibility of their own reasoning; because of this that they don't set their own perspicacity on a pedestal, not because they consider reasoning worthless. They don't trust in their own judgment but defer to God's. That is why One World hates them—their testimony imposes a limit on its aspirations. It reveals that it is not the final arbiter of Truth. It casts doubt on its utopian promise of salvation." Samuel rested his hands on his knees.

Paul refused to engage him on that assertion but pressed his original point. "But it's arrogant to insist that your own worldview is correct and others wrong. It marginalizes everyone else and leads to violence. You should be more inclusive."

"But, as I said, doesn't everyone do that?" Samuel answered. "Don't you say that your way of thinking is correct and mine wrong? Don't you believe that your worldview, that says that science and human reasoning are the sole paths to knowledge and progress and that divine revelation is a fantasy and belief in God childish, is correct?"

"But that's different," Paul protested. "I don't base my convictions on blind belief. I use my mind and reason out my positions while you just believe because a book tells you so. Anyone can follow my reasoning and make a decision for themselves whether I'm right or not, but with Christianity you have to just accept everything. How can you decide if something is true if it is just based on wishful thinking not facts?" he railed. "Atheists are guided by reason; Christians by emotion."

Samuel sat staring at the carpet for a while. "I have a question," he said finally, in a subdued voice.

Paul sighed. "About what?"

"About your religion," Samuel answered.

"I don't have a religion," Paul snapped.

"Okay, your worldview then; I have a question about your worldview."

"What would you like to know?"

"Where do you think life came from? What is your Genesis story?"

"It's not a *story*, it's science, and I'm sure you already know it," Paul replied in a perturbed voice.

"I just wanted you to tell me," Samuel replied, "I want to understand."

Paul tapped the table with his finger emphatically. "Science has shown us that life started in a primordial pool full of chemicals—ammonia and methane and stuff like that. Then a source of energy, lightning probably, triggered a reaction and the first amino acids, the building blocks of life, were produced. Then, over billions of years, propelled by the Subatomic Teleological Force, these evolved into simple cells, the first life. From there on evolution took over—DNA mutations molded by the STF providing new information, generating increasingly sophisticated organisms—fish, amphibians, reptiles, mammals, man."

"And you have proof of all this—the tepid puddle, the chemicals, the lightning, the Force?"

"That's what science says," Paul bristled.

"So you have investigated all these details and found solid scientific confirmation for them?"

Paul rolled his eyes. "Of course there were lots of experiments that confirmed everything. I can't remember them exactly. I mean, you can't expect me to investigate everything we're taught in school, I'd never get through the year," Paul huffed. "Anyway, something like that had to happen or we wouldn't be here now, right?"

Samuel's bushy eyebrows raised. "Okay. I think I understand where you are coming from." He took a sip of his juice. "So we're just material beings—collections of atoms strung together by a blueprint recorded in our DNA?"

"Yup," Paul replied.

"My thoughts, and yours, are just chemical reactions in our brains. There's no *us* apart from our brains. No spirit, no soul."

"Of course there isn't," Paul scoffed. "We can understand everything about humans, or any animal—how we grow, why we do what we do—just by examining the chemicals and molecules in our bodies. There's no need to bring fantastic supernatural claims into it—*souls* or a *creator god*."

"So, if we could look inside a person's brain and record all the chemicals there and had a computer fast enough, we could actually determine what he was about to think by running a simulation of the chemical reactions," Samuel postulated.

Paul paused a moment to consider this. "Yeah, theoretically. Of course, that's way beyond our technological capabilities now but, yeah, if we could take a snapshot of all the atoms in our brains, and if we had a super computer, we would be able to predict everything."

"We are just biological robots basically."

"Yes, exactly," Paul replied. "We don't need a creator god to assemble us when our DNA dictates everything we are and even what we think, ultimately. We're just 'dancing to our genes,'" he added, remembering an axiom from his biology class.

Samuel thought for a while. "Hmmm. I have another question."

"Go ahead." Paul said confidently. He was feeling much the master of the discussion now.

"Why are you angry at Christians for the Inquisition?"

Paul furrowed his brow. It was a strange question seemingly divorced from the conversation's focus. "Of course, because they tortured and killed so many people!"

Samuel shrugged and replied, "So what?" flippantly.

"What do you mean *so what*? You can't mean you approve of that?" Paul said, his voice ringing with disgust.

"No, I'm appalled at it. I wish it had never happened. But what I don't understand is why you are upset about it."

Paul looked askance at him.

"I mean, you said that you believed people were just basically collections of atoms—'dancing to their genes,' you said. If you believe that, then why do you blame Christians for something they had no control over? If their genes made them burn witches, why get angry with the Christians?"

Paul responded immediately. "You can't get out of it so easily. We have evolved to a state where we can go against our animal instincts. We can make choices whether to follow our base natures or to rise above them."

"Oh really?" Samuel responded flipping his eyebrows again. "I'm confused then. Tell me, if our thoughts are just the result of chemical reactions in our brains, as you say—if all we are is determined by our genes—then how can we rise above them? Indeed, what is this 'we' you are talking about that is beyond our genes' control? What is the *we* that can override the chemical reactions in our brains?"

Paul was left open-mouthed. "We, ah…" He waved his hand dismissively, "I just know that we can choose." He was frustrated at how weak his response sounded and wished he could get away and think up a better one.

Samuel shrugged and stared questioningly at him before pressing on. "Another thing: you said we could rise *above* our baser instincts. What do you mean by 'above'?"

"I meant, instead of acting on our base animal instincts, we could employ our reasoning and play to our higher natures, of course," Paul replied. "Instead of working against each other—like in a survival of the fittest mode—we could cooperate with others to make life better for everyone."

"So you think, for instance, helping your neighbor is better, *higher*, than eating him?" Samuel said.

Paul laughed despite himself.

"You laugh but, seriously, why is charity better than cannibalism?"

"We have just reasoned it out, of course. Everyone agrees on that," Paul replied.

"Oh? You reasoned it out? How did you reason it out? Tell me your line of reasoning."

"Oh." Paul laughed nervously. "Well, you know. It's just common sense."

Samuel tsk'd again. "Okay, so you think that, since everyone thinks charity is better, it must be."

Paul laughed helplessly.

"So basic values, right and wrong, are determined by consensus," Samuel asked.

Paul hesitated for a moment. "Yes, essentially. Our societal values generally come from people, or at least a majority of people, agreeing on something."

"If everyone *reasoned* that cannibalism was okay then cannibalism would be the *higher* virtue and charity reprobated?" Samuel queried.

Paul shook his head. "But we wouldn't do that. We've evolved to a point where we are able to discern things better."

"But how do you know that your discernments are *better*?"

Paul didn't understand the question.

Samuel elaborated. "If your thinking process is merely a, more or less, random series of chemical reactions in your brain, as you say you believe it is, then why do you place any credence on its conclusions? By what authority do you pronounce the chemical reactions in your brain

to be morally superior, *higher*, to the chemical reactions in the canni-
bal's brain? If your thinking is completely and exhaustibly described by
chemical activity, what competent facility do you have to judge the efficacy of your thinking process itself? Why should you put any trust in
your belief that your thinking is reasonable?"

Paul understood Samuel's point but didn't know how to answer.
Samuel's questioning gaze bore into him and he felt the heat rising in
his collar.

Samuel sighed and took another sip of his juice. He sat pensive for a
long while.

"Is that how you experience life?" he said softly, almost to himself.

"Excuse me?"

He raised his emerald eyes to Paul. "When you look inside yourself,
do you really feel that you are just a robot, at the mercy of your genes
and unable to do anything, to choose anything, of your own volition?
Do you really feel that there is no intrinsic moral superiority between
charity and cannibalism but that charity is preferred merely because the
chemical reactions in most people's brains favor it at this point in history? What do you really believe?"

Paul returned Samuel's gaze without answering.

"If you really believe that there are positions that are morally superior to others, as you seem to; if you believe there exists an intrinsic good
and evil; if you believe that our thinking is not merely an illusion, that
reasoning is possible, then why do you cling to a materialistic reductionist position that you have verified as impossible? Why do such violence
to your common sense? What is your motivation?"

Paul could only reply weakly, "I… I don't think it's impossible."

Samuel looked hard at Paul for a moment then shrugged and settled
back into his chair.

They were both silent for a long while. Paul took a sip of the juice. It
was bitter sweet and puckered his lips.

It was Paul who picked up the conversation again. "Hasn't all this
been decided though? Don't you know that Darwin has proven that there
is no God." He corrected himself quickly: "I mean, evolution makes it
unnecessary to believe in God since it explains everything without re-
quiring us to believe in supernatural agents—Ockham's razor. That's
really why I find belief impossible. I mean, I know I don't have all the
answers about how we think and such," he conceded, "but I'm confident
science will provide them in time."

"So, basically, Darwin freed mankind from the delusion that his destiny was determined by a higher power. He freed us to build our own narrative," Samuel said.

Paul brightened and nodded, "Yes, that's it exactly! He was the one who allowed humankind to leave the old medieval mindset behind and move forward, guided by reason and science, to achieve that great technological and societal progress we've experienced. Don't you see?" He was conscious of sounding like his professors at school.

"Really? He is responsible for so much?" Samuel said.

Paul nodded eagerly. "He showed us that there was an explanation for everything in the biological world—a natural one not relying on imagined supernatural agents. This showed the old religious myths were just that, myths. Before Darwin, man was unable to account for the diversity of forms in nature and this led him to believe that there had to be a god to account for such elegant designs. After him, man could see these for what they really were: the consequence of a purely natural process, and so he was free from God, finally."

"So you are saying that before Darwin's theory of evolution there was no believable naturalistic theory that could account for the abundance of species so people thought 'God must have done it,' but after Darwin they had a credible explanation of how life could have disseminated?"

"Yes, that is why Darwin made such an important contribution to progress: he validated the atheist position by establishing a scientific explanation for the natural world without appealing to a creator god. It was a revolutionary insight. Mankind could now apply its intelligence to the solution of real problems and not be held back by superstition. Science took off, and the rest is history."

Samuel thought for a moment. "Do you think there were atheists before Darwin? I mean, scientific, thoughtful men."

"Of course there were. There were probably a lot of them, but they were too scared to speak out and get burned at the stake."

"But you said that there was no credible naturalist explanation for the abundance of life before Darwin. Why were they atheists then?"

Paul shook his head in bewilderment, "I, I'm not following you exactly."

"I mean, you said that atheists, in contrast to Christians, derive their beliefs by careful reasoning. But if there existed scientifically sophisticated men who were atheists before Darwin—that is, before there was a credible explanation for the existence of life superior to the God explanation—then they must have chosen atheism in opposition to their reasoning since, as you say, there was no reasonable naturalistic explanation for the proliferation of life. So then, wasn't their atheistic worldview held in opposition to reasoned reflection?"

Paul was a bit piqued but held his temper at bay. "No, of course not! They didn't need to have it all thought out. It was enough that it was clear to them that Christianity, with its miracles and angels and whatnot, was completely unbelievable. They didn't need to have an airtight rationalization for atheism to know that Christianity was wrong," Paul insisted. "When Darwin discovered that there was a logical naturalistic explanation for life, it became impossible for him to believe in God anymore."

"You think that's what led Darwin to reject the theist God—the weight of scientific evidence?"

"Of course," Paul replied.

"But he found Paley's concept of a clock-like cosmos built by God intellectually compelling and the science of his time was wholly inadequate to pronounce authoritatively on contemporary ideas about the mechanism of biological proliferation or, of course, of origins. Darwin's theory, as laid out in the *Origin of Species*, was not generally accepted by scientists in his lifetime, so one had to make a philosophical decision to embrace a non-theistic worldview—one had to take a leap of faith.

"Why did he take this leap," we might ask.

"Firstly, his environment—the nominal Christianism or outright atheism of his educators, clergy and family—narrowed the chasm between his received beliefs and skepticism. It was a small leap from the one to the other. Also, he had philosophical discordances with orthodox Christianity: as a sensitive man, he was troubled by the problem of evil—why there was so much suffering in the world under a supposedly benevolent god; 'nature red in claw,' you see? He was offended that an all-powerful god would allow so much evil—he had even lost a beloved daughter. He was troubled that his family and most of his friends, as unbelievers, would be left out of God's redeeming plan. In short, he greatly disapproved of the Bible account. All this spurred him on to investigate alternative explanations for the natural order—to take God out of the picture.

"At bottom, then, his rejection of the theistic god was based on philosophy and emotion, not scientific necessity. He found the idea of an absent god more agreeable—"

Paul choked down a violent repost. "Even if there was any truth at all in what you are saying it doesn't change the fact that he found the explanation for the natural order that doesn't rely on God or any other supernatural being." He shook a finger at Samuel. "Your hatred of Darwin reveals the typical Christian character by the way. You reject science. Christianity has always resisted science's advance."

Samuel's face registered consternation. "*Hate* Darwin?" he echoed quietly. "*Hate*? Because I disagree…?"

After a pause Samuel spoke. "I think you will agree that modern science was born in the West. Why do you think science flourished there, dominated as it was by the Christian worldview, and not elsewhere; the Far East for instance? Don't you think it strange that it would grow so in an environment that was, according to your analysis, fervently hostile to it?"

Paul rolled his eyes. "It grew *in spite* of Christianity."

Samuel pointed at a spot beyond Paul's head and proceeded as if tabulating the stars. "Kepler and Copernicus, Galileo, Pasteur, Pascal and Descartes, Boyle, Newton, Maxwell, Mendel, Faraday, Bacon, Harvey, Leibnitz, Lavoisier, Kelvin, Planck, Millikan, Fleming, Collins…"

"What's your point?" Paul interjected impatiently.

Samuel leveled his gaze on him. "What do all these men have in common?"

"Yes, yes, of course, they were all supposedly Christian," Paul said wearily, "but at that time everyone was a Christian; you had to be. Who knows how many of those would have been Christians if they had been free to choose—none I'd say. Just look at the scientists of today, there is no Church to lord it over them and, see, they are all atheists," he retorted. "Those *Christians* you are talking about were probably not believers at all, they just acted like they were so they could do their science without being hounded by the Church." He shook a finger at Samuel. "And you have a nerve to mention Galileo, a man persecuted by the Church that you are insinuating *supported* the growth of science." He was immediately embarrassed that he had lost his temper. The old man seemed to know which buttons to push to get his blood up.

Samuel looked aside. "Well, I agree somewhat with you there: most people, scientists not excluded, tend to adopt the worldview of the surrounding culture without serious reflection."

Paul exploded, "I didn't say that! That may be true of primitive or uneducated people, but modern people, especially scientists, don't just accept things. We question everything, weigh the evidence and follow our own reasoning. That's what differentiates us from Christians."

Samuel didn't seem to hear. "Let's look at Newton, a great scientist, yes?"

"Of course. Agreed," Paul demurred.

"But he wrote more about religion than he did science," Samuel said. "He even learned Hebrew and Greek so he could study the Bible in its original language." He looked askance at Paul. "Why did he do all that? If he just wanted to assure everyone of his allegiance to Christianity he could have accomplished that by just attending church on Sunday."

"I don't believe that," Paul replied, "about him writing more about religion."

"Again, you just have to read the history books to confirm it all," Samuel urged. "Mendel was an abbot. Copernicus a churchman, possibly a priest. Maxwell the Evangelical—"

Paul interrupted him. "Anyway, even if it is true, that they were genuine believers, it was probably just because they were raised in that environment. They would have been brainwashed throughout their childhood years to believe."

"So you think that Newton would have been an atheist had he been born today?" Samuel asked.

"Yes, of course. That's what I said."

"So you say you believe that Newton, a man of science, chose his worldview based on what he was taught by others rather than his own reasoning? It seems you have come to agree with my original observation, that the vast majority of people—scientists and other intellectuals included—simply adopt the prevailing beliefs of their age without serious reflection. All men, even educated men, are heavily influenced in their thinking by the culture they find themselves in and few men, even scientists, bother to question its biases and axioms critically. Atheism is the consequence of the blind acceptance of prevailing convention as much as any other religion."

Paul's mouth opened with a groan and the intention to offer a refutation, but then he decided to take a different tack. "You can't deny that your religion is against knowledge though. It says right in your Bible that God was enraged when Adam and Eve ate from the tree of knowledge."

A pained look appeared on Samuel's face. "I'm afraid you haven't examined that passage at all, young man." He waved his hand as if to swat away a bothersome insect.

Paul's eyebrows contracted sternly—he didn't like to be patronized.

"The tree wasn't the *tree of knowledge*, it was the tree of the knowledge of good and evil,'" Samuel informed him, "and God exhorts us to seek understanding and knowledge. Jesus says 'Love God with all your soul and with all your MIND.' Of course you need knowledge of what He is, and an understanding of what He has created in order to truly love Him. That's what motivated these Christian scientists—to know God by examining and understanding His creation. That's what drove Western science, this hunger for knowledge of God."

Samuel returned to Paul's original charge. "The significance of the tree of the knowledge of good and evil was that Adam and Eve were taking to themselves the prerogative to determine good and evil. In other words, they were usurping God's position as arbiter of Truth and morality. They were adopting the position of the One Worlder, deifying their own perspicacity."

"But why should God's morals prevail?" Paul objected.

"Why not? Who else's should prevail? Yours? Mine? One World's? If God is the creator of the world then doesn't he know how it works? Doesn't he know what is good and what evil?"

"Yeah, and God's perfect will is revealed in the Bible, right?" Paul sneered. "How can you accept the authority of the Bible when there are so many obviously wrong-headed things written in it?"

Samuel raised his eyebrows. "Like what, for instance?"

Paul thought for a moment. "Well, like animal rights for instance. The Bible says humans are better than animals and this means you don't have to take their well-being into account. You don't need to be concerned about environmental destruction for instance; that's why Christians were against protecting the environment. One World rejects this speciesism and seeks to preserve animal habitation through conservation. It respects other species and doesn't push a human agenda at them," Paul declared, remembering this from his Environmental Studies classes.

"So you deplore humans forcing their values upon other species?" Samuel responded. "I was wondering if you consulted other species before pursuing your conservation initiatives?"

"Now you are being silly," Paul moaned.

"No, not at all. Isn't it true that this conviction to conserve originates with, and is unique to, the human species? We invented it. You don't see a lion remonstrating for better grasslands, or a duck canvassing for wider wetlands. A sheep is quite happy to forage until the land is bare.

A monkey always dirties his lair," Samuel said. "You talk about animal rights, but what animal supports the rights of other animals? What lion says, 'Oh, I mustn't eat the gazelle because it has a right to life'? In fact there is only one *animal* capable of bestowing rights on other beings, and that is the human animal." He looked challengingly at Paul. "Aren't conservation and rights human concepts that you are forcing on other animals? Aren't you elevating humans above all other animals by presuming to speak on their behalf? Aren't you guilty of the very *speciesism* you deplore in others?"

"But we are the only animal that can reason," Paul objected. "We have a moral duty to look after the environment for the others."

"So you see Man as a kind of custodian, entrusted with the welfare of the world and its inhabitants? Amen! That's what the Christians believe also."

Paul looked annoyed.

Samuel pressed on. "So One World believes humans to be mere animals with no greater claim to authority than any other species and then it insists also on man's responsibility for their wellbeing: theirs and the Earth's. On the other hand, Christians think humans have a different nature and office than all the other creatures, and so a special obligation to care for the Earth and all the animals in it." Samuel waved an open palm at Paul, "Which worldview would you say is more coherent?"

Paul was shaking his head in denial.

Samuel continued. "It seems your main grievance with Christianity is that it does not rely on reason and scientific exploration solely for its source of knowledge. True?"

"Ha, yeah, hardly at all. I don't think anyone should just accept things because they were written in a book."

"Neither do Christians," Samuel replied.

Paul ignored him. "We don't just accept the authority of some unknown, uneducated ancient person."

Samuel sighed and sat silently for a while. Then he had a thought. "Do you recall the French Revolution?"

Here was another of those sudden turns of topic that Paul was becoming wary of. "Of course—Madame la Guillotine."

"How did you learn about it?" Samuel asked.

"I studied it in school of course," Paul answered. "I suppose you are going to say that it shows that non-religious people motivated by 'science and reason' have murdered lots of people in history too."

Samuel smiled. "How exactly did you study it?"

"What do you mean? We read history, reviewed commentary, watched videos, thought about it ourselves."

"How else did you study it?"

"Well, there were lectures."

"How did your lecturers come to know about it?"

"They studied it too, of course," Paul answered.

"So they got it out of books basically, or from others who got it out of books. But I thought you said you do not accept anything just because it was written in a book. So why do you accept the history of the French Revolution?"

Paul answered readily. "Well, of course, some things we can't investigate directly. In historical studies, for instance, we are dependent on the writings of others because we can't go back in time and look ourselves."

"Okay, so for history you believe what the books tell you," Samuel concluded.

"No!" Paul exclaimed. "We check and make sure the facts stand up. We don't just believe it because some *authority* says it is true. We don't accept anything without verifying the facts."

"I see," Samuel nodded. "So you verified the credentials and character of the authors you read when you studied the French Revolution?"

Paul compressed his lips.

Samuel sighed and took up his glass again. "You have citizen enablers of course."

"Yeah," Paul replied reluctantly. Here was another one of those abrupt changes of subject.

"Who are they?"

"Norm and Jean—just a man and woman."

"Are they your natural parents?" Samuel pressed.

Paul's eyes widened. "Of course they aren't! How could they be? Do you think we're perverts or something?"

"How do you know they aren't your natural parents?" Samuel pressed.

"I was assigned to them by Life Center; they aren't my parents," Paul replied defensively.

"Did you have a DNA sample taken to confirm this?"

Paul rolled his eyes. "No."

"So you just believed them without determining it scientifically?" Samuel asked.

"But I had no reason to doubt it," Paul said.

"So you accepted it on the authority of the Life Center unquestioningly," Samuel replied.

"Like I said, I had no reason to doubt it."

Samuel let out a short "hmm" and slid his glass a few inches on the table as if shifting a piece on the chessboard. "Have you ever been to India?"

"No," Paul said.

"But you believe it exists. Why? What investigation have you done to confirm its existence?"

"I've seen pictures of it on TV," Paul replied without thinking.

"Oh, so you believe it exists because the TV said so," Samuel said ironically. "Tell me, when you took math, did you verify that the sum of the interior angles of a triangle is 180 degrees or did you just accept what was written in your textbook? Have you proven that the Earth is indeed, round? What did you do to satisfy yourself that atoms exist?"

"Really, this is silly," Paul said exasperatedly.

Samuel shrugged. "I was just testing your assertion that you never accept anything on authority but insist on verifying everything yourself," he said mildly. "That you are guided solely by reason, not by convention."

"Okay, okay," Paul said. "Obviously, I meant that I investigate things that go against my experience before I would accept them. I wouldn't accept that a person can rise from the dead, for instance, unless I saw it."

"Oh, I see," Samuel said thoughtfully. "So the vast majority of the things you believe, you have just accepted on authority but you investigate the really important things. Tell me some of these other things—the ones that you thought important enough to prove or disprove yourself instead of relying on the authority of others."

"Well..." Paul started, but he couldn't think of anything off the top of his head. The more he tried to come up with something the more it eluded him. He ended up blushing and angry. "It doesn't matter. One World is based on reasoning and scientific study; Christianity isn't, no matter what you say. You can't prove anything you believe is true, or even that this *God* of yours exists, but I can travel to India and prove it does, if I could get travel clearance..."

Samuel sat staring at the carpet for a long while.

"Have you tried to talk to him?" he asked abruptly.

"What?" Paul replied in a shocked voice.

"You wanted to know if God existed. So have you tried to contact Him? I mean, have you tried praying?"

Paul's ire rose in an instant. "I don't want any part of your god," he spat out disgustedly before he could truly digest the question.

Samuel shrugged mildly. "Then you will have no part of Him," he mumbled to himself.

"Don't push that on me," Paul snapped. "He is exclusive. All the good people—as defined by your god—are saved and everyone else burns in hell for eternity. Who would want anything to do with a god like that?" He could hear Gretchen's voice echoed in his own.

Samuel's body leaned forward. "Exclusive? But he offers everyone, regardless of race, sex, achievement—anything—his friendship and eternal life. How is that *exclusive*? And you are mistaken about the part about the 'good' people. There are no good people, as I said before. No one can gain God's friendship through personal piety. No one can, by his purity, oblige God to provide him a placement in heaven. It doesn't matter what your personal virtues and gifts are, God's standard of purity is so far beyond anything any of us could aspire to that our purest works are, to quote the apostle Paul, like 'filthy rags' in God's eyes. No, it is only through Jesus' sacrifice that we might gain heaven." He looked at Paul pleadingly. "You just have to ask."

"It's all a big guilt trip," Paul insisted, angrily thumping his fist on the table.

"But why should you feel guilty, unless you believe that you have done something wrong?"

"It's not fair."

"I trust that my Father will do what is right."

The two were glaring at each other across the table, bodies tensed for the next pass. Samuel's green eyes were wide as saucers. Paul's nostrils flared and his chin thrust out.

Suddenly Samuel's lips trembled and then he started to laugh. Paul was confused at first and thought that his host might be suffering mental dysfunction.

The older man's round stomach shook with laughter, "The look on your face…"

His laugh was infectious and Paul started to laugh also. "You looked pretty ridiculous too."

They talked for a while longer then Paul noticed the time. He wanted to get home before Norm and Jean arrived back from their trip and, anyway, he wasn't sure when the downtown core curfew began, so he informed Samuel he had to leave.

"I hope we can meet again," Paul said. "I'll be better prepared," he warned with a challenging grin.

"Aha!" Samuel laughed darting his arm in a dueling riposte. "Of course. I'm usually here after six; rap on the door whenever you like."

"When do you go to bed?"

"Oh," Samuel chuckled, "I don't sleep too much."

Paul smiled. "Okay, see you later then." Samuel tapped him on the shoulder affectionately as he passed.

Just before the door closed behind him he heard Samuel's amused voice saying, "Your Ockham was a Franciscan friar you know."

* * *

When Paul got home he threw himself onto his bed and lay there staring at the ceiling. His discussion with Samuel had set his brain abuzz.

He was disappointed he had allowed their conversation to wander so broadly. He needed to nail down Samuel's thinking on science and culture but instead had ended up in a heated confrontation.

It was surprising how emotional this topic, Christianity, could become. No wonder there had been so many wars fought over it.

Their discussion had been an eye-opener though. He had believed that his rational mind could easily see through any argument for the devo worldview he would encounter and that it would be able to repulse any incursion against his own. But the old man turned out to be a more formidable opponent then he could have imagined. It was like playing chess with Morris—he kept seizing ground and constricting your position until there was nowhere to go.

He was troubled by the things Samuel had pointed out about his own understanding of the nature of the world. How could he be a reasoning entity if he was in truth merely a robot driven by chemical reactions in his brain? How could there even be such a thing as thought if nothing existed beyond the material realm? How could there be science? He had to solve these problems for his own peace of mind. He had to show that Samuel was wrong about the Crusades and Inquisition too, that it was Samuel's worldview that relied on myths and disinformation, not his own.

Although it would take a lot of effort, Samuel's challenge provided a great motivation to really nail down the positions of each worldview in depth. He felt he would produce a great paper in the end—maybe secure his spot in Trudeau City.

All in all, he considered himself lucky at having stumbled upon Samuel.

His com was blinking in the dimly-lit room; it was a post from Morris. He scanned over his messages—a few news items, a few friends returning notes, lots of junk mail. His enablers left a message saying they had been delayed and wouldn't be back before noon the following day. He regretted not carrying his mobile.

A smile crossed his lips when he saw there was a note from Mel. He clicked it and her dear face appeared in the frame. He frowned when he heard she would be leaving July thirtieth for two weeks—there was a mandatory conference in Muskoka for her vocational cohort.

The message ended and Paul pushed back from his terminal. At least they would have the rest of August together before school started up again. He thought about what would happen after that; where would he and Mel end up?

His hands played over the keyboard of their own volition, clearing the remaining communications. He was about to delete one but the initials O.W.L—One World Library—in the subject line checked his hand. He heart was racing as he slid his chair up closer as if to shield the note from eavesdroppers, clicked the message open and ran his eyes down the page quickly. Near the bottom were the words *Clearance Granted* and instructions on authenticating to O.W.L. services.

He had been granted access to O.W.L. Seven! He couldn't believe it! A low whistle escaped his lips. *Lichter must know someone high up. I didn't think he would come through… not in a million years!"*

All the fatigue of the day disappeared and he bounced up to the screen again and rapidly worked his way through the authentication procedure. He needed to upgrade his cipher package, go through a final signoff and then he was linked to the internal search engine of O.W.L level seven.

He was excited, like a kid at Worldland. *What to look up first? Ah yes, the Inquisition…*

Morning found him with his head on his desk in front of his terminal, fast asleep.

14

DAY 116

HISTORY

It was surreal; what would his friends say if they knew?

Paul had spent the morning reading the first book of the Bible: Genesis. *How incompliant was that?*

Initially, he intended to read the passage that spoke about the tree of knowledge to see if it disparaged knowledge-seeking or if it counseled on another area entirely, as Samuel had insisted.

The concordance at the back of his Bible directed him to Genesis 2:9: *And out of the ground the Lord God made to spring up every tree that is pleasant to the sight and good for food. The tree of life was in the midst of the garden, and the tree of the knowledge of good and evil.*

Paul groaned when he read the last sentence and slammed the book onto the table: "Damn!" he exclaimed. It was the tree of the knowledge of good and evil, not the tree of knowledge.

"Maybe there's a tree of knowledge somewhere else." There was another reference in Genesis 2:16-17: *And the Lord God commanded the man saying, You may surely eat of every tree of the garden, but of the tree of the knowledge of good and evil you shall not eat, for in the day that you eat of it you shall surely die.* "That 'good and evil' tree again. At least God was forbidding Adam and Eve some *knowledge* upon pain of death, but what knowledge did the tree represent exactly?" *Good and evil.*

He scanned ahead hoping to glean a favorable interpretation from the passage, but even with the surrounding text to enlighten him it was hard to arrive at a definitive understanding. He finally turned back to the beginning of Genesis and started reading from there.

The first chapter was like a fairy tale set on an epic scale with God shaping the cosmos and the creatures of the earth. Paul noted God gave man *dominion over the fish of the sea and over the birds of the heavens and over the livestock and over all the earth…* "This is where Samuel got that idea of man the steward of the Earth." Before their discussion he would have been quick to read into this passage the arrogant Christian assertion of man's right to lord over other species and despoil the Earth. But now he recognized in it not just a declaration of man's headship over nature, but his responsibility too, and he wasn't sure that he disagreed—in all practicality, humans *did* occupy the station of stewards of the Earth.

Then came chapter two, the Garden of Eden scene. This showed God once again giving man the responsibility to tend the Earth. God thought a *helper* was needed for Adam because it was *not good that the man should be alone* so he made Eve out of one of Adam's ribs. Paul found this episode objectionable because it seemed to make Adam superior to Eve—she was created for his benefit. That was pretty incompliant. He made a note to challenge Samuel about that.

Now he came to chapter three. As he started reading it all seemed familiar—in everyday conversation there were often references to being 'tempted by the devil' or to 'taking a bite of the forbidden fruit' but he had never read the original account.

It opened with the serpent—it didn't say the *devil*—tempting Eve into eating the fruit—not *apple*—of the tree from which God had forbidden her and Adam. *Again, that tree of the knowledge of good and evil.* Then verse five: *For God knows that when you eat of it your eyes will be opened, and you will be like God, knowing good and evil.*

Paul sighed a defeated sigh when he read that. It was pretty clear now: God's prohibition was not against seeking knowledge, but against assuming you could decide what was good and what evil—taking on the role of arbiter of morality in other words.

Samuel had been right.

"Damn!"

He closed the book and tossed it on the table again.

It made him angry, recalling that day in his Cultural Evolution class where Mr. Harris had stated that the Christian god forbids his followers access to the tree of knowledge. He remembered this clearly because of the point Mr. Harris was striving to make: that Christianity—*devo-re-ligion* he called it—insisted on blind obedience and discouraged critical inquiry. Faith was what was needed, not the acquisition of knowledge. That was the first time he could remember hearing of the tree, but when he thought about it he was sure there had been other instances at school and on the Net where the 'tree of knowledge' had been summoned to witness against Christianity.

He was annoyed with Harris for not verifying his facts but had to acknowledge with some embarrassment that he had accepted what he had be told without question.

Could Harris have deliberately misled the class? He might have made an honest mistake about the tree, but how was it that WorldNet repeatedly got it wrong too?

These were uncomfortable thoughts, but they went no further.

He combed O.W.L. for passages containing references to 'knowledge' and 'wisdom' but was unable to find a single instance dissuading their pursuit. Instead they extolled their virtues with exasperating consistency.

He had half expected as much.

He took up the Bible again and continued on. The stories were so bizarre at times, the culture so unfamiliar, so incompliant, his head spun. They were surprisingly entertaining though.

Chapter four had the Cain and Abel story—the first murder. The disturbing story of Noah and the ark began in chapter six. The sheer magnitude and elemental impersonality of the flood that extinguished all life was terrifying. *It is disgusting that God would unleash such a thing on the world.*

Chapter eleven contained the famous Tower of Babel story. It was a confounding foreign action; inhibiting progress; absolutely incompliant. *How strange that God confused people's language in order to drive them apart and disrupt their plans while One World strove to unite them in one mission. I wonder if there has ever been such a structure—the Tower of Babel.*

He made a note to research it.

The adventures of Abram, a wandering shepherd and clan leader, followed. Paul was amused that he would 'talk to God' at times, as if God was a person standing right in front of him. Later on God renamed him *Abraham* which meant *father of many* according to the footnotes. Paul laughed because Abram was ninety-nine years old and childless at the time. He must have thought God was off his rocker. It was the first time Paul detected any trace of a sense of humor in that otherwise bleak personality.

The Sodom and Gomorrah episode started in chapter eighteen—another disturbing chapter. *It is revolting how God wiped out whole cities that displeased him; he was ruthless and implacable.* In chapter twenty-two God even asks Abraham to sacrifice his only son Isaac, but cancels just as the knife is about to strike. *The whole episode is repugnant*, he felt, but kept reading, unable to tear himself away.

He read on: how Isaac met his wife Rebekah; about the rivalry between their two sons Esau and Jacob—Paul thought Jacob a scoundrel and sympathized with Esau although God inexplicably favored Jacob—Jacob's self-exile and his marriage to Rachel; Jacob's reconciliation with his brother; the adventures of Jacob and Rachel's son Joseph (another scoundrel) who was sold by his brothers into slavery in Egypt. Many years later his brothers come to Egypt to buy grain because there is a famine in their country and find Joseph in command there! In the end all of Joseph's family, the whole nation, moves to Egypt to escape the famine and Joseph looks after them.

Genesis ended with the death of Jacob.

Paul set the volume aside and reclined in his reading chair with his hands behind his head. It had been like being transported back in time. But did that age ever really exist or was it all make-believe?

He was discovering how hard it was to relate to other cultures, especially those estranged from his own by locale and time. It was difficult to understand the motivations and sensibilities of the ancients. *They don't think like us. They don't seem to be aware of their glaring incompliancies.*

This marked the end of a sobering few days of study.

O.W.L. Seven was a whole new world; there were articles and books that had a devo classification; many of them authored by confessed Christians.

The first thing he investigated was the history of the Inquisition.

He was shocked to discover that Samuel's statistics concerning the number of witches burned were essentially accurate—perhaps even too high as they had steadily declined over the years as more documents were recovered. By the time of the Ascension scholarly consensus placed the death toll at less than forty-five thousand of which the Inquisition's victims numbered in the hundreds only. This was a far cry from the millions Paul had assumed.

After the Ascension these records were withdrawn from the public domain preventing further investigation.

The total number of people executed by the Inquisition during the five hundred years or so of its existence was less than six thousand. To put that in context, the number executed during the few years of the secularist French Revolution was about fifty thousand—Paul looked it up. The atheist regimes of the enlightened twentieth century murdered as many as one hundred million.

In modern times the secularists invoked the historic sins of the Church repeatedly to justify the silencing of its voice, yet they themselves never acknowledged the much greater terrors their own philosophy had wreaked upon humankind.

Samuel's description of the Inquisition's operations and procedures was accurate also. While the people of that time would have thought torture a perfectly reasonable means to obtaining a confession, and it was routinely employed in the secular courts, it was rarely used by the Inquisition. In fact there were many complaints about the leniency of the Inquisition and there existed records of people trying to have their cases moved from the secular courts to the Inquisition in expectation of a more lenient prosecution!

If you were brought before a secular court accused of witchcraft your chance of being executed was often high—Paul saw jurisdictions where the execution rate was ninety percent. But if you were tried by the Inquisition it was negligible, certainly less than one percent. The inquisitors didn't believe in witchcraft so they were reluctant to prosecute it unless the perpetrator compounded their transgressions with blatantly heretic acts—demon worship or some such thing.

All this painted a very surprising picture: rather than the secular authorities and populace being repressed and terrorized by a superstitious and cruel clergy, the documents appeared to indicate a superstitious and barbaric secular culture resistant to the civility and rational skepticism of the Church. The true state of affairs was the exact opposite of what he had been led to believe.

Another thing Paul discovered was that the bloody Spanish Inquisition, by far the most prolific of the inquisitions, likely accounting for more than half the victims, was instated by the secular government of Spain not the Church!

The reason for this was, Spain (that is, the various kingdoms which would become Spain) had just fought a seven hundred year war to free itself from Muslim rule—it had been conquered by them early in the eighth century—and it was feared that the Jews remaining in the land might provide a fifth column for the Muslims who still looked across the Strait of Gibraltar with expansionist ambition. This threat, along with extant prejudices against foreigners, hardened public opinion against the Jews and a program of forced conversion was undertaken to expurgate this alien presence within the Christian nation.

So, although religious in appearance, it was actually a political rather than religious imperative—to meld the Jewish people into the Spanish nation and break their sympathies to rival powers.

Those who converted were called *conversos*. Those who refused to convert to Christianity were expelled from Spain as were their Muslim correspondents.

This did not solve the problem, however. The sincerity of the *conversos'* Christianity and their loyalty to the Spanish crown was, of course, suspect so King Ferdinand II engineered a ploy to deal with them: he pressured the Pope into creating an inquisition under his own authority—he would appoint its members and oversee its operation—to prosecute undesirables as Christian heretics. The Spanish kings prevailed in maintaining their inquisition despite the repeated efforts of the popes to shut it down. Failing in this, the Church tried to introduce a measure to allow the Spanish Inquisition's victims the right to appeal to Rome but King Ferdinand blocked it ruthlessly and so the Inquisition remained a weapon of the monarch.

So the church had acted on behalf of accused heretics to protect them from the secular state! Who would have imagined that?

There was one area where Paul thought Samuel had gotten the history wrong, however. While there was some truth in his charge that most of this narrative concerning the 'diabolical' Inquisition which ultimately determined modern opinion was made popular by French *philosophes* like Voltaire and the anticlerical writers who followed them, Samuel had missed, or perhaps didn't want to acknowledge, the role that Protestant Christians had in creating the mythical Inquisition long before the Progressives arrived on the scene.

Here's how Paul understood it: during the sixteenth century wars with Protestant Netherlands, Germany and Britain, the Protestant propagandists, aided by that revolutionary invention the printing press, poured out pamphlets and books depicting Spain as a land of ignorance and barbarity. As part of this effort the Inquisition was recast from the ethical, humane—compared to other courts of the time—institution it had in fact been, to a bloodthirsty instrument of Catholic repression where tens of thousands of Protestants perished horribly. It was all a fabrication—few Protestants even lived in Spain—but it served the designs of the antagonists. *I wonder if Samuel is Protestant or Catholic.*

The Enlightenment writers had merely taken up the tale, ran with it, and in time it became orthodox Progressive dogma.

It was ironic that a legend—it came to be known as *The Black Legend*—created by Protestants to denigrate their Catholic opponents would be adopted later by Progressive writers to denounce Christianity altogether.

Paul discovered that this misrepresentation of history continued through the modern period up to the Ascension. He stumbled across two editions of a book by a self-identified Wiccan priestess—Paul's mind flashed a picture of Cass—who numbered the witches burned to be one million in the first edition of her *Drawing Down The Moon*. To her credit, with more current material in hand, she revised this number to 'between forty and fifty thousand' in a later edition. Paul was surprised to learn that at least twenty percent of these were men, and was further surprised that many of the women brought up on charges of witchcraft had as their accusers other women because he had been taught that the persecution was driven by a patriarchal society's longing to repress independent women.

Even decades after the tales of the Inquisition and witch burnings had been proven to be legendary, gross misrepresentations continued to appear in popular books and respected media outlets. A 1990 documentary called *The Burning Times* declared the number of witches burned to be nine million. In 2003 a popular work of fiction *The Da Vinci Code* said that "During three hundred years of witch hunts, the Church burned at the stake an astounding *five million* women."

These works were widely believed by, what Paul realized must have been, a gullible and historically illiterate populace. What was more troubling was that their authors—educated people claiming expertise in the field—appeared to believe them also, despite hard historical evidence to the contrary. Paul was reminded of what Samuel had said about scientists and other educated people: that they tended to parrot popular opinion like everyone else.

It was disturbing that One World writers had not amended the record either as far as Paul could see. *Why had they not?*

Time was passing quickly so he moved on to his second topic of interest, the Crusades. His understanding was that they were campaigns of bloody conquest driven by religious intolerance against a peaceful neighboring people whereas Samuel painted them as an ineffective campaign to stem the Muslim tide.

Perusing the available literature, he found that the Muslim armies had indeed begun the war in the 630's CE conquering Syria first then taking Jerusalem in 638, Alexandria in 641, Tripoli in 643 and Cyprus in 649—all Christian municipalities. Christian Spain was attacked in 711 and the Muslim advance in the West was only halted in 732 in Southern France.

But Muslim expansion continued elsewhere. In 1453 Constantinople, the capital of the Eastern Christian lands, finally fell opening up eastern Europe to Muslim invasion. Athens fell in 1456 and by 1529 the Sultan's armies were besieging Vienna.

The first crusade didn't occur until 1099, and they effectively ended in 1291 with the final defeat of the Christians at Acre. So they began more than four hundred years *after* the Muslim invasion and ended hundreds of years before the Muslims were finally stopped.

So Samuel was right: the Crusades were not isolated acts of aggression against an innocent foe, they were a military response to a persistent invader.

This made the further contention he had with Samuel—that the trauma resultant from the Crusader invasion caused the hostility of the Muslims towards the West down through the centuries—academic since, if it was the Muslims who initiated the war, they could hardly blame the Christians for prosecuting it in turn. He continued his investigation, however.

As far as Christian atrocities against the Muslims—an oft repeated justification for the modern Muslim hatred of the West—he found the Muslims more than capable of reciprocation. For instance, often cited was the massacre at Jerusalem in 1099—the Crusaders killed an estimated three thousand. But the Muslim forces had done the same thing in 1077 when they had captured the city! When the Muslims conquered Constantinople they raped and murdered their way through the population for three days, as was their practice, before the Sultan stayed his troops.

Also, he noted that one of the original motivations for undertaking the Crusades was to relieve the Christians in the Holy land from the harassment and sporadic pogroms they were experiencing under Muslim rule.

So, he asked himself, rhetorically, *how could twentieth century Muslims lay the blame for their enmity with the West on Crusader aggression and brutality when the Muslim side had initiated the hostilities and prosecuted them with pitiless savagery? What gross hypocrisy!*

It was ironic to note that the success of the first crusade was dependent largely on the military weakness of the Muslims, who were too busy warring with each other to repulse the Christians. The conqueror of the Crusaders, the Muslim general Saladin, came to prominence only after dispatching his Muslim rivals.

So much for the peace-loving Muslim society.

Another surprising fact was that the Crusaders made little effort to convert the Muslims to Christianity; they certainly didn't impose their religion on their opponents. The Muslims and Christians often lived together peaceably and collaborated in commercial endeavors.

Nor did the Christians go on Crusade in expectation of plunder as Progressive writers were wont to charge; it was very expensive to outfit and supply for a foreign campaign and the likelihood of being killed was high. So they undertook the crusade with the very real prospect of financial ruin and death, not of worldly gain.

All the myths fell one by one as he studied. Clearly, despite his vigilance, false impressions had leaked into his personal worldview.

As in the Inquisition, popular culture misrepresented the Crusaders in service to its own agenda. Sir Walter Scott's portrayal of the Crusaders in *The Talisman* (1825) was typical. The Christians were cast as a boorish and devious lot while the Muslim general Saladin, in modern testimony hero to the Muslim nation, was presented as a refined gentleman, in a style consistent with Scott's cultural ideal.

But, in fact, the historic Saladin was as brutal as his opponents and, far from being a celebrated hero to the Muslims, he was quickly forgotten. It took a Western emperor, nursed on romantic stories of valor and chivalry like Scott's, to raise this obscure general to immortal status in the Muslim mind: Kaiser Wilhelm II's fawning visit to Saladin's crumbling tomb in 1898 exported the Crusader legends to the East. The first Muslim history of the Crusades was published the following year—more than six hundred years *after* the Crusaders had departed from Muslim lands.

So much for the enduring trauma of the Crusades on the Muslim psyche. It was clear that modern Muslims had latched on to the mythical Crusades in order to provide a rationalization for their hatreds. Samuel had been right again.

Paul turned his tired eyes from the screen and rested his chin on his hand.

He had learned so many extraordinary things these last few days. History, people's cultures and the interaction between societies, weren't as simple to evaluate as he had presumed and were not delimited by the stereotypes he had been taught in school and World Pioneers.

He realized that his perceptions of people's motivations and his interpretation of events were colored by his own biases. *My own biases!*

With this new insight he believed his ability to evaluate historical record had matured immensely.

So, even though he had found records of Crusader provocations and credible accounts of the witch hunt where churchmen were prominent, he could look at these with a more balanced and sympathetic perspective, understanding the world these people inhabited. Some of the most notorious witch hunters were recognized as men of the highest intellectual ranking—great scholars—and the learned secular scientists and jurists in the universities aided in the witch persecutions. Witch trials weren't foisted on the public; they demanded them—the prince would be negligent if he didn't expunge the threat to his people. So witch burning wasn't just the province of obscurantist churchmen; it was a concern of the whole of society, from top to bottom. The Church was just one player in the drama.

When the Crusaders engaged in slaughter they were behaving no worse than the non-Christians of the time and, in Paul's mind, a good deal better than the nineteenth and twentieth century irreligious had done when they held the reins of power.

Overall, the Christian religion tended to temper rather than enflame the evil in men's hearts.

A more balanced evaluation was needed than that offered by secular commentators, then. One could excoriate the Christians over the fact that, in the nineteenth century in the West, many professing Christianity could be identified in the party supporting slavery—another topic Paul perused briefly—but one should also admit that, upon examining the ranks of the *opposing* party one found it to be manned almost exclusively by Christians! So this was hardly a state of affairs over which the irreligious could assert their moral superiority—although, of course, they did.

He had to acknowledge that Samuel's depiction of events had been more accurate than his own.

He wondered how the old man had learned so much. *I suppose that you tend to know the facts concerning your own worldview better than outsiders do.* That gave rise to the thought, *But do I know the facts about my worldview?* He realized that, despite his pretentions, he had never seriously entertained the thought of himself possessing a worldview with axiomatic beliefs and other baggage; he had continued to assume his own beliefs to be derived solely from reasoning.

It was at this time, perhaps, that it first began to dawn on him how this strange and beguiling religion, Christianity, could have been a forerunner of One World: it encouraged a position of skepticism towards supernatural claims; it professed the brotherhood of all men as God's children and so the equality of men—an alien philosophy in the cultures it displaced—it was the unifying factor that merged people into what became Christendom; the West.

These all pre-staged One World.

* * *

It was late afternoon. Paul had been cooped up in his room for the last few days so he thought he should take a walk and maybe get a bite to eat. He strolled along Morgentaler thinking about the day's work and his next meeting with Samuel.

He had abandoned the idea of confronting him on the religious wars or Inquisition but felt he could press him on the Church's antipathy towards science and on the accuracy of the Bible.

For the former, he would concentrate on the case of Galileo. He felt he had him there: the Church's persecution of the scientist was well documented: Galileo had been forced to renounce what he knew to be true—that the Earth orbited the sun rather than vice versa. It was a clear case of the Church repressing scientific knowledge in favor of blind adherence to an ancient book's teaching. It also demonstrated that the Bible itself was fallible and therefore obviously not *the word of God*. Double kill.

He had reviewed some of the critiques of the Bible's historical accuracy by skeptical authors and selected one as a template to build his case against Samuel.

So he was inspired as he hopped the subway at Summerhill and popped down to Ecology Square.

The square was covered with white tents—an art show featuring the work of mostly local artists. *Art on the Square* was an annual happening *To Promote the Creative Vision of One World* according to the postings. The city was so much fun in the summer—there was always something going on.

Wandering from booth to booth served to distract his mind from weighty matters.

Suddenly someone tapped him on the back. "Hey! What's up?" The familiar voice was the last one in the world he anticipated hearing. He spun around, mouth agape.

It was Calvin.

"What…where…how are you?" he fumbled.

Calvin was grinning like a Cheshire Cat. "Never better."

Paul broke into an ear-to-ear grin too, and then laughed. "Damn(!), what have you been up to?" He grasped his friend's hand in both of his.

"Hey, don't crush the fingers!" Calvin winced.

Paul became serious and looked hard at his friend. "How are you buddy? Okay?"

"I'm okay," Calvin replied sheepishly. He looked straight into Paul's eyes. "I was just pushing too hard, y'know? I needed a break."

Paul's eyes searched his friend's face anxiously for a moment but then his demeanor relaxed. "So, are you doing any gigs around town?"

Calvin waggled his head. "I'm just getting back into it. Petya has a strategy. How about you?"

"Same old, same old. Oh! I've been hanging out with Melanie. I don't think you've met…"

"Oh. New female? *Melanie*? No, I don't think I have."

It was great to see Calvin back in circulation.

15

SCRIPTURE

Paul was flipping through the newscasts: more fighting in Central Africa and China; a rocket hit the One World plaza in Capricorn—minor damage; a chem went off in North Galton curtaining off Haringey and surrounding areas. There were positive stories, too, of course—a new strain of bio-resistant barley growing in Lithuania; the successful repopulation of a town somewhere in northern Italy; an original copy of *The Origin Of Species* found in Munich and a chapel to house it planned for the Museum of Progress in Manhattan—Paul wondered if he would get the clearance to read it one day—but the war dispatches served to remind one that parts of the world remained inhospitable to civilization. *Thank goodness for the Freedom Forces.*

He brought up Kappa news: more war scenes and long lines of devo prisoners and victorious One World forces—the usual stuff. He wondered what it had been like when the Internet existed—there had been such a variety of news sources to choose from then.

His wrist communicator chimed; it was Beverly. He switched to his desk console. "Hey Bev, what's up? Hey, I was thinking about heading down to The Creighton later—check out the band. Wanna go?"

She swept his suggestion aside with an animated, "You'll never guess what's happened!"

"Jays won a ballgame?"

"No, even more astonishing." she giggled. "Kim has gotten a pregnancy!"

Paul glanced skyward and puzzled, "Kim... Kim... you mean Suzanne's friend? That Kim?"

"Yeah! She found out yesterday. Creepy, eh?"

Paul was nonplussed. "Why did she do that?" he blurted.

"She didn't mean to, silly! FreeDom is not one hundred percent effective, you know!"

Yes, Paul knew that. It still seemed a damned careless thing to do though—to go off and get a pregnancy; just before final semester too. "Um so... how's she doing anyway?" he asked awkwardly. "When is the delivery?"

"She's pretty hysterical I hear," Beverly said in a hushed tone. "Understandable of course. I can't imagine how I'd feel if I got a pregnancy." Paul almost laughed at the look of revulsion that spread across her face. "Anyway she's being looked after. I think she's scheduled at Mother next Thursday. Listen. A bunch of us are getting together at seven at Saturne on Emerald. You know it?"

"Yeah, I've been there."

"Come on down if you can make it."

"Yeah, no problem. Seven, right? I'll be there."

"Later," Beverly nodded.

"Whew! It's going to be a wild one tonight," Paul whistled under his breath.

The machine chimed again. Paul glanced at the screen and his face lit up. "Mel!"

"Hi there," the grinning face beamed back at him.

"I was just thinking about you, Kitten. Can you get away tonight?"

Mel giggled, but then her mouth curled down in a pout. "Oh! I'd love to, but—"

"Awk! Don't tell me—more Compliance classes," Paul groaned.

"Yeah," Melanie said with a shrug, "this should be it for a while though."

"We were all heading down to Emerald later," Paul said plaintively. "Oh! You won't believe what's happened—"

Melanie continued her line of thought. "I'm free tomorrow after Doctrine though. How about you? *Garden In Avalon* is showing at the Fox, remember?"

"Yeah, perfect! We can go to the beach, eat, then pop over there."
Melanie nodded quickly, "Yeah, sounds great."
"Yeah, try out that new bikini."
Melanie smirked and turned her head to eye him coyly. "Bye."
The com closed and Paul returned to his task. He had to meet Samuel in an hour and needed to get his thoughts straight.
A silly grin lingered on his face as he worked.

* * *

"I found this book that rebuts a lot of the truth claims of Christianity, *The God Delusion*. A scientist wrote it," he added significantly. "It was quite popular around 200, before Ascension. I figure you were around then." Paul turned the tablet so Samuel could see. "Have you heard of it?"

Samuel's eyes went wide for a moment and his lips parted as if he were encountering a dead acquaintance. An amused look flitted across his face ever so briefly. Paul felt a hollow thump in the pit of his stomach and for a second his mind panicked as if discovering his notes to be missing before a vital exam.

"Um, yes. I was pretty young then," Samuel replied, settling on his couch. "Could you not find anything more authoritative?"

This response did nothing to quell Paul's edginess. He had looked at other sources of course, but had so enjoyed this author's confident dismissal of the Christian assertions concerning the veracity of the biblical account he couldn't resist putting his case to Samuel. It was a further spur that the author dismantling the claims of Christianity was a scientist—it offered the delicious prospect of exposing the Christian in the illuminating light of scientific reasoning: scientist versus religionist.

He set his doubt aside, took a deep breath and, taking on the patrician air of his scientist mentor, announced, "I wanted to examine a few things written in the Bible." He fixed Samuel with his best interrogator look. "You've said you think the Bible is the word of God. So what if I could show you that it wasn't true? What if I could point out contradictions or factual mistakes in the text—wouldn't that prove your belief in it to be misplaced? Wouldn't that show your religion is wrong?" He crossed his arms and glared challengingly at the old man.

Samuel leaned back in his chair. "What have you found out?" he said mildly.

Paul pulled up the chapter he had been studying and scanned over a paragraph. "First," he announced boldly, "the Old Testament said the Messiah would be born in Bethlehem. Correct?"

Samuel nodded.

"But isn't it true that, when the gospels were written, many years after Jesus' death, no one really knew where he had been born? You see, even John says his followers were surprised he was not born in Bethlehem." He waved the tablet at Samuel who remained impassive.

Paul pressed on. "So, we have to suspect the Gospel writers fabricated his birth story to make it look like Jesus was born in Bethlehem so he would fit the role of Messiah. We can see this because Matthew says Mary and Joseph lived in Bethlehem and moved to Nazareth after Jesus was born but Luke says they were living in Nazareth all along, but Joseph was conveniently summoned to Bethlehem for a census in order that Jesus could be born there." He said this quickly as if to forestall any objections Samuel might make, but the old man made no motion to contest anything. "It's pretty obvious that he was just making all this up to get Jesus' parents to Bethlehem for his birth to fulfill prophecy isn't it? I mean, why would Joseph have to go to Bethlehem for a census because he was 'of the house and lineage of David' when David, if he existed, lived nearly a thousand years before Mary and Joseph?"

Samuel looked impassively at him. "Continue."

At this point Paul had imagined Samuel would launch into a desperate attempt to obfuscate the clear implications of his mentor's reasoning, so he was pleasantly surprised that his opponent remained mute and disarmed. His unease subsided completely. "And if that wasn't enough, isn't it true that Matthew, who was Jewish, writes about Jesus' descent from David and his birth in Bethlehem to impress his Jewish readers while Luke, the Greek, tells about virgin birth and worship by kings— things to impress a Gentile readership? They colored their accounts to impress their audiences," he smiled knowingly. "They were hardly unbiased, objective writers."

Paul paused to invite Samuel's engagement, but the old man remained silent so he continued on. "Isn't it true that there were lots of other Gospels—at least a dozen—around that were left out of the Bible because the writers didn't like what they said?"

Samuel stirred. "Which ones?"

Paul was pleased that Samuel had a last roused himself to attempt some defense. "Well—he scanned the tablet—the Gospels of Thomas,

Peter, Nicodemus, Philip, Bartholomew and Mary Magdalen." His eyes lit up. "Oh yes, and Thomas Jefferson—he was an American president—even mentioned them in a letter he wrote to his nephew to encourage him to read them. So their existence was a well-known fact. The *Gospel of Thomas* even has a bunch of stories about Jesus' early life."

Samuel sighed. "Can I see that?" he said, reaching for the tablet.

Paul reluctantly relinquished the machine and re-seated himself while Samuel studied it.

"Hmmmm. Tsk tsk tsk." He flipped the pages. "I haven't read this in years." He chuckled.

"What's so funny?" Paul asked, perturbed.

"Oh, well," Samuel rested the tablet on his lap, smacked his lips and beamed his bright eyes, at Paul. "I was laughing at the suggestion that your scientist makes about Jefferson encouraging his nephew to study those 'Gospels' he has listed."

Paul didn't understand.

Samuel smiled. "Jefferson died in 1826 CE, but with the exception of the Gospel of Nicodemus, their texts were only recovered after 1885—most not until 1945—which would make them very difficult objects for his nephew's study, yes? Ha ha ha."

Paul grimaced. "Okay, even if that is true, it doesn't change the fact that there existed something like a dozen other gospels that were excluded from the Bible," he said, annoyed at Samuel's attempt to sidetrack the main issue.

Samuel glanced back at the tablet. "Do you know anything about them, these *Gospels* your scientist lists?"

Paul shook his head 'no,' reluctantly.

"Okay. *The Gospel of Peter* is a late 2nd century writing and *The Gospel of Nicodemus* was written in the mid 4th century! *The Gospel of Philip* is a Gnostic text dated late 2nd century as I recall. We have no *Gospel of Bartholomew,* and the 'Gospel of Mary Magdalen'—or *The Gospel of Mary* but we won't split hairs here—consists of a very fragmented 2nd century Gnostic text—we are missing most of it. All these were written at least a hundred years after Jesus' death and could not have been written by those whose names adorn them—no one has ever claimed they were, not even your skeptic scientist," Samuel winked at Paul. "They all wildly contradict the writings of the first century Christians who knew Jesus or knew his disciples and they are presented from a worldview antagonistic to the Jewish one from which the Christian gospels sprang; their thought would have been commonplace in the Greco-Roman world that birthed them but quite foreign to Jesus and his disciples." He looked pointedly at Paul. "When the Roman persecution of the Christians came, none of the members of the sects who originated these gospels died in the Coliseum; they weren't considered Christian, either by the Romans or by themselves."

He continued, "*The Gospel of Thomas*—which doesn't have any of those stories that your scientist says it does by the way: it contains one hundred fourteen wisdom sayings and parables apparently spoken by Christ, not a narrative—is the earliest on your list, likely written in the early second century. Much of it agrees with, in fact replicates, the sayings of Christ from the canonical scriptures and the rest is accepted as Gnostic addition."

He looked to Paul. "Why should the Christians accept writings as authoritative authored by those who had no contact with Jesus, or with anyone who knew him, and which contradicted the teachings of those who did know Jesus or his disciples personally and disavowed the religious milieu within which he presented his teachings? Why accept as authoritative texts that were not even considered by the people of their time worthy of preservation? Why accept writings that, according to your scientist"—Samuel read from the tablet—"'were even more embarrassingly implausible' than the canonical gospels?"

Paul looked on, unable to formulate a reply.

"And they *were* embarrassingly implausible; you should read them," Samuel chuckled.

"In fact, there weren't merely 'at least a dozen' of these fanciful gospels as your scientist claims, there were scores of them. There was a whole industry of bogus 'Gospels' and 'Testimonies' and 'Treatises'. The Christians of course rejected these spurious inventions. You don't think it was reasonable for them to do this?"

Paul stared back, jaws clenched tightly.

"It wasn't just these unorthodox *gospels* that were rejected either. So meticulous were the Christians in confirming the validity of their scripture they even rejected the works that *agreed* with the orthodox narrative if their authenticity were in doubt."

None of the authors Paul read had mentioned this.

Samuel sighed. "These gospels were one of the devices used by anti-Christian bigots of your scientist's time to steer the uninformed away from investigating Christianity themselves. None of these Progressive authors seriously believed these writings to be authoritative—none thought the demiurge created the world, that there existed seventy-two heavens, Aeons and Archons, etcetera. They weren't *believers* of these alternative gospels they were proselytizing for," Samuel explained. "They were writing as anti-Christians, not as Gnostics—their sole intent being the subversion of Christianity. To that end they offered other writings, writings they knew to be spurious, to obfuscate the authoritative standing of the genuine gospels. Your scientist fell for their pitch naively."

He motioned to Paul. "I suppose he also told you that there are tens of thousands of mistakes in the scriptural writings, and that the texts were passed down orally person to person, generation to generation, the text being degraded with each conversation, like a children's 'telephone game'. Or maybe he referred to 'Chinese Whispers.'"

Paul looked away.

Samuel sighed. "Let's go back to the beginning of your scientist's attack." He read from the tablet again. He says that 'when the gospels were written, many years after Jesus' death, nobody knew where he was born.'"

Paul nodded.

"But if no one knew where Jesus was born, why was that a 'problem' for the gospel writers? Why didn't they just say he was born in Bethlehem and everyone would have been happy—prophecy would have been fulfilled?" Samuel looked askance at Paul. "Why would Luke make up the census story to get Joseph and Mary to Bethlehem if he could have just said they were from Bethlehem in the first place?"

Paul looked wide-eyed at him. "I'll have to read that part again," he stuttered.

"Isn't it more likely that some *did* know where Jesus was born, or thought they did, so Luke had to clarify things?" Samuel asked.

Paul thought for a moment. "Yes. I think so," he said, "and some people knew he was really from Nazareth, so Luke had to make up the census story."

"But why believe that he *made up* the story? Why not just accept his testimony?" Samuel asked.

"Well, because of the contradiction with Matthew. Obviously some of Luke's readership knew the truth—that Jesus was born in Nazareth—so he had to fudge things to make it agree with the Old Testament."

"But why *couldn't* they have been living in Nazareth and gone to Bethlehem for Jesus' birth?"

"Because Matthew says Jesus' parents lived in Bethlehem all along," Paul said exasperatedly.

"Matthew says Mary and Joseph lived in Bethlehem *all along*?"

"Of course."

"Read that part to me from your Bible," Samuel said.

Paul hesitated for a moment then reached into the secret compartment in his bag and drew out the contraband blue volume carefully. Samuel's eyes twinkled as they followed it on its path.

Paul flipped quickly to *Matthew* to find the relevant passage. The first mention of Mary and Joseph's location occurred in chapter two. "The first thing it says is that Jesus was born in Bethlehem," he said to Samuel.

"But Luke also says that," Samuel replied. "Where were they before that?"

"It doesn't say that they came from anywhere, it starts with Jesus' birth," Paul replied slowly, his eyes lowered to the page.

"So how does Matthew's placing Jesus' birth in Bethlehem contradict Luke's assertion that they travelled to Bethlehem for Jesus' birth?"

Paul lowered the book. "Okay, by itself it doesn't contradict Luke. But isn't it plain that the census is a fabrication—just an excuse to get Jesus to Bethlehem? Luke must have been hiding something or he would not have invented such a ridiculous story."

"Why ridiculous?" Samuel asked.

"Well, who ever heard of travelling to a city to pay your taxes just because your ancestor lived there a thousand years previously?" Paul scoffed.

"Well, people in the Roman world must have."

Paul looked doubtful.

Samuel clapped his hands lightly. "Listen," he said leaning forward, "Luke was writing to people who lived in the Roman Empire. They knew how the Roman taxation procedures worked—they would have been through a census themselves many times. Why would Luke invent a story he knew would be recognized as a fabrication by his readers immediately?"

This point hadn't occurred to Paul. Yes, it did seem unlikely that Luke would venture details that could be so readily contradicted by his listeners.

"About the point your scientist makes about the apostles tailoring their accounts to their audience: with your experience in reading history, do you find it peculiar that an author would write from a particular perspective and with a particular audience in mind—that he would render his account so as to be understandable to his potential readers and detail those items he believes most relevant to them?"

Paul set the tablet aside. "No, I guess not…"

"Of course, there can be no unblemished objectivity—no one can write from a completely detached perspective. What is surprising is that your scientist thinks it a novel occurrence—that a writer is colored by his environment and attentive to his audience's expectations. Is he so unfamiliar with historical writings that this is a revelation to him?"

"He was trying to make the point that they were not reliable historians. Matthew may have fabricated the details of Jesus' descent from David and birth in Bethlehem to impress his Jewish audience while Luke went on about the virgin birth and worship by kings to sell his account to the gentiles. Isn't that plausible?"

Samuel chuckled.

Paul smiled despite himself. "What?"

Samuel laughed. "Well, first of all, Matthew also mentions the virgin birth and Luke Jesus' descent from David. So it is a mystery, if both mention the same details, how your scientist can assert they were fabricating events in order to appeal to their disparate audiences." Samuel guffawed and slapped his knees playfully, "But what's really funny is that it was Matthew, the Jew, who mentions the worshipping kings, not Luke, the gentile. Ha ha. So your scientist didn't even get that right."

Paul startled. He took up his Bible again and rifled back to *Matthew. It's true: Matthew had written the account of the Magi visiting the baby Jesus, not Luke!* He took up the tablet and read. The author believed that "Matthew's desire to fulfill messianic prophesies (descent from David, birth in Bethlehem) for the benefit of Jewish readers came into headlong collision with Luke's desire to adapt Christianity for the Gentiles, and hence to press the familiar hot buttons of pagan Hellenistic religions (virgin birth, worship by kings, etc.). The resulting contradictions are glaring, but consistently overlooked by the faithful."

Paul blushed for the author. *He had gotten it all wrong and then compounded his error by following it with a stupidly arrogant jab about the carelessness of the 'faithful' in examining their sacred texts!*

"I'm sorry," Samuel said, drying his eyes with his handkerchief. He sighed audibly. "You know what I found most surprising about this book when I read it those many years ago?"

Paul tossed the tablet aside, no longer eager to pursue the line of investigation he had prepared. "What?"

"I wasn't so much astonished by the ignorance of the author concerning even the basic elements of the Christian faith"—he flashed a mischievous side glance at Paul—" although I'd have to say his callowness exceeded all my expectations.

"I also wasn't overly astounded by his lack of understanding of history—he was a biologist after all, not a historian, and you must understand, by his time one wasn't expected to be conversant in the humanities to be considered an intellectual, one could just be competent in one's own narrow field—to be a PHD in something."

Paul smirked despite himself.

"One might expect an intelligent person to make at least a cursory study of their chosen topic before holding out on it authoritatively but this"—he pointed to the tablet—"was common fare for the popular anti-Christian writings of his age; the author was simply parroting the myths and recapitulating the biases of the tribe to which he belonged knowing that his Progressive audience would accept such tripe unquestioningly."

"So that's what surprised you the most about the book—the superficiality of the arguments?" Paul surmised.

"No!" Samuel laughed. "What really amazed me was his incompetence as a logician—his inability to formulate a coherent argument. I thought at least he would have achieved some proficiency there considering his profession and reputation. But in chapter after chapter he revealed himself mystified by the elements of sound argumentation. While his book is worthless as a resource in its intended field, I think you could employ it profitably as a sourcebook for the study of logical fallacy. It's a catalogue of special pleadings, rushes to judgment, appeals to motive, chronological snobberies, false dichotomies, ad hominem attacks, circular reasoning... one long non sequitur in other words."

"But it was so popular," Paul mumbled half to himself.

Samuel stared knowingly, sadly. "Yes."

"So many people, scientists, recommended it ... glowingly—look at the testimonies." Paul turned the tablet to Samuel again.

"And you believe what is written there because of the esteemed profession or fame of the reviewers?"

Paul shrugged. Again, he remembered their first meeting when he, Paul, had insisted on not blindly trusting authority.

Samuel shrugged resignedly. "Such was the reputation of Science at that time—as today—that the common man assumed the scientist competent to hold forth authoritatively on subjects for which he, in fact, had no academic qualification or acumen."

He sighed. "As I recall, near the beginning the author challenges the reader to go through his book and see, upon completing it, if they still believe a reasonable person could believe in God." He turned to Paul. "Well, I pass the same challenge on to you. You've read some of the Bible and begun an exploration of the relevant literature. Now finish reading his 'rebuttal,'"—he pointed to the tablet—" this state of the art argument against Christianity by the famous atheist apologist lionized by the doyens of progressivism; this giant of progressive thought. Read *The God Delusion* in its entirety and tell me how you think this champion does in proving the case against Christianity."

* * *

By the time Paul arrived at Saturne the place was packed. He spotted Beverly in a group of eight or nine others from the window before he entered. He knew them all from school.

A lanky guy in a Leafs jersey slapped him on the shoulder. "Hey Paul, what's happening?"

"Hi Roger." Paul cuffed him back. "Morris here?"

"He's in the washroom I think. He's just back from Foucault."

"Yeah, he gets around," Paul replied absently. Beverly was engaged in conversation but acknowledged him with a wave and smile. He slipped into one of the stalls.

He was late arriving because he had been reading *The God Delusion* and lost track of time. The jaunt to Saturne was welcome because he needed to take a break and clear his mind.

His eyes roamed across the room taking in the panorama of the yammering, gesticulating youth but he didn't feel the desire to join in the trivialities of social interaction in his present mood.

There were paintings on the walls executed by local artists; the restaurants along Emerald were obliged to host them. The one on the wall beside him was a somber canvas depicting a desolate landscape. Paul thought its earthen palette and empty horizon quite effective in portraying a hopeless and profound loneliness. One World depictions were often of this genre, it seemed. It was an image to ponder but Paul's attention was captured by another canvas in the corner, lit by a candle. It was a cross with a Jesus hanging upside-down.

He hadn't noticed Christian imagery in public spaces before; at least, if he had they hadn't registered strongly in his mind. This particular image seemed to insinuate a profound truth. Paul squinted mentally to decode its message, but in the end he sensed the true depth of its dissemination to be mere and pointless vandalism; the temper tantrum of a superficial mind with nothing substantive to relate. If this harsh verdict was uncharacteristic of Paul, perhaps this afternoon's studies had exhausted his charity.

"So what's up with you?" Beverly startled him.

"Oh hi. I was just thinking… How's things with you?"

Beverly sat opposite. "Oh same old, y'know. I've made some great progress with my paper."

"Oh, figures you would; always the keener," Paul jibed. "It's One World cinema you were writing on wasn't it?"

"Yeah. Well actually, the role of the second generation in cinema."

"Oh yeah, right." Paul tried to catch the conversation of three girls close by who were talking about Kim.

"You were doing some religious thing."

"Oh. Yeah. A comparison of pre-Ascension culture with modern culture—specifically, the pre-Ascension worldview versus One World."

Beverly's eyebrows shot up. "Now there's an interesting topic; a bit arcane, but interesting. What are you discovering, anyway?"

Paul shrugged and tossed his arms impotently. "I really don't know…"

Beverly rotated the salt shaker slowly to catch the candlelight in its crystal facets. "Not getting on too well with it?"

Paul drummed his fingers on the table. "No. Well, I'm getting on okay I guess… I just don't know where it's going really."

Beverly stopped rotating the shaker. "Where it's going? Well, hopefully it's going towards a completed paper and a placement in Trudeau!"

"No, that's not what I meant." He placed his elbows on the table and rested his chin on his hands. "I just… well, I've dug up a lot of material. It's not like I'm stumped for ideas or anything."

"So what's the problem?"

"No problem," Paul muttered. He was wary of saying anything incompliant to Beverly. He slid the salt shaker over. "I just hope the Committee will approve of where it's going."

Beverly grinned nervously. "What do you mean?"

Paul tapped the shaker on the table a few times and left it there. "Well. I figured I would just distill the two worldviews down to their basic tenants." He glanced at Beverly. "You know, right down to base axioms: what makes them tick." He looked down and began to fidget with the shaker again. "Then I'd provide an analysis contrasting the, um, Christian with One World, to give a concrete demonstration of cultural evolution."

"Sounds great. So?"

Paul studied the crystal facets. "I don't know. I need more time to digest everything."

Beverly shook her head, nonplussed. "Well as long as you get *digested* before Induction; you want to be ready for Trudeau."

Paul nodded tentatively. "Yeah. I'm sure I will."

Beverly's wandering eyes caught sight of someone across the room. "Oh, excuse me a bit, I see Rachel over there; I have to get my HaloCaster back. See you later." She skipped off.

No sooner had he taken up his drink then someone else plopped down in the chair Beverly had vacated. "Hi."

It was Harmony grinning from ear to ear beguilingly. She raised her sunglasses so they rested on the luxurious hair on the crown of her head.

"Wha… oh, I didn't…" Paul started. The sunglass thing at night was a new fad.

Harmony laughed. "No, it's normally not my crowd. Jim Hooper brought me along. You know him?"

Paul nodded, "Yeah. Well not too well." Her low-cut shirt exposed her breasts invitingly and he could see a pendant wedged between them at the end of a leather cord. It appeared to be a zodiac medallion.

"Well, he was coming down and brought me too. Then I saw you over here," she smiled. "So what's up? I haven't heard from you since…" She giggled. "…since Anne's place."

Paul grinned back. "Oh yeah, well, I've been really busy…"

"Been to the gym lately?"

"Just a few times last week; not as much as I would like to. I've been working on my exit paper; that's taking up a lot of my time." He was tempted to mention Melanie but didn't.

"Yeah, I remember. You're graduating this year. So you are writing about us Christians?" she asked archly.

Paul chuckled nervously. "Yeah."

She rubbed the rim of her glass with her finger studying the contents. "If you need any help on that," she said without looking at him.

Paul fumbled for words. "Oh thanks, great. It's okay though, I found someone who knows quite a bit about it."

Harmony looked up. "Oh who? Gretchen?"

Paul blinked. "Yeah, I interviewed Gretchen. I found someone else too though."

Harmony looked at him suspiciously. "Who?"

Paul hunkered down over the bar list. "Oh, someone I met coming out of your church, after seeing Gretchen. *Hey, they have Henley Stout on tap.*"

"One of the other congregants?"

"No, just a man, an old man, who has been a Christian for a long time and studied a lot about it. He's into history and science and stuff too." Paul was feeling restless and wanted to return home to his studies.

Harmony looked concerned. "I don't know who... what does he look like?"

Paul looked up sheepishly. "A little like Santa Claus."

Harmony's eyes lit up. "Oh I think I know who you mean." Her mouth soured. "I've seen him a few times, I think, on Ecology."

"He lives along there."

Harmony looked at him carefully. "So what's he saying?"

"Oh, we're just talking about history—like where the Bible came from, y'know?" He glanced at his watch. "Oboy, ten twenty. I was supposed to be home at ten thirty," he said, rising. "An out-of-town friend is coming over. I'm supposed to meet him."

Harmony clasped her hands on her lap. "Oh."

"Yeah. Hey, message me when you are heading out to the gym sometime," he said throwing his coat over his shoulders and heading out.

"Yeah sure," Harmony looked after him. "Well, I should get back to the others then..."

16

SCIENCE

"**B**ut why frame the case in those terms 'a confrontation between Science and Religion'?" Samuel asked. "Both ramparts were manned by Christians: those who urged the censure of Galileo were Christian and those who defended Galileo were Christian; those who suppressed Galileo's book and those who published it. He was denounced by some Christians and he was sponsored by others. The principle antagonists, pope and scientist, were both Christian and," he darted a glance at Paul, "both were scientifically astute. So calling the quarrel between the church and Galileo a confrontation between religion and science is like, I don't know… like calling a game between the Yankees and Red Sox a confrontation between New Frankfurt and baseball."

Paul laughed. "Okay. But weren't the church leaders promoting dogma over science; wasn't the Church anti-science in that sense? Didn't the Galileo case prove this?"

"If the Church was *anti-science*, as you say, then I don't understand why you are so upset that it would silence Galileo who, as a member of the Church, must have been *anti-science* himself by your reckoning. How is the repression of an ignorant anti-science bigot—a Christian in other words—like Galileo to be interpreted as an attack on science?"

Paul's lips curled wryly. "You know what I mean; the Church tried to shut down scientific progress."

"The Catholic Church's official position on the question of Ptolemaic versus Copernican astronomy was in accordance with the scientific consensus. If it was anti-science then the vast majority of scientists of that time were also anti-science," Samuel countered. "Why limit your indictment to the Church then? Why not brand the scientific community *anti-science* for all times and in all places, on the same particulars?"

"Okay, okay. Some scientists, maybe even most, may have disagreed with Galileo—that's natural in science—but it was the Church that insisted he be silenced, not them," Paul asserted. "That's the point: they didn't try to stop open discussion, the Church did. It has a long history of persecuting scientists."

"What other scientist besides Galileo has the church persecuted?" Samuel asked unexpectedly.

Paul's mouth opened and hung ajar for a moment. "Even if I can't think of any off the top of my head the Church's treatment of Galileo still reveals an enmity towards scientific enquiry. Didn't they ban his books because they contradicted the Bible?" he urged. "Weren't they afraid of science because it exposed the mistakes in their scriptures?"

"Which mistakes do you mean?" Samuel inquired.

"Well, where the Bible says the Sun orbits the Earth for instance," Paul replied promptly.

"Where does it say in the Bible that the Sun orbits the Earth?"

Paul waved his arms in exasperation. "I don't know where, but everyone knows it does. I mean, that's why the Church persecuted Galileo wasn't it? He was saying that the Earth orbited the Sun and that contradicted their Bibles."

"Galileo didn't believe he was contradicting the Bible, he thought he was contradicting Aristotle," Samuel answered, "and that's what the scientists in the universities thought too, and why they denounced him and goaded the Church to take action against him."

Paul shook his head emphatically. "Why would they do that? What does Aristotle have to do with science anyway? He was a philosopher."

Samuel sighed audibly. "In order to comprehend the Galileo affair you must understand the societal environment of that time, the mindset of scientists; what they believed science was."

"I don't know what you mean; I know what science is," Paul insisted.

Samuel's eyebrows shot up. "Oh? What is that?"

"It's when we use observation and reason to find out how the universe works," Paul replied.

"So you would say it's the search for how things really are—*reality*," Samuel offered.

Paul nodded. "Yeah you could say that. Science is concerned with what can be proven."

Samuel shook his head and cast around the room as if seeking allies. Suddenly a delighted grin transformed his face, he winked playfully at Paul and disappeared through the door between the sitting room and kitchen. Paul heard another door slam then the rattle and scrape of something being dragged across the wooden floor. The door burst open.

"Help me with this," he huffed.

Paul rushed over and took a corner of the contraption. In was a small legless pool table, surprisingly heavy as the base had compartments for pocketed balls. Samuel swept some books off the coffee table and they deposited the artifact on top.

"It looks like a kid's game of pool," Paul laughed. "Where did you get it?"

"Oh, I found it," Samuel replied unconvincingly. He produced a yardstick from somewhere beneath and reached up to the top of a bookcase to retrieve a second. These he carefully taped together along one edge and then wrapped the tape completely around one end making a long v-shaped channel. He was smiling as he retrieved a ball bearing from his desk drawer—obviously enjoying the whole exercise. He rested one end of the yardstick assemblage on the edge of the pool table forming an incline.

"Okay, watch please... a little experiment." He set the metal ball at the top of the trough formed by the yardsticks and gingerly released it. It accelerated down the incline and impacted the cushion at the bottom with a thud.

"Ha, ha, it works! Okay let's try again." He placed the ball back at the top and released it. It rolled down and impacted the cushion as before. "Again," he said, "but now..." He placed the ball half way down the incline, smiled quickly at Paul, then released it. It traveled down the yardstick striking the cushion with noticeably less force than before. "Aha! Science!" he whooped.

Paul laughed too. "Okay, I think you are testing how long the ball takes to get down the incline; but why? What's the point?"

"Ah, the point." He raised a finger again. "You were talking about Galileo. This is an experiment Galileo did. He was studying the motion of falling bodies, in particular how they accelerated."

"Ah yeah. Right."

"And do you know what his conclusion was?" Samuel asked.

"That the Earth went around the Sun?" Paul replied deadpan.

Samuel grimaced.

"Okay, what did he find out?"

"No, no, no. You mean 'what bit of *reality* did he uncover'? We are seeking absolute facts—truth—through science, remember?" Samuel continued. "First: what did he observe?"

Paul shrugged. "He observed that the ball sped up as it hurled down the incline obviously; the higher up the incline it is released, the greater its momentum at the bottom."

Samuel rolled his eyes. "Yes, yes, but be more specific—*science* remember?"

Paul squinted and thought for a moment. "Well I can't quite remember. Mr. Zeno—he was my physics teacher—talked about something like this…"

"Wonderful!" Samuel exclaimed mockingly but with good humor. He held up the officiating forefinger and proclaimed, "what Galileo was trying to discover was the rate at which a falling object accelerates; but how to measure that? You see the problem?"

Paul stared blankly.

"Yes, how to measure that?" Samuel repeated. "If you dropped a ball—as legend says Galileo did—from the tower of Pisa, how could you mark off how far it had traveled in each unit of time so you could calculate its rate of acceleration? I mean, it is over so fast."

Paul saw that—it would not be possible to accurately determine how far the ball had fallen each split second.

"So what do you do?" Samuel asked. He didn't wait to see if Paul had a suggestion. "Obviously, you need to slow down the speed of the falling ball."

Paul nodded. Yes, that seemed reasonable, however difficult to accomplish.

"But how do you slow it down without distorting the characteristics of its fall? I mean, you could drop a ball in water but obviously it wouldn't fall the same way it does in air: a ball dropped through, say, one hundred meters of water would strike the bottom with the same velocity as one dropped from twenty meters. Not so one dropped in air, correct?" Samuel looked for the affirming nod from Paul. "So how can you slow the falling ball without altering the natural progression of its descent?"

Paul supposed the answer to involve the yardstick experiment.

"So," Samuel announced proudly, as if he had been the originator of the solution, "what Galileo did was to roll the ball down an incline, as we are doing here. The ball takes much longer to descend a certain distance if it is rolled down an incline, rather than dropped straight down, so it is easier to time its progress."

Paul interrupted at this point. "But he wanted to determine the rate of acceleration of falling objects, not those rolling down an incline."

Samuel smiled and nodded eagerly, "Yes! But he had deduced an interesting fact beforehand, which is this:"—the punctuating finger shot up again—"the speed of the ball at the bottom of the incline is the same as the speed of a ball dropped straight down from the same height! So the characteristic of the fall is not altered with the interposition of the incline; it is just strung out over a longer period."

Samuel was becoming increasingly animated. Paul had expected to find passion for religion and for science in completely opposite personalities, but here they coexisted.

"That doesn't seem possible."

Samuel chuckled. "Oh, but it is true. Galileo deduced that fact from other experiments."

"How did he do that?" Paul pressed.

"Ah. Yes, I am encouraged that you don't accept this assertion on my authority," Samuel grinned, "but I don't want to digress from our quest here, so I will direct you to the relevant literature on that point. For now, I ask you to accept that it is true."

Paul nodded reluctantly. He was curious to peruse the pertinent *literature* however.

"Okay. Let's move on quickly. What Galileo did was to roll a metal ball down an incline and time its descent with a water clock he had so cleverly devised for accurate measurement. He rolled it the full length of the incline; then half the length; then three-quarters, etcetera, timing each descent." He looked to Paul who was following the discussion closely. "You can see that by doing this he could interpolate how far the ball would have travelled for each unit of time had he rolled it down the whole incline or indeed, dropped it from the tower of Pisa. For instance, if it took three seconds to roll down the whole length of the incline and two seconds to roll down one half the incline, then he could calculate that the ball rolling down the whole length took two seconds to roll the first half but only one second to roll down the second half, etcetera. So we have a methodology with which to locate the ball's position at any point in time."

Paul nodded.

"So he calculated that, for the first unit of time—at the start of the incline—the ball would travel, say, one unit of distance, yes?" He flipped his eyebrows at Paul. "For the second: three units. The third: five. And so on—the odd numbers in other words." He turned to Paul. "So that was the finding of his scientific investigation. What truth can we extract from it? How have we been enlightened as to the nature of the universe?"

Paul furrowed his brow then said hesitantly, "Well, we should be able to express the ball's motion mathematically so we can predict how far it would travel given a time. We could come up with a law governing falling bodies."

"Yes, yes," Samuel nodded rapidly. "You are thinking just like Galileo. So how far did the ball go after one unit of time?"

"One unit of distance," Paul answered.

"And after two?"

"Another three. So four altogether," Paul answered.

"And after three?"

"Ummm, well, that would be four plus five. So nine," Paul responded.

Samuel nodded and wagged his finger. "So, to review: Galileo found that, for successive equal periods of time, the distance the ball had traveled from the beginning was one, four, nine, sixteen, twenty-five—"

"Thirty-six," Paul interjected.

"Yes, exactly!" Samuel folded his arms in front of him with another curt nod. "This is what Galileo observed. So what truth have we discovered?"

"I remember it now. We've learned that the distance a falling body will cover is proportional to the square of the time it has been falling." Paul answered. "Now we can apply this formula to predict where the ball will be, given the time it has been falling."

"Yes, his Law of Falling Bodies," Samuel nodded, "but what truth have we discovered underlying it all? Remember, we were discussing the struggle between religion and science—the truths of science intruding on the dogmas of religion. So, what scientific truths can we deduce from our experiment—what victims for religion's savagery?"

Paul laughed. "I don't know what you mean. *That's* the truth: that the ball's distance will be equal to the square of the time. Through scientific investigation we have discovered a law of gravity basically."

"But why do you say 'discovered'? Why not *formulated*?" Samuel interrupted.

"Well, *formulated* would imply that scientists make up the laws; but scientists don't *invent* the laws of the universe, they just discover them. Gravity would work the same way whether scientists had discovered this law or not."

"So the laws are there and scientists just find them?"

Paul nodded.

"And these laws reveal reality?"

"Yeah," Paul nodded again.

Samuel waggled his head. "Prior to Copernicus science had discovered that the Sun orbited the Earth. It was irresistibly logical and experimentation proved it: scientists could use their mathematical models to predict the position of each heavenly body with impressive accuracy. That the Sun orbited the Earth was scientific *fact*." He terminated the word with a crisp 't.'

"After Copernicus it was scientifically proven that the Earth orbited the Sun, as we have seen." He looked to Paul. "Since you assert that scientists discover laws that reveal truth you must believe that, prior to Copernicus, the Sun orbited the Earth but after the Earth orbited the Sun."

"Of course I don't believe that!" Paul laughed.

"So, the laws these scientists *discovered* which explained their observations of the motion of the planets, did they reveal Truth?"

Paul stared blankly.

"Before Newton a moving object would maintain its motion only if acted upon by a constant force. After Newton the same body would maintain its motion indefinitely if not acted upon by another force. Then came Einstein and Newton's laws were over-turned—light no longer had a fixed speed, time passage was no longer uniform, etcetera." He looked at Paul. "So, did the nature of the universe change between Aristotle and Newton, and between Newton and Einstein?"

Paul uttered a quiet, 'No.'

"Say I owned a nice house with a bay window in front," Samuel continued. "Every weekday I look out at precisely eight o'clock and Mr. Smith from up the street passes by. At eight fifteen he passes going the other way. I observe this phenomenon day after day, week after week. Sometimes the weather is bad and Mr. Smith is late. I know on these days to expect him at 08:05. So I can predict the location of Mr. Smith's body within these narrow timeframes with some accuracy. Have I then discovered a law, the Law Governing the Position of Mr. Smith's Body?"

Paul laughed.

"You might not think so, but I say, 'Yes, certainly.' And what is the nature of my *law*? Isn't it merely a tool I've invented from my observations, useful if I have the need to intercept Mr. Smith? This is the utility of science—it is Galileo's science. Laws are labels scientists hang on their observations; they don't disclose the true nature of the universe; they elaborate observed effects rather than their causes."

The point Samuel was making, had been making all along, suddenly burst on Paul's mind like an apple off Newton's pate: Laws weren't things scientists gleaned from the universe, they were invented by scientists to summarize their observations, and those observations are constrained by human and technological limitations. *Laws are not discovered, they are created.*

Samuel watched Paul's face closely and saw this realization register there.

"But the scientists of Galileo's time did not proceed by observing phenomena and deriving laws from their observations. They did things the other way round: they reasoned about causes and assumed their observations conformed." He smiled at Paul. "It is as if we tried to discern the reason for the motion of Mr. Smith's body—maybe there's a newspaper box on the next corner and its drop off time is 7:50—and then assume the location of his body based on this understanding of the nature of Mr. Smith vis-à-vis his orderly habits and reading requirements. This would be thinking like Aristotle. You see?"

Paul nodded weakly, "Yeah…I suppose. It still seems a strange way of doing things though. Why not just observe whether they were correct and form laws based on that?"

Samuel smiled. "To a modern mind focused on technological progress and the Utopian Enterprise this way of proceeding seems obvious. But to a scientist of Galileo's day, searching for Truth, the reverse seemed obvious: you had to discover the cause of the phenomenon in order to understand the observations. They were more interested in discovering the basic essence of the universe—why it did what it did—than in forecasting effects. What we call modern science—the science of observation and measurement—was considered low brow by the scientists of Galileo's time because only natural philosophy—their science—dealt in actualities. Accordingly, mathematicians—*measurers*—like Galileo, were less esteemed than natural philosophers because their art focused on the mundane rather than the absolute." He looked to Paul. "It was an understandable bias: science had descended from philosophy as philosophy had once issued from religion. It was only after this new science had proven its mettle in producing these useful technologies that it came to be respected in the scientific community. But that was still in the future."

Paul's head was nodding slowly, indicating he was following the discussion.

"So science was rooted in Aristotelian philosophy. If you wanted to be a scientist and understand why the physical world functioned as it did you studied Aristotle. Aristotelian thought formed the basis for scientific study for hundreds of years.

"We might say, before Galileo, science had been a search for causes, but Galileo made it a search for laws—for the *what* not the *why*. For if absolute Truth is always beyond man's certainty—which is what Galileo believed—why not look for that which is useful instead? Why not credit one's laws as adequate gauges of reality for the purpose of achieving technological benefit? My yardsticks here are not thirty-six inches exactly—only in the abstract are they so—but they are nevertheless useful in carpentry This was a revolutionary idea that seemed likely to turn scientific orthodoxy on its head and, like all revolutions, it provoked the enmity of those whose worldview and livelihood were anchored in the threatened paradigm. The scientists tried to silence him by argument and, failing to best him there, attempted to get him dismissed from the university." Samuel tapped his finger on the table. "It wasn't his anti-Christianism that provoked the reaction against Galileo, it was his anti-Aristotelianism."

Paul had listened patiently to Samuel's exposition but was compelled to speak now. "So where does the Church come in? I mean, it did persecute him, that isn't a myth, right? If it was just a quarrel between scientists about scientific methodology, why did it silence him?"

Samuel smiled graciously. "As with our discussion about the Inquisition and the Crusades, the true story of Galileo is much more nuanced than the Progressive narrative of religion versus science would concede. There were other factors—the religious upheaval of the Reformation and resultant political turmoil in particular, and the personalities of pope and scientist." He nodded to Paul. "Galileo himself believed his impeachment to be the result of a misunderstanding between himself and his friend Pope Urban VIII."

"Really," Paul mouthed skeptically.

"So, to answer your question, 'Why did the Church persecute him?' we need to go back and examine the events leading up to his trial." Samuel paused to compose his thoughts; Paul could see he was getting ready to launch into another historical narrative.

"Copernicus came before Galileo. In, I believe, 1543 CE he published his opus *On the Revolutions of the Heavenly Spheres* laying out the hypothesis of the sun-centered galaxy. He had delayed publishing for many years, fearful of ridicule from his peers—his hypothesis not only flew in the face of accepted scientific knowledge but common sense also—but the pope urged him to do so."

Paul furrowed his brow.

"His book circulated for almost one hundred years but failed to convince scientists. Then came Galileo.

"At that time storm clouds were gathering. There was continued unrest over the Protestant states which had split from the Catholic unity.

"It was into this environment, in 1610, that Galileo released his *The Starry Messenger* documenting his discoveries that the moon was not perfect but had craters and that Jupiter had moons itself—things that contradicted Aristotelian cosmology and lent impulse to speculation that perhaps the Earth was similar to Jupiter: a rotating planet with an orbiting satellite."

Paul cut in. "It also must have enraged the Church authorities because this implied that the Earth was just another planet and not at all special."

"Why would that trouble them?" Samuel queried.

"Well, they were always saying humans were so important to God that everything revolved around them. It must have pissed them off to have humanity knocked off its pedestal."

"Quite the opposite I think," Samuel replied. "Common people of that age believed that God's realm existed above the Earth in the heavens beyond. The further from the Earth you were, the closer to God's perfection. Hell was actually the center of the universe; down there," he said pointing to the floor. "Placing Earth out in the heavens with the other planets would have actually *elevated* man's position in their eyes. No, the idea that the Church was perturbed at Galileo for ousting humanity from its privileged position is a modern myth."

He pressed on: "Galileo's hypotheses were challenged and some opponents produced scripture passages like"—he rolled his eyes to the ceiling—"*He set the Earth on its foundations so that it should never be moved* to augment their philosophical and scientific arguments and tried to enlist church officials against him. Galileo's response to this tactic was to say that, although he knew the Bible to be inerrant, people's interpretations of it were not necessarily so. He believed the Church shouldn't champion either side in a contest of scientific opinion since scientific opinion was always changing. If you had asked him which hypothesis—Copernican or Ptolemaic—the Bible supported he would have undoubtedly answered 'Whichever is the correct one.' He thought this should be the position taken by the pope.

"But, in offering these opinions he left himself open to the charge—which was made by his opponents—that he was assuming the prerogative of the pope, even the authority to pronounce on the true meaning of scriptural passages—something that was discouraged in the Catholic church to which he belonged." He looked to Paul. "As you might know, one of the points of contention between the Catholics and the Protestants was just this: without putting a fine point on it, the Protestants believed everyone had the right to form their own opinion of scripture passages while the Catholics believed it was the function of the church hierarchy to do so—that it was something that needed to be trusted to those authorized and learned in the field, not laymen, even if they were scientists." Samuel chuckled, "After reading *The God Delusion* you can perhaps sympathize with this viewpoint."

Paul smirked.

Samuel continued. "Galileo's perceived foray into theology brought scrutiny from the Catholic Church and in 1616 he was summoned and reprimanded. It was his friend Cardinal Bellarmine who delivered the decision from the Inquisition: he was forbidden to present the Copernican hypothesis as proven fact." Samuel explained to Paul, "You see, they thought he should continue his scientific investigations but let the Church judge whether sufficient evidence existed to warrant the assumption of a heliocentric planetary system which would not only require obliterating the foundations of contemporary science but also the altering of church thinking which was informed by that science." He nodded to Paul. "Everything was intertwined because the Church had not followed Galileo's recommendation concerning its refereeing contentious scientific debate—to instead remain above the fray.

"Anyway, Galileo swore to comply with this stipulation and so was free to go his way."

Samuel leaned forward and took a sip of water before continuing.

"Years later his friend Cardinal Barberini was elevated to pope. By this time the storm clouds had broken; Europe was embroiled in the Thirty Years War and things were not going well for the Catholics.

"Galileo approached his friend, now Pope Urban VIII, with a proposal to publish a book detailing the case for the Aristotelian, that is Ptolemaic, system versus the Copernican. The pope, being an ardent follower of scientific progress, agreed enthusiastically. He favored the Aristotelian system himself but thought the discussion could be advanced profitably if someone of Galileo's expertise and eminence were to lay out both cases in print.

"And so Galileo published his *A Dialogue on the Two Chief World Systems*. As the title suggests, it was in the form of a dialogue between a proponent of the Ptolemaic system and one of the Copernican. Also, there was a third character whose job was to supply a neutral perspective." Samuel turned to Paul. "This was a common *oeuvre* in those days—to present an exposition of contending viewpoints in the form of a discussion between their spokesmen. It was an ideal vehicle for Galileo as it enabled the author to appear as the disinterested presenter of the views of others rather than as an apologist for his own.

"But"—he held up his finger—"as the book progresses, Galileo piles up the evidence, argument upon argument, fact after fact, all on the side of the Copernican system confounding the bumbling Aristotelian—who Galileo has aptly named Simplicio—and even swaying the neutral participant. It seemed obvious that the author's intent was to present the Copernican system as irrefutable fact, something that Galileo had sworn not to do back in 1616 at his first run-in with church authority. To compound his indiscretion irretrievably, at the end of the book he placed a pro-Ptolemaic argument, which the pope had made to him, in the mouth of the battered Aristotelian and then proceeded to have his hero mock it in the most humiliating way."

"Ouch," Paul muttered.

Samuel shrugged. "An unfortunate decision rendered disastrous by another occurrence." He smiled grimly at Paul. "You see, someone—one of Galileo's opponents—found a document from Galileo's earlier encounter with the church authorities that stated he had agreed to refrain from instructing on Copernican astronomy. He presented this to the pope and you can imagine how everything must have looked to him." Paul looked impassive so Samuel explained. "The pope must have believed that Galileo had expropriated his consent to write his book knowing that he had already been prohibited any such undertaking. In short, that Galileo had played him for a fool, then openly taunted him in his book."

"Oh" escaped Paul's lips.

"Anyway, an angry pope ordered Galileo to Rome to answer for repudiating his earlier vow."

Paul sniffed and nodded.

"But the trial didn't go as planned. Galileo produced a document from his first trial which indicated he had *not* been restricted from teaching about Copernicanism, contrary to what the pope had been led to believe. This affidavit was signed by Cardinal Bellarmine himself. The prosecutor's document from those proceedings which stated Galileo was indeed forbidden to do so was not even notarized and so was trumped by Galileo's. In view of this, Galileo was offered a kind of plea bargain: he could admit that, in his enthusiasm, he had gone too far in his advocacy of the Copernican system and then he would be let off with a mild rebuke." Samuel winked at Paul. "It was a face-saving ploy. Galileo, embarrassed that he had offended the pope and that he could be suspected of any kind of anti-Catholic agitation, agreed readily and the case seemed settled."

Samuel took another sip of water. "Now the story takes a fateful turn. The pope, believing Galileo to be thumbing his nose at him, and facing pressure from his political allies to show firmness in the face of any questioning of Catholic authority—they were still at war remember—ordered that Galileo be charged with suspicion of heresy based on the obvious fact that he did hold, what was still considered to be, un-substantiated doctrine—namely that the Earth moved—to be fact." Samuel explained, "He wasn't charged with heresy, but suspicion of heresy, which was not as serious; Urban wanted to make an example of him and discourage others from taking papal authority lightly. It was a comedy of misunderstandings really: poor Galileo had not intended to give any offence or question the pope's eminence. He thought he really had not been prohibited in his first trial from putting forth the Copernican system.

"In the end Galileo was sentenced to house arrest, prohibited from publishing, and enjoined to recite the seven penitential psalms each week. Despite this, he did in fact produce other writings, including his most important book *Discourses and Mathematical Demonstrations Relating to Two New Sciences*, which was published while the pope's guards looked the other way. He lived comfortably on his church stipend and died at home aged seventy-seven."

Samuel sighed and reclined in his chair and the room fell silent but for the muffled sound of traffic outside.

After a long while Paul spoke. "Why didn't the pope support Galileo with all the evidence he offered in his book?"

"The pope was likely familiar with most of the arguments in Galileo's book beforehand—he was a scientifically literate man as I said—but they weren't conclusive. For instance, in his book one of Galileo's prime evidences for his belief in the Copernican system was his theory concerning the ebb and flow of the tides. He believed the tides provided clear evidence of the Earth's rotation: the waters slushed after the rotation of the Earth like water in a rotating bucket. He had such confidence in this that he had originally titled his book *On The Tides*. Of course he was wrong—it is the moon that affects the tides. So from a purely scientific viewpoint, given the available evidence, the pope was justified in his rejection of the system Galileo championed.

"You understand that the pope had to be sure Galileo was correct if he was to launch an undertaking to revise the orthodox understanding of the scripture passages that had been taken to mean the Earth stood still. Science cannot allow the overturning of its established precepts easily and neither can the church. Both are conservative in their approach—neither jump at any unproven hypothesis and declare it *gospel* as it were. Both resist unorthodox encroachment. Your scientist friend, the author of *The God Delusion*, might loudly condemn the church for its repression of Galileo, but he himself often insisted on the silencing of dissenters from orthodox scientific consensus in his own time." He grinned at Paul. "In a way the Galileo affair has been repeated again and again, down through the centuries; scientists of the established order enforcing orthodoxy."

"Yeah, I get it," Paul said, "but isn't it also true that Galileo was overturning Christianity itself? Wasn't the progress of the Copernican hypothesis another example of religious dogma being forced to retreat in the face of scientific discovery?"

Samuel chuckled, "No. You are assuming what you are trying to prove—that the hero in this case perceived a rift between knowledge gained through scientific investigation and that gained through reflection on scripture. But neither Galileo nor the pope believed this. They believed there was one reality, one truth, undergirding the universe but

212

many ways to approach it. Modern secularist scientists believe there is only one—scientific observation—but no scientist at that time believed that. To them science was one method for furthering their knowledge of reality, revelation another, but the two could not contradict each other. They couldn't because there was only one reality to be understood."

He turned to Paul. "You see, the pope and Galileo both believed the interpretation of scripture must not contradict what had been discovered through science, but they disagreed on what science was telling them at the time. The pope upheld the established scientific understanding that Galileo was endeavoring to overturn. It wasn't religion versus science but established science versus new science.

"And as we've seen, to scientists it was even more than that. Galileo wasn't just overturning an outmoded scientific hypothesis, he was altering the very essence of scientific enquiry. He was putting the quest for practical knowledge ahead of the search for elusive Truth, which Galileo thought could not be discovered solely through science anyway. His opponents accused him of elevating observation over reason. It was a radical change and, understandably, it provoked a backlash from scientists—their discipline was being degraded and their worldview invalidated.

"So, if anything, it was scientific dogma receding in the face of scientific discovery."

Paul had been listening intently with the semi-glazed look in his eyes of one peering deeper into the mystery of things than ever before. "So if the Church had accepted Galileo's advice and not taken sides in the scientific dispute, the historical record would have been quite different and the perception of the Church being anti-science would not have risen," he reflected.

Samuel smiled wryly. "Do you think so? Given the historical distortions required to transform the pious thoughtful Galileo into an anti-Christian martyr to philosophical materialism and his scientist antagonists into obscurant religious authoritarians, do you think historical fact to be a sufficient barrier to the dissemination of popular anti-Christian apologia?"

The question was of course, rhetorical.

There was one more thing Paul felt he needed to say. "There's still the emotional force of the Galileo story." He raised his eyes to Samuel. "I just have this vision of Galileo, an old man, being bullied and silenced by the Inquisition. After he was forced to recant, when he was being led away, he muttered under his breath 'But, it does move.'"

Samuel chuckled, "Only in the movies."

The room was quiet for a while.

Samuel broke the silence. "Who do you think is right?"

Paul looked questioningly at him.

"Who do you think is right?" Samuel repeated. "Is reality grasped though scientific observation solely, as your scientist would insist, or are we in fact abandoning the search for reality by limiting our field so? Must the search for Truth employ other methods in addition to science? Who is right, Galileo or the modern scientistic?"

Paul smiled warily but deemed not to answer.

Samuel smirked. "Possibly the ancients understood the essence of science better than modern scientists."

Paul smiled in return. "Maybe Galileo understood the essence of theology better than the pope."

"Ha! Yes maybe."

With this the company fell silent again. They were both all talked-out.

Later, Paul reflected on everything. The ancients were interesting. They were thinking people, just like One Worlders; maybe even better informed.

It was funny—about Galileo. The Church was branded 'anti-science' for repressing his book but, if anything, it had reacted the way it did because it held science in such high esteem.

He remembered a quote offered at the beginning of one of the chapters of *The God Delusion*. It went something like 'The religion of one age is the entertainment of the next.' But, unlike science, religion—Christianity—had not changed its precepts in two thousand years.

How much more true that quotation would be, he wondered, *if the word 'science' were substituted for 'religion.'*

17

DEATH

The call came in to the police line at 09:00 that sunny Tuesday morning. Two squad cars arrived at the World Conservatory of Music at 09:20. The detectives arrived soon after.

On the third floor, in a little studio, they found the body hanging; the rope around its neck secured to the exposed water pipe overhead.

"Looks like he jumped off the piano," the detective commented dryly. "Melodramatic. Anyone know who he was?"

One of the policemen answered, "The music teacher who found him said he was a performer who used her studio sometimes when she was away."

The other detective had walked over to the body and was peering up at the dead face. "It's Calvin Wong," he said.

"Calvin who?"

"Calvin Wong. I've seen him play," the other answered. "My female drags me out to these things." He scrutinized the pinched eyes and clenched determined jaw. "He was one of the up-and-comers from what I gathered…a future star." He paused a moment. "But I think I heard he had dropped out for a while—stopped playing for some reason."

"Humph. Well I guess he decided to drop out permanently," the first muttered scornfully. He had seen it all before—too often. "What's with kids nowadays? They're looked-after from cradle to grave, handed a career on a silver platter, and then this. Ungrateful, incompliant…"

The other shrugged.

* * *

Scores of red lights pulsed in the gray-yellow cloud that enveloped the Museum of Human Rights in Astral City. Paul switched the monitor off, lay down and stared at the shadows on the ceiling.

It was never openly discussed—you overheard someone whispering about it or noticed the vacant seat of a classmate or a public personality would suddenly be gone. Word of it spread through the grapevine. No one was terribly shocked—it was quite common. Paul thought everyone must have an inkling that something was wrong. *This shouldn't be happening.*

They are probably churning out another Calvin down at Mother now. He was angry at the whole damn system. *Why didn't they just leave him alone.*

Death. How could one fathom it? The molecules that composed Calvin's body were still there. What had been lost? Why was he sad? Somewhere in its deep recesses his mind was replaying a discussion with Samuel. *Atoms; was there nothing else? Anything to mourn?*

* * *

Later that afternoon Paul met Melanie at the Layton Center. They ate quietly with little conversation then walked in the park hand in hand amongst the flowers. Paul's enablers were gone for the weekend and Melanie's were in Kevorkia until Sunday afternoon so they went over to his house and settled into the couch in the bay window as the light was fading.

"Cass says our souls are gathered into the Great *One*." Melanie formed an 'O' with her hands. Her unfocused eyes rested on the hanging plants above the window.

Paul looked straight at her for a long moment. "But what do *you* think happens to us after we die?"

Melanie rested her hands on her pelvis. "I don't know," she sighed. "We won't know until it happens. I guess we return to wherever we were before we were born."

She turned her head and looked at him with those cloudless blue eyes. "Do you ever wonder who your parents were?" she asked, "I mean your biological ones."

The abruptness of the question disarmed Paul. His heart thumped hard once. "Do you?"

Melanie compressed her lips, dimpling her cheeks, and her soft eyes drifted off mistily into the distance again. They suddenly refocused on him and she tilted her head in that cocker-spaniel way of hers. "Doesn't everyone?"

Paul smiled faintly. "I don't know. I guess lots of people wonder who their progenitors were."

"Do you?" she asked again.

Paul shrugged. "I don't know. There's not any point to it is there?" He looked away. "We'll never know anyway."

He felt Melanie looking intently at him for a moment. Then she sighed and settled back on the couch with a cushion under her head, looking at the plants.

They sat alone with their thoughts for a while.

Suddenly Paul's body stiffened and he jumped up. That impish grin she loved spread across his face as he skipped over to the com. He selected some music and dimmed the lights while Melanie's eyes followed him with amused curiosity.

He nipped back to the couch and offered his hand. "Dance?"

"She giggled, then looked at him carefully. "Okay." He cavalierly brought her to her feet and their bodies pressed together as the initial strains of the violin wafted from the speakers. And then they were swaying slowly in the dusky room while the melody wisped them on a vaguely nostalgic haze back to another starlit honeysuckle evening.

"What is it," Melanie asked in a hushed voice, "the music?"

"*Ashokan Farewell*," he replied.

"It's beautiful," she sighed.

"You're beautiful," he whispered.

18

DAY 104

ESCALATION

"There's a real danger of the revolution failing." Every eye round the triple oval drew to the speaker.

"Oh yes," she said, her head turning, her eyes scanning each cohort, "we can still lose; we can still be pulled back into the grim morass of the pre-Ascension. Of individualism. Of economic competition and uncertainty. Of national posturing." She stopped and looked directly at the senior officers in the first tier. "Of the clamoring democracy of the masses."

Her eyes began to scan again. "The forces of reaction are determined. Even though they appear weak they have commitment and endurance. That's the important thing: spirit, not numbers or guns." The overhead lighting rendered her facial features distinctly feline.

"An established civilization does not succumb to military force; it has to be undermined—hollowed out spiritually—before it can be overthrown. The decay works from within through lax discipline, relaxed vigilance, the toleration of injurious views—negligence of duty. Incompliance." The word lingered like a plague.

"Doubt arises in the face of adversity. Needful actions are no longer attempted. The will to defend core values are gone. In the end all that is needed is a bold thrust to accomplish its demise." She nodded to the company. "We all know that. It's clear that the enduring society has to be pure. Cancer must be eradicated."

She swept her hand over the assemblage. "Look around you; look around." Croydon shifted his eyes along the triple tier of faces, all glowing white, drawn, mask-like in the illumination.

"I put it to you that we have not been worthy of the trust placed in us. We have not discharged our duties with the commensurate gravity or utilized fully, ruthlessly, the resources at our disposal." Her voice sharpened and her black eyes burned with the ferocity of the fanatic. "We have compromised our Truth."

She put her hands on her hips. "What must we have? A more disciplined society—everyone—without reservation or compromise—efficient and committed. We have to deny the devos any foothold, deprive them of soil in which to sow their poison." She shook her fist. "No compromise, no quarter—our desire can only be for total war."

She drew up to attention. "Let's dedicate ourselves anew. Remove all obstructions. Purify our motivations. Purify our struggle."

Croydon cringed—to be lectured by this sanctimonious princess like school children. His eyes panned the faces nearby. Some were staring dispassionately; some had eyes closed and might have been sleeping; many, especially the younger ones, were held in rapt attention, that idiot ardor burning in their eyes. Pitiful.

"So I urge you to acclaim the protocol to Zone. Repeal *GraceNost*. I *demand* it for the sake of the people."

Croydon could barely restrain himself from guffawing at this final flourish of idealistic pabulum. *Does she think that stringing up naïve citizens—'enemies of the World'—will stop food getting to the devos?*

For the past decade One World had nurtured compliance through holistic education and compassionate intervention and, when necessary, careful excision. Through this strategy the battle for hearts and minds was being won—for the vast majority *devo* was the most heinous label imaginable. Behavioral compliancy was improving year after year by any measure. Sure the devos were getting more daring in their attacks, but it was a recklessness born of desperation; he was confident of that.

This patient molding wasn't enough for the gung ho new-style cops and their ivory tower apparatchiks, however. *Will their 'deep surveillance' and 'enhanced policing' programs calm troubled neighborhoods? How could their 'zero dissidence' or 'heightened awareness' measures not foster discordance? Their stupidity will ruin everything.*

He looked around the room again in search of prospective candidates—someone to take the floor against Banderjee. They all knew she reflected the views of many there and had solid backing in the hierarchy. Opposing her was dangerous. He himself would have to stay silent and bide his time—he could do more good in his present position than he would in risking a confrontation. In any case, he recognized that nothing said here would have any bearing on policy anyway; the decision had already been made at Central—*GraceNost* was dead. This was just a stage on which to parade one's fervency.

A young officer motioned to the silver-haired officer at the convergence of the ovals.

"Officer Stenson," the chair recognized him.

The tall dark-uniformed trooper stood. "CS Yellow." He cleared his throat. "I'm strongly for the protocol." His eyes rolled over the company. "Before, we did not have the technical capability or manpower to enforce compliance but now, with White Night, cyber-C, and the auxiliaries we can dominate the streets and cyberspace. We just need the authority to do our job. That's all we ask. Give us the chance to eradicate the devo presence completely."

He sighed haughtily. "I know there's been talk, once again, about *heuristic* approaches and *evolutionary* transformation, but isn't this just defeatist talk? Doesn't it really say we lack the will to go all out for One World?" He nodded briskly. "I hope our zone won't be seen as lacking resolution—that we've lost the faith." As he took his seat he stole a glance at Banderjee who didn't acknowledge him.

Croydon looked at the faces flanking Stenson—he hated the imbecilic look of smug superiority he read there. *Callow morons.*

Another officer on the third tier motioned to the chair.

"Officer M'Bago."

"CS Blue," he announced. "I just wanted to add this thought." He spread his huge hands in supplication. "I believe we're at a crossroads in the Transformative Revolution. So we need to ask the question: How will history remember us? How will future generations judge us? If the revolution falters and future generations look back and examine the causes—when they dissect the corpse as it were—where will they pinpoint the beginning of its decline?" He left the question hanging. "This is where we stand now, at a fork between glorious ascension and regress; honor or disgrace. We need to rededicate ourselves to the mission." Suddenly he punched his fist skyward heroically. "We are ready for the sacrifice! Total war!" A smattering of hands from the upper oval swelled to a hooting and applause which he acknowledged with a dazzling display of white teeth on his black face as he sat down.

When the clamor subsided another young officer moved to speak, but the chairman glanced at his watch and said, "Okay that's it." He surveyed the assembled cadre. "Thank you everyone, and the speakers especially for your candor." His granite visage relaxed into a smile. "I salute the junior officers for injecting a much needed spirit into these proceedings… much needed." His face hardened again. "Adjourned."

A multitude of jackboots hit the carpet. Croydon looked over to Banderjee. Another officer had thrust a document to her attention and was hanging over her shoulder as she read. A smile formed on her lips.

Croydon's eyes gleamed like cold steel.

* * *

A sullen Kim sat immobile.

"They wanted her to carry it for a few months. Can you believe it?" Belinda scoffed.

Kim sobbed, dry heaved and bolted from the room.

"Jeepers! What's wrong now?" Belinda moaned.

"God, Belinda!" Suzanne exclaimed exasperatedly. She hurried after Kim.

Belinda shrugged, "She's so touchy about everything." She looked for a consoling nod from Paul. "If she had taken her MorningAfter she wouldn't have had any problems."

Paul turned away. The room was silent except for the click-clicking of Belinda fidgeting with her compact.

"Kim?' Suzanne called softly into the darkened room. There were suppressed sobs coming from the corner.

She edged over to their source, lowered herself to the floor and held the trembling girl to herself.

"I keep thinking about *him*," she warbled.

"Who *him*? You mean Helmut?" Suzanne asked.

"No!" Kim bawled.

Suzanne held her convulsing friend and looked at the narrow slits of sunlight seeping through the shutters.

Paul left Suzanne's house early. It was all pretty depressing—Kim's hysterical outbursts; Belinda's griping. It was too much to take in the wake of Cal's death. Bev hadn't shown up either.

He walked to a nearby park and sat on one of the benches beneath the towering chestnut trees. The warm July sun soothed his pallid skin. He would have liked to have taken his Bible out and read, but that was out of the question here, in public.

He had been reading it a lot lately.

Another man came and sat close by. He resented this intrusion, but the stranger turned his back to him, intent on his own reading thankfully.

He had spent a sleepless night thinking about Cal—reviewing his life. Suzanne's invite offered an opportunity to get out of the house and shut away the demons troubling his mind. He had half-hoped Suzanne would be there by herself.

Besides his remembrances of Cal, when they didn't tend towards Melanie his thoughts circled and circled around the impenetrable problem introduced during his first conversation with Samuel: if he was a biological robot, where was the space for free will or reason? He could make no progress on this conundrum.

He wondered what Samuel would make of Kim's behavior.

Suddenly there was a cacophony of voices nearby and the clack of jackboots approaching along the asphalt path. Was it a counter-insurgency sweep? Paul shot a glance around to see the reaction of his neighbor but the bench was empty. He had left unnoticed.

A troop of blues double-timed by. Paul could see two bedraggled prisoners amidst them—young people not much older than himself. He strained to catch a clear vision of them but suddenly a dark blue object obstructed his view. "What are you looking at?" the angry voice snarled from behind the visor. The policeman thrust his register into Paul's face. "Comply!" he demanded.

Paul pressed his palm to the device which responded with a reassuring beep.

"What are you doing here?"

"Visiting..." Paul stammered.

"Who?"

"Just some school friends."

"Where?"

"On Springhurst."

"What do you have in there?" he growled, ripping the bag from Paul's hands.

Paul's reflexes made a feeble gesture to retain it, but in a split second he realized it was not his bag—it was green. Somehow he had gotten someone else's bag.

The cop rifled through the sack—Frisbee, water bottle, bag of soy chips, pair of socks—then stuffed the contents back in and slapped it against Paul's chest.

"Shove off!" he ordered.

Paul hurried away. When he was a ways off he chanced a quick glance back to see if his bag was resting by the bench, but it was nowhere in sight. The person who had sat there beside him must have taken it. He hustled out of the park.

In the excitement he momentarily lost his bearings and wandered down an alley. He was still rushing along, wishing to be far away from the park, when an angular script scrawled on a red brick wall flashed by and stopped him in his tracks staring confoundedly at the bizarre inscription. In what looked like white chalk he read:

> *We have no struggle*
> *We have no want*
> *We have no children*
> *We have no family*
> *We have no charity*
> *We have no purpose*
> *We have no love*
> *We have no future*
> *But we have One World*

He stood there for dangerous seconds trying to fathom the meaning. *It is from the devos for sure,* he thought. *Obviously incompliant.* Immediately he became cognizant of his surroundings: the buildings were decrepit and dark. He had probably wandered into an un-reclaimed neighborhood. There was another message scribbled on one of the other walls: WE WILL NOT COMPLY! Icy tentacles of fear gripped his stomach and he bolted out of the alley, escaping into the sunlight on Richmond. He kept running until he reached the safety of Emerald.

It was quarter to nine when he finally rushed through the door, still shaky over the day's incidents. The loss of his bag and Bible drove him to the edge of panic. He had been scared about coming home—afraid the police might be waiting for him. What if the person who took his bag discovered the Bible and turned it over to the authorities? There was no identification in it that could lead to him but what if the cop in the park remembered him? He had scanned him! What if they did DNA tests?

A desperate examination of the green bag revealed no clues as to its owner.

He tried to master his nerves and carry on as usual, grabbing a bowl of Honeycombs without milk and sitting down in front of the screen.

Coincidently, he had planned beforehand to study the devo contribution to the so-called Neo-Darwinism that plagued the natural sciences before Ascension. DNA figured large in that investigation.

He was taught that the absurd concept of random mutations and natural selection was an artifice erected by devos to impede the investigation of the Subatomic Teleological Force and to subject Evolution to ridicule. It wasn't until they were rooted out of positions in the scientific journals and the academies that Neo-Darwinism was exposed as a purely ideological proposition without any supporting empirical evidence. Soon after, the Subatomic Teleological Force was discovered. It explained the obvious sequencing of DNA that couldn't be accounted for by Neo-Darwinism without appealing to fabricated constructs or impossible chance.

So Neo-Darwinism had been another of those instances where Christians had tried to waylay scientific progress, and it succeeded in this for the better part of a century.

That's what he had been taught anyway.

But Samuel turned this on its head saying that the random mutations natural selection theory had been advanced and rabidly defended by *Progressive* scientists and that it was Christian scientists who questioned its capacity to generate the complex information required in the DNA for higher species to emerge. It seemed an outlandish charge, but Paul's reading of *The God Delusion* seemed to confirm Samuel's claims. Could it really be true that, as in the Inquisition's witch burnings and the Galileo affair, One World had effectively inverted historical events and used the devos as scapegoats to paper over its own predecessor's culpability?

Willing himself to set aside his anxiety, he pulled up the O.W.L. portal and agile fingers typed user id and password. When the search engine panel popped up he set his access level to seven, selected the *religion* domain and clicked *Go*. The panel loaded as he munched another handful. Suddenly an alarming SECURITY VIOLATION: UNAUTHORIZED

ACCESS LEVEL message popped up. For an instant he thought he had keyed his password incorrectly, but the system had already accepted it. The access level was correct: seven. He set his bowl aside and selected *7* and *religion* again and clicked *Go*. Once more the search engine screen cycled back to the bold red-lettered message. Now he was sure his authorization had been revoked. *Why would they do that?* The lost book bag and Bible shot to mind. *They must have tracked them back to me. They must have ruled me incompliant.*

He hastily clicked back to his mail box and ran down the items expecting to see a note from O.W.L. but there was nothing. *What to do?*

He thought for a moment then, tossing caution aside, flipped back to the O.W.L. portal. There was a *Contact Us* link there that enabled him to brave an enquiry: *I am trying to switch to level 7 security access but I get an UNAUTHORIZED ACCESS LEVEL message… it was working this morning.* He clicked *Send* and camped on his in-box for a few minutes. There was no reply, so he got up and took his bowl back to the kitchen. When he returned there was still no reply.

He waited for an hour all the while thinking about his missing bag and wishing he could talk to Melanie about it. Finally he dozed off.

There was still no reply by morning. He would have to speak to Mr. Lichter.

19

ARCHIVES

As he approached the door Paul heard Mr. Lichter speaking with another student inside so he settled into one of the chairs just outside the classroom and checked out the SpaceFleet situation on his tablet to steady his nerves. It was a hot one outside. He wished the air conditioning was operating but the power situation mandated only essential systems.

A few minutes later he caught snippets of parting salutations so he slipped his tablet back into his bag. The other student—Paul couldn't remember his name—emerged and gave him a 'hi' on the way past. Paul took a deep breath and knocked on the door.

"Yes. Come in," Lichter's voice called from within.

A smile spread over Mr. Lichter's face as he poured over the message on his tablet. When he looked up and saw Paul it wavered a moment before reasserting itself. "Paul. Oh, I'm glad you came in." He deposited the tablet on to one of the neat stacks of paper on his desk.

Paul leaned against the edge of one of the student desks with his arms crossed in front of him. "My access was revoked—my access to World Lib for my paper," he said abruptly.

Lichter looked away. "Yes, I know."

"Why was it taken away?" Paul continued, barely restraining the tone of recrimination.

Lichter's demeanor steeled instantly. "Obviously the administrators decided that it wasn't in your best interest to have access," he said haughtily. "That's what they are there for." He looked over his glasses at Paul. "I don't know how you got clearance in the first place. That stuff you've been reading is pretty extreme; hardly the thing for a future leader to be displaying an interest in."

Paul roused to speak but Lichter cut him off. "I warned you in the beginning it wasn't smart to pursue this topic," he snapped. He discarded his glasses and his hand moved to massage his temple. "Who knows what they think of you at Zone. And not just you but me and this whole institution," he snapped. "Did you ever think about that?" He lowered himself into his chair and stared at the desktop with his hands clenched tightly. He hadn't meant to blurt that out.

Paul was taken aback by the anger and desperation in Lichter's voice. He hadn't known him to lose his cool; ever. A dead silence ensued, so complete that neither seemed to be breathing.

It was Paul who finally braved some words. "You have always told us not to be afraid of pursuing knowledge wherever it leads," he began haltingly. "I don't know why this is—"

Lichter exploded. "Oh! You don't know! You don't know!" he sputtered. He sprang from his chair and flew towards Paul menacingly and stomped his foot on the floor just short of him. "You will stop this right now!" He wielded his finger threateningly. "This thesis of yours is done! Do you understand!" he screamed, eyes wild as Africa.

The rage manifest in Lichter's face cowed Paul.

"You understand!" he roared again.

"Yes," Paul replied meekly.

Lichter remained posed like a bird of prey over Paul, looking like he might burst from his body for what seemed the better part of a minute. Finally his arms fell to his side and his voice assumed a weary, defeated tone. "Understand, it's not a question of concealing knowledge, it's just that you lack the experience to interpret what you are reading. You are not ready. You can end up with an incorrect understanding." He looked hard at his student. "You might turn incompliant."

Paul remained frozen, fearful of setting the older man off again. It was like engaging a bottle of nitro-glycerin.

"That's why we don't have just anybody perusing through the archives," Lichter continued in a fatherly tone. He looked for an empathetic response, but Paul averted his eyes.

Lichter signed. "Okay, we'll talk about what to do about your exit paper later. Just go home now." He put his hand on Paul's shoulder. Paul nodded weakly, slipped from beneath his hand and exited the room.

Lichter was left staring at the closed door. His lips twitched madly, but there were no words for them to pronounce. Finally he strayed back to his desk and slumped down in the familiar chair. "Everything will be okay," he assured himself. "It will all be okay."

* * *

"So he blocked your access?" Samuel asked.

"Lichter? No, he doesn't have the authority for that. It had to be O.W.L. Well, maybe at his recommendation." He looked at Samuel. "I was surprised… really shocked… I'd never seen Lichter lose control like that."

Samuel resumed pacing. "Why do you think?"

Paul compressed his lips together. "He was frightened about how it would look… I mean, if one of his students went off the rails…" He sighed. "He said I could go incompliant." He looked to Samuel. "I guess I never fully appreciated the pressure teachers are under."

Samuel continued to pace while Paul sat on the dilapidated couch. "So. What about your paper? What will you do?"

Paul looked around the dim apartment. "I want to finish it; I want to finish the investigation anyway."

Samuel waggled his head. "Maybe you should put it aside for now," he said gently.

Paul reclined on the couch. "I won't be able to use it for my exit paper, for sure," he acknowledged. "On the other hand, I don't have anything else to work on now, so I have time." His shoulders slumped. "But I need resource material and there's no way to get it." He slapped the arm of his chair. "I'm dead in the water except for what I can learn from you."

Samuel had listened intently enough when Paul recounted the events in the park with the police, but had refrained from commenting or expressing interest in Paul's speculations about the stranger who had stolen his bag.

The old man stopped in the middle of the floor and fidgeted with his keychain absent-mindedly. Paul could see he was grappling with something.

Samuel finally spit out, "So, *ahem*, if you had the books, you would continue your study, even though the-powers-that-be have prohibited it?"

The blatant incompliancy of such a course of action jolted Paul alert. He looked hard at the old man like a bloodhound sensing game. "Yeah. Yeah, I think I would."

Samuel stroked his beard thoughtfully and went back to pacing and flipping through his keys. At one point he stopped suddenly and looked intently at Paul and seemed about to speak but then resumed his pacing.

He stopped again. "Well, books. You need books." He smacked his lips and shuffled over to the door from which he had produced the pool table on Paul's earlier visit. Paul assumed it was the way to his living quarters. The hinges squeaked as Samuel wrenched it open. "Come, come," he motioned back to Paul as he waddled through the doorway.

There was a curiously narrow, poorly lit hallway beyond leading to the back of the house. Paul surmised the original hallway had been divided between Samuel's apartment and one adjacent, which accounted for its claustrophobic breadth. Paul tripped a few times on the frayed carpet as he navigated in the wake of Samuel's dark silhouette—evidently the ceiling lights had fallen to the neighbor's allotment.

"Ah," Samuel grunted to himself. Paul heard his keys rattle then a sliver of light appeared and widened until they could pass into the room beyond. "My sanctuary," Samuel said proudly.

Gauged by floor area it wasn't a large room, but Paul found himself looking up at an astounding wall of books, rising up to the ceiling about four meters above. Three of the room's walls were covered this way—with books from floor to ceiling. The volumes presented a dazzling mosaic to Paul's eyes; he had never seen anything like it. There was even a ladder mounted on a rail that traversed the bookcases enabling access to each elevation.

Samuel had settled behind the oak desk, also blanketed in books, nestled on the remaining wall. A large cartographic print in a gilded frame hung behind him; the land was copper and the oceans metallic blue. A gold cross hung beside that and, on the other side, a skeleton suspended from a stanchion added a touch of the macabre to the decor. Paul took it all in with eyes agog.

"I can't believe this!" he exclaimed, "Where did you get—?"

"Ha! I've had a good long while to accumulate them—you know: a book here, a book there." He smiled reminiscing. "There used to be a lot of second hand book stores around where you could get anything you wanted. It was like that before… before Ascension"

Paul was pouring over the titles. "Aristotle. Origen, Cicero. And over here: Eusebius, Livy and Tacitus." Paul slid a thick volume out and read, "*Contra Celsum*." He flipped through its numinous pages carefully before returning it to its place. "Hobbes, More, Voltaire." He moved to the next shelf. "Heidegger. Sartre." He paused and pronounced slowly: "Simone de Beauvoir?"

Samuel shrugged. "You have to read the other guys too."

Paul's eyes took in the literary trove. "I can use all these?"

Samuel waved his arm expansively. "Use whatever you like; we have no *prohibited sections* here," he laughed.

Paul grinned back but then a thought caused him to sober instantly. He looked intently at Samuel. "You're taking a risk. If anyone found out you had these…"

Samuel's eyes searched his. "How will anyone get to know that?" he said quietly.

Paul's gaze wavered then came back to Samuel. "No one will, of course."

Samuel fumbled in a drawer and pulled out a little canvas satchel. "Take this," he said offering it to Paul. "You can conceal books in here." He was holding the bag open and showing an almost invisible flap that divided the main compartment from a smaller bottom one. It worked even better than his stolen one. "No one will see them if they happen to look inside," he explained. "Just don't take too many books at a time—no more than two of the softcover ones, one hardcover—and you should be okay. You don't want it to get too heavy."

Paul reached out and took possession of it. "Thanks Samuel. I'll be careful." Samuel grunted and sat down again.

Paul looked up at the three walls of books looming over his head once more. There were so many he would like to read; which should he pick to make best use of his time? The titles ran riot across his vision. The more he searched the more anxious he became. He was used to using a computer where the volume of information was concealed behind search engines, but here he was confronted physically by the oppressive weight of extant knowledge.

"Yes, daunting isn't it?" Samuel's voice came from behind. "So much information."

Paul looked around. "Yes. I don't know where to start," he admitted. "What do you think?"

Samuel was silent for a moment. "What is really essential… well, maybe first you have to read a few books so you can begin to understand." He went over to the first wall and selected two thin volumes. "Maybe you can start with these; something general," he said handing them to Paul. "They will give you a start. After that you can jump into something more advanced." He paused for a moment and added enigmatically, "But what is really essential for you to learn is not contained in the pages of any of these books."

Paul looked askance at him. "I don't understand."

"These will help you see through those objections to Christianity you have."

The reply caught Paul off guard. *Is that what I'm seeking?* "What if they don't?" he heard himself ask.

Samuel's face was blank for a moment then he shrugged. "Then you were never meant to." He left the words hanging in the air, shuffled back to his chair to bury his nose in another tome. His posture intimated he had nothing more to say at that time and curfew was drawing near so Paul stashed his two books beneath the concealing panel of the satchel and left the room, noiselessly closing the door behind. He found his way down the dim corridor to the sitting room and stepped into the now darkened street.

As soon as Paul was gone Samuel looked up from his reading. He had lived a long life in a precarious environment. He knew his time here was surely drawing to a close and he would be moving on.

He put his book down.

He had prepared his whole life for this passage, neither turning to the right nor the left—it had been an arduous journey—so the prospect wasn't unwelcome.

Still, he pondered over the young man, Paul. *What will happen to him after I'm gone? Will he follow The Way or will he be lost?* The old man tried to penetrate into a future he could perceive but darkly.

In the end he knelt on the threadbare carpet to pray.

* * *

It was just after nine when Paul slipped through the door. There was no one in the living room, so he stole upstairs and locked his new bag in his cabinet before creeping back downstairs to see if his enablers were home.

He heard voices on the back porch so he took a deep breath and crashed through the screen door.

"Hi Norm, Jean," he said nonchalantly. They were lounging at a small table with a platter of cheese, crackers and pâté and each held a glass of wine.

Norman smiled and saluted, "Hi buddy. We just got back about an hour ago. Want some cheese?" he said pushing the platter towards Paul.

"Sure, thanks." He selected a white cube. It was real cheese. How they got goodies like this he never knew—both worked as inspectors for some government urban planning department. It was suspicious; at times he wondered if he was being incompliant not reporting them.

"We wondered where you were," Jean asked, her eyebrows assuming that hog's back line they always did when she was concerned.

"Oh, just downtown visiting a friend," Paul explained. "I wanted to be back before you got here but, well, I guess we got to talking and..."

"Hey, no problem," Norm grinned. "We had a great time in Florida," he said, winking at his companion. "Jean really loved the Keys, didn't you?'

"Yeah, I love the parks. Oh, and the seafood!" Jean kissed her fingers. "You have to try a Strength Through Joy excursion when you have the merits. I think you'd enjoy the Florida leg. It's really hot though." She flounced her long frizzy red hair.

They are probably the only ones who choose to go to Florida in August, Paul smiled to himself.

He had always gotten along well with Norm and Jean—he had been with them for almost four years—but his sensibilities varied from theirs and often he wondered how the Life Center had managed to match them up. Likely, there had been a shortage of enablers; it was a persistent problem. In any case he was thankful that their relationship was a cordial, if not penetrating, one. They left him alone to do his own thing for the most part.

"Oh, by the way; the roof in the den is still leaking," Paul informed them.

"Oh? The Kappas haven't been by?"

"Nope." Paul reached for another cheese square.

Norm sighed. "Geez, this place is falling apart. I'll check on the work order in the morning." He shook his head. "I'm almost tempted to go up and fix it myself." Jean laughed. It would be quite a spectacle to see Norm's Alpha hands trying to mend the shingles.

Paul was anxious to get at the books he had brought from Samuel's, so he chatted just a bit longer, had a few more snacks then slipped back up to his room.

With his bedroom door secured he retrieved his book bag and extracted one of the volumes from the secret compartment. Before locking the bag up once more he stashed a few political pamphlets and a pen and notebook into the main compartment so if someone ever looked inside they wouldn't be curious about his touting an empty sack. That completed, he settled into the large lounging chair under the reading lamp and broke open the volume.

It was written by the twentieth century Christian apologist C.S. Lewis and titled *Mere Christianity*. It was pleasant to read an actual book rather than use his monitor; he liked the feel of the pages and the serene impression of the inked words on his eyes.

The introduction said it was a transcription of some broadcasts Lewis made on British radio during World War Two explaining what Christians believe, and why. *How strange the world must have been back then, when a devo was allowed to speak on national media!*

Paul was somewhat surprised that Lewis went about things like a philosopher: establishing premises, drawing conclusions from them, building his argument. Although his acquaintance with Samuel and the snippets of a few Christian authors had gone a distance to divest him of this stereotypical view, a part of him had still expected to be presented with a litany of imperatives with which the author would expect one to conform uncritically. Lewis didn't take that approach at all—he invited the reader to reason with him. He was like Samuel in that way.

A few of the things Lewis said stuck with Paul immediately. At one point he was contrasting the Christian understanding that there is an absolute morality determined by an omniscient god which all humans understand but inevitably neglect, with the alternative understanding that human morality evolved in concert with humanity's biological evolution and was merely a product of utility and consensus. The proof offered in support of this latter position—one that occurred immediately to Paul—was that *We don't burn witches anymore. Doesn't the fact that we no longer torture and execute helpless women because of some supposed malignant power in their possession prove that morality has advanced steadily?*

But Lewis pointed out that, in this case, humanity had made a leap forward in knowledge, not in morality. The people who burned witches

really believed that witches had the power to harm people so they removed them to protect their society. One World wasn't a great evolution
in thinking concerning the value of human life or human rights but
rather a loss of belief in the ability of witches to really do harm.

A stray thought crossed Paul's mind: *Does One World represent a
higher morality than that of the witch burners? Does it treat people it perceived as threatening—devos—in a more humane manner? Has morality
evolved or has witch burning merely modernized?* He wasn't sure.

Another point that piqued Paul's attention was something Lewis
mentioned in passing. He said that both worldviews, the materialist and
the religious—*interesting that Lewis puts it that way: materialist versus
religious*—had existed through all ages. Paul had assumed that materialism resulted from the culminations of man's reasoning and scientific
knowledge—ancient people were credulous and religious and 'spiritual';
modern people scientific and atheist and materialistic. Theism evolved
to atheism. Having studied some of the ancients now he realized how
uninformed his opinion had been, and Lewis' remark merely brought
the point home. He knew the ancients were no more credulous than One
Worlders; that the great men of science were, almost without exception,
religious; and that materialism could only provide definitive resolutions
to all the vexatious questions of existence to the superficial mind.

Lewis dwelt at length on the phenomenon of the human perception
of the existence of a *real* moral right and wrong independent of personal preference and beyond mere expediency. Even the most recalci-
trant atheist would exude righteous anger over some supposed wrong
committed against his person even though his worldview excluded the
notion that moral wrongdoing could exist objectively. For Paul it under-
scored the difficulty in living a genuine atheistic life with integrity—one
had to proceed as if each person had no more worth than a lamppost—
they were both just collections of atoms; that one's experiences of sen-
tience and personhood were delusional, the product of random chemical
reactions; that freewill was impossible and so also reasoning and moral
liability. *How could a sane person live out these beliefs?*

He wanted to explore this further, but his weariness compelled him
to lock the book away again and go to bed.

He had gotten into the habit of reading his Bible before sleeping so
his missing book bag intruded into his thoughts now, as much as he
would prefer that distressing situation remain forgotten. He wished he
had asked Samuel if he had a Bible he could borrow earlier, but dis-

tracted by the bounteous provisioning of his library, it hadn't occurred to him. Suddenly his body lurched with an electrical thought: *I wonder if he has* The Origin of Species? *That would be the ultimate read!*

Sleep continued to elude him. He was elated but also apprehensive about continuing this investigation. He knew he had to pursue it while he had this chance because the opportunity was unlikely to reoccur, but at what cost to his future career and peace of mind?

In any case, he would try to lay low and keep out of Mr. Lichter's sight to delay his re-assignment as long as possible.

His mind passed to thinking about Samuel, alone in that room with all those books. *All the things he must have studied. What thoughts developed in a mind like that? He would surely make a fascinating study subject himself. Perhaps I should write Samuel's biography and submit that as my exit paper!* He laughed out loud.

Paul recalled what Samuel had said—about the books not being the essential thing. *What did he mean by that?* He would ask next time.

His exhausted mind finally slipped over the threshold of wakefulness with one parting thought: *Melanie.*

20

Day 95

LIFE

Paul had been mulling over *Mere Christianity* for about a week.
Lewis drove home the point that Samuel had already made: that
ninety-nine percent of the things you believe, you believe on another's
authority and that EVERY historical fact is believed on authority. It was
true. Paul could no longer insist that his own beliefs were anchored in
the bedrock of objective and independent reasoning untainted by societal bias or personal whim and desire; he had to justify his own worldview as much as any Christian.

Lewis' observations often left Paul's mind looping around a kind of
mental Mobius strip: *Why do we believe that some of the things we do are
immoral? If I think the thing I'm doing is bad, then why do I do it? Is it because it is useful to myself and therefore 'good'? But if 'the good' is merely
that which is useful to me then why do I often feel, when I do the thing
that is advantageous to myself, that the thing I should have done instead
was the moral thing?* He often thought about the poor old lady that day
with Harmony and Anne and felt bad he hadn't risked ridicule and gone
back to help her.

*Where do our moral imperatives originate if not from personal pref-
erence? If from personal preference, then how could I think anything I
choose immoral? I want to do good so how can there be this dissonance
between what I do and what I believe to be good? Is there, then, a standard
of behavior established outside of myself that I'm conscience of transgress-*

ing? If this thing outside of myself is the state, and it determines what is moral according to its own advantage, then I should not disapprove of any of its actions on moral grounds. But I don't believe the state to be beyond censure and so clearly I don't really believe it is the final arbiter of morality. But doesn't this mean I believe there is a moral authority beyond the state—beyond One World? What authority is that?

Around and around it went. All of these musings of Lewis had an acidic relationship with one's ironclad presuppositions.

Faith. For Lewis, faith was the fruit of critical thinking. Having faith meant holding on to the things your reason once accepted despite your changing mood. Without reason faith could not be, for faith was birthed in reason and maintained by resisting emotional revisionism. This was a total inversion of what Paul had been taught—that faith was the maintenance of wishful thinking in defiance of reason.

Which of these two definitions—reasoned conviction or wishful thinking—are reflective of Lewis and Samuel's beliefs, now that I understand them better? Which describes Gretchen's? Of more acute relevance: which describes Dr. Bright's?

Another intriguing topic: sin. Lewis didn't define it as Paul would have guessed—as 'doing bad things.' Instead he said sin meant putting something else before God and inevitably abandoning God's counsel in pursuance of this other. We choose to walk apart from God and define our own reality: what is good and what evil. But God created everything, so his reality IS reality and our own machinations merely obfuscate that fact to our own detriment. All the evils of the world stem from this, even death, for God is the source of life and when we choose to separate from him we cannot sustain our lives because each of us has no life of his own, we just maintain the one we've been given. We are cut off from our source of life because God cannot mingle with sin and remain God any more than white can merge with black and remain pristine. A chasm is opened between us and Life.

Jesus sacrificed himself to repair this rift. He cut himself off from Life so that we might be joined again. He died in our place and his sacrifice fills the chasm between us and God.

That's what Christianity says, anyway. It was a perplexing contrivance, this doctrine, trampling all of one's predilections; grating on one's pride.

Maybe Lewis was right: Christianity was too strange and unpalatable to be made up.

The troops were still unable to push into North Galton. Paul clicked the monitor off and looked over to Melanie lying on the couch, eyes closed to feel the sunlight on her face. He was holding back, apprehensive about speaking for fear of alienating her and embarrassing himself—maybe even appearing incompliant in her eyes. But if he couldn't confide in her then how genuine was their friendship?

"Mel?" Her eyebrows flickered. "What do you know about Christianity?"

Her body lurched as if pricked and her eyes popped open. She broke out laughing and sat up. "Boy! I never know what you are going to spring... where did that come from?"

Paul looked at her sparkling amused eyes and felt ashamed, but pressed on. "Just something that's come up at school," he explained, "a project I'm working on."

"Oh yeah, I remember, your exit paper. You asked once if Cass knew anything—"

Paul nodded impatiently. "Yes, but what about *you*? What do you think?"

Melanie cocked her head to sense if Paul was being serious or pulling her leg. She reclined once more and slipped her hands behind her head. "Well, let me see..." She flicked her eyebrows. "It's a religion that taught to be nice to people—to give to poor people and help those in need, I think." She nodded to Paul. "That was okay then I guess—they didn't have a government that would look after everyone. But it also taught some pretty terrible things... burning witches, stopping science, saying people will burn in hell. Really nasty. I read that on Worldpedia," she assured him. "What's your project about exactly?"

"Oh, just looking at their—the Christians I mean—beliefs. You know: how they differ from modern people."

"Sounds pretty interesting," Melanie said languidly. She propped herself up on her elbows. "So what have you found out?"

"Well, I did some research—which was good—but I couldn't find any material written by Christians themselves; it was always by others."

Melanie yawned and stretched. "And that was important?"

"Well, I didn't want to rely on someone else's word, I wanted to get the story straight from them—from some Christians."

Melanie shuffled up and rested her back on the arm of the couch. "Yeah, I can see that makes sense. Of course Worldpedia is the final authority, but it's nice to actually interview people to get it in their own words. I can see that. So what did you do?"

"Well," Paul began then stopped. He laughed nervously. "Oh, well. I went to a worship."

Melanie's jaw dropped in astonishment. "Really? That's creepy!" she squealed. "At a church?" She pronounced church as if it had quotation marks.

"Yeah, right downtown; the Church of the Affirming Spirit. It's part of the Inclusion Church."

"Holy...!" Melanie gasped. "I mean, I've seen some churches around, but I didn't think you could just walk in. Didn't you feel weird? What did they do anyway?"

"It wasn't really that much different from Cassandra's sessions," Paul replied thoughtlessly. He realized immediately he had blundered.

"Oh, don't say that."

"Sorry, sorry. I meant the worship was very, um *spiritual*," Paul explained. "I thought it would be more, you know, sin and hell and all that. Instead they talked about everyone being part of the One and everyone evolving towards that, with Science as our guide. Stuff like that."

Melanie listened.

"I even talked to the priest afterwards."

Melanie's eyes widened again. "And? What was he like?"

"It was a *she* actually. We talked about equality and science and evolution, living on through our genes—nothing too far out. She was pretty much normal."

"So you think Worldpedia is wrong?" Melanie said in a shocked tone.

Paul clasped his hands in front of him and bowed slightly. "Umm, well you see Mel, I don't think the Inclusion Church is really what I was looking for. I wanted to talk to real Christians but I don't think they represent the Christian worldview at all."

Melanie's brows shot up. "Why? Religions change, you know."

Paul didn't take up Mel's line of thought, instead he dove in with, "Well, for one thing, they don't believe that Jesus—you know him?—rose from the dead."

Melanie laughed. "Yeah well, I guess they're not completely crazy then!"

"But I think the resurrection is pivotal to their religion; nothing makes sense without it." He signed. "Listen," he said wetting his lips, "there is someone I'd like you to meet."

"Who?" Melanie giggled. "Jim the Baptist?"

"Just someone. You'll get it when you meet him."

Melanie eyed him warily. "Can you give me a hint? Who is he?"

Paul grinned shyly. "Someone I met after I went to the church. I think you'll find him pretty interesting."

Melanie shrugged.

"He's pretty old; he was around long before Ascension. There were still some Christians back then who took the Bible seriously," Paul explained.

Melanie's eyes blinked in recollection. "Oh yeah, the Bible; that's what it was called. That was their holy book. They thought that… like God wrote it."

Paul grimaced. "Yeah, something like that."

Melanie smirked. "Does he believe Jesus rose from the grave?"

Paul sighed. "C'mon Mel. Just come and meet this guy—his name is Samuel—he's not what you think."

Melanie crossed her arms at her chest and weighed her options. This was obviously important to Paul and she had learned to trust him even when she didn't understand. If she went along things would become clear. "Yeah okay, I'll go," she conceded haltingly, ending with a flash grin.

Paul clapped. "Alright! He lives down on Ecology. Let's go!"

"Whoa, you mean you want to go now? I was hoping we'd spend some time here." She lay back down on the couch and smiled playfully at him.

Paul sighed. "I told him I'd come by today. Really Mel, we should go."

"Okay, okay." There was a note of annoyance in her voice, but she was pleased Paul was so elated. The next minute they were marching hand in hand down Davisville Avenue.

Paul jolted when the door opened immediately in response to his knock. Samuel was also startled at finding his threshold blocked by the two teenagers.

"Oh, oh," he exclaimed, recognizing Paul. "You scared the daylights out of me!"

"Ha, sorry Sam. We were in the neighborhood and thought we'd check in on you."

Samuel's bright green eyes scanned Melanie. He appeared agitated.

"This is Mel," Paul said, putting his hand on her shoulder. He wondered if he had made a mistake bringing her along unannounced. He probably should have asked beforehand.

"Oh, Mel… Melanie from the party…" Samuel stammered. Paul flushed and nodded affirmatively. Samuel gazed hard at the pretty blond stranger again who bounced his stare right back at him. Apparently satisfied he said, "Come, come along then," and rushed off.

Paul tripped after him, Melanie in tow. "Where are we off to?"

Samuel's stride had an extra hop in it today; a lively spirit animated his person. "Ha ha, to the greatest thing!" he exclaimed. In a more subdued voice he added, "Never mind, just come. You'll see."

He led them to Singer and headed up a few blocks before stopping by a lamp post and waiting, peering down the street. Paul and Melanie's eyes followed his. "What are we waiting for? The streetcar doesn't stop here."

Samuel glanced at his watch then resumed his vigil without responding. It was uncharacteristically chilly for a July evening so Melanie slipped her sweater on. She caught Paul's eye and gave him a *What now?* look.

A group of Kappas were fixing a pothole on the other side of the street, about twenty meters down. Paul wished they would get around to fixing the roof at home. *I guess it's like Dr. Bright was saying: there's a shortage of them.*

The light at Ecology changed and a few cars passed by. Then a dark shadow turned the corner and headed their way. It was a black maria. It seemed to Paul to be approaching in slow motion, like the frames of a movie played at quarter speed. His heart beat fast remembering his missing book bag and he drew Melanie close. When the car was level with them it was within a meter of where they stood. He had never been this close to one before. The windows were impenetrable. It slipped by noiselessly without pausing. Paul watched its red tail lights float up the avenue until it was several blocks away.

Suddenly, he realized Samuel wasn't there. His heart shuttered and he looked around for the old man fearful of finding the maria had swallowed him up. There was a rattle in the alley and the gray figure of Samuel emerged haltingly. Paul could see his breath came in quick shallow draughts. He glanced at Paul briefly, checked his watch then resumed his posture looking down the street as if nothing had happened. Paul looked hard at his face trying to read in it some sort of explanation, but Samuel ignored his entreaty.

Suddenly a blue car screeched to a halt in front of them and Samuel flung open the door and leapt inside. His hand waved to them out of the dark interior. "Get in!"

Paul looked at Melanie whose countenance had taken on a concerned look. "It's okay," he heard himself saying with more assurance than he felt, "Let's go." He sprung in and Melanie tumbled in after and the car lurched forward immediately and sped off.

The interior was hot and dark except for the dim green glow of the instrumentation. They couldn't see the face of the driver and no words were exchanged. Paul realized the car's windows were blacked-out—some kind of mat-black tinting—that's why it was so dark inside. Samuel sat mute at his left elbow. Melanie's hand grasped his in the darkness. It felt cold and damp.

The car sped along Singer then turned east along a side street that Paul couldn't identify. Soon it turned right, then almost immediately, left. It was mandatory that all cars use GPSnav to steer the most efficient route and avoid forbidden zones, but this driver zigzagged for, what Paul reckoned to be, about fifteen minutes, following some sort of sanctioned route like a corvette picking its way through a minefield. Any chance of Paul reestablishing his orientation was completely obliterated by the rapid course alterations.

The vehicle made a sharp turn throwing all the passengers together and lurched to an abrupt halt. Samuel flung open his door. "Come."

Paul tumbled into the cool air with Melanie in hand. The car sped away immediately. They had been dropped at the entrance to an alley where a van was idling with one of its rear doors open. There were no landmarks to enable Paul to fix his location.

"Follow me," Samuel ordered, scampering towards the vehicle.

Paul held back. "I'm scared," he heard Melanie whisper.

Samuel paused before climbing into the van and turned back to Paul. "You wanted to know what Christianity was all about—to see it in its naked light. Here's your chance. Come."

Paul was holding Melanie's hands in each of his own. He looked into her pleading eyes. "I trust him," he said doubtfully.

Melanie's hand disengaged his as he moved towards the van. Samuel had already disappeared inside. When he gained the threshold Paul looked back at Melanie hanging there in the alley looking helpless. Suddenly she darted towards him and they leapt into the inky blackness together and the door clanked shut.

The van bobbed and squeaked as it sped along into the dusk; it obviously wasn't sticking to legal roads either. It seemed to be gasoline powered so, with its range, they could end up anywhere. Inside, the occupants felt around in the darkness seeking a handhold. A dim ceiling light flickered on and illuminated the company in a faint yellow glow.

They were sitting on a bench running the length of the van. Samuel was to his left and Melanie was holding his right hand. Across from him sat a young man, likely not much older than himself, staring intently at the floor. Beside him, across from Samuel, there was a heavy set woman in a shapeless monochrome coat with a bonnet strapped under her chin. The shadow cast by the hat concealed her eyes, but Paul deduced from her jaw line and figure that she was an older woman. There were others there too.

Samuel suddenly piped up, "Elizabeth!" He leaned forward extending his arms towards the woman.

"Well I'll be…" she exclaimed, "…it's you! I didn't recognize you in the darkness." She reached out and clasped hands.

"No, I didn't recognize you immediately either," he laughed, "but you haven't changed a bit."

"Oh, still the charmer!" she giggled. Her head rolled back with the effort, and Paul caught sight of a friendly matronly face with dusty brown eyebrows and ruddy chubby cheeks. "What are you doing here?"

"I know the family," Samuel explained. "I knew them…" He glanced at Paul and Melanie out of the corner of his eye. "Well, I've known them for a long time now."

Elizabeth pressed on un-self-consciously. "It's their third I believe."

"Fourth," Samuel replied. "Two girls, one boy."

"Oh wonderful." Elizabeth sat beaming with her hands folded on her lap.

"So you are assisting?"

"Yes." A sudden lurch of the van almost tossed her off her seat. "Oh, this is hard on the old bones," she groaned. "I was called in late. The other couldn't get through."

Samuel nodded, fully understanding.

Paul and Melanie listened intently, trying to piece together the storyline of the drama they had blundered into. The man opposite raised his head slightly at one point to examine his fellow travelers but then returned to his original position without speaking. Paul saw the tension in his fingers which grasped the edge of the bench between his legs like a bronco buster to arrest the effect of the wildly swaying van. Paul would have liked to talk to Melanie and see how she was, but he felt constrained in that company.

Elizabeth's head turned slightly in his direction and he knew she was surveying him, although her eyes remained hidden. Samuel must have noticed also. "They are with me," he said to her. "My friend, Paul and his friend, Melanie."

Paul was comforted Samuel referred to him as *my friend*.

"Melanie?" She looked questioningly at Samuel for a moment then her lips turned up and broke into a friendly smile. "Oh, it's so nice to see young people."

The van slowed abruptly then pitched forward. "We are going underground," Paul thought. The van leveled out and crept forward slowly before finally lurching to a stop. The doors burst open immediately.

"Hello!" a jolly voice bellowed. "Just in time for the party. Hi Liz! Hurry! They asked for you." The young man followed Elizabeth out of the van; then Samuel.

"Samuel! Long time no see!"

"Nicolas!" The two hugged each other. Paul caught sight of a man dressed in a black felt overcoat and black beret. He must have just arrived too.

Paul stepped down and helped Melanie. They were in an underground parking lot as expected. It was unlit except for a red bulb glowing above a nearby door.

"I brought two young people Nicolas. It's okay?"

The bereted man became serious. He looked them over quickly and broke into a toothy grin. "Okay? The more the merrier! What a night! What a night! A little chilly, eh? Come, come, come," he urged as he skipped off like a leprechaun towards the door where Elizabeth and the others had exited. Paul and Melanie followed everyone inside leaving the garage silent but for the ping ping of the cooling van.

The hallway was poorly lit, the concrete damp, the paint peeling. Their shoes echoed noisily in the still night. They marched down two flights of stairs then burst through a fire door into a startling light.

A middle-aged man and women, grinning from ear to ear with arms around each other, disentangled from the rest when they saw Samuel. "Hey Sam! Just in time!"

It was a carnival atmosphere. Samuel was busy pumping hands, hugging, slapping people on the back and being jostled in return. He tossed his coat in the corner and pushed through to a larger room where the crowd was even more clamorous.

Paul figured it must be a celebration of some sort. "What's happening?" he shouted to Samuel.

Samuel face was animated, joyous. "It's a birth!" he exclaimed wide eyed.

Paul didn't understand.

"A new life is coming into the world," Samuel explained, "another image of God."

"I think someone is birthing!" Melanie whispered into Paul's ear.

Samuel nodded an exuberant "Yes!" and threw his arms around her lifting her off her feet.

Paul's mouth went agog in disbelief. "A birthing? Outside of Mother? Can you do that? You can't do that..." he stammered.

Samuel dropped a disheveled giggling Melanie and turned to him. "*Can't? We can't?*" He flicked his nose with his stubby fingers. "We thumb our noses at your *can't*! We defy the pompous powers-that-be! We renounce and denounce your state-sanctioned surrogate 'mother' with her cold tentacles smothering her human commodity. We take back our own, our families; we take back our humanity!" He winked and laughed haughtily and plunged into the crowd.

Paul knew that people had once produced children themselves, generations ago. He hadn't seen a baby before, except that time at Mother—from a distance. It was an exciting prospect, to actually see a baby close-up; a self-birthed one at that.

Another thought thrust to mind: *These people are devos—that's why they are doing this—they don't want the child to be integrated into One World.* A shiver ran down his spine and he felt vulnerable at that moment, in alien country without support.

Samuel reappeared and called to them. "Come over here! You will see!"

Paul and Melanie, hands clasped, nudged shyly through the animated company. It got even more congested as they inched toward the door with the small round window that seemed the focus of the guests. They couldn't get close enough to see what was happening inside so they huddled together while their heads pivoted frantically to take in all the chatter.

Then they heard it: a plaintive bawl like a primordial exclamation point—like nothing they had ever heard before. The crowd hushed.

"It's a boy!" an unseen voice declared. They stood on their tip toes, straining, straining to see.

Nicolas nudged to the center of the room and gestured for everyone to be quiet. "Please, please everyone…" The voices were stilled. Nicolas stretched out his arms as if to embrace the company. "Everyone… in accordance with the occasion, let us give thanks to our heavenly Father, who gives us life." They gathered around and lowered their heads. Paul and Melanie exchanged glances and lowered theirs also.

"Most gracious Father, we praise you, the creator and sustainer of life. We thank you for this gift of new life. Instruct us as we seek your will." He chuckled as the newborn's howl pre-empted his devotional. "Oh most merciful God, we ask that you take this child into your bosom and shelter him under your mighty wing. May these, your people, guide him and instruct him in your ways. May he enjoy your presence; may he pursue the straight path and come to the place of peace. This we pray, by the Spirit, in the name of your son Jesus Christ, our Lord— Amen."

The room echoed with a communal "Amen."

Nicolas skipped over to the door with the little window and peered inside as if looking for a signal. The minutes stretched on. Then he stepped back adroitly and the door opened as if enchanted. "Brothers, sisters." Nicolas took the door and his eyes lit up and his teeth dazzled, "Meet your newest brother…Erastus!"

The crowd pressed to the door. "Order, order, don't push" Nicolas cautioned them laughingly. Someone had brought the baby out and Paul and Melanie could hear everyone nattering and cooing over him. They strained to catch a glimpse, but there were too many pressing around.

Suddenly, the body in front of her shifted and Melanie found herself staring into a little cherubim face not two feet away. Its eyes were pressed tightly shut and its nose crinkled up. A little doll hand rested on the woolen blanket. She reached out shyly then stopped and looked up at the woman holding the baby. The smiling face nodded back so Mel let her forefinger brush against the back of the miniscule hand. The skin felt silky and hot. The baby snuffled and puckered its mouth, and the little hand stirred and closed around Mel's finger. Mel gasped and looked at the other woman who laughed. Melanie laughed too.

"Why are they so obsessed with it?" Paul whispered to Samuel. "Lots of babies are born every day." He was contrasting how efficient the birthing process had been at Mother.

Samuel darted a glance back at Paul. "It's inherent in the Christian character. Perhaps, in some way, it defines it." An impish grin spread over his face. "It's an addiction to life."

Paul didn't have time to inquire further. The women and child had moved on so he and Melanie stuck close to Samuel as he squeezed through the crowd into another room. The place was a hive of labyrinthine passages and alcoves.

The chamber they found themselves in was quieter than the others. People were standing in small groups or sitting on the chairs that ringed the room in places, conversing. There was a small table with a few pitchers of water and some glasses. Samuel circulated around, speaking with one, patting another on the back.

Melanie noticed a woman off to one side. She was an older lady, perhaps sixty, sitting in a motorized wheelchair although Melanie couldn't ascertain her injury. Her head and plump calves, swollen feet and the tips of her fingers were the only things that protruded from the plaid quilt she was bundled in. The strangest thing was, except for her facial expressions, she didn't seem to move at all. Others stooped down to have a word with her but she would reply without moving her body. Melanie strained to try to hear what she was saying but her voice was faint.

After a while she turned her attention to five people standing by the opposite wall talking to people as they passed. The group consisted of two adults—male and female—and three children. What interested Melanie was that the adults would touch and hold hands and the man stroked the woman's hair at times and even put his arm around her waist so casually. More curious still, they both rested their hands on the children's shoulders as if presenting them to the company—there was a prideful glow in their faces when others took interest in the children. Added to this, Melanie noticed that one of the girls and the boy looked a lot like the woman and the other, who was fairer and stouter, resembled the man in many ways.

Melanie realized they were the children's biological progenitors! She was appalled. *How can they parade their 'family' so brazenly, right in public!*

When she got past the shock she was surprised that her feeling of revulsion was not as strong as their behavior warranted. She felt ashamed staring at them, but the interactions between the members of the group captivated her—the deference of the adults to each another and the trust between the children and the adults. *They are a little society unto themselves.*

"Ah, here you are!" Samuel startled her. "Let me introduce you to some people," he said taking she and Paul by the hand and leading them towards a young woman in a deep blue silken dress with long blue-black hair and graceful red lips. "This is Priscilla. How are things in Derbe? How's Aquila?"

Priscilla smiled broadly revealing ivory teeth. She glanced quickly at Paul. "Ah yes, we miss you there. You haven't been by in…"

"It's been a bit difficult…"

"Yes, I know," the girl conceded. "Aquila is doing well. He's just completing his degree."

"Aha! What, two years ahead?" Samuel exclaimed, "He was always such a clever boy." He turned to Paul and Melanie. "I brought two young people. This is Paul," he said patting him on the shoulder.

"Nice to meet you," Paul nodded. She was almost as tall as he.

Priscilla's speckled gray eyes twinkled.

"And this is Melanie."

Priscilla look perplexed for a brief moment but recovered and extended her hand with a cautious smile.

Melanie shook the taller girl's hand. "Nice to meet you."

"They're not believers," Samuel explained.

"Ah, yes," Priscilla emitted, coloring slightly. Her hands smoothed down her skirts. Paul suddenly understood the reason for Priscilla's confounded look: it was Mel's name; it wasn't a biblical name.

"Paul is a graduating student. He is writing his Induction paper on Christianity," Samuel offered.

Priscilla's smoky eyes widened in astonishment. "A very curious topic for an Induction paper."

Paul grinned in response. "Actually, I'm comparing the Christian worldview to the modern one… you know, trying to compare and contrast the basic beliefs of each." He cringed sheepishly and felt a bit silly explaining his paper to her, not at all like the sophisticated politico he esteemed himself to be.

"Oh, very interesting," she replied. "You are fortunate to have Samuel then." Her eyes sparkled with a note of humor. "So what have you concluded to be the foundation of both? What is the essence of each?"

"Um, well I'm just getting started. Samuel's lent me some books," he fumbled.

Priscilla grinned mischievously. "So, have you learned anything to-night?"

Paul grinned back. "Yes, well, I've never been to a birthing before."

A silvery laugh erupted from her lips. "No I guess you wouldn't. It must seem strange to you."

"No... well, yes," Paul laughed.

Priscilla laughed out loud again.

"I think I'm starting to understand something that I didn't really see before..." Paul felt for the words. "Christians say 'God is love,' but what you mean is 'God is life'?"

"Oh!" Priscilla's eyes became more earnest. "You could say that." Her stenciled black brows straightened. "Everyone's path is predicated on how they respond to one ultimate decision: to choose Jesus or to choose death. But, I suppose, each of life's smaller decisions reflect that larger choice also. In these smaller decisions we Christians choose life also. You understand?"

Paul desperately wanted to understand, but Melanie was becoming impatient with the company and Samuel cut in. "Oh, here's someone else," he interjected, hustling them away. "Later, Priscilla," he winked. Priscilla narrowed her eyes and gave him a side glance in response.

Samuel brought them to two young people, a boy and a girl, perhaps thirteen or fourteen. "This is Nethanel and Miriam. Nethanel is a musician; he plays piano." Samuel ruffled the boy's sandy-haired head. "And we believe Miriam is to be a physician. How are things, dear?" he said to the elder.

Paul noticed how similar Mariam's features were to Nethanel's. "Lots of studying, Uncle Samuel," she began. "Hey! I won the Luke last semester; did you hear Uncle Sam?"

Samuel laughed, "Of course. Don't you think I keep track of my kids?" He winked at Nethanel who smirked back.

Mariam continued, "I'm doing fine but I can't wait for summer break." Her face lit up. "We're going to go to Laodicea next spring; Iddo says anyway..."

"Ruth is there, right?"

Mariam clapped her hands. "Uh, huh. I haven't seen her since Three Taverns."

The boy had remained quiet, following the conversation with his eyes, so Paul tried to engage him.

"So you want to be a musician?"

Nethanel hesitated before speaking as if gauging if it was appropriate to respond. "Yes, that's what I hope."

Paul thought of Cal. "It's a demanding profession; when were you told you were going to be a musician?"

Nethanel looked confused.

Samuel stepped in. "Nethanel has always loved the piano." He looked at the boy. "I think it was when you heard Lee Song perform that time, at the Forum, remember?"

Nethanel's eyes lit up. "Yes, that's the first time I think I really felt I wanted to be a pianist!"

Now it was Paul who was perplexed. If he understood correctly, Nethanel had just chosen his own career without the necessary genetic analysis and vital early conditioning—on a personal whim. *How could they know if he was going to be any good at it?* he wondered to himself. *Perhaps that's why you never saw any devo pianists performing at Huxley Hall.* He realized how stupid that would have sounded and found relieved confirmation in the attentive faces of the young people that he had not spoken aloud.

Melanie was likewise troubled by Nethanel's disclosure. "Are your birth agents here?" she blurted out, suspecting his delinquency to be consistent with just such an aberrant social arrangement.

Nethanel's face froze. His mouth shut tightly and Melanie saw his eyes grow watery. He covered them with his sleeve and turned away. Miriam moved to put her arm around his shoulders, but he sloughed it off and walked away. The girl looked apologetic at Melanie. "I'm sorry. He's had a very hard time coping. It has only been three months."

Melanie stood rooted, pained in the uncertainty of her transgression.

"Mister and Mrs. Franklin were taken by the police," Samuel explained gravely. He hugged Miriam who buried her face in his jacket and sobbed. An elderly woman saw her distress, approached and questioned Samuel who spoke quietly to her. She glanced quickly—Melanie thought accusingly—at her and Paul, then led Miriam away.

Samuel shrugged awkwardly. "Well, there's others you should meet."

"Do you know what happened to them," Melanie asked, "their birth agents?"

Samuel's expression was pained. "The Ministry of Equality captured them. They were outside in… well, in a park. They used to like to walk there in the evening. A detachment of MoE descended on them before the sentinels could react. They failed to scan."

Melanie understood that adult devos—she knew that's what they all were here—would be detected immediately by police scanners because they had inactive transponders. She had heard that some of them were not chipped at all. "So where are they now; where are they held?" She felt responsible for their wellbeing somehow.

Samuel stared blankly at her.

"Did you know them?" Paul interjected.

"Yes. I was the godfather of Mr. Franklin." He looked sadly at Paul. "Ah well." He looked around the room. "Oh look, here is someone else you should meet," he said "Your namesake practically. Mel, meet Mel."

They turned and the woman in the wheelchair was there. "This is Melinda," Samuel announced proudly.

"Hi," Melanie said brightly, reaching out her hand. The other smiled but her body remained motionless. Mel's hand fell back to her side awkwardly.

"It's okay, Melanie. Melinda is paralyzed from the neck down," Samuel said.

Melanie nearly jumped back.

"MS," Melinda's weak voice added.

"Multiple sclerosis," Paul said. "It does something to the brain..."

"Yes. In very bad cases, like Melinda's here, you can lose all your motor capabilities. She's had it since she was, oh, twenty-five, twenty-six?" Samuel looked to Melinda, who nodded. "She was a business executive—finance I believe." Melinda nodded again and looked nostalgic. "She keeps an eye on things around here now—watching the perimeter."

Paul was flabbergasted in the presence of this rare specimen—he had never spoken with a malfunctioning human before. He subjected her to a close scrutiny.

Melanie had been looking at Melinda's motionless hands and now edged closer to the wheelchair.

"Can you feel?" she asked meekly. She reached out and touched the fingers of Melinda's left hand. It felt cold.

Melinda nodded and smiled, "Oh yes; that works." She beamed contentedly. "Good to feel another hand on mine—the warmth."

Melanie rubbed the old woman's hands. "It must be hard for you to keep warm when you can't move."

"Ah, good for the circulation," the older woman purred.

Melanie grinned down at her, then at Paul. *She's forgotten about the scene with Nethanel. It hasn't made her afraid of talking with these people,* he thought, fondly. *She sure has a… dauntless character.*

Melinda's chair suddenly skirted forward a few inches.

"How did you do that! How did you make the chair move?" an astounded Melanie exclaimed. She had been watching Melinda closely and hadn't detected any body movement.

Melinda laughed delightedly at Melanie's bewilderment. "Just a slight tilt of my head, dear."

"She doesn't have a biblical name," Paul whispered to Samuel.

Samuel grinned. "You've noticed that."

"That you all have biblical names, yeah," Paul said, "but I don't recall a *Melinda* in the Bible."

Samuel shrugged. "Yes, well, it's better if one of us is captured that they don't know the names of the others." He chuckled. "We even try to forget our own names if possible." He looked at Paul significantly. "Melinda came to us late. She doesn't go out."

Paul understood immediately; a person as severely damaged as Melinda would be reported and given relief immediately. These people were keeping her alive for some reason, as if her life had some value to them irrespective of its circumstances. His first reaction to this propping up of this husk of a person was revulsion—there was something ghoulish about it. But alongside that was another, barely palpable perception: he could sense a bond between the helpless woman and the rest that was different from any he had encountered. He knew, somehow, they needed her as much as she needed them; somehow they were benefitting as much as she from the relationship, as insane as that seemed. He felt compelled to linger there and tap into that energy if he could, whatever it was.

Melinda was chatting with one of the other women who had bent down close to hear her diminished voice. Paul watched them getting on. *How hard it must be for someone like her,* he pondered, *and yet she keeps going on. A testimony to the irrationality of the human spirit?* He wondered what he would do if he were in her place. *Would my life be worth living?* Maybe it was different looking from her side of the ledger—she did have this community to support her.

Samuel left them for a while—he had some business to attend to—so they filled the time observing the various conversations and interactions of the denizens. It was a lot more fun than Culture Studies class. Melanie wanted to see the baby again, but he had been retired for the night.

Samuel finally returned. "How do you keep this place secret?" Paul said quietly.

Samuel smiled. "It's not really a *place*, it's a community. It occupies different places at different times."

Paul wasn't sure he understood.

"God knows there's an endless supply of unused buildings." Samuel glanced at his watch and exclaimed, "twelve twenty-five!" He turned to Paul and Melanie. "We have five minutes to get back! Come, come." He led them hastily through the gathering, nodding here, smiling there. They tossed their coats on as they hurried up the stairs and the narrow twisting hallway back to the underground parking lot. A dark blue van was idling there under the solitary bulb and an attendant was just closing the rear door.

"Hold it, hold it!" Samuel called. "Three more."

They jumped into the back and the door closed behind them immediately leaving them feeling around in its shadowy confines, looking for a place to sit. There seemed to be five or six others there. A few shuffled over to allow the trio adjacent seats as the van started on its way.

As his eyes became accustomed to the light Paul could make out several of the other commuters. Two girls, around Paul and Melanie's age, chattered quietly. An older man snoozed in the corner, his cap drawn down over his eyes.

It is like a secret transit system, Paul thought, '*the devo express.*' An alarming thought crossed his mind: *What if we are stopped by the police?* He and Mel didn't have travel permits. He looked around at the others again. They seemed unconcerned by the prospect; perhaps they were frequent travelers. *At least Mel and I would scan*, he assured himself. He remembered Samuel's hasty retreat into the alleyway earlier that night, when the maria drove by. *He wouldn't scan.* It was the first time he had admitted this to himself.

He considered the situation of these people. *They must live their whole lives on edge like this, knowing they could be arrested at any time. Generations of them living like this. What must that be like?* He looked them over again. They weren't overtly agitated. *They must get used to it*, he thought, *like prisoners in a death camp.* It was startling that that comparison suggested itself.

The sound of a siren nearby disrupted his thoughts. The others quieted. It rose to a crescendo in front then faded to the rear. Paul leaned back in his seat, relieved. Melanie gasped and wrenched her hand from his sweaty grip. The two girls began to talk again. The man still slept.

Paul reviewed the night's happenings. He felt he had learned more about Christianity tonight than he had in reading all his books even though there had been no talk about their religion—no metaphysical dissertations; no creedal formulations; no quotes from the Bible. It had all come out in their manner and speech.

Their obsession with life was a new angle. What was it Priscilla had said—*a constant choosing of life*? It had something to do with what Samuel had said once: a sanctity of life ethic versus a quality of life one. He remembered that phrase but couldn't grasp the implications of it completely. He suspected Samuel intended Melinda to be an illustration.

Their grouping into families based on biological relation seemed essential to their worldview also. He had to try to understand that. The way the 'parents' interacted—the trust between them all. *That must be what happens when people are together so long*, he reasoned.

He realized immediately the danger of the family cell to the greater society—the autonomy of the parents and their authority over the children. *How does devo society hold together when the state's power is so constrained?*

The van finally lurched to a stop. "We get out here," Samuel said as the door opened. The three exited hastily and a man in a balaclava slammed the door after them then scurried back and hopped into the passenger side and the vehicle squealed off into the night. It had a tight schedule apparently.

The trio were standing on a deserted street which Paul did not recognize. A car rushed through an intersection a few blocks away. It looked like a major thoroughfare.

"The subway is just a few blocks up that way," Samuel said gesturing in the direction of the intersection. "You need to get out of downtown by curfew." Their shoes clop-clopped on the sidewalk as they walked—the city was quiet out this far from the core. The air remained surprisingly crisp and heavy for that time of year.

When they got to the intersection Paul recognized it as Darwin Street West; there was a church tower to the east he remembered from a party he had attended.

With Samuel leading, they walked the short distance to York Road and crossed to the north side of Darwin. "The subway is just there," Samuel said pointing to the luminescent green triangular sign just ahead of them. Paul and Melanie walked on but Samuel didn't follow.

Paul stopped and looked back and saw him standing on the corner. "You coming, Sam?"

"No. I'll see you later."

Paul stood there a moment looking at the old man still and silent, totem-like, beneath the street lamp.

He wouldn't scan.

Paul turned and walked with Melanie to the subway.

They rode the train in silence, both lost in thought. Thankfully, no police questioned them. At Davisville they emerged and found themselves standing in a park looking up at the summer sky. They had been transported there as if in a dream. Neither had spoken; neither wanted to go inside.

Melanie emerged from her reverie. "It all just seems so unreal... this night."

Paul nodded but said nothing.

They were silent again for a long time before Melanie spoke. "All those people... they were all just... it was like a big celebration..."

"Of life," Paul said quietly.

Melanie pulled him closer to keep warm. They stood there a long while, arm in arm, staring up at the glittering stars.

21

Day 91

Love

"**B**ut shouldn't a woman have the right to choose then? I mean, if she wants to have a baby she should be able to; if not, she should be allowed to get an abortion. That way everyone can choose which is best for them personally; no one is forced to do anything they don't want to do," Paul urged.

Samuel threw up his hands in exasperation. "This isn't about *choice*! I believe in choice as much as you do; more so even. I believe a woman should be able to marry whomever she wants, read whatever she wants, learn what she wants, pursue whichever career she desires, raise her own children. How many of these 'choices' do you—does One World—countenance?"

He glared at Paul. "What *choice* does the child have?"

Paul stared back.

The old man scowled. "A true culture of choice would insist on freedom of action, yes, but also on the obligation to take responsibility for one's actions. But the pro-abortionist wants their unborn child to assume the liability for their actions and endure the consequences. So they are hardly seeking a culture where personal autonomy is respected but rather one where choice is demeaned. They abhor real choice, with all its obligations, as it would oblige them to expand beyond their self-absorbed little worlds."

It was a bizarre discussion—whether a woman had the right to terminate her pregnancy. *Baby* was too abstract an entity to have any weight in ethical deliberations in One World so Paul had to imagine living back in proto-Ascension times, when Christianity still influenced the public's thinking, and work up into their mindset in order to experience the force of the arguments. The visit to the devo colony (*Catacomb*, Samuel said it was called) with Mel and seeing there the families and the newborn helped a lot. He had also reviewed the reproductive justice units from his Cultural Evolution classes to familiarize himself with the historical arguments.

"I just believe a woman should have the right to do what she wants with her body," Paul persisted. "Why should she be restricted by someone else's religious beliefs?"

Samuel pounced. "*Her body* you say? How is the child growing in her, *her* body? Every cell in a body contains a copy of that body's unique DNA, like a fingerprint. But the fetus' DNA is distinct from its mother's; it is a separate organism. It is also autonomous, directing its own development. So on what grounds can you call it part of her body? What is its bodily function?" He waved his hands in the air flippantly. "Is it a component of her vascular system? Is it perhaps used to regulate the metabolism? Maybe it's a third kidney."

Paul's lips drew taut in the face of Samuel's drollery.

"If you believe the fetus is just part of her body and not a separate being why do you call it *abortion* anyway? Why not *amputation*?" He looked challengingly at Paul. "No, the very terminology used by pro-abortionists reveals they are perfectly aware that the fetus is not part of the woman's body. Clearly, the pro-life and pro-choice positions don't differ concerning what a woman can do with her own body, they differ on what she can do with her unborn child's body."

He sighed wearily. "As do all pro-choice advocates, in order to exempt yourself from presenting a reasoned defense of your position, you seek to dismiss the pro-life case out of hand saying it is argued from a position of religious belief only. Fact"—he held up one finger—"the unborn is human. Fact"—adding a second digit—"the embryo pursues its own development from conception to birth and therefore, fact: life begins at conception. Fact: the embryo is not part of the woman's body it is a separate being with its own unique DNA." He held his extended fingers before Paul, "Which of these facts are *religious*?"

Paul didn't take up the challenge. "But you can't compare a fetus to a baby. Most abortions are done within the first trimester when it's just a clump of cells."

"Clump of cells?" Samuel cried. "Within three weeks the baby has a beating heart! By the fifth week its brain has developed, it has sexual organs and developing limbs and it hasn't even reached the 'fetus' stage yet!" He was staring wide-eyed at Paul. "*Clump of cells*! Do you understand what an abortion is? Do you know what is left in the abortionist's pan after he has completed his deed?"

Paul buried his hands in his pockets.

"How is its age even relevant? What mere 'clump of cells' can fashion itself into a living child?" Samuel scowled. "Surely you can discern the uniqueness—the potential—of the fetus."

He re-seated himself and continued in a more subdued voice. "If you are motivated by reasoning and science and you believe in human rights then why do these facts not determine your position on abortion?" He thrust out his chin. "What science backs your claim that the fetus hasn't a right to life? Present your reasoning please."

Paul waved the challenge aside. "Okay, the fetus is a human being and not part of the mother's body, I'll grant that, but that doesn't mean it is a person."

Samuel signed. "What do you mean 'person'?"

"I mean, the fetus isn't really conscious, it's not fully aware of its surroundings, so it doesn't really qualify as a person."

"Oh, I see," Samuel replied. "A two year old isn't fully aware either; tell me, is it a *person* then? How about a seventeen year old? I ask because the brain doesn't mature completely until eighteen years at the earliest—are you a *person*?"

Paul was un-dissuaded. "But a two-year old is much more aware than a fetus so it is a person and has rights."

"So a two-year old is a person but a fetus isn't," Samuel repeated mincingly. "Tell me, how does this happen; when does a human become a person? Can you witness its personhood arriving? Can you, say, detect it with a blood test or an X-ray?"

"The government sets the guidelines," Paul replied obliquely. "I believe it's about sixty days after birth. By then they know if the baby has any problems."

"Oh, so personhood descends from on high!" Samuel responded ironically his arms raised heavenward. "What you are saying is, if the technicians judge the child to be a useful addition to One World they bestow the attribute of *person* upon it. Conversely, if the child exhibits some defect or deformity which might hinder its progress personhood is not bestowed, and since the child is not a person, it can be exterminated without violating moral principle."

Paul glared at him defiantly. "Yeah."

Samuel frowned. "Don't you find your reasoning circular? If it is true that personhood is just an endorsement of the child's worth in the eyes of its judges why not just say plainly that we kill the child because we don't think its life will contribute to our happiness? Why fabricate this fiction *personhood*? Why discard your logical razor now?"

Paul looked steadily at his interrogator who continued. "Hitler said Jews were not persons and so could be exterminated. What criteria did he employ to determine if they were persons? The same as the pro-abortionist: if they were undesirable they were *non-persons*. Gypsies were also non-persons. Neither were the mentally handicapped nor the physically disabled, persons." He nodded sharply to Paul. "The *non-person* designation discloses more about the person employing it than it does his victim; it says more about the pro-choicer than the fetus.

"No, the essence of the fetus lies not in its person-ness, but in its humanity."

Paul sighed. "I just don't think people should be able to impose their personal views on others. People have rights. I mean, maybe I'm personally not comfortable with abortion either, but I don't think I should be able to impose my views on someone else."

"So if your neighbor believed in slavery your position would be 'Well I don't personally believe in it but I won't question your right to engage in it'?"

"No, but I don't see how that's the same…"

"Don't you? The pro-abortionist says there are two kinds of humans: those with rights and those without; that the position of the fetus vis-a-vis the mother is the same as that of the slave towards his master—the master has life and death authority over his human chattel. This is the essence of the evil of slavery in a nutshell. Can you really see no similarity?"

Paul shrugged.

"In fact, isn't the pro-abortionist even more radical in this regard since the slave owner degrades a stranger only, whereas the abortionist dehumanizes his own child, reducing it to sub-human status."

Samuel paused for a moment to calm himself. "You were refer-

260

ring to 'human rights', but if someone holds your right to life in their hands, how real are any of your other rights? Abortion annuls human rights comprehensively. So I have to ask again—"

A siren's wail interrupted him. Both sat rigid as it approached. It whined by and faded out in the distance.

Samuel's form reanimated like a statue returning to life. "So I have to ask again, why do you, an intelligent, logical person, support abortion? It can't be because abortion is not the unjust taking of another human's life—murder—because you know the fetus is human and you know it has done nothing to warrant execution. It can't be because the fetus is not a person because you know that 'non-person' is merely a label we attach to humans we desire to be rid of; it doesn't offer a justification for our assumed right to do so. Again, it can't be because of a reluctance to impose your views on others because in other cases, such as slavery, you have no such scruple. It can't be because you believe in human rights because abortion obliterates all human rights by denying the most basic human right." Samuel looked to Paul challengingly. "So, given all this, why are you *pro-choice*?"

Paul hardened his brow. "Say the woman was raped. Surely you would agree she should be able to get pregnancy relief? I mean, how cruel would that be to have to carry a child who would remind you of that every time you looked at it."

"Yes, it isn't fair to the woman," Samuel concurred. "She'll be wounded for the rest of her life by the crime. It's a daunting task, to have the child; it would take a lot of love on her part. But can you take away the life of someone because of the crime of another? Is it just to say that the children of rape victims should be executed?"

No answer materialized.

"No. Murdering the child doesn't reverse the injustice of the rape; neither does it erase the trauma. It in fact doubles the injustice and the trauma—killing an innocent child in addition to the original emotionally scarring assault." Again he looked to Paul.

"The question you are posing is 'what should we do with people who remind us of a painful incident?' What do you think? Should we dismember and dis-embowel them?"

Paul grimaced. "It doesn't seem fair to the woman but, I guess, killing the child isn't right either."

Samuel nodded. "You must know that the pro-abortionist's appeal to extreme cases like rape was a common ploy intended to expose the supposed fanaticism of their opponents. Of course it was just a ploy—the number of such cases was miniscule, and if their opponents had amended their position to allow abortions in extreme situations it wouldn't have placated the pro-abortionists one whit since the gist of their reasoning was that human life should only be valued if it did not imperil the parent's autonomy."

He sighed. "What do you think?" he said turning to Paul. "Is papering over our moral obligations to the weak and defenseless the most compassionate way to proceed? Is it the most enlightened or merely a capitulation to shabby expediency? Does it advance us towards that state of greater humaneness that Progressives preach on about or is it a retreat from same?"

He rose from his chair and began pacing. "You see, we all have this propensity to slant the world to our advantage; to look to our own needs first. We're self-centered; it's the human condition. I don't think you would contend otherwise." Paul mounted no protest. "Progressive society reinforces this disposition for selfish pursuit; that's why it can tolerate abortion. After all, what can be expected from people living in a community that esteems self-fulfillment above all? How can they choose the wellbeing of another over their own?

"In our progressive societies *choice*, by which we mean applied selfish individualism, is elevated above love, and all the malignancies of such a society springs from that reversal."

He paused in front of Paul. "Christianity fosters a disposition to look to the needs of others. It attributes value to everyone, not just the strong and unblemished—the *wanted*. It dampens our natural selfish inclinations. As our society turned away from Christianity our lust for self-gratification was given free reign; it was encouraged and pronounced normal, healthy, *natural*."

He resumed pacing. "All the arguments made by the pro-abortionists back then were merely attempts to rationalize their selfishness." He nodded to Paul forcefully. "In truth they supported abortion not because they held a mistaken view of the humanity of the fetus, or of its right to life, or believed in any of the other sophistries. The prochoicers' shrieking denouncements of pro-lifers, their determination to silence them, and their rage when confronted with graphic images of the products of the policy they championed revealed that they knew abortion to be evil and were aware that the plain facts, if disseminated, would confirm their guilt.

"No, in reality abortion was supported because, in their lust for their own comfort and felicity—their *rights*—they could no longer allow themselves to care about others."

"But it did give women the right to control their own lives," Paul objected weakly.

Samuel halted in front of him abruptly. "Abortion gave women the *right* to be cold and uncaring."

Paul was silent for a while. When he finally spoke it was with a discordant levity. "Whew! I can see how things got pretty emotional back then." He bobbed his head enthusiastically. "I think I'll be able to really make use of this in my paper."

"Paul," Samuel asked quietly. He had returned to his chair and sat studying his guest.

Paul responded warily. "Yes?"

"Paul. We've been debating what was, I believe, a pivotal junction in our society's unfolding—when it chose to abandon the sanctity of human life ethic. You've been playing the part of the Progressive pro-choice advocate to my Christian pro-life one adequately, but what do you really feel about this subject?"

Paul turned away and busied himself organizing his book bag. "I don't know."

Samuel peered at him with a concerned, hungry, look.

Paul didn't care to engage Samuel on this front anymore, and this provided the incentive to steer their discussion to another topic; one which he had been anxious to confer on however reluctant he was to reveal his interest.

"What about marriage?"

Samuel did a double-take and his bushy eyebrows flipped up in astonishment. "What about it?"

"I saw the 'families' at Catacomb. The adults were married, right?"

The knowing look Samuel gave him embarrassed Paul. "Yes. Marriage is central to Christian community. It came to western society via Christianity."

"That's not true is it? Didn't the Romans have families?"

Samuel put his feet up on the stool and settled back on the couch, hands resting on his stomach. "Not in the same way. The Roman family was a looser confederation. In pagan culture the woman was inferior to the man, and the father owned his wife their children and their property. If he walked away from the marriage the family was left destitute. All is was quite different from the Christian situation.

"Roman marriage was often undertaken for social or political connections and to produce heirs. Divorce was an acceptable means to forge further profitable alliances. Also, it was common to seek sexual gratification outside of one's marriage. This differed substantially from the Christian ideal of two partners becoming one entity physically, socially, economically, spiritually, in a permanent union."

Here was Paul's chance to get to the subject that most interested him. "They are supposed to stay together their whole lives?"

"Yes."

"But how can you expect people to stay together forever? What if they marry, then find after a while they no longer love each other?"

Samuel smiled faintly. "When you talk about *love* you are talking about romantic feelings, but the Christian concept of love goes beyond emotion. Jesus commands us to love others but feelings cannot be commanded so, clearly, he means something other than to 'have warm gooey feelings' towards them." Paul listened attentively. "Christian love involves the sacrifice of one's interests for another. When Christians marry they are not proclaiming their romantic feelings for each other solely—that's what Progressives do—instead they promise to attend to the interests of the other. They promise to serve the other as Christ served us—he sacrificed himself out of love; he did not act to please himself. Love is evidenced more by action than it is by emotion. It is in this serving of the other that we display love most clearly."

Paul didn't pursue this last thought but continued, "Isn't living together the same thing as marriage? Why get married anyway?"

"The same as committing to marriage? No," Samuel answered. "In marriage you are promising to love your partner forever. You are saying 'I love you enough to dedicate my life to you, to give up my own interest.' In co-habitation you are saying 'I like the things you do for me, but I don't love you enough to sacrifice my own preferences.' The two couldn't be further apart. Christian marriage is about love; Progressive marriage about self-gratification."

Paul had leaned towards him, listening closely.

"So you see, the dynamic of the relationship is completely different. In marriage you have the security to be yourself, to really let yourself be known and to really get to know yourself. With co-habitation, where the other person can break off the partnership whenever they choose, you have to keep proving yourself to the other, so you never have the freedom to let yourself be known. It's a buyer-seller relationship. You understand?"

Paul nodded, "Yes, I think so. But what do you mean by 'really get to know yourself' exactly?"

Samuel chuckled. "When you live with another in such an exposed state they will get to know you better than any person ever has or will, so you have to take their observations and critical commentary seriously. Not only that but you will also be more honest in acknowledging your shortcomings and be motivated to improve, a project itself leading to yet more self-knowledge. So marriage will reveal you to yourself."

Paul laughed warily. "I don't know if I would like to get to know myself that well."

Samuel laughed too. "If you want to mature you will." He smiled openly at Paul. "When you can reveal the real you, with all your warts and foibles, to your wife and know she still loves you then you are free. You can hear her out because you are in a committed relationship and you are loved despite your flaws. This love is like the love of Jesus for us. So, for Christians, marriage is one avenue to a greater understanding of God and it's a vehicle for the honing of a more Christ-like character." His eyes elevated to the ceiling as if reciting from a higher guide. "For Jesus came to serve, like a groom for his bride, and marriage offers us the opportunity to walk the same path." He looked to Paul. "If you want to learn to really love, if you want to be genuine, free, then let marriage spur you on."

Paul was quiet, discomforted by the intimacy of the appeal.

Samuel rocked gently as he sat pondering. Suddenly he stopped. "You were wondering how you'd know if you really loved the other person before you commit to marriage, but you don't really love the person you marry."

"Huh?" Paul startled.

"I mean, at the time of your wedding you don't really know the person well enough to know if you love them in the way you are thinking. Likely you love the image of them you have built up in your mind. You're excited by the physical attraction and delighted at being with a beautiful girl who acknowledges your wonderfulness. True?"

Paul laughed but wondered, *Is that the way it is with me and Mel?*

Samuel continued on. "But we are always changing. The person you marry will be a different person in a few years, and you will too."

"That's discouraging," Paul sighed. "But I don't get it; are you saying it doesn't really matter if you like the person you marry?"

"No. I'm saying you should adjust your criteria for selecting a wife. Don't stake your choice on physical attractiveness, which is temporary. Choose someone whom you can serve and who can take that journey of mutual discovery and spiritual maturation with you."

An "ah" escaped Paul's lips. "Why are Christians so hung up on sex?" The question had been welling up inside him for a while and now spilled over.

Samuel laughed at the abruptness of the query. "What do you mean *hung up*?"

"I mean they insist that you only have sex with your spouse. But people are wired to want to have sex with lots of people. Sex with one person becomes boring after a while doesn't it?"

"It can get to be boring I suppose," Samuel answered pensively, "but having sex with a lot of people is so inevitably."

Paul laughed. "Well, I don't know about that…"

Samuel directed a sage look at Paul but didn't expand on the point. "Christians get an undeserved bad rap about sex. They believe their god invented sexual intercourse and instructed them to 'go and populate the world' after all, and if you've read your Bible you will see it's hardly the journal of a prudish people. Did you know that, before Ascension, Christian couples consistently scored highest in surveys tabulating sexual satisfaction?"

Paul smiled wryly. "That I would have to see. So then, why all the fuss?"

"Why the insistence on sexual fidelity you mean?" Samuel nodded. "There are many reasons. Even if you are a committed Darwinist, you can acknowledge Nature's primary intent for sexuality to be procreation. In order to enlist the father in this self-denying enterprise—I mean raising children—he had to be assured that the children were his own and it was imperative that the parents remain together to ensure the resources, material and emotional, were available. So, for the rearing of children and the furtherance of society, sexual fidelity was essential." He looked to Paul. "This model, a man, woman and their children, is the driving force of the ascent of nations and its disintegration marks their decline."

Paul wondered where One World stood along that spectrum.

"But beyond that the exclusive nature of the sexual relationship between husband and wife is one of the bonds that hold the relationship together. The Bible says 'the two shall become one' physically and spiritually. It's another illustration of that total self-giving that we were talking about earlier. A spouse who shares himself with others in a sexual way has not entered into the state of marriage any more than the co-habitor because the one situation is self-centric, the other spouse-centric. The adulterer says 'I love you but not enough to surrender my sexuality to you.' But this is not love at all; and it is not marriage."

Paul roused himself here. "Isn't that just the Christian societal standard, with its spouses and families? Why should that be the norm? Don't we do all that—raising children, enjoying sex—much more efficiently with the Life Center model?"

"What do you think?" Samuel smiled confidingly. "You can see the practicality of the Christian family even if you do not ascribe to Christianity. The children have a safe environment with people who are fully invested in their wellbeing. The parents have the financial and moral support of each other and the motivation for personal growth. The children see the parents and they know that love—I mean the self-sacrificial kind we have been talking about—is possible. This environment fosters a culture which encourages service and responsibility and raises societal institutions to advance these. It creates more mature, self-giving—better—people. Everyone enjoys autonomy within the family which provides security within, and with other institutions like the church, a bulwark against the tyranny of the state."

"Hold on," Paul cut in. "*Tyranny*?"

Samuel's eyes lit up. "Yes, yes, exactly what you need to understand for your paper! Let me see..." He stroked his whiskers thoughtfully. "Ah yes," he said returning to Paul, "our focus these past weeks has been on the two prominent worldviews instrumental in shaping our present culture; let's call them the Christian one and the Progressive one." Paul nodded. "At the core of each is their understanding of the basic nature of the person—the person being the fundamental building block of society. This understanding determines how each society pursues its goals and, indeed, which goals it deems worthy of pursuit."

He stood up and began to pace again. "The first, the Progressive one, sees people as basically good or at least capable of becoming good given the correct environment—education, material wellbeing, etcetera. So the direction Progressive society takes is intended to refine people, to make steady improvement in their manners and in their material provisioning and so to evolve a better society. The goal is this perfected society and the means is the heuristic betterment of man—the evolution of mankind."

"Yes, I think that pretty much describes it," Paul said. "What about the other one, the Christian?"

"The Christian worldview sees people as limited in their knowledge and clouded by sin; beings, left to their own ingenuity, incapable of the kind of transformation the Progressive desires."

"That sounds pessimistic," Paul said.

"Or realistic," Samuel enjoined. "So the goal is for people to acknowledge their sinfulness and submit to One who knows better."

Paul rolled his eyes. "Right."

"What do these societies look like in practice?" Samuel asked rhetorically. "The Progressive culture relies on experts in each field—scientists, sociologists and political overseers—to guide society towards its intended goals. The people surrender their right to direct their own lives to these experts. So Progressive society is only pluralistic in the sense that everyone is free to make their own decisions in trivial matters—important ones being the purview of the state—and it is only tolerant in that its citizenry is compelled to respect those practices the ruling elite have deemed worthy of toleration." He gestured to Paul with an open palm. "You see how the rule of experts works?"

The option didn't look as sunny to Paul now.

"The Christian society minimizes the power given to anyone since all are sinful and so cannot be trusted with absolute authority. So, instead of the state educating children for instance, in Christian society their education is the responsibility of their parents. A truly diverse citizenry with varied opinions is created rather than the homogenous herd bred by the Progressive state. Institutions exist where people of like mind can gather; differences of opinion are respected. There is a truly pluralistic and truly tolerant society."

"And *tyranny*?" Paul prompted.

Samuel nodded quickly. "Yes, as I said, in the Progressive society, with its heuristic approach to refining, perfecting, each element of society—what the citizens eat, what they drive, how they dress, which entertainments they partake—everything must be blessed by expert authority and any opposition to the state's prescription has to be crushed." Paul made to interrupt, but Samuel anticipated his question. "If it didn't do that, if it allowed unreformed areas to exist, it would be abandoning its mission," he explained. "For instance, if you believed that benign therapeutic liberal Christianity was the correct choice for an advancing society, then you cannot allow orthodox congregations to exist because they would doom cultural evolution to stagnation. All competing viewpoints must be corrected and brought into line. An atheist institution can exist in a Christian society—the atheist is just another flawed human as is the Christian himself—but a Christian one cannot be allowed to exist in a Progressive society because the Christian blights the society's perfection. This correcting of divergence, in service of the perfected society, is what Progressives mean by 'societal evolution'—*progress*—correct?"

Paul nodded a slow uncommitted nod.

"You see, in the Christian society, the Church and the family and other social institutions provide a check against the government's power. The political elite are unable to indoctrinate the youth because the family is responsible for their education—they are their children after all; they created them. The government cannot dominate the financial affairs of its citizens because other institutions, like the family, provide for their members. The state cannot intrude into their personal lives because the family is seen to exist before the state and so has a validity and authority independent of the state's sanction, etcetera.

"This liberty is anathema to the Progressive who sees the state as the provider of all social goods. For him, the family has to be made subservient to the state. Marriage, rather than being an institution existing prior to and independent of the state, becomes a social good provided and defined by the state according to its own perceived advantage. With the emasculation of the family the children become wards of the state to raise as its apparatchik see fit. Religion is no longer a check on the arrogance of the state but—as in Roman times—an instrument of the state—the various deities being interned into the Progressive pantheon. In this way, by folding everything into itself, the government is able to usurp the authority of all."

Paul was pondering the process of transforming Christian society into One World. He cut in. "The Progressive state sounds dictatorial, but if the devos thought Christian society was preferable why would they go along with the Progressive program? Why would they allow their freedoms to be taken away?"

"In an advanced Progressive society people cannot fight back because they have no organizations to represent them as these are all instruments of the state; you would have to fight the world."

"I know. But before that," Paul asked, "why didn't they fight back before it got to that point?"

"Oh." Samuel shrugged. "In short, I think the answer is self-interest; selfishness."

He plopped down on the couch again. "In pre-Ascension times we wanted sexual liberty so we allowed the state to redefine marriage to accommodate our desires—I'm speaking about no fault divorce. Not only did it undermine the stability of our unions, but in acknowledging the state's authority to re-define the institution, subjugated marriage to the state and so obliterating its ability to counteract the state's power. Similarly, homosexuals wanted self-esteem so they agreed to—no demanded—marriage's abolition and replacement with a self-affirming, Progressive institution also, confusingly enough, called *marriage*.

"Parents wanted to be relieved of the burden of tending their children, so they let the state daycares take them off their hands and also entrusted their education to the state's schools—they outsourced their parenting responsibilities. Not surprisingly, in time, they found they no longer had the right to educate their own children or raise them in their own values; the state had appropriated parental authority."

He continued his litany. "We could be looked after in our infirmity if we just turned all responsibility for our healthcare over to the government; so we did. It would decide who could have access to which medical care and, in the end, who should live and who should die.

"We agreed to allow the government to appropriate our wealth and our family's property through escalating taxes in return for the promise of security. And so the state confiscated the proceeds of our labor and reduced us to dependence."

He looked to Paul. "Oh yes. We begged them to take over our lives and relieve us of the burden and responsibility of looking after ourselves.

"Ah!" Samuel exhaled. He had remembered another anecdote. "I recall reading about the Progressive president back then. He said 'Never let a crisis go to waste,' meaning: 'Never miss an opportunity to extend government control over more of people's lives.' Progressive bureaucrats took up the cause for more stringent state controls to aid us running our lives for, we were told, there would be dire consequences if we didn't rely on their expertise to do this: it was a *war* to save our society from extinction, from racial unrest, from environmental destruction, from financial collapse, from inequality—whatever—and wartime justified extreme measures and the dictatorial powers they demanded."

He sighed. "We were complacent back then. In our prosperity we didn't appreciate how precarious our freedom was." He shrugged. "We thought we could improve on marriage by discarding the covenantal aspect relieving ourselves of any responsibility. We thought we could enhance sex lives by refusing to commit to the entanglement of relationships. Renouncing the sacrifices inherent in the rearing of children with our barren partnerships; renouncing struggle, never having to be inconvenienced, we embraced the primacy of self-actualization. We could all be takers instead of providers. The state would provide; all we had to do was surrender our liberty.

"In short, we fell victim to our appetites, our greed. Our selfishness."

"Why didn't the church step in?" Paul asked. "You said it should be the conscience of the people. It was supposed to provide a bulwark against the state."

Samuel nodded. "Like the other peoples of God in the Bible, modern Christians forgot where their security originated. They neglected to instill an understanding of their religion into their children and, in time, knowledge of Christianity faded in society. They were then vulnerable to the Progressive allurements—promises of self-fulfillment—being floated by its proponents. Sex was one of the prime allurements; a wedge that precipitated much of the rush to Progressive philosophy."

"Sex? Okay, you have to explain that," Paul chortled.

Samuel grinned good-humoredly. "Here's an example: let's go way back to the 1950's. It was a heyday of religious observance, if that is to be measured by church attendance—the churches were packed. The Christian sexual ethic—marry, raise children—which was responsible for our civilization's flourishing was an accepted societal norm; it made sense to people." He looked to Paul. "Take sexual abstinence outside of marriage for instance. If you had sex outside of marriage you were risking the chance of having to deal with unwanted children. There was no way around this given the state of contraceptive technology. So it made sense to everyone to restrict sex to marriage—or to get married if a child came along." He nodded to Paul again. "The thing that people thought most accommodating to their own desires coincided with what the church was teaching."

Paul nodded. "So far so good."

Samuel continued. "Then along comes the sexual revolution of the 60's. Contraceptives—the pill—are readily available—first to married couples in an effort to hold the line with existing moral standards, but they quickly become available to everyone of course. People could now

-225- James Tennant

have sex without having to risk pregnancy and unwanted parental responsibility. We could all live the Hugh Hefner lifestyle."

"Yeah," Paul grinned approvingly. In his Cultural Evolution classes he had learned about the pioneering efforts of Hef in liberating the West from devo sexual restrictions.

Samuel checked him with a censorious look. "So a course of action very much against the church's teachings—having sexual relations outside of marriage—was feasible."

Paul smirked. "So I would guess the church's teaching would lose out."

"Yes. People perhaps continued to attend church services although they no longer supported the church on this, I would say quite pivotal, topic."

"So really, full churches don't necessarily indicate a high commitment to Christianity," Paul said, more to himself than to his friend.

"No. But a full church does signify a certain pragmatic acceptance of Christian norms," Samuel answered.

"Yes, I see," Paul replied slowly. "So the church could have a strong influence on society even if people weren't real believers."

Samuel nodded. "So what had been shown was—what had always been true for most churchgoers—that they were not following the Bible's guidance because they thought it authoritative by virtue of its divine origin, but that it corresponded to their own thinking. The contraception issue just brought this fact to light."

Paul nodded inviting Samuel to continue.

"People started to say that the church was 'behind the times' or 'living in the dark ages' etcetera. Of course, the question wasn't about the church being out of date but whether the Bible was the authoritative exposition of God's will."

"Right," Paul interjected. "If you believed the Bible to be out of date you could hardly assert that it came from God—it was just the opinions of some ancient sheep herders. So then your Christianity became more of a philosophy, or personal ethic, rather than a religious claim to absolute Truth."

"Exactly," Samuel grinned, pleased that Paul was tracking with him. "So here was another one of those pivotal revolutions in our culture, like no fault divorce, that went unnoticed at the time. Religion became, as you say, a matter of personal preference or opinion; it had been privatized so to speak. It became one of those trivial decisions left to us—whether to

272

do Jesus or Buddha or Mother Gaia or some combination of the bunch. Trivialized so, it could no longer exercise an effective restraint on the state's hegemony over public discourse. Another safeguard to state tyranny had fallen."

"*No-fault divorce*. What was that exactly?" Paul asked.

"Ah. Our national government introduced no fault divorce into law back in 1986. This stipulated that either spouse could terminate the marriage without justification. The idea was to make it easier for disenchanted couples to dissolve their marriages without the lengthy and costly legal wrangling inherent in the process."

"Sounds reasonable on the surface," Paul said.

"But as we've said, without a binding commitment marriage is a completely different relationship—it's one of personal convenience rather than of self-giving—and none of the benefits of marriage can be realized under a regime devoted to self-fulfillment. No fault divorce simply renamed co-habitation 'marriage.' A revolution in our culture had taken place and no one noticed: from that point on we were all co-habitors."

"Ah, I see," Paul said pensively. He thought for a moment. "So the societal rot advanced by stealth through the industry of well-meaning individuals—often by Christians divorced from the Bible."

Samuel nodded, "Yes. Well put. As with abortion, no fault divorce elevated choice over love. It was a precursor to the *choice* revolution, from whence came revolving-door divorce, abortion, same-sex marriage, polygamy, euthanasia, intergenerational sex—all the relationships of self-actualization, *choice*." He looked at Paul remorsefully. "When it came time to ban marriage there was nothing of consequence left to defend.

"In its fervor to be seen as *compassionate* and *relevant* the Church jettisoned the Truth that had been entrusted to it and rushed to prostitute itself to the idols of selfish pursuit."

Paul picked up the thread of the conversation. "I suppose the Christians wanted to dispel any ideas that they were the narrow-minded killjoys they were accused of being by people who wanted to abolish the morality that, as you say, had been the foundation of their society. They didn't want to look stupid; like they were holding evolution back."

Samuel nodded emphatically. "Yes. You can understand why they would be susceptible to that. After all, the Church *had* been wildly successful in advancing positive social change."

"Like the abolition of slavery you mean," Paul said.

"Yes, exactly," Samuel said, "but also poverty alleviation, woman's rights, public health care and education, etcetera. The Church's accomplishments were stellar. The problem was that the Church got it into its head that salvation could come from conscientious societal management and that bringing about this Utopia was the totality of the Christian mission distilled down to the rubric of 'social justice.' As you can imagine, it was much easier to promote social justice—which was really a euphemism for self-gratification—than to proclaim the gospel in the teeth of the sexual revolution or in the glow of the civil rights successes. We wanted to be players in the emerging Utopia project. We wanted to be *relevant*.

"Once this social justice gospel had been injected into the veins of a congregation its progression proved irresistible and its consequence fatal." He pressed his fingers to his temples. "We substituted the gospel of love for the one of self-fulfillment; gave up Heaven for the allurement of Utopia."

"I see," Paul mumbled vaguely. He was lost in his thoughts momentarily—thinking about Gretchen and Harmony. "So the church was no longer about spreading the Gospel, I mean talking about God's work, it was about improving mankind's material wellbeing on Earth. In other words, it was on the same mission as the Progressives—the subversion was complete."

"Yes, exactly." Samuel nodded and smiled as a proud tutor would at an accomplished student. "If Christian duty could be reduced to the furtherance of the utopian cause du jour then the church must be counted as a vassal of the Progressive state." He shrugged resignedly at Paul. "And so it was."

A thought presented itself to Paul. "It seems to me the people themselves changed through all this. I mean, they had originally been willing to give up their time and money to raise children, but I can't imagine people at the time of, say, pre-Ascension, doing that."

"Yes! Yes, we had lost the majesty of character for that," Samuel nodded.

"You see, the successful individual in Judeo-Christian culture is one who puts his talents to profitable use in the service of his family and his community. The successful individual in Progressive society—indeed all utopian societies—is one adept at extracting sustenance from the state. The one cultivates the giver, the other the taker.

"Our liberty had to be sacrificed to achieve One World, as, say, the Russians had sacrificed theirs to their utopian dream before us. Like

them, we believed the experts could fix the world by scientistic management so we surrendered our liberty to them. But they couldn't fix
the world because they couldn't fix themselves. Like the communist,
Progressive culture made people self-seeking and dependent and in
the end, like them, we welcomed the tyranny of One World to rescue
us from the consequences of what we had become."

Another thought occurred to Paul. "You lived through all this."

Samuel nodded sadly again. "I remember once when I was a young
man… the leader of what is now Zone 53 brought in a public school
program intended to condition primary schoolers to affirm, what were
then considered, deviant sexual activities. I had a friend who had three
children in state schools at the time and I remember him writing the
leader to say it was inappropriate for children to be learning about anal
sex in grade four. Well"—he rolled his eyes—" the leader wrote back
something to the effect that 'We believe our children have the right to
be informed of alternative lifestyles.' Ha!" He nodded to Paul who was
grinning in expectation. "There was of course that royal 'we' that all
tyrants use, as if he himself were the embodiment of the people's will,
but there was also that 'our' in *our children*. That was when it became
clear to me what we had squandered. Twenty years previous the 'we'
would have been met with derision and the 'our' would have been political suicide, but now our children belonged to the state and we had
been relieved of our right to object." He tsk tsked to himself.

"We sold our children—our families, our homes, our lives… our
freedom—for a worthless promise of ease and security."

Both sat quietly for a long while as the sunbeam cleared the edge of
the carpet and fell full on the rough wooden floor. Dust was suspended
like tiny snowflakes in its wake.

"Do you ever wonder who your parents are?" Samuel asked suddenly.

Blindsided by the question, Paul could only stutter, "I don't know."
He was thankful Samuel didn't press further and took the opportunity
to steer the discussion elsewhere. "You said the parents in Christian
society were 'partners,' but I've heard that the husband was supposed
to be the 'head'? What does that say about Christian equality?"

Samuel laughed out loud. "You think that makes the woman subservient, but even more is asked of the man; he must *sacrifice* himself
for his wife. So who is the master and who the servant?" He winked at

Paul. "In any case, in Christian society it is the servant who is exulted, not the master."

They were silent for a while. "Were you ever married?" Paul asked.

Samuel looked down and smiled tenderly. "Yes." He didn't offer more.

Paul reviewed their conversion on the train home and after when he was lying in bed. It had been a rambling discussion that would require consolidation to get down to something he could present articulately. He was beginning to appreciate the difference between Christian society, based on marriage, family and personal virtue and One World Progressive society based on self, government and regulation.

He reconstructed the particulars along the path Samuel had outlined in the evolution from Christian culture to One World—the dissolution of rival institutions like marriage, family, private property, the Church, and finally representational government, and how it all had been done—substituting choice for marriage and family, utopian aspiration for Christianity, security for liberty; selfishness enabling the government to achieve mastery over our lives step by step.

Often his mind wandered to thinking about Catacomb—silly fantasies really; incompliancies. *What if Melanie and I became devos; would we be allowed to live at Catacomb? Which character traits would I look for in a mate if I could be allowed to marry? Could Mel be the one to show me who I really am like Samuel said or is there someone else for me?* His mind offered up an image of Priscilla. *Could I stay with Mel as she grew; could I love—serve—what she would become—always?* It would be a difficult pursuit to be sure, but he sensed a certain fineness, even nobility, in choosing that path. One World seemed sordid in comparison—a society based on self-interest solely.

None of this can ever be, of course. I can't fight the world, as Samuel says.

What about my paper? How should I record these observations there?

He stared up at the shadow cast by the light fixture overhead. *Samuel said Christianity was an addiction to life. Somewhere along the line Progressives have lost that addiction. They have lost their connection with life.*

He looked over to the black window. He wished he could have known his parents.

276

22

CASSANDRA

"So he's talking a lot about devo religion?"

"Yeah, well, quite a lot, yeah." Melanie flushed. She had run into Cass after class and stayed behind in one of the deserted classrooms to chat.

"So what does he say?" Cass spoke calmly, but Melanie detected an edge to her voice.

"Well, he has done a lot of research, you know? He's found out a lot of things that, well, some pretty surprising things."

"Like what, for instance?" Cassandra pressed.

Melanie thought for a moment. "Well, he thinks the idea that the Christians were all against knowledge and science...you know...that they just followed the Bible and didn't think much—is not true.

. He found that the really important people who established the foundation for modern science were Christians; like Galileo and Newton. They just wanted to understand God, so they looked at the things he had made to see what he was like," she explained. "Did you know a lot of the early scientists were priests?" Cassandra didn't respond. "It's true. They were educated and had the time to roam the land collecting and cataloguing specimens and whatnot."

Cassandra scowled. "Yeah, well, everyone should have a hobby." She folded her arms across her chest. "You should be careful believing everything he says. You need to research this stuff yourself."

"I have been—"

Cassandra rolled her eyes. "So what else has he been saying about their religion?"

Melanie was hurt by her friend's tone—as if she were admonishing a child. "Well, he has read some of their Bible." Cassandra gasped in disgust, but Melanie was determined to be heard. "At first it took some getting used to, he told me. It's pretty bizarre—God helping the Jews to wipe out whole nations in war; priests slaughtering hundreds of animals for their sacrifices; weird rituals—but after a while he started to understand them. He said he had to familiarize himself with their world a little at first and try to imagine himself in their shoes. He says that we modern people rush to judgment before understanding the problems other societies had to deal with." Just then she remembered: she had promised not to tell anyone about the Bible.

Cassandra maintained an unblinking stare.

"He says their worldview isn't at all as primitive as he thought it would be. In fact he thinks they were a positive force in the evolution of our culture and that a lot of the good things we take for granted originated with them."

Cass rolled her fingers over and examined her long black nails. "So what do you think about it—their religion?" she said casually.

Melanie was wary. "Oh I don't know. It's all pretty different."

"Different from what?" came the immediate reply.

Melanie was really beginning to resent Cass' attitude. "Well, like I said, different from what I had been led to believe." Cass' eyes narrowed but Melanie plunged ahead. "Their god is like a person. It talks to them," she explained. "I mean, they are really quite spiritual; not like I expected. They don't just follow the Bible blindly…"

Cassandra's jet black eyes flamed up, and her pretty face turned severe and ugly. "You're actually buying his stories aren't you?"

Melanie assumed an identical, hands on hips, stance. "No, I said *I don't know.* I don't know enough about it. Why are you so upset? You've studied many religions and you're always telling me that I should learn from them all, so why are you so angry that we're learning about Christianity?"

Cassandra was livid. "Don't you lecture me Miss High'n… who do you think you are!" she spat. "You don't know anything!" She looked poised to strike out at Melanie.

Melanie recoiled in alarm. "What's the matter with you?"

"What's wrong! What's wrong!" Cassandra sputtered. "These ideas, this religion, it's the repudiation of everything we've ever talked about; everything I thought you believed! How could you, someone who has been initiated into the mysteries and felt the power of the One, go traipsing after their blood-sucking god... their *male* god?! It just makes me sick!" She was panting and, indeed, did look unwell. Her eyes burned with hatred. "What are you going to do next, hold a witch burning?" she raged.

"It's not that way at all," Melanie flustered. "They don't think like that at all. You should hear—"

"You, you...," Cassandra huffed. She drew herself up menacingly and pointed a dagger sharp finger at her. "Beware this... this... closing of your mind," she hissed.

Melanie cast out her arms and looked pleadingly at her friend. "You're not being fair," she sobbed, "Jesus—"

"Jesus?" Cassandra vomited the word back. Her head shook back and forth violently repeatedly trying to cast it off. A guttural howl erupted from her twisted pained lips then "Jezuzz! Jezuzz! Jezuzz! Jezuzzz!" spewed forth in a tortured child-like voice. Melanie was terrified. Cass' eyes expanded into steely black crystals glowing with primordial fury. "Jesuzzzzzzzz!" Her head thrust back and her eyes rolled back macabrely. "Jesuzzzzzzzzzzzzzzzzzzzzz..."

Melanie's feet delivered her from Cassandra's presence before she knew what was happening. She cowered as she ran, expecting to feel Cassandra's sharp claws raking her back. Her friend's awful remonstrations pursued her all the way down the hall until she crashed through the doors and emerged into the sweltering heat outside. Tears poured from her eyes. She headed for Paul's house.

* * *

"No, you didn't see her," Melanie persisted. "She was... I thought she had gone mad. I mean, she changed so.... I didn't know her. It's like she wasn't even human."

Paul listened intently.

"I'm scared, Paul," she confided.

"Scared she might hurt you?"

Melanie stared wide-eyed. "I don't know."

"She's probably upset you've been hanging out with me so much; you two used to be inseparable."

Melanie flushed. "Yeah. I suppose," she said resignedly, "but you should have seen her."

"Well she does have that way about her," Paul said breezily. "She has that *presence*."

Melanie's mouth flashed a grin before recomposing. She leaned against the bay window sill and stared at the floor.

"What I don't understand," she said finally, "is why she's so violently opposed to Christianity. I mean, she's always been the one saying—she mimicked Cassandra's cadence—'No one religion has all the answers,' so 'We need to explore all paths to enlightenment' and so on." Her eyes were red from crying.

Paul sat in the sofa chair pressing his fingers together and looking pensive. He wasn't surprised at Cassandra's reaction.

"You should come with me and talk to her," Melanie urged.

He looked at her doubtfully.

She crossed her arms at her chest. "I think it would do her good to talk to someone better informed," she nodded decisively. "Take her down a notch or two." She clapped her hands. "Hey! What about Samuel?"

Paul looked alarmed.

"No I guess that wouldn't be safe for him." Paul's eyes followed her as she paced the floor. "Cass should have been there and seen those people, you know, that night I met Sam and… the birth," she said wistfully. "She would see things differently then."

Paul shrugged. "Do you think that would have changed her mind?"

"Do I think..?" Melanie's mouth was agape. Paul looked steadily at her and she held his gaze. "I don't know," she said faintly. She plopped down in the chair opposite.

Suddenly, she startled and looked anxiously at her watch. "Eleven-thirty! Damn!" She leaped off the chair. "I need to get going!" Paul remembered that her ride would be coming early in the morning to take her to Muskoka and she still had to pack.

They rushed downstairs. It was still hot outside. They hugged and kissed on the porch. "I'll be back on August fourteenth," she said breathily with a sly grin. She turned to go.

"I'll miss you," Paul said quietly.

Mel looked back and smiled at him then turned to face the night again. "Me too."

He stood there on the porch in the darkness watching her cherished figure receding from him, fading more and more until it was lost.

23

DAY 74

TESTIFY

In the weeks since Mel's departure Paul had immersed himself in his studies and talked to Samuel regularly, continually expanding, reviewing and refining his knowledge.

The problem of the impossibility of the existence of free will, and of reasoning itself, given the deterministic understanding of the human organism's functioning required by his materialistic worldview remained intractable and continued to trouble his thoughts. *If I am but a biological robot, how can any of my opinions or decisions be relevant?* What could justify the confidence of the scientistically managed society in the competence of its 'experts'? What was the sense of scientific exploration; how could there be any connection between the products of the chemical reactions in his brain and the external world out there that 'he' was 'observing'?

Also weighing on his mind was his personal experience of the existence of evil and good. Could he reconcile himself to believing that—to borrow from Samuel: *charity and murder were ethically interchangeable?* If not, what justification could he offer for his preference beyond personal convenience?

Could he defend his belief in the historical progression of human civilization and, most importantly, the ethical evolution of the human creature itself? Did the evidence around him suggest that mankind was evolving towards an Omega point or did it support the Christian claim that mankind's very nature was permanently compromised and incapable of such a transformation? Had the quality of the creature advanced alongside its technological achievements or did its technological attainments mask its moral stagnation? Were we all kinder, more enlightened people or just cavemen with machineguns? What did the evidence—the abortions, the genetic typing, the Peace Center (KIDS), the Compassion Directives, the war—around him suggest?

In his studies he had gone back to re-examine the abortion question and one item had stuck in his mind: studies taken during the proto-Ascension showed that the two most common reasons women gave for seeking abortions were financial burden and 'I'm not ready for the responsibility of motherhood'—basically, that their baby was an impediment to self-gratification. The abortion movement hadn't been about women's health, or rape or any of the high ideals Progressives ascribed to it; it had been about personal convenience and entitlement. The women wouldn't even trouble themselves to carry their child to term and permit adoption; they had allowed their unborn children to be dismembered, disemboweled and decapitated rather than taking responsibility for their *choice*.

It was disconcerting to compare the view of children held by those in Christian culture to those in Progressive society. The first saw them as a gift and a joy while the second saw their children as intolerable impositions. A young woman shouldn't be 'punished with a baby' the American president had said. *No*, thought Paul, *she had the 'right' to luxuriate in her own fancies with no regard for the agony inflicted on others.*

He could discern the coarsening of the human heart and mind in the progression from the one society to the other.

These illuminations dogged his thoughts during his frequent solitary walks in the urban landscape between his study sessions.

As emotionally encompassing as his investigations had become, he welcomed the diversion offered by Beverly's call to meet at a favorite hangout downtown that afternoon.

Paul would have liked to have gotten her opinion on some of his questions but was careful to explain his paper in general terms without confessing the struggle he was having defending the One World worldview in his own mind; he didn't want to appear incompliant. For her part, she was pleased that he appeared to be making progress.

Beverly took a sip from her straw. "Oh, I met Suzanne yesterday at

The Hall," she said with a smirk and a wink. She was in the habit of dramatizing Suzanne's smitten state in regard to Paul.

"How's she doing?" he asked drily.

"Oh, party party party," Beverly replied spritely. "I don't know how she keeps up the pace—her and Belinda. You wouldn't believe the guys they go through." She smiled teasingly at Paul.

"What about the other one? You know, Kim."

Beverly's smile and good humor evaporated instantly. "Oh, yeah. She mentioned Kim." Beverly shook her head wearily and sucked on her straw again.

"So, she's still depressed," Paul surmised.

"Yeah *depressed*, that's an understatement. I mean, she's just like a kid most of the time—she cries at the smallest things. At other times she's like a zombie. I think that bothers me more—she just sits and stares blankly into space." She sighed. "I just don't get her problem."

"Maybe she's upset she had her baby killed." Even Paul was surprised at the bluntness of his response.

Beverly's eyes widened to the point of exploding. "Sorry? What did you say?"

Paul averted her look. "I mean, maybe she had doubts about going through with it—her pregnancy relief." He looked up. "I mean, I've heard that some women—"

"What the hell!" Beverly snapped. "That's not what you said. You said she 'killed her baby.'" She slammed her cup to the table. "What do you mean by that?"

At this point Paul preferred to withdraw, but he knew Bev wouldn't allow him so he plunged in. "Well, that's what pregnancy relief is, isn't it? An unwanted baby is killed."

Beverly's hands gripped the tabletop tightly. "Whatever!" she snapped dismissively. "You said it like you were judging her. What right have you—"

Paul warded her off. "Whoa. I was just stating the facts: a pregref kills a baby."

"That's mean spirited!" Beverly blasted. "A woman has the right to do whatever she wants with her body. What's with you anyway?"

"But how is the fetus *her* body?" Paul heard himself replying. "Its body has a different DNA from hers and it directs its own development from conception on—fetus, child, teenager, adult, old age, death. It's an independent organism we are killing."

Beverly strained to master her rage. "This is outrageous! Killing a fetus isn't like killing a human being."

"Why not?" Paul pressed. "All the scientific facts would place the fetus in the category of 'human being.'"

"It hasn't developed into a person yet," Beverly asserted shrilly.

Paul was getting angry now too. "Oh, so basically your point is that you can kill it because it isn't old enough to protest," he ripped back sarcastically.

"Don't be stupid. It doesn't even know it's alive yet. It's just a dumb lump of flesh," she hissed back.

"We were all like that when we were its age. Why does its age give us entitlement over its life?"

Beverly began to shout. "You, you can't understand. You're not a woman—"

"Well, you're not a fetus!" Paul snapped back.

Beverly froze in mid-sentence, a shocked, wounded look on her face. Paul was sorry he had lost his temper.

"You can't know what it feels like... to have... little parasite growing in you," she whimpered.

Paul was nonplussed. Had Bev had a pregref too? He looked around at the others who had turned to listen and tried to defuse the situation. "Listen, I have to work these things out for my paper," he explained.

"So that's what this is all about—that stupid paper of yours!" She swept her cup onto the floor angrily and flew to her feet jarring the table with her thighs. "You want women to all be slaves... like *Handmaid's Tale!*" she screamed in his face. "Well, you know what you can do with your ... paper..." she spat with a hurt note in her voice and stormed off leaving Paul cringing under the censorious looks of the other patrons.

Later, at home, he thought about what had happened. The conversation with Beverly certainly had not progressed well. His need to have a rational foundation for his beliefs had spurred him on and he was surprised that Beverly didn't have a reasoned reply to any of his challenges as he had always considered her to be of a kindred temperament.

She isn't able to consider the situation logically.

Now he could appreciate how the pro-choice advocates before Ascension had advanced their cause—through emotional bluster and dogmatic prescription to shut down reasoned debate.

He wasn't overly worried about their friendship; she would come around in time he was sure.

In any case, things would be looking up soon; *Mel will be back tomorrow.*

24

The Highway

"It's Melanie, Paul... She was hurt in a car accident... bad."
The voice on the com sounded otherworldly, like it came from the opposite bank of a river. A sick sick feeling clawed at his guts.

He didn't recognize her at first; she didn't look herself. "Beverly?"

"We're at Friendship Emergency. Just get over here." The com went black.

Paul stood frozen with his hand pressing his forehead, his mouth agog, the dead com in his other hand, unable to will his body to move. He thought he must be dreaming and wanted badly to wake up. Finally he stumbled down the stairs, managed to rip his coat from the hallway closet and staggered outside.

A hundred meters down the road he started sprinting.

Night was falling as he flew out of the Life subway station. He hurled down University towards Friendship. Five minutes later he dodged past the unadorned *Emergency* beacon and burst through the doors.

He head throbbed as he squinted in the glare of the bright lights, trying to locate a familiar face. There were people of every description and configuration sitting reading or bundled up waiting for their number to be called. He saw the check-in station and started towards it, but then spotted Beverly and Paige sitting side by side on the hospital green vinyl chairs against the window. He stumbled altering his course and stopped in front of them gasping with sweat pouring down his forehead.

They were crying. He felt dreadful. He heard his breathless fearful voice say, "Bev, what's happening?"

Beverly raised her bloodshot eyes, "Oh, Paul!" she cried. She struggled to her feet, wrapped her arms around him and buried her face in his chest and bawled. Paige stood and patted Beverly's shoulder.

As he held her he could see their reflection in the window against the dark avenue: the green chair, her shuttering body, his terrified and maddened eyes.

Finally he mustered the courage to say, "How is she doing? Is she going to be okay?" Beverly cried all the harder. Then he was crying too.

"Oh Paul…Paul…Paul…" she sniffled. "Paul, she's dead. Melanie is dead. They told us just before… just before you arrived…" She began to wail again. The two bawling girls held each other while Paul slunk into one of the sick green chairs. His eyes bulged and his hand clutched his stomach which felt like a gurgling cyst. His throat constricted.

He remembered the rest of that terrible night as if it were a dream: his feet carrying him away from that humid pit of a room; drifting in the darkness unaware of the rain, a thousand images of the life they had shared for such a short time singeing his mind. Constellations floated in the black sky; shadows rushed past; black birds congregated on the telephone wire—watching; her face glowed in the night.

He somehow awoke in his bed next morning—the morning Melanie was to return. His com was flashing in the dimly lit room—there were messages waiting. He watched it blink in the graying dawn.

Paul learned the details of the accident days later.

Mel was returning home on the Z-400. She was in the front passenger seat. On a bad stretch of highway a pickup truck swayed and clipped their fender causing their car to veer sharply and strike the concrete pillar of an overpass. The driver was killed instantly. Melanie was taxied to Friendship where she was diagnosed as having a broken neck. The prognosis was that, at the end of a long and uncertain rehabilitation, she would be left a quadriplegic; she would never lead a normal existence. In light of this, the attending physician made the decision to terminate her life in accordance with the Compassion articles of global directive GC432-7T222-24420.

25

CONFESSIONS

The sun shone down mockingly as he sat on the bench and looked far off at the sail boats skimming the crests out on Lake Obama. A skinny teenaged boy was endeavoring to launch a kite and imperiling those sprawled on their beach blankets in the process. Gaily-colored umbrellas kept the sun off the backs of the others taking in the activities lounged on portable chairs. People strolled past on the boardwalk.

It was all so incongruous to his mood.

Since Mel's death Paul had avoided the company of his fellows. He hated the sorry looks those he encountered gave. He had attended classes only when necessary and Mr. Lichter had uncharacteristically neglected to burden him further with a new exit paper assignment. He was reluctant to broach the subject again, no doubt.

He hadn't worked on his unofficial paper either; it just didn't seem to matter anymore.

The ring of feminine laughter drew his attention. There were two girls lying on blankets with a trio of boys gathered round. Despite the sun-bleached hair Paul recognized Harmony under her shade hat and sunglasses and determined the other, in her red baseball cap worn backwards like a catcher and dark glasses, to be Anne. The girls were in high spirits, obviously basking in the attentiveness of their quite captivated audience. Suddenly they all sprang up and bounded over the hot sand towards the water. Harmony's voluptuous figure, barely contained in her pink leopard print string bikini, commanded a lot of attention while Anne held her own in a tiny lemon-colored thong with a ruffled waistband.

When they reached the water two of the boys charged in followed shortly by the third. Anne screeched and took the icy plunge. Harmony waded into the deeper water gingerly until she was submerged to her shoulders.

Numbly Paul watched them rollicking and splashing in the water. The biggest boy managed to hoist Harmony up on his shoulders and she squealed as he spun around and around before tipping her off with a splash. Anne was occupying the attention of one of the other boys. They paddled out deeper into the mazarine wash until Paul could only see their two heads bobbing in the water.

The scene seemed surreal to Paul, like watching an extended holiday advertisement while intoxicated. How could life go on as usual? He yearned for the occurrence of some incident, anything, to prick his delirium and assure him that the world was still real—some thunder erupting from angry skies. Instead there were carefree people lazing contentedly under a luxurious sun.

As he watched Harmony and Anne frolicking with the boys he felt a pang of jealousy which made him despise himself further. It was silly, he knew, to mope like a jilted lover over some girls he had barely met. He didn't even have much regard for Harmony, who was a nice enough girl, with a terrific body, but pretty superficial. And Anne was, well, who could know what went on behind that unremitting smile.

He began to reflect, once more, on how little substance his relationships had. There was little need to delve into a girl's heart or to empathize or forge any deeper bond. Again, he didn't feel his experience was exceptional—from all he could see, none of his friends had purposeful relationships either. The sexes never really related to each other on that level. How could they in One World?

A stray thought: *What did women do when they grew middle-aged and could no longer compete with younger women? Where was their place in One World then? Where companionship?*

How trivial his schooling had been. '*Sex Ed*,' what a laugh; '*Fuck Ed*' was more like it.

He knew these thoughts were incompliant—triggered by his recent readings. For some reason he had gone back to the Old Testament and Genesis—Samuel had supplied him with another Bible—and noted, again, how the concept of family presented there differed from his modern experience. The idea of two becoming one; children. One World unburdened everyone of all that but did it also divest them of something in the process? He still thought about Nethanel and Miriam, about all those Christian people at the birthing, the families.

The willingness to sacrifice one's own advantage for others; the longing for something beyond personal attainment.

He wished he had a father to talk to.

His mind wandered like this around the periphery, balking at the entrance to his deeper consciousness. Part of him wanted to think about her death—Melanie. It wanted to come back again and again to confirm what it had found there, rummaging in the recesses of his mind. To experience once again the hollow feeling of crushing loss— that was real anyway: the tragedy of youthful beauty snuffed out; the unyielding idiocy of it all—death. In five billion years the sun will go out and nothing he had ever done would matter.

Mel's life wouldn't matter.

And then, there it was laid open—that feeling of... relief. That was the most horrible of all. She had not survived. He would not have to stand by her diminished husk. He was rid of the cripple.

He wanted to know himself. These past weeks he had advanced greatly in that undertaking at dreadful expense.

You who are evil, Jesus had said. Paul understood intimately what he meant.

But it was people like himself who shaped One World, pressing it into the templates of their soiled natures. *What chance did it have, then?*

What was our culture cultivating?

Perhaps that was how he could understand One World—by looking inside himself and examining the twisted pilings—the darkness within.

The Christians at Catacomb had some quality he lacked. They were able to support Melinda despite the demands a physically dis-functional human placed on their lives. *What was it, this quality? Were they just naturally more caring?*

Whatever it was, he had lost it; One World had lost it, somewhere along the line.

His disgust with his ambivalent feelings about Mel's death provided consolation though—perhaps he wasn't totally beyond rehabilitation.

He would recall it whenever the weight of his despondency threatened to crush his desire for life.

The squirrels rummaged in the grass. He couldn't recall ever seeing them fight. *What of natural selection then?*

His thoughts remained disjointed, his mind feverish. He glanced out to Harmony and Anne and the boys.

A youth walked by with a spaniel on a leash. The dog nosed the ground happily and zig-zagged back and forth to greet everyone it encountered with a wide-eyed expectancy and a frantic wag of its truncated tail. *Dogs are so happy and carefree*, Paul reflected. *What is it that makes people dissatisfied with their lot?* He guessed Samuel would say something like *'Because they know their lives are not what they were intended to be; they know they are meant for something higher.'* What would One World say? *That they needed more engaging entertainments?*

Isn't the whole object of One World policy to transform people to more closely resemble the dog: happy, docile, mindless? Compliant.

The bathers had tired of the water and came scurrying back over the hot sand to their towels. They were laughing and talking animatedly. Harmony slipped on some sweat pants and a tee shirt while Anne donned a miniskirt—Paul wondered if she owned any pants—and threw a light jacket over her shoulders. They deposited their towels into their bags and began to walk towards the boardwalk where Paul was sitting, chatting gaily with the boys all the while. He turned away and watched out of the corner of his eye as they approached hoping they wouldn't recognize him under his sunglasses and hat. At one point Anne's gaze paused on him and he waited for the dawn of recognition to appear on her face. It never came though; her eyes moved on and she passed by.

Although he was relieved he had not been recognized, the feeling of abandonment re-asserted itself.

How insignificant he felt. Weightless.

His eyes continued to survey the scene before him mechanically, but his mind had ceased registering any of it. Instead it was pervaded with remembrances of Mel. Her serious look when she was reading. Her musical laugh. Her sashaying walk. Her dimpled grin. The long talks at night. What anguish he felt knowing this was lost forever. For a fleeting instance there was clarity: he knew that, in the end he had really loved that girl.

It was possible: love.

But then that feeling was gone too—a fleeting obsession.

"Hi stranger."

The intrusion startled Paul. His head snapped up displacing his glasses. Bev was standing there with a look of empathy on her face. "Oh hi, Bev," he answered squinting against the sun.

"I stopped by the house and figured you might be here." She sat beside him.

Paul adjusted his glasses, pulled his hat lower and looked out over the water. He didn't really want the company and despised the empathy.

She peered out over the whitecaps too. "Summer's almost over," she sighed.

Paul nodded slightly and sat silently for a few moments before finally resigning to talk. "I always feel sad this time of year. There are still a few weeks of hot weather left, I know, but it's the prospect of winter coming on—the long gray months ahead—that gets me down."

"Yeah, I feel it too," she acknowledged. "I always try to get out during the winter though; do some skating and snowshoeing. It gets me my activity credits," she added.

Paul nodded. "Yeah, I do the weights. At least I can do that all year round." He lowered his eyes. "I'm sorry about the spat last time."

She turned to him. "Oh. No, it's okay. I was pretty rude too. It's an emotional subject for everyone."

"Yeah," he said quietly and looked back out over the rolling surf. Her eyes remained on him.

"You still working on that paper?" she asked suddenly.

Paul crossed his legs and rested his clasped hands on his knee massaging one thumb with the other. He was surprised at the question. "I don't know... I think so," he said finally. "I can't really think about that now."

"I thought about it after, you know with Kim and... well with everything lately..." she flustered. "I would be interested to read it when you are finished."

Paul felt a pang in the pit of his stomach. He remembered how Mel's death had struck Beverly. They reached out simultaneously and took each other's hand and sat there looking out over the water.

"I miss that girl," Paul said quietly.

"Yeah."

They sat for some time in silence, staring out over the foaming surf, hand in hand. The sun sank lower in the west and people started to pack up their belongings and leave.

"You would really like to read my paper?"

"Oh… yeah."

"Okay."

26

SAMARITAN

The late summer sun was hot on his skin although a coolness in the air hinted of autumn.

Paul wandered through the Layton Center that morning and sat by the fountain at Alliance Square for a while watching the shoppers. Gretchen's church was just outside, but he had no desire to visit it again. He paused to listen to a few of the street musicians at Ecology Square before resuming his stroll.

A sense of déjà vu had dogged him all morning and now, as he headed up Morgentaler, he thought about that other Sunday, three months ago, when he had gone to church with Harmony and Anne. They had walked this same stretch of road then. He hoped he didn't run into them this morning; too much water had passed under the bridge.

As he approached Gandhi he saw an elderly woman, frail and sparse, toddling towards him. As far as he could make out it wasn't the same one he and the girls had encountered after church that day; she didn't have a cane for one thing.

She stopped suddenly and began to cast around frantically as if seeking shelter from an imminent downpour. Paul glanced over his shoulder and saw two policemen advancing up the street and realized immediately she was incompliant.

Nearby, a group of young adults were huddled in a pocket made by a recession in the storefronts. Paul strode up to the lady and murmured

"Come this way." Her searching eyes latched on to his and he managed a reassuring smile. "It's okay; they haven't seen you. Come, move this way."

She cowered behind his frame as he edged her over to the young people and positioned himself between her and the street. "Yes, it looks like summer is almost over," he said as casually as he could. She nodded a terrified affirmation. Paul heard the clop of the cops' boots on the pavement and heard their voices as they brushed past. His companion's bottom lip trembled terribly and she looked up at him, imploringly. Paul continued the conversation. "Yes, I know how you feel; I hate the cold weather too."

One of the teens looked down at the elderly woman and then at Paul suspiciously. Paul grinned at him, but the youth's countenance remained fixed and unsmiling. Finally, he turned back to his friends.

Paul glanced over his left shoulder and located the cops standing at the corner waiting for the light to change. The traffic passed agonizingly slowly. As soon as the intersection cleared the cops crossed against the red light. Incompliant.

By then one of the girls had noticed Paul's companion. He saw her nudge her friend and whisper in her ear. Her friend looked at the trembling women then at Paul. The boy beside her saw them staring and turned to see what the matter was. The conversation dropped off perilously.

Paul held out until the cops had disappeared then muttered "Let's go." The young people stood mutely watching them move off.

When they were out of earshot he said, "I'm Paul." It was then he noticed his voice was shaking; in fact his whole body was shaking.

The old lady looked bewildered. Her eyes darted to the right then the left. "Alicia," she answered cautiously in what seemed to him a surprisingly youthful voice. He hadn't heard many old people speak.

Paul managed to still his tremors. "Do you live around here? Do you have a place?"

She looked hard at him, searching his face. Paul looked back and she quickly lowered her eyes again. They walked on. "Yes; a few blocks over," she replied at last. "I went out to find something to eat. Then I saw them…"

Paul didn't press for details; he could see plainly the woman's distrust of strangers. They walked on and came to a corner store. "You're hungry?" he asked.

"Oh… yes. I can't… I mean…." There were tears forming at the corners of her eyes.

"You won't scan?" Paul said quietly.

She sobbed. "No. The doctor wouldn't renew my living. He said I was too old. My… well, I'm not well."

"It's okay," Paul said gently, "I can get you something."

She looked hopefully at him.

They found an alley beside a store where Alicia could wait. "Just stay here." He began to edge away cautiously worried the old woman might bolt.

He halted suddenly. "Um, you have a place to cook?"

Alicia didn't seem to understand him at first. "Yes. There is a way," she replied finally.

"Okay." Paul left her in the alley, hurried into the store and bought a dozen eggs, milk, some fruit, and a few other items. The clerk looked at him warily, not recognizing him as a local. Paul appreciated his mistrust—one had to be vigilant so as to avoid transgressing any of the food dispensation laws. He knew he was endangering himself buying for an incompliant. Luckily, with all his studying he hadn't been eating much lately so none of his purchases were flagged by the checkout scanner.

When he emerged he was relieved to find Alicia hiding in the alley still. *She has nowhere to go*, he thought to himself, *and there's no one to help her.*

Alicia led him to a one room apartment off an alleyway on Sherbourne. "I'm sorry for the mess," she said. "It's not my place."

"Oh, it's okay," Paul answered. The apartment was really quite orderly. "I'll put the groceries over here." He set the bag on the counter and put the eggs and milk in the refrigerator which was vacant except for half a lemon. It was difficult to part with the eggs because the protein was indispensable to his body building and he couldn't get more until the following month. *She needs it a lot more than me, though.*

Alicia had collapsed on a chair in the living room. Her skin looked damp and deathly pallid. "Oh. I'm so tired," she moaned, "so tired." Paul let her sit quietly with her eyes closed.

After a while she awoke with a jolt startled to find him sitting there. "I'm sorry. I get tired over the slightest physical activity anymore." She sighed wearily. "I wasn't always like this, y'know. I used to be able to walk all day without any fatigue at all."

"It's okay," Paul said "Would you like something, a drink?"

She brightened up. "Oh, water would be nice," she smiled. Paul got up to get it for her. "And some lemon; it's in the fridge. Just squeeze it in."

Paul filled a glass, squeezed the lemon into it and took the concoction back to Alicia who had managed to sit up.

"Oh thank you," she beamed as he handed her the drink. She took a small sip as if to test the temperature then gulped down three quarters of it in one go. "Ah," she smacked her lips crisply, "picks you right up."

Paul smiled at the old woman's show of gratitude.

"Oh!" she startled, "did you turn the tap off completely?"

"Ah, yes," Paul assured her.

"Oh good."

Paul realized she was worried the water consumption would alert the authorities to her presence.

"Is there anyone else to help you?" he asked. Alicia looked guardedly at him for a moment then began to unburden herself of her sad history.

She had been an executive in the real estate business, but the company was disbanded after Ascension and the workers assigned to the One World Housing Provision Office of the Department of Social Justice—part of MoE. The years passed by, but then she had gotten sick—cancer—and was dismissed. Her doctor had cut her living allowance when it became clear it would be too expensive to treat her disease and she had stubbornly refused euthanasia treatment. She went into incompliancy.

Her friends helped her as best they could, but they were getting old too. Many of them had already been taken away. In time they all disappeared except for Kathy, an old associate of her husband, who was allowing her use of her apartment while she was away and Beatrice, a woman she had met a few months earlier. Who knew how long old Kathy could keep going, though, and she hadn't heard from Beatrice in five weeks and feared the worst. There was no one else.

"You were married?" Paul asked incredulously.

Alicia startled slightly, surprised at his boldness. Her smile spread wide displaying largely intact although discolored dental work. "Well! For thirty-seven years," she announced proudly.

All existing marriages had been voided about ten years ago, so Paul assumed she had been married for thirty-seven years previous to that although he had heard of some radicals insisting on the validity of their marriages even after the Annulment. She didn't look like that sort of person though.

"He's been gone for, what, eight or nine years—my Vick." The smile illuminated her face as her eyes peered into a time long departed. She blinked back to the present and looked to Paul. "He was a doctor. We had the most beautiful home in Rosedale."

The Rosedale neighborhood was where society's elite lived—scientists and One World political bigwigs. Paul imagined the juxtaposition between Alicia's lifestyle then and her current state.

"We used to go down to the Esplanade, to a bar there where they had the greatest selection of beer. He liked his beer. You could get real imported beer back then." She smiled fondly to herself.

Paul had to grin at the thought of the figure before him guzzling beer. A flash thought crossed his mind that he could go out and get some but he knew the scanner would most certainly raise an alarm.

They talked for about two hours, and he was surprised at the general lucidness of her thinking since he had imagined old people to be mentally vacant. He wondered how old she might be; she must be older than Samuel.

As he listened to her story he became increasingly angry realizing it must surely echo the plight of many elderly. What their lives must be like! He had just never thought about it before—there wasn't anything about them in the World Curriculum. He saw now how his society marginalized those no longer able to contribute—unwanted people—and longed to do something to alleviate her situation. Momentarily his mind flashed to Melinda.

"I know some people who might be able to help," he said as he was leaving.

Alicia's face glowed with hopefulness. "Oh, if there was anyone…" She began to sob softly.

Paul felt awkward in the face of the women's distress. "I'd better go. I'll see you later," he said, gathering up his coat.

He paused in the doorway and turned back to her. "Did you ever know any Christians?"

Alicia dabbed her eyes with her hanky, blinked, and looked confused.

"Never mind. I just wondered." He stepped into the hallway and closed the door securely.

As he was leaving he heard the deadbolt slide into place.

* * *

"So that's what happened. I couldn't just leave her there to starve."

Samuel had been listening intently to Paul's story, stroking his beard all the while with a twinkle in his eye.

Paul grimaced. "Well, I couldn't, right?"

Samuel smiled a faint smile.

"Okay, why the look?" Paul asked impatiently.

Samuel reclined back on the coach looking contently at the ceiling. If he had had a cigar Paul would have imagined him blowing smoke rings.

"Say something," Paul urged. "Can you help her?"

Samuel laughed. "Yes, we'll see what we can do. I mean, it's not easy, but we'll see."

Samuel's emerald eyes studied Paul who began to feel uncomfortable under their scrutiny. He was relieved when they finally closed.

Suddenly he recalled something he had meant to tell Samuel earlier. "Have you heard of *White Night*?"

Samuel's eyes remained closed. "Yes."

"So you know they are going to be able to activate everyone before they even leave Mother?"

"Yes. Do you think it a technical advance?" Samuel said, still without opening his eyes.

Paul's mind didn't register the question. "Doesn't that make it impossible for you to recruit young people?"

Samuel's eyes opened. "Difficult yes; impossible no," he snorted. "But we intend to raise our own children, as you've seen." His eyes closed again. "There will always be a Church."

It was the answer to Paul's unasked question.

Paul saw he was tired. *Old people need to sleep a lot*, he thought. He noiselessly stuffed his books into his knapsack and tip-toed to the door. "Don't forget about Alicia," he said quietly but Samuel was already dozing. He closed the door softly behind him.

27

Truth

Paul stopped dead in his tracks. There were several police cruisers parked in front of his house and a MoE van was just pulling out. Norm and Jean were nowhere to be seen. His hand released his satchel and it fell to the sidewalk.

"You there, come here!" A stern MoE officer was pointing at him.

Paul's initial reflex was to bolt, but his feet had rooted themselves to the pavement.

"Come here!" the officer shouted again. A black-clad trooper appeared at his side.

Paul left his bag there, concealed as it was behind an eco-bin, and willed his legs to carry him towards the two MoE operatives.

The officer waited, standing imperiously, akimbo. "You're Paul," he growled when Paul had drawn near.

Paul nodded affirmatively.

"Can't you speak?" the officer bellowed.

Paul cleared his throat. "Yes sir. Yes, I'm Paul, sir."

The officer looked him up and down and sniffed contemptuously.

Some cops came out of the house and got in their cars and a second MoE trooper appeared. "Bring him," the officer ordered. Paul was trembling as they marshaled him over to the blue sedan. A three car convoy was formed and they headed back towards Morgentaler.

Paul was wedged between two troopers, his head locked in position forward leaving only his eyes unrestrained. He didn't doubt they were taking him to an unpleasant place. They had undoubtedly discovered his O.W.L accesses and likely found his treasure box.

At Morgentaler they turned left and headed downtown. No one said a word. He thought briefly about how smooth the car rode. Through the corners of his eyes he could see people and buildings pass by. Paul felt like the condemned who rode the tumbrels through the streets of Paris; street after street moving past. *But I still have some time to live.*

When they turned right at Ecology Paul surmised their destination to be the Strong Building.

They pulled into the north compound. He had walked past it often but never imagined he would be seeing it from the inside so soon. The escorts looped around and departed. The MoE officer spoke briefly to the duty officer there and two guards emerged from the building. They marched Paul past the heavy steel doors into the maws of the beast.

"You are a discerning man; what do you think?"

Paul remained too terrified to reply. The interrogation was taking place in a finely-upholstered office somewhere in the heights of the Strong Building—he understood it to be an interrogation although his inquisitor was polite, his timbre patient and their surroundings improbable for such an activity.

"Come, come, what is your opinion? What have you uncovered in your studies?" the voice probed.

It was asking Paul about his One World Library readings—what did he think of the devo worldview. Paul knew his fate depended on answering satisfactorily, but he couldn't think of a compliant response. "I… I didn't really have time to learn much before I… before my access was taken away." A trickle of sweat slithered down his forehead.

His examiner's voice was very quiet, seemingly conscientious to conduct the interview in strict confidence, but by some facility undiscovered by Paul there was no difficulty hearing every word he spoke clearly. He seemed to be able to transmit his voice directly to its intended target without the requirement of an intervening medium.

"Oh come, come. You're a bright boy. I know all the files you accessed at O.W.L. What did you think of their beliefs—the Christians I mean. What did you think of those people presuming they had Truth all neatly circumscribed by their little book? How did you feel about their 'sanctity of human life' dictum, blowing the importance of this miserable species all out of proportion? Did your inner self rejoice when you read of the enlightenment thinkers—Hume, Spinoza, Voltaire—coming along and putting them in their place? Oh, and then there was Darwin of course. But you were not authorized for that. Did you then appreciate the deliverance from irrationality that One World secures?" He paused then reiterated rather ironically, "The *freedom* of One World."

He looked hard at Paul who remained petrified and mute. "Yes, of course. You're afraid to voice your opinion," he sighed, "just like the rest of them. You're a true product of One World," he added condescendingly. "I don't blame you really."

The comment, uttered in such a patronizing overtone, stung Paul as it was undoubtedly intended to. He choked down the compulsion to retort.

The other emitted a pointed "humph", sat down and crossed his legs. His chair creaked as he swiveled side to side with his earthbound leg and studied Paul. Suddenly he swept the room with one arm. "Well here it is," he said expansively, "the Strong Building, nerve center of zone fifty-three. What do you think?" He shrugged at a motionless silent Paul. "I mean, it's where it all happens, where you are striving to be some day. What do you think? Feel the power, eh?"

Paul felt he must answer but did not know what to say. The other sat staring at the floor expectantly.

Paul stole a glance and saw he was middle-aged—he placed him around forty-five—tall, stately, and of lean musculature, well maintained, polished and elegant like his office. His hair was pitch black and his skin unblemished and smooth but for the heavy furrow above his brow. He had an aristocratic air which bespoke of efficiency rather than inhumanness; an intellectual. Paul was intensely interested to know what a man in his position thought about it all—Christians, human rights, abortion—and longed to engage him openly but dared not.

"Look," the other said sternly without raising his eyes, "you have to talk to me. You understand?"

Paul searched for something to say. "Are we? Are we more free? Are there no irrationalisms, no dogmas restraining us?" he heard his voice inquire timidly.

The other reclined in his chair and re-crossed his legs. "What do you think?" he punted the question back. "We've broken the stifling grip of the priests haven't we?"

"What's the difference?" Paul muttered incoherently.

"How do you mean?" the other pressed.

Paul had probably surpassed the limits of prudence already but the man's manner, his evident disdain for polite conformity, suggested he might possibly be someone to reason with. "Haven't we just traded masters? I mean the Christians bowed down before their god and his rules, and we submit to whoever precedes us in the hierarchy and their rules... people with PHDs." He didn't know why he had added that; perhaps a stray thought of Dr. Bright.

They sat staring fixedly into each other's faces. Paul feared he had misread the other's propensities and braced for the imminent explosion. Instead his lips drew up at the edges and he finally broke into unrestrained laugher which terrified Paul all the more. "*PHDs, ha!* That's good!" He slapped his knee jovially. "Yes, yes, we revere the *specialist*—the person who endeavors to know more and more about less and less. That's what you mean, eh?" He smiled his agreeance to Paul. "That's who we consign our destinies to; quite true. Ya 'Gotta Serve Somebody' as the song goes," he chuckled. "Who better?"

Paul felt a constriction in his throat. The feeling he was being drawn into a disclosure he needed to avoid swept over him.

"Who better?" the other repeated firmly.

"Themselves?" Paul ventured in a shallow voice. It was a desperately incompliant submission.

"The common people?" the other chortled. "Why trust them to conduct their lives? What credentials do they have?"

Paul stared back.

"No, we cannot trust our enterprise to human folly. Give the people what they want—that's what government boils down to—grant them what they crave and they will allow their betters to rule over them. That's it in a nutshell, isn't it? Isn't it the best way? Of course you have to implant the proper cravings into them: woe to those who desire other goods—or is that other gods?" he laughed.

Paul suspected he was playing on his susceptibilities to draw him out; he knew everything he had read after all. "But we"—he was careful to say *we*—"take away their freedoms. What gives us the right?"

The other sighed. "I think I see where you are going." He clasped his hands together. "You are brooding over the idea of natural rights, existing prior to human government"—*you see, I know what you've been reading*—"that humans have the right to life that cannot be annulled by government for instance. That's what you mean by *their* freedom, correct? You are thinking it isn't the government's purview to designate their rights but to protect their inalienable ones. You would favor negative rights instead of positive rights—that humans should be free to do what is not prohibited by law, instead of being prohibited from doing anything not prescribed. You think the government should butt out as much as possible."

This articulation exceeded anything Paul could formulate but didn't diverge from his own thought at any point.

"But that's all been tried as you know," the other continued, "and what was the result? Social injustice, sexual inequality, environmental degradation, economic inequality, cultural inequality…" He nodded to Paul, "in short, all manner of inequality. In order to have equality government power must be absolute. Equality must be enforced."

Paul raised his eyes. "Is that what we have, equality? Is our society more egalitarian than what came before?"

The other laughed out loud. "Yes, well you see clearly then. Equality isn't the point—not our concern. It's just a useful abstraction; a way to take away what we want to take away." He tapped his exquisitely manicured fingers on the desktop. "When you say *we* took away their freedom you mean us politicos." He chuckled. "But it wasn't just us back then—for we are talking about the pre-Ascension times of course. We had lots of help: the church mice, the *oh so* liberal media, the politically correct politicians, all the absurd 'public intellectuals'—all the useful idiots. *Progressives.*" He laughed derisively. "All shepherded along by the *equality* mantra. But you see through all that. Good."

He sighed dramatically. "That's the vanity of the public intellectual isn't it?—this drive to convince the masses that what their common sense shows them to be false is really true. Only an intellectual—someone immersed in the world of ideas and convinced of his own genius—can overrule his common sense and believe his own absurdities."

A thought triggered another laugh. "There's a funny quote I read from a Soviet dissident once—you remember the Soviet Union?" Paul nodded cautiously. The conversation had become so disjointed he was having trouble following the speaker's intentions. The other grinned and continued. "This man—this dissident—had enjoyed the acquaintance of many engineers during his lifetime. He said that, before the

Russian revolution he would listen to them talk about engineering, yes, but also art, music, philosophy—whatever would interest an intellectual disposition." He glanced at Paul to confirm his attendance. "After the revolution, when the old corps had been purged and the profession's ranks filled by the imbecilic sons of the dim proletariat, he found that they could only talk about two things." He paused to accentuate the punch line: "engineering and *wodka*." He laughed. "Such are the 'intellectuals' of the utopian society."

He looked for a response from his reticent audience and, finding little, returned to the previous tract of their conversation. "So what was our concern back then, us *intellectuals*?" he asked Paul. "I mean, in service to One World; what untruths did we have to make true? What was our mission? What were we seeking to subtract?" Thankfully, he continued without waiting for a response. "To convince the people to fob off their real political rights for trivial, *private* ones." He smirked at Paul. "That was it in a nutshell, yes? They would surrender their right to property, their right to family, of free thought, their very individualism and finally to life itself for the right to fornicate." He drew himself up straight. "In sexuality, libertarian; in all else, authoritarian," he pronounced solemnly. He grinned at Paul. "Our motto."

"Authoritarian... like the Soviets..." Paul muttered.

The other winked at him. "Yes, of course; after all, the Progressive is merely a Bolshevik who is too squeamish, or lacks the political clout, to utilize the firing squad. His goal is the same—the acting out of his utopian designs on an earthly stage."

He clapped his hands. "But really, *freedom*? A nebulous concept that. What we really want—what YOU want—is the license to do whatever we like. That's the only freedom that really counts. You agree?"

Paul didn't know how to reply. The conversation was so unwieldy and so wildly inconsistent with the One World Curriculum; so incompliant.

The other laughed. "Sin is merely that which wanders from the ideal of those in power. My freedom is your servitude. Freedom belongs to the master, and to the master only."

"It's all just for our own benefit—" The words fumbled from Paul's lips.

"Oh no! What was best for us all," the other corrected him in a schoolmasterly way, "everything for the people." The ironic tone mocked the spoken orthodoxy however. "What gives us the right? Science, utility—those are the instruments we wield that justify our mastery—"

"*Utility*?" Paul blurted out. "Is it efficient to raise children like we do, via disinterested strangers instead of committed parents? To maintain this unending war against dissenting opinion—the constant culling? Is the endless scanning and the stifling micro-management of all the petty minutiae of life productive? Does this statist totalitarianism motivate our people? Does it benefit our economy? *Science?* Is our science flourishing in this scientistic ghetto? What great benefits has it provided humanity since Ascension? White Night?" He looked goggle-eyed at his interrogator.

The other was visibly impressed by the younger man's outburst, his mouth hung ajar for a moment. He grinned, "Yes you see. The commandments have not all departed with… with the Christians and their ridiculous book." He looked up at the rows of officious—looking volumes on the high bookcases ringing the room. "They had only their meager ten. We have…" He gestured at the books. He smirked at Paul. "The demise of virtue precipitates the eminence of law."

He strode over to the window and peered out. "Quite right. I'm glad you see that. It certainly isn't utility, still less science, that inspires us; they are just slogans. It's hedonism—the satisfaction of desire—that sustains our enterprise." He turned back to Paul. "We offer utility, science, reason, progress as comforting myths for the comrades along the way, but we venerate power only, and we rule through desire." He chuckled. "And even then we cheat them of their desire's reward in the end."

"Doesn't it degrade man—leading him around by his appetites? Using him?" Paul said quietly.

"As if our mission is to facilitate man's freedom to, what, *to achieve his potential*?" the other guffawed. Paul recognized the phrase from the One World catechism. "Our government's mission is not to *free* man, it's to *enslave* him to serve our great experiment," he sneered. "Perhaps our greatest success in pre-Ascension western countries was this shifting from representative to dictatorial government. Here, but for the griping of various Christian affiliations, we were able to accomplish this with hardly a whimper—just with a slogan, 'equality,' to anaesthetize the masses, and a Charter to crush the rest." He laughed.

"The Rights Revolution," Paul muttered.

The other laughed out loud. "Yes! Yes! Brilliant, don't you think?"

He clapped his hands together jubilantly. "*Multi-culturalism*—what better way to introduce divisions where none existed and what better way to mold society to our preference than to oblige each tribe to petition our Progressive judges for their piece of the public affirmation? Our courts simply validated those views they felt useful to the revolution and denied all others," he announced triumphantly. "No one noticed that they hadn't the authority to do so," he laughed. "What hilarity: the spectacle of them bickering over their inconsequential sexual 'rights' while their very freedom was being taken away; in their rush to assert their rights and freedoms demanding the destruction of the very institutions that secured these in the first place. Brilliant!" He laughed heartily.

"As for White Night, do you really offer that as an exhibit to the glory of our science?"

This was a riddle to Paul. Samuel had also seemed unimpressed when he had mentioned White Night. What did it mean?

Paul continued to be astounded by the contemptuous undertone of his interrogator's speech—incompliant, mocking the revolution. He never imagined encountering someone like this here: an unbeliever. Again, it was also possible that he was leading Paul on to incriminate himself but it seemed increasingly unlikely. In any case, at this point he figured he had little to lose and felt he had to know: how deep was the faith in One World at HQ?

"Why do you go along with it?" he asked quietly.

The other paused, surprised at the directness of the query. "Why not," he smiled wickedly, "I like my perquisites."

Paul looked fixedly at his interrogator. Was he being sincere? "So it's a lie, then."

His interrogator leaned forward, clearly relishing the exchange. "What is?"

"All of it. One World's reason for existence. The evolution of mankind; the compassionate society."

The other guffawed but ignored his question. "You see our conundrum?" Paul didn't. "Is it even possible to preserve one's integrity as an intellectual in One World? Can an inmate of a utopian society, given his conditioning, transcend its confines and become cognizant of its excesses and inadequacies—in short, its untruth—and—still more difficult—having done so, survive?" He looked aside to Paul and confided, "That's your sin you know—daring to think."

Paul directed a questioning gaze at him but he turned his eyes away again. "You see how hard it is to fit in—the intellectual; the artist? No totalitarian regime can tolerate them and maintain its authority. It needs to project its own reality, its own myths and verities, and these have to be believed." He turned to Paul. "You need to understand this. It must shatter the spectacles of the intelligentsia, crush the freethinker or anyone who might see through to the truth. It needs intellectuals who have learned not to think." His voice had crescendoed and now subsided again. "And so we have the *specialist*, the pantomime artists and the other ersatz *intellectuals* the totalitarian society allows itself." He stopped and sat staring at the floor pensively as if personally affronted by this spectacle.

"It's servitude, then, all the way down… tyranny," Paul said almost inaudibly. At last he was beginning to perceive the intent of the other man's communications: he was revealing to him what his future vocation would entail. To what end? To ascertain his reliability?

"Oh?" The other revived. "Ah truth. It's so refreshing, yes?" He smiled.

"But if this is how it is, if this is the people we are to be, then we've given up our own freedom also. No one is free." Paul looked askance at the other.

The other emitted a noncommittal "Hmmm." He crossed his legs again. "So we are back to our original question: what did you think of the Christians?" One of his elegant long fingers shot up. "A better question: why do we hate the Christians so? Surely you've noticed our especial antipathy towards them?"

"Their philosophy impeded One World every step of the way," Paul offered routinely.

The other chuckled. "Yes, yes, I suppose. But why hate them with such vehemence? After all, they were needed you know; all utopian societies require an enemy to mollify its failures—the Jews, the Bourgeoisie, the Christians." He looked at Paul significantly. "Make sure you do not fill that prescription; One World needs enemies still."

Paul stared back bravely.

"…like your friend Samuel."

Paul's stomach lurched. A faint smile tickled the corners of his tormentor's lips. "Yes, of course I know all about him. That little library he keeps in the back; not too smart." He tsk tsk'd.

Paul slouched.

His interrogator checked his joviality abruptly and looked at Paul, thoughtfully. His mouth opened to speak then stopped before any words came. He thought a moment longer. "It's a comforting myth—God. But there's nothing there. There's nothing there, right?" He looked for Paul's response without expectation. Paul gazed back questioningly. Finally he sighed, "and so we go on..."

"What about truth?" Paul said meekly.

"What is truth?" the other answered morosely. His demeanor had sobered completely. His gaze captured Paul's. "This is truth: in five billion years the sun will go cold and everything we do here, everything everyone has done and will do, will mean nothing."

Paul held his gaze. *I thought the same before...*

"You understand this don't you?" He studied Paul's face closely. "God is dead: eat, drink, for tomorrow we die."

Paul didn't respond.

The other exhaled a "humph" and walked over to the window. "Truth is whatever power mandates," he pronounced. He stood there peering over the skyline with his back to Paul and hands clasped behind.

Paul startled when the door opened. A black-garbed guard appeared. His time was up.

Croydon surveyed the city below and replayed the interview in his mind. He had studied Paul's dossier when Lanton's actions had come to his attention. Still, he was surprised—pleasantly surprised—at the aptitude of the young man. Paul had gone a long way to figuring things out himself, but he would help him the rest of the way as best he could.

He smiled nostalgically thinking how alike Paul he had been at that age; even that naïve idealism—that stupid stubborn idealism. He half admired it but knew it wouldn't do in a politico. It was dangerous—so many things were dangerous now—especially with the repudiation of GraceNost—but he also knew it would surely fade in time. Abiding in the corridors of One World would accomplish this metamorphosis. Like acid wearing on steel, nothing could resist its corroding power finally; he had seen it all before, again and again.

An image of Lanton popped up in his mind. Had *his* idealism faded? But he was a strange bird really; quite unique. Croydon smiled to himself at the old party standard bearer getting his wings clipped for staring into the Christian sun too long. He could only be amused

imagining the frustration and befuddled bewilderment that stolid so-
cialist brain must suffer in attempting to comprehend any belief which
was motivated by concerns beyond creaturely comfort. What dolts they
were, those paper-hanging, rainbow-flag-waving, do-gooder drones of
the revolution. Still, they were useful.

Like Paul, Croydon had been fascinated by Christianity back in
his school years. It was uncommon for a One-Worlder, of any caste,
to have anything but a cursory understanding of the tenants of any
of the devo religions, but it was prudent for a man in his position to
understand them—the devos. He was a rare bird in a way also—his
breadth of knowledge marked him so. Perhaps he would have passed
for a renaissance man at that point in time, if such a species could be
suffered to exist, but he knew what a poor specimen he would present
if examined in the light of historical precedence.

Wodka.

This skepticism of Paul's, his questioning nature, was encouraging
really. For through the years of doubtful seeking there would arise a
greater appreciation of the inevitability of it all; a greater conviction.
It would lead him to a more thorough acquiescence. One had to walk
through the valley of hope to become a true believer. He knew all this
from experience of course.

But he must ensure Paul didn't succumb to the same myopia as
Lanton or he could be lost to the other side.

He watched the crane below moving a massive concrete stanchion
into place. Beyond he could see the Kappas setting the steel rails into
its comrades. He had watched the work progress day by day as the barrier drew closer to ringing the Strong building completely—an extra
protective skin in the face of rising devo activity.

He let his eyes range over the city. *Christianity*, he smiled to himself. How he envied them in one way—the Christians. They were the
only ones who could pursue their ideals genuinely. Everyone else had
to betray their professed beliefs in order to live. The atheist had to appeal to human reasoning for his morality although he knew his ability to reason to be illusory in the deterministic universe he occupied.
He would extol the potency of science while denouncing any doctrine
which would oblige the chaos to conform to his mind's contrivances.
Even knowing that in a short time every atom in his body had been replaced by another, he would yet greet himself in the mirror each morning as if it were the same individual who had peered back at him the

month before. In short, if he were a man and not a lunatic, he would strive, all his life, to live in accordance to the maxim that everything he believed was untrue.

Croydon smiled ruefully. *We are all apostates but for the Christians.*

He sighed and turned away from the spectacle. It was plain that things were not going well at 53 HQ. He slumped down on his chair. *It is all so stupid—those who take all this so earnestly. What does it really matter—whose vision prevails? Why can't everyone just get along? There's enough for everyone; why risk it all? If the government controls everything, it could be blamed for everything. What madness.*

But, however he calculated his prospects, he could not avoid concluding the other side was winning. And in this struggle it didn't do to be numbered outside the cadre of zealots.

Of course he would sacrifice the others to protect himself if things got to that.

It was the encounters with young people like Paul that gave him hope for the future. They needed more like him to take their places in the hierarchy—allies. They were the only chance.

He had brought Paul to the Strong Building knowing the others would be watching. It was better to do things out in the open. In any case he had accomplished his mission to defuse any repercussions the young man's actions might have wrought.

He would watch over Paul as best he could.

* * *

The sudden knock at the door startled Alicia awake. She sat bolt upright, without breathing. The late afternoon sunlight streamed in through the kitchen and bedroom windows and spilled into the living room where she sat. She listened to determine if it had really been a knock or if she had dreamt it.

Another rap on the door dispelled her doubt. A young woman's voice called from the other side. "Mrs. Forrester? Mrs. Forrester, I've come to help you."

Alicia's heart raced. She rose slowly from the chair and then froze not knowing where to go—where to hide.

"Mrs. Forrester. It's okay," the voice said. "Kathy sent me."

Alicia remained fixed to the floor. "Kathy?" escaped from her mouth weakly.

"Yes, Kathy told me you were here," the voice responded.

Alicia was confused. *Kathy sent someone? Kathy didn't say she would send anyone. That young man Paul said he would. No, she said she was from Kathy, not Paul.* What could it all mean?

She shuffled cautiously over to the door and listened.

"Mrs. Forrester—*Alicia*—Kathy couldn't make it. She'll be away for another three days. She told me to check up on you."

Alicia's fingers alighted on the deadbolt. It did seem strange. There was that young man Paul. Now this girl… Her fingers played on the bolt. Maybe there were still good people left; someone who cared…

She drew the bolt back cautiously.

The door burst open and the head of a pixie-faced young woman with a toothy smile and huge brown eyes under an auburn bob appeared. "Hi, how are you feeling?" she asked.

"Oh, I'm, I'm okay…" Alicia stuttered, attempting to offer an appreciative smile.

"I'm Yolanda," the girl announced pertly. When she emerged from behind the door Alicia saw she was wearing the white uniform of the Department of Health and Compassion and her eyes swelled in horror.

The young woman hooked her arm under Alicia's. "Oh, it's okay," she assured her, "we're here to help."

Two husky men in white uniforms entered the apartment. Alicia lurched when she saw them and tried to break free but Yolanda held her firm. "It's okay," she repeated soothingly, as if to a child. "Everything is going to be just fine."

"No, no…" the old woman sobbed piteously.

"Alicia, Alicia, don't worry. Everything will be better soon," Yolanda purred.

Alicia kicked with all her might and wailed but the men held her fast. Yolanda turned aside and reached into her bag. When Alicia saw the needle she bucked and yelled all the louder.

"Oh hush, hush," Yolanda scolded her gently as she injected the contents of the syringe into Alicia's emaciated arm. "There, there. All better." The old woman's body convulsed once, then went limp.

Yolanda pressed a stethoscope against her chest and listened for a few moments. "Okay she's gone," she nodded to the men. They efficiently encased the limp body in a black bag and carried it out.

Yolanda lingered behind, surveying the apartment. She loved her job, working in the field instead of a stuffy office; helping others attain to compliancy. It had other advantages too. She peeped inside the fridge and her eyes went wide at the sight of the egg carton. *Three eggs!* The carton disappeared into her bag.

She looked around the room again. *Hmmm… a little off the beaten track but serviceable.* She had a friend who was eligible for a place downtown and had assured her she would let her know if anything suitable might be coming up on the listings. *We'll have to see.*

She slipped out, locking the door behind her.

28

DAY 7 CONTINUED

TWILIGHT

"What was this gentleman's name?" Samuel asked.

Paul had been relieved to be beyond the confines of the Strong Building, free again. He chanced a glance over his shoulder expecting to see a squad of police coming to haul him back but no pursuers followed. As soon as he cleared the square he broke into a trot. After hours of wandering downtown, elated just to be alive, he stole back to his house.

His book bag was still on the sidewalk where it had fallen. Scouting around the house he discovered that his enabler's possessions were gone but could detect nothing of his own missing; even his treasure box appeared undisturbed.

It was eerie, this sudden excision of the entities he had known as Norm and Jean from his world. He remained uninformed about the details of their transgression but knew he would never see them again.

Fortunately he would be assigned another enabler for the rest of the semester so he didn't have to return to Mother.

Finally he had made his way to Samuel's.

"I don't know," he answered despondently "Someone pretty important; and he knows who you are. He knows what you are." Then in a quieter voice: "He knows about your library."

Samuel was leaning towards him listening intently. "What did he look like?"

Paul closed his eyes. "He was white, with straight shiny black hair. I'd say he was about one point seven or eight meters; pretty lean; forty-five-ish."

"Any accent?" Samuel asked.

Paul thought. "No, but he had a distinctive voice. It was soft but carried well. Strange. Like he could throw his voice right into your head."

Samuel raised his eyebrows.

"You know who he is?" Paul asked.

Samuel had turned aside. Paul thought he hadn't heard his question at first, but before he could repeat it he responded with a quiet "No. No I don't." The tenor of his voice led Paul to doubt the answer. He stared at the older man, but he would not offer more and Paul sensed that pressing the question would avail nothing.

"What should I do now?" he said finally.

Samuel shrugged. "Of course, you have to stop your investigation."

"I can't do that!" Paul protested.

"Just for now. Let things quiet down," Samuel urged.

Paul kneaded his bottom lip with his fingers. "I can't. If I did that I would never know."

"Never know?"

Paul sighed. "You know; the truth." The statement sounded naïve in his hearing at that moment—after all that had transpired at the Strong Building.

Samuel shook his head. "It's too dangerous now."

"Yeah. I know," Paul answered quietly, "but it was always dangerous." He looked at Samuel. "It's what I have to do."

Samuel looked concerned.

"This man, the guy at the Strong Building... he doesn't really believe," Paul confided.

Samuel's gaze remained leveled on him.

"How many there are like him—living a lie?"

Samuel didn't response.

Paul sighed. "What else could he do anyway? He's trapped. We're all trapped."

"Maybe it's what he really wants, though; the depths of the human heart are treacherous to trawl," Samuel offered. He settled back in his chair. "Whatever it is that dominates your thoughts and time—whatever consumes your life—that is what you become in the end. You are what you worship; it's what traps you."

It seemed grotesque that someone would expend his life on an enterprise he secretly despised. *What you worship; what was it his interrogator worshiped?*

Suddenly he recalled something that had come to mind after his interrogation. "The White Night chips; they are just a hoax! Mother could have safely activated our transponders when we were kids. It's some kind of game." A look of consternation spread over his face. "You knew?"

"Yes."

Paul waved a hand in exasperation. "How did you...?"

Samuel seemed distracted. "Well, the technology has been around for a long time. Even before Ascension people were bugging their children to insure against foul play. It wasn't hard to figure out—"

"But we were never told..." Of course, he had been fed whatever One World wanted. How could he have failed to see that?

"...in many ways it imitates God," he heard Samuel mutter to himself.

"What are you saying?" Paul asked.

"I was just thinking how One World often mimics his ways while inverting their true essence. It's a distinguishing feature of the work of..." The explanation had been directed mostly into thin air, but now he refocused on his guest. "God always leaves room for you to reject him. He won't coerce you. You have to come of your own free will, or not at all."

Paul caught the gist of Samuel's meanderings. "You think that's what One World is doing—that they delay the transponder activation so we have the opportunity to voluntarily submit..." His body shivered as he remembered his upcoming Induction ceremony, one week away.

Something else occurred to him just then—something he had wanted to ask Samuel before. "Why did you pick me?"

Samuel looked questioningly at him.

Paul sensed Samuel had understood his question but offered a clarification anyway. "Why did you approach me that day outside Gretchen's church? There were lots of others there—religious types—you could have pursued."

Paul thought he detected a slight curl in the tips of Samuel's lips, as if he was going to smile, but his mouth immediately recovered its firmness. "They will not listen," he said with finality.

"Why won't they listen? I mean, you could reason with them; show them the books..."

Samuel blinked then lowered his eyes slowly. "No, no..." he parried the suggestion. Paul stared at him expecting some word of explanation but Samuel just sat there, his eyes lowered, his hands inanimate on his lap—a picture of resignation.

Paul waited silently. Finally, the old man said quietly, "They can't listen."

Paul shrugged. "Some would see the light," he said in an upbeat, almost ironic, manner.

Samuel looked up quickly and their eyes met. "They are afraid of the light... afraid of what it might reveal... about the world... about themselves..."

The words impacted Paul's mind heavily, sobering his mood instantly. He was anxious to explore their meaning but suddenly remembered he had to get home before curfew—he no longer trusted his transponder to leave his movements veiled—so he stuffed the books into his bag and reluctantly turned to go.

When he reached the threshold he stopped and turned back to Samuel who was still looking intently at him as if he wished the conversation to continue. "How do people come to faith?" Paul ventured.

Samuel's mouth hung open for a moment, then he exhaled heavily. "It's different for everyone. Some are born with the awareness of the Spirit. Many come to faith through the industry of others—their friendship and mentorship; their prayers. Some are drawn by the Word. Some have a mystical experience." Samuel's gaze captured his own. "Some long for Truth."

The two stood staring at each other as if something further needed to be said but neither could produce the appropriate formulation. Finally, Paul broke eye contact and turned to go. "I'll see you... maybe after Tuesday." He passed through the doorway into the dark hallway.

Samuel looked after him. "Yes. Maybe," he said quietly.

An uneasiness caused Paul to pause on the street just outside the door; a premonition of evil events, or presentiment of some vital matter unaddressed and threatening dire consequence. The twilight was just beginning to fade to darkness. There were few people on the street. He waited a few moments there, his senses acute, listening. A cool breeze tossed the leaves in the gutter. The world was changing, the season wearing and fading to gray. He felt it falling away and drawing into a coming desolation. His body shivered and his breath came in shallow draughts.

He started off into the gathering darkness.

29

MIDNIGHT

A lister Croydon strolled along in the night, his hard-soled service issue shoes clip-clopping on the pavement as he walked. He knew it wasn't the most prudent thing for a senior officer of O.W. to roam Parkdale at this hour—there had been several incidents involving devos in the area recently—but he possessed the careless bravery of one whose life proceeded under precarious circumstances. He found it comforting to envelop himself in the protecting darkness, to disappear for a while. It was a delusion he knew—thanks to the microchip in his right palm they always knew precisely where he was—but he didn't allow that certainty to prevent him from savoring the illusion.

He loved the big city. The first time he set foot on the sidewalks of the surging metropolis and felt the energy he was hooked. He had been sent to attend high school and was happy to be selected to return after university. 'University'—a strange word that, he thought to himself. Unity in diversity. It was all a sham of course—since Ascension. What should it be called now; a 'uniformity'?"

He had always enjoyed strolling in the quietness of the night, after the bustle had dissipated. The placid stillness served to amplify his perception of the pulsating energy beneath.

There was power here.

As he continued his walk he reviewed the day's proceedings. In short, nothing of importance had happened at HQ. There had been the

321

usual rumors of reorganizations in the chain of command, certainly—
that kind of thing went on in perpetuity at One World; they were always
organizing and re-organizing as personnel were shuffled, procedures
amended and initiatives launched from Central. The orders trickled
down the chain of command and everyone scurried to comply with
feigned devotion as per usual. *Everyone just trying to cover their ass*, he
thought. *Just a mindless machine.* The words escaped his lips: "A mindless machine." The wind blew them safely away.

At least there hadn't been anything to be terribly alarmed about this
week so far—it had been quiet in his immediate cell. *Perhaps too quiet*
his subconscious prodded him. *Perhaps I should have heard something.*
He drew his trench coat collar tight against the cool breeze that whispered along the almost deserted street.

When he turned off Emerald onto a tree-lined avenue the wind
dropped off and the cool night air hung like a leaden curtain. There
were few lights in the adjacent houses—everywhere they were battened
down against the bluster—so the street was a deep blue washed with an
effervescent moonlight.

The elevated devo activity made zone fifty-three look bad. It gave the
zealots an impetus and they steadily gained dominion. He thought of
Bandergee and his lips drew down; he knew their approach would just
birth more devos, but he seemed helpless to influence policy. *Everything
needs to be done quietly, with no fuss*, he recited to himself.

He hadn't heard the car approach until it slowed beside him. He
knew immediately what must follow. The tires screeched as it braked
hard and the doors flew open. He just managed to catch sight of the
black sedan before the hood descended over his head. He had barely
resisted; it didn't seem worth it after all. As the syringe drained into his
arm his fading mind registered one final thought: *It had all been done
quietly, without a fuss.*

30

DAY 2

THE APOSTLE

The Reverend Gretchen Teasdale stood in the lectern of The Church of the Affirming Spirit, raised her eyes and beamed a welcoming smile over her congregation this glorious autumn morning. Sixty familiar pairs of eyes beamed back at her expectantly, awaiting her words of consolation and healing.

Her smile faltered, ever so briefly, when she felt the presence of the unfamiliar figure ensconced in one of the central pews about six rows from her station. It was an elderly man, unsettlingly familiar though she could not place him. He had a full white beard and glowing eyes seemingly fixated on her person.

She adjusted her golden robe self-consciously then smiled out over her flock once again, her arms flung wide and her voice rose in greeting. "May the light from the mind of god stream down and enlighten our minds!"

The congregation rose and sixty voices rejoined: "May we gain god's knowledge."

"May the love of god stream down and saturate our hearts!"

And they responded: "May we exude god's love!"

Her voice climbed to its greatest height. "May the will of god be done on earth as in the higher realms!"

"May god's will be done!" the company confirmed.

"Amen!" Samuel sounded preemptively.

"Amen," Gretchen's voice asserted with finality.

"Amen," the rest echoed.

The congregants looked discomforted and glanced at one another and shyly at the stranger, sensing in him a fractious presence. They settled uneasily into their seats.

The screen behind the celebrant changed to a panorama featuring a Buddhist temple in a Tibetan mountainscape and a mesmeric chant wafted in like fragrant incense. "Brothers and sisters, welcome to this house of god, of love"—her smile extended—"and inclusion. A special welcome to our visitors—to all seekers." She nodded graciously in Samuel's direction.

"I'm a *finder!*" he said happily, panning those nearest.

Gretchen continued with an uncertain "Oh, yes" before reestablishing her beatific smile and proceeding on. "First off, as you can see in your bulletins we have lots of exciting activities on the menu the next few weeks. I encourage you to take advantage of them to further your personal growth—our theme this month." She nodded pointedly at her audience.

"On Monday night the Native Spirituality series continues in the East Chapel under the direction of elder Beatrice Starlight. It's at seven o'clock. Remember to bring your mat if you have one as we have a limited number. And on Wednesday Bishop Alexander continues her series on Jeremiah. Note the start time: seven-thirty."

"Yes that seems relevant to our times," Samuel interrupted, nodding to the others around him, "to make clear the consequences of sin, eh?"

Gretchen ignored this commentary and continued. "And remember—I've mentioned this before—on Thursday at seven we have Reverend Pangels from Holy Progress to speak on the Gnostic Gospels."

"Yes it's good to be informed about the counterfeits," the vexing voice from the pews offered helpfully.

With some effort Gretchen composed her features and scanned through the remaining announcements silently. "Well, you can read the rest in the bulletin." She shot a dagger sharp glance at the intruder.

The smile returned to her lips. "Our first hymn is one of our favorites I'm sure. Let's all stand and sing *Power of Creation.*"

But for the stranger, the congregation rose in unison; he struggled to his feet after them, grinning self-deprecatingly at the woman nearest, obliging her to smile back nervously.

This part of the service, one of the most anticipated, especially by the younger members, many felt spoiled by the mis-singings of the visitor this day. Not a few felt the onus to project louder in order to drown his oblation beneath their own, but despite their efforts his robust intonations would often break through the surface marring the spiritual ambience. For instance, when they sang *Praise Everyone* the stranger failed to accent the 'everyone' resulting in, what must be interpreted as, a universal call to worship rather than the call to universal worship intended. Worse still, at one point the incompliant voice took to interposing 'God' between the two producing a chorus uniquely suited to the purpose of chafing the sensibilities of the spiritually unbiased.

That the final strains of the music saw them immersed in a euphoric bath despite these vexations must stand as a witness to the habituation of the congregation.

The golden figure had mounted to the pulpit and stood ready to offer her sustaining heat to the ecstatic brew. "Praise E-V-E-R-Y-O-N-E. Yes *everyone*." She shot a quick glance at the newcomer. "We are all carriers of the spark. We *all* are to be praised. And we praise Jesus who showed us this truth: that we can look beyond our mortal vestments and discern the godhead in each of us." She raised her arms and proclaimed, "Praise be to Master Jesus, the one who shows us the path to glory."

"Praise be to Lord Jesus Christ, Son of God!" Samuel enjoined thrusting his arms to heaven, "Who takes away our sin!"

The congregation was stunned to silence. Some looked terrified as if expecting some calamity to descend from above and crush them all. An old woman near the back scampered off to gain the exit ahead of the impending tribulation.

"All glory, laud and honor to the Son of God who takes away the sins of the world!" Samuel reiterated rapturously, expectedly, to the crowd.

They moaned and cast around for deliverance. Their pastor roused to arrest this abomination. "We don't speak of sin, we speak of love—"

Samuel waylaid her proclamation, "—and since we love him we obey him. We repent, for the kingdom of God is here. Repent and believe the good news: for God so loved the world that he gave his only Son, that whoever believes in him shall not perish—"

Gretchen: "We don't believe Jesus was—"

Samuel wheeled to confront her. "Whoever denies that Jesus is the Christ is the antichrist!"

Gretchen staggered and impotent little hoots proceeded from her madly trembling lips.

Samuel had turned back to the audience. "Go forth and spread, make disciples of all nations—"

"We believe in tolerance, not religious bigotry," Gretchen sputtered haughtily. "Peace, not animosity," she hissed.

"*Peace, peace*, but there is no peace!" Samuel exclaimed. He addressed the congregation. "Do not suppose that I have come to bring peace to the Earth. I did not come to bring peace, but a sword." They all gawked leadenly at him. "The word of God is sharper than any double-edged sword; it judges the thoughts and attitudes of the heart. You see?" His audience remained mute, mystified. An anxious pall spread over his face. "Brothers, sisters: a light has been shown us! A great thing has been done! And so, renouncing the wisdom of the world, we resolve to know nothing except Jesus Christ… and him crucified."

At this last affront one woman gasped and crumbled to her seat, her attentive neighbor catching her up lest she spill onto the floor. Gretchen trembled in morbid disconsolation for her dear sanctuary, defiled so savagely. Her nostrils sealed up as if that mutilated body had been deposited there before her.

Samuel appealed to them again. "Brothers, sisters: when we were dead in our sins God made us alive with Christ." A wretched 'no' was bleated in protestation. "We now have a high priest in heaven who intercedes for us!" He tried to take them up on his own faithful shoulders. "Glory to the Son who takes away our sin!"

Gretchen's teeth clenched, her visage contracted into a mask of impotent rage and her pallid eyes darted about for a path to salvation.

"Do I hear a hallelujah!" Samuel called to the barren silence. His arms were wide open, beckoning their approach. His body turned, inviting each member of the cowering assembly in turn. A great ecstatic flame enveloped his person; his tongue was no longer his own. A voice issued forth and filled the dim sanctuary: "Come to me all you who thirst, for I am the fountain of living water. I am true food and true drink. Whoever comes to me will never be hungry; whoever believes in me will never be thirsty." An old lady whimpered. Samuel's arm extended towards her, but she drew back in revulsion. Another bowed her head and covered her ears with her shriveled hands and sobbed while her companion stood immobile at her side with a sardonic smile lodged on his face. The others huddled in the murky gloom, clinging to the shadows. Some of the younger ones, their faces mottled in consternation, tried to decipher the message emanating from the oracle's mouth, but in the end it was too much for them; it was all too foreign.

An anguished look descended on Samuel's face as his eyes searched the faces in the gloom imploringly. His tears began to spill down. It was too much to bear. He knew. *They are dead. All of them. Dead.*

Suddenly two burly black-uniformed wraiths barged noisily through the ancient doors and bore down on the old man standing with his back to them, arms opened to embrace sinning humanity. Gretchen watched with hands clasped desperately to her bosom as they each locked an arm around the interloper's and hustled him off to the exit. The heavy doors crashed shut after them, securing the company against the world's impositions.

The congregation remained transfixed, benumbed by the finality of the vision cast by those sealed portals. Gretchen herself remained frozen, stunned by the deliverance so miraculously rendered.

Then she blinked and slowly, tentatively, the smile returned to her lips. "People of the light," the soothing tones of her voice poured its balm over them. She thrust her arms wide, "We are the light of the world."

They all turned as if awakening from a troubled dream. "We are the image of the enlightened masters," they mimed back, feeling the comfort of blessed corporeality's return.

Gretchen beamed steadily over her people with reverent thankfulness. They were hers again.

31

Day 1

"Mary"

Morris had returned in triumph from Port Gorbachev the day before and was filling Paul in on his adventures there while Paul caught him up on local happenings in turn. Michelle had gone back for an ice cream.

"Where did you meet her?"

Morris smirked, "Oh, you know... I can't even remember..."

Paul chuckled. "Well, I guess there are advantages to being a famous wood pusher." He had noticed an elevated sense of confidence in his friend's manner—the swagger of someone whose star was on the ascent.

Morris laughed. "Buddy, you wouldn't believe!" He took a prestigious chomp out of his hamburger. "She's low grade Beta," he added surreptitiously. "Dumb as shit but well, you know..."

For some reason Paul recalled that they used meat in the burgers before Ascension. He wondered what that was like—eating meat. Perhaps Samuel knew. It was incompliant to be wondering about eating meat—animals were our fellows. Recently, he had found himself slipping into this habit more and more—incompliant thinking. It was alarming how he had grown to savor these transgressions.

Morris put his burger down and took a swig of Coke. His eyes made a quick pass around the room. "So, have you seen Suzanne lately?" he said casually.

"Just around school a few times. We didn't talk." It seem indiscreet to mention Suzanne had glanced back over her shoulder at him in the hallway, gyrated her hips and winked the last time he saw her.

Morris took his Big Mac up again. "She's pretty hot, eh?"

Paul laughed uncomfortably. "Yeah, yeah, she looks pretty... hot."

Morris whistled softly. "Yeah." He drummed his fingers on the table then finally broke out with, "You know, I could never figure you out there. She makes it pretty obvious she wants to screw, but you just basically brush her off. What's up with that?"

Paul shrugged. "I just don't really jive with her."

Morris nearly choked. *"Really jive?"* he gasped. The women at the table beside them looked over. He leaned in towards Paul. "Are you nuts? She's hot and ah-vale-lah-bull. So what's your problem? Do you have a better—?" He immediately checked himself. "Oh sorry..."

"It's okay," Paul replied avoiding his friend's eyes.

"I was in New Frankfurt when I heard. I'm sorry man. You two had it going..." He didn't really understand his friend's obsession with his dead chick girlfriend—there were so many other available females—but felt obliged to empathize.

"It's okay. I've moved on," Paul assured him quietly. It would be absurd to unburden himself on his friend.

An awkward pause in the conversation ensued wherein Morris pretended to be engrossed in devouring his Big Mac. With some effort Paul restarted the conversation. "Hum, so New Frankfurt and Port Gorby went well. What's in store for you next?"

Morris cleared his throat. "Yeah, well, it went as well as could be expected; I'll get in the premiere league this year for sure. That's what I'm concentrating on now: get some more tournament play; make a little lucre."

"It's great to have a job you're really passionate about," Paul murmured in a far-away voice.

"Yeah, for sure."

Paul lurched recalling something he had wanted to ask before. "It must be hard having to compete—to win—all the time. I would find it difficult to be under that pressure to perform."

Morris finished off his burger. "Well, it's the same for everyone."

It was one of those offhand comments Morris had a penchant for—ones you wanted to take away and chew on for a while. Paul continued, "Yeah, but for you it's so black and white—no pun intended," he grinned. "I mean you either mate, or the other guy mates you; there's no brownie points for 'I played swell but lost.'"

Morris nodded. "Yeah, it's tough. But that's one of the things I like about chess—the integrity of the game. You can't hide your failures behind fluffy rationalizations, 'I was unlucky' or whatever. You either put up or shut up. There's no bullshit in chess."

Paul chuckled. "You might have been a poet if you hadn't been a chess player."

Morris laughed but then his face took on a serious expression. "Listen. I'm not under any illusions here. I know it won't be easy to hold down a place in the league. There will be other, younger players coming after me with better conditioning and improved eugenics profiles." His eyes travelled past Paul. "God knows what they are cooking up down at Mother." He had a far-away look as if he could see that great white cube in the distance.

Paul was attentive to Morris' point but at the same time he was struck by the fact he had mentioned 'God.' *What is it, this vestigial verbal incompliancy? Evidence of Christianity's lingering presence?*

"I can win… at least they can't take that away," Morris mumbled.

"Sorry?"

Morris blinked. "Oh; nothing."

Paul had placed his elbows on the table and cradled his chin on his folded hands while he studied his friend. "Does that bother you that your life is like, I don't know, a production line where last year's model is rendered obsolete?"

Morris shrugged. "Not so much, I guess." He looked at Paul. "Aren't all our lives like that?"

"Yeah, I suppose you are right," Paul murmured. *Hadn't Cal's life been like that, after all?* He felt a rising exasperation. "Don't you wish everyone would just lighten up? Why do we need this frantic push for progress?"

Morris didn't flinch at Paul's outburst. "Progress with a capital 'p' you mean." He folded his hands on his lap and sighed. "I don't know about all that; all I know is, I have to concentrate on the job at hand. I can't get distracted by politics or metaphysics or whatever; that's someone else's job."

Paul slouched and buried his hands in his pockets. Something had changed between them. The intimacy had gone out of their relationship, like they didn't really know each other anymore. He wondered when this estrangement had occurred. *When did we become strangers?*

Despite his grand designs, Paul sensed the smallness of Morris' world.

"Did you hear about SpaceFleet?" Morris offered.

"Yeah, it's gone." Everyone knew that SpaceFleet had been expunged from the Net—something about it encouraging incompliant attitudes. Paul wondered what the players would do now; where might a virtual starship captain be re-deployed?

"Yeah, I guess it's old news," Morris said morosely. "Hey! Want to go to the Firkin? It would be like old times."

Paul looked at his watch. "I really have to get home." In truth, he didn't have anything pressing at home but just wanted to be alone.

Morris looked sad but not entirely disappointed. "Okay." He sucked the last of his Coke up his straw noisily. "Catch you next time then." He waved to his companion who was on her way back with a cone.

"Yeah. Next time." Paul watched him slip an arm around the girl's waist as they hit the street.

He sat a while longer. The meeting had left him in a melancholic mood. Adding to his despondency was the realization he couldn't think of anyone he could confide in at that moment; not even Bev.

What would it be like to have a father?

He emptied his tray into the eco-container absent-mindedly, strayed out on to Morgentaler Street and started towards home. His intention to board the subway at Ecology lapsed as his feet carried him past the station. He passed College, Gandhi—he thought about looking in on Alicia but walked on instead—and Darwin in the same way and finally ended up walking all the way to Davisville.

The sun was setting when he arrived home; the house dark and quiet. He went up to his room and tried to read, but restlessness easily overwhelmed his resolve. There was a rumor going around that the Rights Museum in Astral City had been destroyed, but there was nothing on the Net. He couldn't find anything else to occupy his attention, so he just lay on his bed staring up at the ceiling.

He heard a squirrel run across the roof. It hadn't been repaired yet so when the rainy weather came... *Everything is falling apart. Samuel said it was different before Ascension.*

No one owned anything now. No one has anything to show for their labor—it was forfeit to One World. How does the One Worlder's social standing differ from those who built Pharaoh's pyramids, then?

Induction was tomorrow. He knew it was the reason for his unrest. He should be elated at the prospect—finally he would have the authority to manage his own affairs, to have his own money and maybe, in time, be able to get his own place. If things went inordinately well, he might be allotted a car. *Imagine the girls who would be available.* He should be ecstatic at gaining full citizenship but he was strangely disinterested; too many questions remained.

Suddenly it dawned on him: it was time. He had learned enough about the devo worldview and it was time to summarize his findings—to make an end of this project that had consumed his life these past months.

He took up his tablet. *Where to begin?*

Perhaps the first thing would be to establish the basic structure of each society, One World and the Judeo-Christian one. It was a relief to have found something to occupy his mind.

One World seemed simple: it had two layers. The first consisted of the state—the MoC at the top directing the myriad bureaucrats in the thousands of departments controlling every aspect of life: work, education, finance, health, leisure—everything.

The other layer, subservient to the bureaucracy, consisted of the rest of the people. One World was a society sustained by state authority and regulation, all in deference to rational utility—the experts ran things.

As a politico, he had studied this system thoroughly in school and now, with Samuel's help, he was truly awakened to its essence.

Superficially, Christian society was similar in that it also had a government layer and a people layer, but it interposed a third between these two; Paul called it *the association layer.* It consisted of, what were mostly, voluntary associations like artistic, sports or other clubs, professional bodies, independent schools, media and even political organizations and, of course, religious communities and family.

This middle layer altered the character of society dramatically as it fostered a significant autonomy of the bottom layer from the top. The scope of the state's jurisdiction in the affairs of the people was limited and its authority exercised only obliquely since it did not control the substantial aspects of life that fell under the prerogative of these institutions.

So the structure of the Christian society functioned to protect the individual freedoms of the citizens from governmental infringement while One World's facilitated such intrusion.

In his estimation, the two most important of these Christian institutions were the family and the church. The first established the basic worldview of the citizenry, independent of the state's aspirations, through parental mentorship and the exercise of educational prerogatives. These actions were made possible by the existence of familial authority and financial resources—private property—not available in One World. So everyday life tended to proceed under the supervision of the family rather than the state.

The second, the church, provided autonomy from the state through its social relief offerings—soup kitchens, hostels, hospitals, schools—and further impinged on the opportunity for state mandated morality by postulating a higher authority.

The result was a citizenry manifesting diverse opinion and of heterodox conviction as to societal goals and mores, all to the frustration of state hegemony.

So effecting the transformation of Christian society to One World was as simple as subtracting one from three: just destroy this middle layer. That's how all utopian societies—the Nazis, the Soviets, the communists—had done it and that is exactly how the Progressives did it.

He would have to find a place to talk about the destruction of the family through the redefining, privatization and final abolition of marriage; the imposition of governmental control through confiscational taxation to hamper the family's influence; and compulsory public education to indoctrinate the youth into anti-family lifestyles. He could detail the Church's abdication from Jesus' gospel to Progressive doctrine; and the Rights Revolution which annulled natural rights, like the right to life, and substituted others at the government's discretion—along with human rights commissions to enforce compliance with Progressive mores.

This all reminded him of the need to illume the divergent perspectives of those raised in these alternative societies, for it wasn't just the societal structures that were different, the peoples' mind-sets were too; they had to be because different qualities were needed for survival in each, and each nurtured those characteristics deemed beneficial.

For instance, since their relationship to the state was of paramount importance to the One Worlder—it provided all sustenance and diversion—compliancy was the only necessary virtue.

But Christian society was less regulated, encouraging personal wisdom and virtue rather than relying on external coercion. In consequence, the Christian needed to be more outward-looking because his flourishing depended on relations with others—his wife, his children, his associates. Christian society inspired an aptitude for service and sacrifice in the interest of others while One World instilled an instinct for self-preservation only—altruism's obligations already being borne by the state and there existing no family members to demand one's beneficence.

He had been scribbling down these thoughts as they occurred to him. Now he paused and read back all he had written and was reminded how bleak his vision of One World had become. There was no doubt in his mind which worldview nurtured human excellence and which strangled its flourishing.

He wandered over to the window. It was black outside so the only distinguishable feature was a neighbor's porch light across the yard.

What about my friends? If they had taken the same journey these last few months—read the same books, sat in on the conversations with Samuel, seen Catacomb—would they have the same feeling as I do: that this society we're were living in is foreign to our natures and damaging to them?

He imagined Morris would brush such an idea off, crack a joke and ask for a beer. He was satisfied with the role One World had assigned him. But would even Beverly, the level-headed one, be open to ideas that contradicted all her schooling. *Perhaps Melanie...* He turned away.

This was why he was feeling more and more estranged from his friends—he no longer bought into their worldview. Neither had he committed to an alternative one, though, and this accounted for his restlessness.

He sighed. Maybe he was just tired. Maybe he should just go to sleep and continue in the morning when things might look different.

But Induction was tomorrow.

He resigned to continuing his brainstorming but immediately found himself impatient with the whole exercise—this summarizing and contrasting of the two worldviews. It didn't seem to be the most important thing anymore—which was most profitable to society's flourishing. He wanted to get right to the bottom of the matter: *Which worldview reflects reality? Which is true?* That was the vital issue.

When he moved to weigh the two, immediately the old problem—the one he had christened the *Intractable Problem*—rushed in: *If I am merely a robot whose every action is determined by chemical reactions in my brain—if I am merely 'dancing to my genes'—then how is reasoning possible? What faculty do I have, independent of my electro-chemical brain, that could direct my thinking?*

These—the deterministic, naturalistic, reductionist explanation of the world and the role of science and reason as the sole purveyors of knowledge—were indispensable to the One World worldview. But he realized the two concepts were mutually exclusive. In fact, when he thought about it, in the One World lexicon *science*—applied reason in a purely deterministic environment—was an oxymoron. He had to smile—*a one word oxymoron. You could either believe in philosophic naturalism or you could believe in the existence of human reasoning; you can't believe in both.* As a life philosophy One World was incoherent, then; its claim to objective truth was, at best, a pious secular profession.

Then there was a second consideration which had been troubling him: if there was no God, as One World insisted, then there could be no objective morality either; moral standards had to be the mere derivatives of the subjective biases of those powerful enough to enforce their own preferences.

But who really believed that to be the case? Paul asked himself, rhetorically. *Who believed that charity and genocide were morally equivalent but for the prescription, or proscription, of the government? Who could be persuaded to believe the extermination of the Jews was 'good' because of the Nazi government's endorsement? But by what authority could the imposition of one's own verdict on this matter, in opposition to that of the government, be justified in what had to be, in actuality, a morally relativistic universe? Why is my opinion more valid than theirs? Or, to take it to the logical end: why should the products of the chemical bubblings in my brain be considered of nobler issue than those of Nazi brains?*

Who really believed that their own strongly held convictions were merely personal preferences without objective foundation? Even the leaders of One World didn't believe that: weren't the devos wrong and even evil?

But how could one disbelieve it and not hypothesize a higher source of moral values trumping human caprice? You couldn't. It didn't need to be God, this higher authority, but it needed to be someone pretty much like him—not some 'thing,' for how could the impersonal inform the personal; how could you get ethical imperatives from a stone? No, it had to be some 'one.' A scary thought.

So One World demanded moral absolutes while denying the existence of any rational foundations for them. How befuddled was that?

A third nagging concern was One World's obvious revisionism in historical interpretation. As a result of his access to original sources, most of what he had learned in school about the origins of science, Christianity, the Crusades, the Inquisition, witches, etcetera, had been stood on its head.

He had learnt that all witnesses had their bias—not even Samuel was free of it—but even in the historical episodes where the iniquity of the Church seemed most palpable—in the witch craze for instance—the written record revealed a much more nuanced reality than that extolled by One World. He recognized the 'history' he had learned was more properly classified as cultural propaganda—the mythology of his Utopian society. It was like something out of *Nineteen Eighty-Four*—Samuel had lent him a copy—where historical fact is manufactured real-time to fit the unfolding political narrative.

But the historical documentation was available to One World scholars, so why was I lied to? Why did the historical record have to be locked away in the inaccessible vaults of O.W.L anyway?

There was another troubling thing that cut to the core: One World's institution of pregnancy relief—*abortion* Samuel said they called it before Ascension.

The old Progressive platitude that 'a woman has the right to do whatever she chooses with her body' no longer satisfied him since the child was clearly an individual human life and not part of her body—to say otherwise was a denial of scientific fact—and to postulate the absence of another requisite quality, 'personhood' for instance, to justify the annulment of the baby's basic right to life was to subscribe to a myth, a fabrication resting on no logical or scientific foundation but rather the desire to conceal the abhorrent nature of the crime.

How easily Progressives discarded science and reasoning when it suited their purpose to do so.

So One World's scientific underpinning was a sham. But without that foundation—without Science's sanction—what validated its rule?

Beyond all this, Paul's growing insight into the underlying mindset of the pro-life and pro-choice—to use Samuel's terminology—antagonists and how these served to illustrate the Christian and the One World natures had a jarring impact on his allegiance to One World. He realized that one manifested a spirit of giving, the other of selfishness; the one sought to serve, the other entitlement; the first honored life, the other self-fulfillment.

With this commodification of the human individual, attitudes towards abortion and euthanasia as well as related areas like palliative care, assistance to the physically handicapped and the intellectually disadvantaged became subject to utilitarian considerations which deliberations increasingly told against the weak and powerless, like Alicia or Kim's baby. The baby had no utility, therefore it was expendable; the frail and aged lacked worth also.

A society results in which human life in general is de-valued, for the relationships between all people are tainted by this utilitarian valuation of others. Life is cheap for everyone.

Paul considered: *If one had to capture the spirit of Progressive society succinctly, to provide an iconic image, one couldn't do better than a photo of a disemboweled fetus. How better to illustrate the self-absorbed, unfeeling essence of the culture?*

He knew he wasn't free of this disease either; this was perhaps the most enlightening insight he had gained. When he looked inside himself he didn't see the basically good person, but for proper education and sustaining environment, that One World proclaimed. No, instead he recognized all the evils—the covetousness and selfishness; the greed; the pride; the callousness—that Christianity exposed. He wasn't more virtuous than other men despite possessing that universal propensity to believe so. He also knew that, no matter how hard he tried, he could never eradicate these failings. His nature was a sinful one, as the Christians said.

That was the truth.

Ruefully, he smiled to himself. *The Christians, then, were right about the true nature of man. This is one Christian doctrine that can be verified through personal observation anyway.*

Utopian societies like One World, or like the Soviet Union before it, got this fundamental factor wrong—the nature of man—and so they had to murder tens of millions in the attempt to impose their will on reality.

One World was a reflection of the flawed humans that built it as were all human civilizations; it was not an improvement on them. It was not a rung on the great evolutionary ladder to societal perfection, rather it was the contemporary expression of the iniquity of man. His cohort and those like them—politicos, the shapers of society—could only offer what they were; they could only bring forth the society that reflected their own inner brokenness.

The intractable—free will—problem; the existence of moral principle; the implausibility of One World's ethical and metaphysical postulations; its biased historical interpretations and its naïve estimation of human pliability and goodness—in view of these, how could he accept One World's narrative concerning the nature of the world? It didn't reflect reality. Clearly it was merely a contrivance, a useful compilation of Progressive myth that preyed on people's weaknesses so as to enable the powerful to rule over them, just as the man in the Strong Building had said: *Submit to us and there will usher in a just, prosperous and peaceful new world*—the pledge of all utopian tyrannies.

...Plato's Republic, Rousseau's Social Contract, the Communist Manifesto, Trudeau's Just Society, One World...

He was trapped. He could never be like the man in the Strong Building, selfishly procuring his portion but knowing it was all a lie. Nor could he bury his head in the busy pursuit of life's rewards, which were really One World's pacifiers, and overlook the inconsistences and injustices like Morris or Roland or Beverly could. He couldn't satiate his need for meaning with therapeutic illusions like Harmony and Gretchen and Cassandra.

He couldn't just go with the flow. Things had to make sense; they had to be real. This was the burden he labored under—he wanted to live genuinely; to walk in Truth. To stop pretending.

'*By their fruit shall ye know them.*' *Jesus had said that, or something like that*—Jesus' words often intruded into his thoughts now. These were the fruits of One World: far from being a corrective of all that came before, One World regurgitated all the iniquities of the past with the plagiarist's ineptitude to originality—the abortions, the euthanasia, eugenics, utopianism, nature worship, occultism—in short, the rituals and practices of the culture of death—that's what Samuel had called it: *the culture of death*—as they had been played out in the brutal, pagan, pre-Christian eras. In modern times the Nazis and the Soviets had followed the same program, merely brushing a gloss of scientific nomenclature over it. One World wasn't evolution, then, it was recapitulation. All this had happened before, again and again. As Morris had said, *There's nothing new under the sun.*

Was it another dark age coming on, then?

He was growing increasingly weary but his mind continued to race.

The repudiation of One World left him adrift on a sea of nihilistic despair. *But what is the alternative? It is fine to excoriate One World for its excesses and incoherencies, but what about the other side? Maybe all worldviews are incoherent, wishful illusions.*

Turning to Christianity, he had to admit Christians didn't have to wrestle with the *intractable problem* because they believed humans were more than just chemical reactions; they had a soul and could exercise free will.

Neither were they troubled by the apparent existence of objective morality: God was the essence of goodness; he was the transcendent reality. In their universe there was a good and an evil, an objective right and wrong. This was in total concordance with actual human experience—all humans had an innate sense of the very real evil that One World denied objective reality to; everyone lived as if they believed objective morality existed. So one had to reject reality to make peace with One World. That's what the devos, like Samuel, had refused to do. That's why One World hated them—the answer to the question the man in the Strong Building had asked.

So, in these aspects Christianity provided a much better explanation for the world as he experienced it than did One World. But in order to avail oneself of this integrity and coherency one had to accept the existence of God. Once one did this all the impediments to Christian belief—the miracles and the outrageous incompliancies—disappeared.

God. That was his one objection to Christianity—his stumbling block; he could see that now. Christianity's case was palatable as long as he could think of God as a hypothesis rather than a person. A hypothesis could be worked with, but a person was not so easily subdued. Further, a person of such potency demanded reverence. But there just wasn't enough evidence that God existed to warrant the surrender of one's autonomy this way; it would be irrational to.

His mind was feverish.

The heavens declare the glory of God, Samuel said. But could *he* discern God's attendance in the creation's artifacts?

He took up his Bible and flipped through the pages for a moment before letting it fall to his lap. He didn't know what he was looking for. Did he hope to find some incontrovertible evidence as to the surety of God's existence?

It was very late. He glanced down at the volume and wearily picked it up again and read. It had fallen open at chapter twenty in the Gospel according to John; *The Empty Tomb* it said above the text. He began to read how Mary Magdalene discovered that the tomb of Jesus had been opened in the night. It was a passage he remembered reading before.

Mary ran and told Peter and John who rushed to the tomb and verified her report: Jesus' body was not there. The two men departed leaving a distraught Mary. "They have taken my Lord away," she wails, "and I don't know where they have put him."

She notices a stranger, Jesus actually, but somehow altered so she doesn't recognize him. He asks her why she is crying. Still not recognizing her master through her distress she asks if he knows where Jesus' body has been taken.

Then comes verse sixteen: *Jesus said to her, "Mary."*

Paul stopped abruptly. His brain tingled as it did sometimes in the afterglow of a particularly elevating discussion or when a song would somehow reveal a deeper truth barely comprehended by the cognitive mind and there occurs a moment in time when the universe seems simple and intelligible—a moment of enlightenment.

It was the first time he had fully appreciated it—how Mary's world changed when she heard that voice speak that one word, *Mary*. She must have recognized it immediately—the familiar intonation. She had heard Jesus say her name many times before.

Think of it: she had travelled with Jesus and heard him speak and seen the miracles—so they claimed—and stood captivated with the adoring crowds. She, all of Jesus' followers, had felt such promise for the future.

Then it all ended. Her beloved master was dead—cruelly, humiliatingly, executed—and the disciples scattered; their world invalidated; crushed.

Then came that one word—"Mary"—and everything changed. Suddenly the world was something different than she had supposed. Reality stood revealed. Truth.

These reflections stirred his thoughts and caused the question that had been simmering all that night, just beneath his conscious mind, to burst the surface: did *he* believe it was all true? He had never dared ask himself that question before. In the beginning such a question seemed silly. Then it seemed profane. In the end, after all he had learnt, he was just apprehensive of what the answer might be.

He wished he could have been there to hear that word, *Mary.* How simple things would be then.

What a story was mankind's story! He sat on his bed looking out the window at the pitch black night while his mind reviewed the players: the citizen enablers; the scientists; Galileo; the crusaders; the witches; the abortionists; the man in the Strong Building; the apostles; the saints; Jesus. *God.*

When he tried to formulate some acceptable synthesis between the fabrications of One World and the fantastical claims of Christianity— two equally foreboding alternatives—the effort proved time and again to be beyond his genius. It was like mixing oil and water.

Alternatively, when he turned his back on One World and endeavored to approach Christianity he understood what Samuel had meant when he said the books were not enough: to have any chance of committing to such a relocation he needed something solid to grasp—a safe ledge to leap to. He had to make contact with... what? God?

Samuel had counseled him to pray; but that was impossible. Yes, it seemed the most natural thing on the surface—to ask and see if there was any response; to knock and see if a door opened. It could even be said to be the scientific approach. But this insight availed little because how ignoble a capitulation to unreason, how desperate and craven would that be—to stoop to the irrationality of prayer? What unendurable humiliation?

His frantic thoughts cycled once again: the intractable problem; good and evil; Samuel; Catacomb; the children; Priscilla; Dr. Bright; science; the Strong Building; Mother... The hours passed and still Resolution held itself aloof. His body was cold as if his vital essence were draining out. His mind cycled again and again and again: Ascension; Induction; KIDS; Alicia; Calvin; Mary; Jesus....

When he reached the limit of his endurance, it occurred: a reflex triggered by fatigue and desperation. "God. If you are there..." He stopped, deflated by the deafening silence. "I don't know what I want... help me."

The room was still as if time had ceased. A voltaic disturbance, barely noticeable at first, like a small quiet voice, kindled in his temples and from there blazed forth combusting his skull and then radiating throughout his body, filling him to the brim. A guttural groan of, what was almost pain, escaped his lips. Like a magnetic field reversing itself, his soul wavered, inverted, and a calm assurance, like a sigh, floated in on the tide.

He was insensitive to time's passing as he remained there before the window staring out upon a world remade. But then the first rays of the sun appeared on the horizon.

The first day.

32

INDUCTION

It was a brisk autumn day, the vivacity of which formed an apt backdrop to the august proceedings in the large auditorium where the company had gathered.

In fact there were two assemblies present. On one side of the great hall the confirmed citizens of One World reposed in their resplendent vestments pavilioned under champagne-colored lights. The masters in their red gowns occupied the front rows in all sobriety. Paul saw Mr. Lichter there. Behind them were the other luminaries: academics, politicians, clergy—there was a bishop from the Inclusivity Church sitting regally, self-important in her white mitre and green surplice—and their adjutants. Gray-uniformed men of martial bearing were deployed altogether in company—the Ministry men.

On the other side of the auditorium, barely discernible in the dimmed lighting there, the candidates sat—row upon row of eager-faced youth ripe with wonder and expectation.

These two hosts were separated by a wide intensely-illuminated aisle that ran like a shimmering stream between them. In its center there was a raised section with a podium festooned in the red, green and gold blazonry of One World and a single file of chairs occupied by the presiding officials. Access to the platform was provided by a stairway ascending from the golden aisle. An elevated walk to the rear of the platform bridged the gulf to the seating area of the One World incumbents.

Paul wore a green gown with the '225' of One World on the right breast and all his fellows were communally arrayed. The low hum of subdued but excited voices electrified the shadow world they inhabited and above them airy spiritual-sounding music drifted in from the intercom and spread mistily.

The music and verbal cocktail evaporated with the extinguishing of the lights on Paul's side—the ceremony was commencing.

The first official, Dr. Dew, the principle of Eastview, approached the podium. He spread his notes there, surveyed the audience then donned his glasses and launched into the introduction graciously welcoming each association in turn then exalting the fortitude of the aspirants and lauding their attainment to this grand collaboration—that is, One World citizenship—and auguring their future accruance to its welfare. Preamble discharged, he turned to the line of officials—"And now an introductory word from Deputy Minister Magan"—and led a general applause.

The slight figure in the light blue uniform of the Ministry of Truth took her place at the podium. "Greetings students," she beamed brilliantly. The students returned the salutation. She released a great sigh as to declare some immense labor accomplished, then began in a voice that was grander than anticipated: "In the beginning there were only disparate molecules floating in a primordial ooze. Then, gathered by the great Sub-atomic Teleological Force, ignited by a fortuitous atmospheric incident, the first amino acids, the constituents of proteins were formed. From there rose spontaneously RNA, the recipe of life, and the first cell—the first life. Fueled by mutation and the STF, refined by natural selection, the great creative factory of evolution propagated the abundant tree of life we know: insects, fish, amphibians, the great reptiles, birds, mammals, apes, and finally humans, the culmination of evolution's travail."

The synopsis swept past Paul's sleep-deprived brain without imprinting any new revelations or provoking a response but for the vague thought that he needed to solicit Samuel's opinion about this genesis.

"… in time forming bands for mutual support—for food and protection; community. Biological evolution begetting social evolution." She paused to allow the initiates to digest that morsel. "They grew to be villages; then towns; cities; nations—holons coalescing into greater holons until the time for the revealing of the greatest society: One World, the apex of Evolution, the culmination of history."

346

Paul's eyes wandered to the faces closest. He knew that, for most of them, and despite all their conditioning, these lofty principles cast upon their waters were squandered. They merely wanted to get their due—their stipend; authority to buy and sell. They just wanted to get chipped. One World made them that way.

He thought of Catacomb at that moment—the families—and surveyed his classmates again. *One World will be their parent now. It will provide for them; nurture and protect. But unlike the children at Catacomb, they will remain children always—never to seek beyond their confines. Never to venture their selves for another. Never to love.*

"…Galileo—the martyr for Science, the Enlightenment when we threw off superstition and dogma, the inevitable march to knowledge and truth. Darwin"—her eyes rolled heavenward—"blessed Darwin…"

Paul heard these words pronounced in the voice of Gretchen.

"…equality, fraternity, compliance… with Science always to guide us, one for the many, many for the one…" She paused again, dramatically. "One World." The minister acknowledged the applause smilingly as she returned to her place.

Other officials were called to the podium in turn and pitched their salutations and inducements with comparable ardor. The students grew increasingly restless even as the line of speakers steadily diminished. Paul found it harder and harder to resist dropping off as he had not slept well for several weeks and not at all the previous night. Finally the last orator was returning to his seat and Dr. Dew rose once more and the fervor of the students revived.

Resuming his station, he adapted a magisterial carriage in concordance with the gravity of his commission. Paul noticed the spiritual music had resumed. "And now we come to the summit of this gathering—the Induction proper." A cheer went up from the candidates. Dr. Dew beamed proudly under his spotlight, as if he were the object of their remonstrance. Finally, he motioned them to quiet. "To assist us with this sacred task we have Doctor Robert Sentinel, Vice Director of Compliance, Zone 53, with us today." The applause of both hosts acknowledged the pre-eminence of the personage moving to the podium: a robust looking man of military bearing in a charcoal uniform with the indigo epaulettes of the MoC.

The Vice Director accepted the tablet from the other doctor. The aspirants sat tense while his metallic voice announced the first inductee: "Burton Abdullah." A short dark-featured male rose from his seat hesitantly, glanced to either side, then proceeded down the aisle bravely. A uniformed woman ushered him to the stairs leading up to the stage. As he approached the podium the next name was read out: "Aldous Acardi."

Burton stood before the dignitaries and repeated the Oath of Compliance: "I, Burton Abdullah, chemist, joining the ranks of the great planetary civilization of One World, hereby pledge my undivided allegiance to its leaders and my unflagging obedience to its directives. I vow to pursue my vocation conscientiously and to hold no thought, sympathy or relationship not faithful to my duty to One World; to dedicate my life to the progress of One World; to be compliant in all I do." He took a breathless pause here before concluding: "If through evil intent I break this solemn vow, then let the stern just punishment of One World, and the universal hatred and contempt of its citizens, fall upon me." After that his right hand was pressed to the register then he turned to salute the assembly by raising his arm and displaying his open palm so they could see the lamp on his transponder blink green. A cheer and applause went up from the witnesses. Burton crossed the bridge and spritely mounted the stairs to take his place among the host of One World while Aldous recited the oath.

The names continued to be announced and the summoned to mount the stage and swear allegiance. On and on it went. Paul grew increasingly agitated as each name was called leaving a smaller and smaller un-enfranchised remnant. He couldn't shake the feeling that they were going to skip his name. They must know he doubted his society's values; they knew his apostasy. With dread, he imagined all their eyes turning to him afterwards, sitting alone there—the only one not affirmed.

But then again, how many apostates were there in the Strong Building? How many in the audiences here? Perhaps they all were—apostates.

The summons continued while Paul agonized. Then: "Cassandra Lisle."

The familiar name snared Paul's attention. A statuesque figure rose instantly, passed along the row noiselessly, and floated down the stairs. Eyes turned to study the apparition, the pallid skin and wild claret lips incongruous to the civilized hunter green gown. Her countenance was calm and impenetrable, eyes fixed on an invisible light that drew her up the stairs to receive the token of community. The oath was pronounced full and elemental from those savage lips. Paul looked for any hesitation in her voice or manner, any sign of doubt, any hint of defiance. There was none. Afterward she held the audience spellbound as she advanced to the front of the stage and offered her open palm dramatically to each section of the candidates' seating area, proclaiming the augmentation of One World's power by her own. Wild cheering broke out around the unaffected Paul. *Doesn't anyone see?* he thought. *She has no power. One World let her have her harmless cult as it let Gretchen have hers.*

Performance completed, she turned and drifted up the stairs to the realm of One World and the individual he had known merged into the collective and ceased to exist.

The pang in his stomach hinted that Mel had somehow ceased to exist with her.

The names continued relentlessly. Finally: "Roland Malton."

Paul's friend rose and proceeded down the aisle with a stiff determined gait. Paul felt his world constricting as Roland earnestly pronounced the oath and executed the obligatory salute. When the green light pulsed his serious face broke into a relieved grin. *He will be able to pursue his career in eugenics—another Dr. Bright. In a few years he will be lost to rational entreaty, his humanity sacrificed to his consuming mission. And what was that exactly? To make slaves of all our descendants as we are slaves of our ancestors. So will they all expend their lives forging the chains of their own prison.*

It was strange hearing the tenor of his inner voice, the contempt he felt towards One World. Like his estrangement from Morris he wondered when it had happened; when it had seeped into his being.

The robot voice continued to call them to the stage and each obeyed its summons and passed to the other side. *Like crossing the Jordan*, Paul thought. *Or baptism.* He couldn't think clearly. *All that is holy must be profaned.* He didn't know where that thought came from and was startled that he might have spoken it aloud. It was something his interrogator in the Strong Building might say; or maybe Samuel. He needed to talk to Samuel.

"Beverly Morrison."

Paul lurched in his seat. Beverly moved along the row confidently, grinning at acquaintances, and started down the aisle like it was the most natural thing in the whole world. Paul was angry to see her embrace oblivion so callously; it was a betrayal. She strode up to the podium and happily pronounced the oath. As the green light welcomed her to One World she waved her palm to the crowd with an exuberance that sickened Paul. The feeling of estrangement heightened as he followed her figure on its progress up the heights of One World.

She would never read his paper now.

"Victor Morozov."

He thought about Catacomb again; the families there. *Priscilla. Melanie.*

"Phillip Mortimer."

Paul's hands shook and his heart beat painfully in his temples. It was hot. His chair felt damp. His head reeled in the constricting atmosphere. He should have gotten more sleep… he was so weary…

"Suzanne Mrzowski."

The name shook him alert. He had drifted off. How many names had he missed? Fortunately they still hadn't gotten to his.

Suzanne rose from her seat just a few rows in front and moved along to the steps. He watched her sunny blonde hair sway as she walked. Her voice was quiet as she took the oath. The green light flashed, and she raised her palm above her head and held it there for a second, head tilted winsomely. Then she proceeded up the steps to One World. Paul felt a sense of loss but was glad she was gone—no longer an enticement somehow.

"Bobby Nabor."

Paul's fingers gripped his chair tightly to keep from tumbling. He wondered how he would make it to the dais when his name was called.

"Heather Natal."

He blinked and thought he saw Melanie rise and move along the row towards the stairs but it was another girl; someone he didn't know. What would Mel think if she knew his thoughts? What would she think of him? *Better she is gone.* A lump formed in his throat.

"Timothy Newton."

He vaguely registered Tim's figure descending the stairs. He had known him from a few classes but could no longer recall any particulars. The peppermint scented electric air and the wispy music spun a kaleidoscope behind his aching eyes. Through the fever he looked up to see the ascended floating under their canopy of light. The room rocked and tumbled like the deck of a ship.

"Paul Norris."

No one rose. All eyes scanned over the remaining cohort of graduates sitting there in the darkness.

"Paul Norris." A murmur rose from the attendees and heads turned to each other in consternation. The Vice Director fidgeted on the stage.

A blue uniform stepped behind him and whispered something. He cleared his voice.

"Zeta Norton."

He was hurtling down the cement stairs at the front of the school, almost colliding with someone coming the other way. "Paul!" she called out as he barreled past.

He stumbled over his feet at the bottom turning to see who… it was Harmony.

"Harmony! What… what are you doing here?" he gasped.

"Jim is graduating so I thought I'd come over. Y'know—offer moral support," she grinned. "Where are you off to?" Her mouth fell open in surprise. "Hey, aren't you supposed to be graduating too?"

He just wanted to get away. "Oh.. yeah… it's a long story. I gotta go, okay?" He turned and bounded off.

"Hey. I saw your friend 'Santa Claus' on Sunday. He came to church!" she shouted after him.

He stopped dead in his tracks and turned to her. "What did you say?"

"You know; the old guy with the gray beard—he was at church on Sunday. Hey, you look really tired…"

"Samuel? You mean he went to your church, the Church of the Affirming Spirit?" Paul stammered unbelievingly.

"Yes," she said snidely. "Well, he caused quite a commotion. The police came and dragged him out. He's crazy!" she snickered.

Paul's face turned gray. "I gotta go. Bye." He rushed off in the direction of the subway station.

As he ran he glanced back frequently to see if the police were pursuing. He stopped just inside the door and checked again. There were two men about fifty meters away striding towards his position. Panic set in and he tore across the floor and held his palm against the reader. It didn't work! They had shut him down. What could he do? Where could he run? *They will be here soon.* In a panic he passed his palm over the reader again. The light turned green and the roundabout released. He must have not held it long enough the first time. He flung himself through and hurled down the stairs.

Luckily a train was just preparing to leave. He barely squeezed between the closing doors and stumbled into the car, managing to steady himself by grasping the bar in the center of the car. *Made it!* There was no way the men could have caught the same train. He stood there gasping for breath.

When he looked around he discovered the car was only half full. He felt the others' questioning looks upon him—it was incompliant to stand when seats were available. Thankfully, there was a vacancy nearby, so he deposited himself into it and sat staring straight ahead at a poster on the opposite wall. Quite improbably, it was advertising excursions to the Astral City Human Rights Museum.

He had time to consider his reasons—for running out of Induction. His feelings had seemed so compelling then, but now upon sober reflection, he wasn't so sure. *Maybe I should go back to the school.* He could say he was not well, which was true. *Would they allow me to take the oath then? What about all the other things that had gone on—my paper; my access to O.W.L.; my friendship with Samuel; the books; even the thing with Norm and Jean: Why didn't I bring my suspicions to the authorities? Surely, they would discover everything if they pried. How could I explain it all?* He would be ruled incompliant for sure. *If only I hadn't missed Induction.*

He needed to see Samuel.

The train shuttered and slowed. Paul looked around alarmed. Everyone remained unconcerned, viewing their tablets, talking to companions or dozing. The train sped up again. Soon it rumbled into Rousseau station and the doors swooshed open. Paul half expected some police or a MoE official to charge through the door but an old lady with a white poodle was the only boarder. His tension heightened for a moment realizing she must have influential political connections since it was so difficult to get clearance for cross-species companionship. But she settled into the seat across the aisle without taking notice of him. The dog sat on the floor between her feet. The doors swooshed shut and the train lurched off again.

Paul took the time to reflect: *Why would Samuel go to Gretchen's church? To break up the worship service?* He furrowed his brow. The poodle peered at him and furrowed its brow.

Damn! Why would he do such a reckless thing, drawing attention to himself? he agonized. *Everything will be investigated now. It will be the end. At the very least I'll be reevaluated Beta... Stupid, stupid, stupid... leaving Induction.*

The train rolled into Summerhill and two of the passengers got off; two women. The train continued.

A thought waylaid him: *Maybe I should have gone home and hid the books. They might go there looking for me and find them. No. No, I have to see what has happened to Samuel.* They already knew he had books anyway. He had missed the Induction. *How am I going to explain that?* He might as well take this opportunity to find out how Samuel was before things caught up with him.

The train stopped at Rosedale. Having made up his mind on a course of action he felt more relaxed but was still impatient to get to Ecology. When the train arrived there he bolted out and shot up the stairs, relieved to still be free.

The buzzer rang hollow on Ecology Street. He rang again. Still no response. It was quiet as a tomb inside. Paul looked around nervously. He felt exposed standing outside on the street so he tried the handle. Surprisingly, it turned and the door opened. He listened and still there was no sound within. He peered up the street once more then took a swallow and slipped inside. The noise of the street faded as the door closed behind him.

The room was a shambles. Debris was strewn everywhere. The carcass of Samuel's green sofa was tottering over a chair, gutted, and the rug underneath shredded. The old table clock was smashed, disemboweled against the wall. In the kitchen the refrigerator was laying face down in a pool of oily green and scarlet ooze, its severed door thrown into the corner. Ceramic shards littered the floor. Strangely, there was no paper.

Paul froze in shock, afraid to move lest he rouse the spirits of the place. Then his attention went to the door at the back, the one that led to the hallway and library. He willed his feet to carry him to it and stood there listening in the shadows for a moment before nudging it aside with his shoulder and passing into the twilit hallway beyond.

The temperature seemed to fall ten degrees immediately. He could hear his own breathing as he edged along in the semi-darkness. Once or twice he stumbled noisily on unseen objects littering the floor. At the end of the hallway he paused again at the door to Samuel's study before giving it a shove. It was pitch black inside. He felt for the light switch and hesitated a second before flicking it on crisply.

The light revealed a room stripped bare except for the splintered wood planks—the remains of Samuel's bookcases—and the weighty oak desk which was largely intact but heavily scarred. Despite the general carnage there was no paper here either—not one scrap. The books had been removed prior to the pillaging, apparently. Paul shifted the debris to confirm their complete and utter disappearance.

He checked in the drawers of the desk. Nothing was there. He returned to the middle of the room and surveyed the mess, wondering what to do next.

Suddenly, the door to the hallway creaked, and he heard footsteps advancing rapidly up the hall. He had lingered too long. He looked around frantically for a place to hide, but none presented itself readily. Finally, he rushed to duck behind the desk; too late. The door burst open and two men, the two he had seen at the subway, stood there blocking his exit.

He was caught.

33

The Call

Paul kept the desk between himself and his adversaries, alert for any opportunity to bolt.

The stouter one switched off his flashlight, handed it to the other and approached the desk warily. "I'm Ezra," he said opening his great palms to Paul.

Paul was bewildered. Why should he care about his name?

Ezra stopped a few feet from the desk and waited, his eyes interpreting Paul's face. "We are not MoE," he assured him.

Paul's mind couldn't register the meaning of Ezra's words. His calves tensed, ready to spring. Time was short—there would, no doubt, be others arriving soon.

Ezra spread his massive arms. "We have been watching over you. Remember the park?"

Paul blinked. He heard the words *the park*. Which park?

"Titus switched your bag," he said pointing to his partner. "Remember? He didn't want you to get caught with the books." Ezra stepped right up to the desk and faced Paul head on. "We're friends."

Paul's head drew back. "Friends?" he repeated weakly.

"Yes. We're here to guide you."

Paul looked dumbly at him. "I thought you… you're not MoE?"

"No. We're friends of Samuel," Ezra repeated.

"Samuel! Where is he?" Paul looked around anxiously.

Ezra glanced quickly at Titus. "He was arrested a few days ago at Gretchen's church."

Paul's mouth was agog. "Gretchen's church?" Then he remembered. "Yes, yes, I heard that… why would he go there?"

Ezra clasped his hands together. "It was something he felt drawn to do."

"He went there to confront her for me," Paul said distantly.

Ezra waved the thought aside. "No, not for you. For everyone. For love."

"I told him about her," Paul moaned.

"About Gretchen? He knew about her all along."

"I have to go and see what's happened to him."

"You can't do that," Titus snapped, drawing a stern glance from Ezra.

Paul focused on Ezra. "Where have they taken him?" He felt helpless, in a fog, but if he could just see the old man, to talk with him, things could be set right.

"To KIDS," Ezra said with a note of finality.

"I have to go there," Paul insisted, moving around to the side of the desk.

Ezra shifted to block his path. "There is nothing for you there anymore."

It was like a great door swinging shut. Paul was struck dumb for a moment. "I have to go," he reiterated emphatically, rapping his fist on the table and glaring at the larger man.

Ezra held his gaze for a moment then moved to step aside. Paul barged forward, brushing against him. Titus made way reluctantly— Paul heard him say "You're being stupid" as he bolted down the hallway.

In a moment he was out in the cool air and casting about frantically trying to get his bearings. He had to go east. When he started to run he remembered that other night, not too long ago, another nightmarish dash to the hospital. Panic seized his brain, propelling his legs faster.

The sense of deja vu was still present as he barged through the doors at KIDS.

"Young man!" he heard a feminine voice cry. "Young man, is there something wrong?" A burly guard blocked his path forcing him to an abrupt halt.

The nurse at the reception desk behind the glass asked again, "Young man, what is the meaning…"

"I'm looking for a friend," he blurted out breathlessly. He looked around the tiny room; there was no one else there.

"You have a friend here?" she asked. "Where? A commitant?"

Paul nodded. "His name is Samuel."

"Samuel? Samuel who?"

"I don't know," Paul answered truthfully—he didn't even know if Samuel was his real name—"just Samuel. He's old; gray beard, long gray hair to here; looks like Santa Claus…" He rolled his eyes wearily.

"Well, I don't remember anyone like that," she sniffed nodding to the guard who resumed his station by the door. "Let me check…" Paul approached the glass and she began to search her computer screen.

"Samuel, Samuel, Samuel. Just today?"

"What?"

"You said he was committed today?" the nurse repeated impatiently.

"Oh. No, Sunday probably," Paul stammered.

The nurse shook her head in exasperation. "Oh well," she sighed, "let me see…. yes. Samuel Ecker, is that it? Ecology Street West?"

"Yes, yes, that must be him. Where is he? Can I see him?"

The nurse scanned the screen and dashed a pointed look at the guard.

"No. No, I'm afraid that's not possible." She swiveled her chair around turning her side to Paul and buried her face in a dossier indicating their interview was at an end.

"But I just want to know if he is okay. Is he injured?" Paul persisted.

The nurse swiveled back and looked at him sternly over her glasses. "I'm sorry. He was retired a few hours ago."

Paul stared at her incomprehensibly.

She peered into her screen and tsk'd. "Sixty-six years old. Poor thing. A long life."

Paul heard himself say, "You mean he's—"

The nurse looked up over her glasses again, annoyed at the continued intrusion into her very busy schedule. "He was unburdened this afternoon," she repeated sternly.

Paul exhaled hard. "But… but he was okay. He wasn't sick or anything."

"He was old. He lived a good long life…" the nurse replied as soothingly as she felt capable.

"No. There wasn't anything wrong with him!" Paul huffed.

The nurse's eyes shifted to the guard. Paul sensed his approach and turned away, stepping past him and making for the street.

"My, what a rude young man," the nurse remarked. The guard returned to his post and she turned back to her duties.

The day was fading. The frigid air numbed Paul's face as he stumbled along College street but he didn't care. The pillars of his world were fractured and everything was crashing down. He crossed University without consulting the streetlights. He paused there and stood on the sidewalk looking back towards KIDS. He could see the tall gray smoke stack. A little black puff billowed from it as he watched.

He drew his eyes away and passed down a side street. A morbid sense of loneliness pressed down on him—not merely a feeling of being alone but of being an outcast. He drew his chin down and pressed on into the icy wind and blowing leaves. The sound of laughter and music wafted in between gusts—a Mexican restaurant off to the side. It quickly faded behind him. The blocks grew more decrepit as he plunged onward; fewer streetlamps functioned. He could be in devo territory now for all he cared. He would be more likely to meet a police patrol. He didn't care about that either.

Now there were old red brick warehouses on each side, all dark and silent. As he was passing one of these a massive hand reached out, collared him and drew him roughly into the alley. Strong bodies enveloped his and hauled him behind the eco-bins. He struggled wearily, half-heartedly, but they were on top of him, his arms were pinned and a strong hand covered his mouth. His head was pressed to the icy concrete.

Out of the corner of one eye he saw a glowing illumination spread across the entrance to the alley; there was a vehicle approaching. The light grew brighter and brighter. He tried frantically to shake his mouth free and yell for help but his assailants held him immobile.

"Shuddup!" Ezra growled in his ear. He lay still.

From beneath the bin he saw the tires of the car draw across the alleyway entrance. It stopped there as if listening. He could see it was a black sedan; a maria. Paul peered unblinkingly at the phantom car registered sideways in his field of vision. It stayed there a long moment peering into the stygian darkness of the alley. Then he watched it slide slowly past—a cobra tracking for prey—and the red taillight receded.

"That one was for you." The hand on his mouth loosened and his subduers clambered off his body. When he managed to roll over, Ezra and Titus were standing there buffeted by the bitter wind.

Paul's back hurt, but he staggered to his feet and looked to where the maria had passed. He didn't doubt the truthfulness of Ezra's assertion.

His right hand felt numb but now he realized it had been encased in a black mitt; they had somehow got it on him during their scuffle. "What is this?" He started to remove it.

"Don't do that!" Ezra cautioned. "You'll bring the marias."

He looked intently at the younger man. "You know the life they are leading you to," he said quietly. "Do you believe in it?"

Paul looked down at the black asphalt, a plethora of conflicted thoughts traversed his mind. He pressed his cold hand into his pocket.

Titus sniffed the air nervously. "We have to get moving," he said anxiously.

Ezra waved to quiet him and turned back to Paul. "He's right, we can't stay here." He extended his hand. "Come with us."

The wind had dropped so the *come with us* echoed supernaturally in the alleyway. Paul knew what was being offered—the path that was being offered him—to become a devo.

"You've been pursuing me, you and Samuel, all this time, trying to recruit me. Why me? Of all people..." Paul looked pleadingly at them. "What made you think I would ever choose to become one of you?"

"We prayed for you," Ezra said quietly.

Paul's angry rebuttal checked in his throat. For a moment he glowered at them defiantly but then his shoulders drooped in resignation.

"His sheep heed His call," Titus said.

Ezra nodded. "Come with us, Obadiah."

Paul looked up cautiously. "That would be my name? Obadiah? I can't remember—he was one of the old testament prophets..."

"The *servant of the Lord*," Titus answered. "He prophesized against those who rejoiced over the calamities of God's people."

Paul thought for a moment. "...prophesized against those... So you hope I could be someone like that—someone who speaks up against the evils of One World? Is that why you want me to become Obadiah?"

Ezra smiled. "Nothing so dramatic I'm afraid; we just assign names alphabetically. The last two postulants were *Micah* and *Nahum*."

Paul's face was blank; he appeared not to hear. His mind had wandered on to other things.

"What about my friends? What about Beverly and Morris...?"

Ezra looked sadly. "They have already chosen whom they will serve."

"We have to go," Titus reiterated urgently.

Ezra nodded to him then turned back to Paul. "Everyone must choose," he said. Paul stood frozen. "You understand that now? Everyone must make their choice. It is why we are here. Everyone, from the beginning of time, in all places… everyone is faced with these same two paths, these same two masters. Everyone must choose." The two men's eyes remained locked for a long moment. Then Ezra turned and proceeded to follow Titus along the alleyway.

Paul hesitated a moment longer, then followed after them.

Epilogue

Three years later…

Just after 18:15 the SWAT team crashed through the door of a dilapidated dwelling just off Emerald West. The single room on the second floor bore the debris of recent habitation—there was a disheveled cot, garbage in the wastebasket, and a newspaper on the chair—but the target had fled. They combed the dwelling for forensics, ransacking the bedding, even prising up the floorboards in the effort. One of the policemen found a large blue faux leather notebook in the drawer of the table. It appeared to be a draft for a novel.

An officer from MoE arrived just then so the policeman went downstairs to issue his report. "There's no one in the house, sir, but he was here earlier; we found a copy of today's *Oracle*. We also found this." He handed him the volume. "It looks like he was writing a novel or something."

The officer opened it and began to read silently: *This is late, I know. I finally completed it…*

He leafed through the pages, pausing here and there to read a few paragraphs, while the policeman stood attendant.

"A strange item for a pastor to carry," the cop finally remarked. "Anything important, sir?"

The officer read another paragraph, paused, then flipped through a few more pages and paused again. His brow furrowed. "No," he answered haltingly. "No, I don't think so." He closed the book absent-mindedly and stood examining the floor for a few moments. Then he snuffed his nose and finally looked up. "Check the neighbors and the houses across the street; someone must have seen him."

"Yes, we're already on that sir," the other replied, a hint of annoyance in his voice. He was happy to dash off leaving the MoE operative alone with his thoughts.

The officer stood there a while with the volume cradled in both hands. Then Lanton slipped the book under his overcoat and stepped out into the damp evening.

CPSIA information can be obtained at www.ICGtesting.com
Printed in the USA
LVOW11s1050160914

404170LV00002B/27/P

9 781927 684115